For Pascoe and Kerry

PART ONE

1984

Heather BURNSIDE

Blood Ties

An Aria Book

This is an Aria book, first published in the UK
in 2018 by Head of Zeus Ltd
This paperback edition published in 2019 by Head of Zeus Ltd

9 7 5 3 1 2 4 6 8

A catalogue record for this book is available from
the British Library.

ISBN (E): 9781786692559
ISBN (PBO): 9781789541496

Typeset by Silicon Chips

Printed and bound in Great Britain by
CPI Group (UK) Ltd, Croydon CR0 4YY

Head of Zeus Ltd
First Floor East
5–8 Hardwick Street
London EC1R 4RG

WWW.HEADOFZEUS.COM

1

Adele was serving a seven-year stretch in Styal Prison for the manslaughter of her father. Many of the inmates were currently in the visiting room, which made the rest of the prison uncharacteristically quiet. She walked into the cell of her fellow prisoner, Louise, thinking that they might keep each other company while the others were away.

'Are you OK, Louise?' she asked.

Louise was sitting on the edge of the bed with her back to Adele. Her head was down and her shoulders rounded. On hearing Adele, she raised her head and glanced quickly over her shoulder before turning away. That brief glimpse was enough for Adele to notice her tears.

'What's the matter?' asked Adele, stepping towards the bed.

Louise turned to face her, the scar on her right cheek magnified under her glistening tears. Adele watched the river of tears change course as they traversed the scar, which dented Louise's right cheek and stretched the surrounding flesh taut. Louise's tears then circled her chin, diluting the stream of mucus that gushed from her nose and across her lips.

Despite her concern, Adele felt a momentary repulsion. Louise always had this effect on her. She was skinny and had one of those faces that would be considered pretty if it had been better maintained. Although aged twenty-four, Louise had a childlike demeanour, but this child had been forced to grow up quickly, and it showed.

Her complexion was sallow, her teeth discoloured and her eyes encircled with dark rings. Today Louise's hair was even tattier than usual; the natural blonde highlights lost in a sea of grime and split ends. In contrast, Adele's dark locks shone with vitality and her face had a healthy glow, which enhanced her attractive features. She was slim, 'but with curves in all the right places', as her boyfriend, John, used to tell her.

Louise gave a loud sob, which came out as a snort and drew Adele's attention back to the situation. Adele took another step forward and sat next to Louise with her back to the door, drawing her into her arms and over-compensating for her intense scrutiny.

'She didn't fuckin' come!' sobbed Louise, nuzzling her face into Adele's chest and smearing her top with a mix of tears and mucus. Adele felt another tug of repulsion but tried not to let it show.

'Who didn't come?' she asked.

'My mam. She's been promising for weeks,' Louise sobbed. 'She said she'd bring Becky, too. I was really looking forward to it.'

Adele sympathised; she didn't have any visitors either but it was something she was learning to accept. Becky was Louise's three-year-old daughter, and Adele knew how much she missed her. She couldn't imagine how difficult it must be, stuck in prison when you had a child on the outside.

For Adele it was bad enough that she never saw her mother or her former boyfriend, John. Adele's mother, Shirley, refused to visit and Adele held out no hopes of her changing her mind. Those hopes had vanished as soon as she was convicted of the violent killing of her father. And John had split with her once the guilty verdict was given.

The only person who had visited Adele in the few weeks since she had been inside was her brother, Peter, but he couldn't make it today. He had a bit of business to attend to, apparently. Adele had her own ideas on what that business might be.

Before she became lost in her thoughts, Adele checked herself and tried to concentrate instead on the young woman sitting next to her. 'Did she contact you to say why she wasn't coming?' she asked.

'Did she fuck! Got better things to do than come and see me.'

'You don't know that,' said Adele. 'There could be all kinds of reasons why she couldn't make it. Try not to upset yourself till you find out why.'

But even as Adele tried to console her, it sounded phoney: false platitudes that she felt obliged to utter even though she didn't believe them. What did she know about Louise's situation? The most likely reason Louise's mother hadn't visited was because, like the parents of many of the women in here, she just didn't care.

Adele was still getting used to life inside and she was often shocked by the stories that some of the inmates told. Although her own childhood hadn't been exactly idyllic, at least she had avoided many of the forms of abuse that other prisoners had had to contend with. Her parents' faults were numerous but she did have the advantage of being brought up by family, including a loving grandmother, rather than having to live with foster parents, in a care home or, even worse, on the streets.

It was obvious her words hadn't brought any comfort to Louise, who continued to weep as she buried her face further into Adele's chest, saturating her top. At a loss as to what else to say, Adele just held Louise close, stroking her hair.

After a while Louise's weeping ceased and she lifted her head and gazed into Adele's eyes. Adele held her gaze and tucked a stray lock of hair behind Louise's ear.

It was an attempt at reassurance but she realised, too late, that the young woman had misread her intentions. Louise raised her head further, her lips hungrily seeking those of her comforter. Adele drew back but Louise's lips were already on hers.

Before Adele could pull away, she heard someone yelling her surname. 'What the fuck d'you think you're playing at, Robinson?' the woman at the door demanded.

It was Denise, Louise's girlfriend. Adele didn't have an opportunity to explain before she heard Denise advancing towards her.

Adele quickly prised herself from Louise and raised her bent right arm. With no time to turn round, she judged Denise's position from the sound of her footsteps. Then she drew her arm back swiftly and jabbed her elbow hard into the soft flesh of Denise's abdomen.

Adele didn't give the other woman a chance to retaliate. She rose from the bed and stood to face Denise, who was stooped low, her hands gripping her stomach and her breath coming in short gasps. Before Denise could recover, Adele followed up with an uppercut to her face, which knocked Denise off balance and she crashed to the ground with her nose pumping blood.

Then Adele adopted a defensive kickboxing stance; left leg in front of the right, and hands forming fists in front of her face with her elbows covering her ribs. As she waited for Denise to recover and charge at her, the adrenalin was racing around her body and priming her for action.

'Stop, stop!' shouted Louise, dashing up to Adele and grabbing ineffectually at her left arm. 'It's not what you think,' she called to Denise, who was now sprawled across the floor, still clutching her stomach.

Adele stepped back but maintained her defensive stance while she awaited Denise's reaction. She could feel her heart thumping but she tried to focus on Denise.

'What the fuck is it, then?' gasped Denise.

'Everyone knows I'm not gay, you silly cow!' said Adele. 'I was trying to comfort her, that's all.' Then she rounded on Louise, saying, 'But I won't fuckin' bother in future if that's all the thanks I get.'

She stormed out of the cell, leaving Louise to do the rest of the explaining to her girlfriend. A small crowd had gathered at the cell door: prisoners who had just returned from visiting. On the outer periphery of the crowd Adele could see two prison officers. One of them was Prison Officer Fox, otherwise known by the inmates as Sly.

Nobody liked Sly because of her attitude towards the prisoners, which was hostile and condescending. Sly was middle-aged, overweight and had a matronly bearing. She had plain features and her hair was short and brushed back from her face in a style that was more practical than fashionable. Sly had been married for thirty years and her sex life, or lack of it, was a constant source of speculation and amusement amongst the women.

'What's going on here?' Sly demanded as she approached the crowd.

The women began to disperse and Adele quickly pushed her way through them and strode up the corridor. A confrontation with Sly was the last thing she needed. As she walked away she could hear Prison Officer Fox quizzing the prisoners around her. After a few paces Adele felt a tug on her arm and she swung round, ready to defend herself again. But it wasn't Denise or Louise. It was her friend Caroline.

'Adele, stop!' Caroline said.

Adele turned to face her, her complexion now ruddy and her palms sweaty.

'You all right?' Caroline asked.

'Yes, just a misunderstanding,' snarled Adele. 'I'm sure Denise will realise that once Louise has explained herself.'

'Do you want to talk about it?'

Adele looked into her friend's face, and noticed how the soft folds of her features had settled into a frown. Seeing Caroline's motherly concern, Adele couldn't stay angry for long.

'OK,' she said. 'I think I could do with a chat after that carry-on.'

They entered Caroline's cell, where she poured them both coffee from a flask.

'Get that down you,' she said, smiling at Adele.

Adele forced a smile in return.

'What was it about?' asked Caroline.

'She was upset because her mother hadn't showed up again. I was just trying to comfort her, that's all.'

'Ah, right. And Denise got the wrong end of the stick?'

'As far as I was concerned, yes, but she may have spotted Louise trying to kiss me.'

'You're joking!' said Caroline, stifling a giggle.

'I know. Hilarious, isn't it?' Adele responded, joining in Caroline's laughter.

'It amazes me how she could try it on even though everyone knows you're not that way inclined. Not to mention the fact that she's already in a relationship with Denise.'

'I know,' laughed Adele. 'And even if I was that way inclined, I don't think Louise would be my type,' she added, pulling a face to display her repugnance, then glancing down at her snot-stained top.

Then Caroline's tone changed. 'It was good of you to comfort her, though,' she said. 'Especially considering you didn't have any visitors either.'

'Thanks. I think that's why she turned to me.'

'You miss your mum, don't you?' asked Caroline.

'Yes, but it's something I've just got to accept. It's hard trying to patch up differences while I'm in here. Maybe when I get out I can try to make her understand.'

'I know what you mean,' replied Caroline. 'And it's

also hard to feel that you won't be with your loved ones again for years. Visits are one thing but it's not the same as being with them every day.'

Adele noticed the wistful look in Caroline's eyes. 'You really miss your kids, don't you?' she asked.

'Oh, yeah.'

'How are they? Are they OK?'

'Yeah, they're muddling along but I've missed so much of them growing up.' Adele spotted a tear in Caroline's eye as she quickly switched the subject away from herself. 'What about John? Have you not heard from him either?'

'No, and I don't expect I'll ever hear from him again.'

'Well then, he's not worth the trouble,' said Caroline.

'I can't blame him really. After all, who wants a killer for a girlfriend?'

'I'm sorry,' said Caroline. 'I can tell you really miss him but I'm sure you had your reasons for doing what you did.'

It was Adele's cue to talk about what had happened but she couldn't. Not yet. Not even to Caroline, who she confided in so much. In the weeks since she had been inside, she had tried her best to block it from her memory.

It wouldn't do to focus on it too much because, every time she did, all she could picture was her father's bloody, battered head. And, no matter how badly he had treated his family, Adele couldn't find the words to justify why she had killed him so brutally, bludgeoning him over and over till his brains spilt out of his shattered skull.

But Caroline seemed to understand how Adele felt. 'Don't beat yourself up over it,' she said, covering Adele's hand with her own in a comforting gesture. 'The memories will ease with time, I promise.' Then she quickly switched topic again.

'I tell you what else I miss,' she said, gazing at her mug and grinning. 'A bloody decent cuppa. That's one thing I'm looking forward to once I'm released.'

Adele smiled back and clinked her mug against Caroline's. 'I'll drink to that,' she said, relaxing her strained features.

It was strange how Caroline had a knack of always making things seem better. Adele had gravitated towards her from day one and now the ex-schoolteacher was Adele's closest ally in prison. Caroline radiated warmth and had a way of always putting people at ease. Maybe it was the schoolteacher in her that had taught her how to relate to people. In the short space of time that Adele had been inside she was already finding Caroline to be loyal and trustworthy.

Although Caroline was in her early thirties, and a good ten years older than Adele, she got along with her better than any of the women her own age. However, Caroline's motherly nature could never make her a replacement for Adele's mother, even though Shirley had never been particularly maternal. But it was good to have somebody mature and level-headed to confide in.

The other thing about Caroline was that, like Adele, she wasn't an addict. That made them unusual in the prison environment where most of the women were hooked on drugs, tobacco or alcohol. It also gave them an advantage as they didn't have to constantly trade goods or favours to get a fix.

Adele enjoyed a drink, and access to moonshine could certainly help to brighten up an otherwise depressing evening behind bars. It could also help her fall off to sleep when the deafening noise from inside the prison kept her awake. Thankfully, though, she didn't need it in order to function.

While she had been inside, Adele was pleased to find that she got along with most of the prisoners. The majority were OK but they were often flawed in some way or other. There were many like Louise, who had been abused as children.

Louise's life experiences had left her with a raw edge that was often hidden beneath a vulnerable façade. Adele had soon learnt that although the girl was likeable, she wasn't to be trusted. She leant on her dominant girlfriend, Denise, and was anxious to please her.

Louise was also a drug addict and, like most addicts, she would do almost anything to get her next fix. As Adele was gradually finding out, life behind bars could be vicious, and drugs often drove people to commit extreme acts of violence. Even people who weren't drug dependent could get sucked into the brutality of prison life. Unfortunately for Adele, she was about to become one of those people.

2

Louise approached Denise tentatively where she lay on the cell floor still clutching her stomach.

'You all right?' she asked.

'No, I'm fuckin' not!' Denise gasped as the blood from her nose circled her lips and coloured her teeth.

While Louise hovered over Denise, she continued to lie curled on her side. Then, after a few deep breaths, she rolled onto her knees, using her hands to lever herself up. 'Give me a fuckin' hand then,' she snapped at Louise, who was still standing over her.

Louise put out a hand to help Denise up. Denise grasped at it, pulling herself upwards until she was on her feet. Just as she rose, Prison Officer Fox walked into the cell.

'What's going on here?' she demanded.

'Nothing,' Denise and Louise replied in unison. 'It was an accident,' said Denise. 'Louise shut the door as I was walking in and I banged my nose.'

Sly looked sceptically at her. 'Aye, and pigs might fly,' she said. 'I hope you've not been fighting, my girl, or you'll be in trouble.' Then she assessed Denise before adding, 'Get yourself cleaned up.'

Once Sly was gone, Denise covered her nose with her right hand. 'My fuckin' nose!' she complained. 'And look at the state of my top. It's a fuckin' mess.'

Louise looked at the blood spatters on Denise's top. 'Do you want me to get you a clean one?' she asked.

'Leave it for now! Help me clean up my face first.'

Denise's dark complexion was smeared with blood. She was boyish in appearance, which was accentuated by her cropped hair, her clothing and her larger-than-average muscular physique. The only make-up she wore was thick black eyeliner, narrowing her eyes to menacing slits.

Louise was anxious to ingratiate herself, knowing it was her fault Denise had reacted the way she had. She should never have tried to kiss Adele, but she hadn't been able to help herself. She knew there'd be repercussions from Denise, who was very jealous and possessive.

Louise hoped that Denise hadn't seen everything. Fortunately for her, she was so slight that she had been hidden behind Adele's body so all that Denise would have been able to see was Louise's arms wrapped around Adele's back and Adele stooping over Louise, comforting her. But that had been enough for Denise to lose it.

'What the fuck were you playing at anyway?' demanded Denise, while Louise dabbed at her bloody face with a damp flannel.

'Nothing. She was just comforting me 'cos I was upset, that's all.'

'Well, in future, when you're upset you fuckin' come to me, right?'

'Yeah, sure,' said Louise. 'I didn't go to her anyway. She came in here, then before I knew it she had her fuckin' arms around me.'

'Yeah, well, that bitch had better watch her fuckin' back if she knows what's good for her,' hissed Denise. 'No one fuckin' smacks me like that and gets away with it.'

'Are you gonna get her?' asked Louise, becoming animated.

The prospect of a bit of trouble excited Louise, as long as she wasn't on the receiving end of Denise's temper. In a place where boredom soon took a hold, the inmates found their own ways to entertain themselves.

'No I'm not. What kind of a fuckin' mug do you think I am? She's a kickboxing expert, isn't she?'

'What you gonna do, then?'

'I don't know yet. Let's just play it cool for now, pretend it's all forgotten. Only, it isn't, is it? And one day I will get her, when she least fuckin' expects it.'

★

Peter took his seat at the head of the dining table in his plush apartment, and looked around at his men. To the left of him were Mickey and Sam, who had proved to be worthwhile members of the team since they started working with him. To his right was David, one of his oldest friends.

He and David had been through a lot together since they were teenagers. David, along with another friend, Alan, had accompanied Peter on some of his earliest crimes when they had started carrying out house break-ins and snatches on shopkeepers. At that time Alan was their unofficial leader – until he had stabbed a man to death during a house burglary. He was still serving his sentence for that crime.

Once Alan was inside, Peter had carried on working with David, using a squat as their base after Peter's father had thrown him out. Then Peter had enlisted Mickey and Sam to help them carry out larger jobs together and they had continued working with him. They all regarded Peter as their leader.

The trouble with David was that he had always been a bit of a loose cannon and, as the years went by, he was getting worse. Peter was sure it had something to do with his drug habit although David would never admit it.

Further to Peter's right and the next along from David sat Glynn, the newest member of the gang, who was puffing on a cigar. When he handed his cigars around Peter turned down the offer, opting instead for the cigarette he had already lit.

Although Glynn hadn't been with them long, Peter liked and respected him. He was charismatic and smart, and was a savvy operator. His rugged good-looks enabled him to ingratiate himself with many people, especially women, but what impressed Peter most was his sharp mind and the fact that he was well-built and could handle himself.

In the few months since Glynn had worked with them, his input had been invaluable. Rather than just following instructions like the rest of the men, Glynn would come up with fresh ideas for ways to do things. It felt good to Peter to have someone so switched on. It meant that on the rare occasions that he missed something, he could almost guarantee Glynn would have it covered.

Peter had never appointed a number two but now he was considering doing so. As they became involved in increasingly lucrative crimes and he took on more men, it was evident that he would need someone who could help him lead them. The problem was that David, as his oldest friend, would automatically expect to be handed the job. But Peter was beginning to realise that Glynn was far more suited to the role.

David was already becoming demanding, asking for a greater share of the spoils for each job, though Peter wasn't prepared to increase David's share if he didn't add anything extra to warrant it. They had almost come to blows when Peter had pointed this out.

As he surveyed his men through a thick pall of cigar and cigarette smoke, Peter knew that this was going to be one of his most difficult meetings. Someone had double-crossed him, and that someone was currently seated around his dining table.

'Right,' he said. 'There's a reason why I've called you all here today. It's to do with the Binkley warehouse job. We're due to hit it next Saturday night, as you know. Only, some bastard's beaten us to it.'

He watched the men's reactions. Mickey, Sam and Glynn seemed shocked, whereas David remained unresponsive as he repeatedly tapped the edge of a coaster on the table top.

'Not only that,' Peter continued, 'whoever did it had inside info. From what I've been told, their modus operandi was very similar to what we had planned.'

He paused for a few moments to gauge his men's reactions before speaking again. 'That can mean only one thing,' he said. 'Someone in this room was either involved or they provided information to the team that hit the warehouse.'

He heard one of the men suck in air as he digested his words, but it wasn't David.

'Might be a coincidence,' David said.

'I don't fuckin' think so!' snapped Peter. 'There were too many similarities.'

'Like what?'

'The day of the week. The time of day. And the method of entry.'

David didn't say anything further, but continued to fiddle with the coaster, turning it over in his hands then tapping each of its edges in turn against the table top.

'So, has anyone got anything to tell me?' Peter asked.

'Not me,' muttered each of the men, apart from David, who carried on playing with the coaster.

'David?' Peter prompted.

'What the fuck?' David snapped back. 'What you askin' me for?'

'Because you're the only one who hasn't denied it.'

'Didn't think I had to. How many years have you known me, for fuck's sake?'

'OK, so is that a denial?' Peter asked.

'Course it fuckin' is. You shouldn't even need to ask.'

In the silence that followed, Peter stared at each of the men in turn and the tension in the room grew. The only sound was the repeated tapping of the coaster hitting the table.

'For fuck's sake, put the bastard thing down!' Peter ordered.

David slammed the coaster down hard on to the table top. 'What you having a go at me for?' he demanded.

'Because it's you that's making that fuckin' awful noise,' Peter barked back.

'Fuck this shit!' cursed David, getting up. He then

slammed his chair under the table and headed towards the door. 'Let me know when you find out who it was,' he said before he departed.

'Wait, I haven't finished yet!' Peter shouted, but he was wasting his time. David kept going until he was out of the apartment.

Peter gazed at the other three men. 'Well, any of you know who it might be?' he asked.

The men shrugged and shook their heads. Peter's interrogation was now half-hearted. He knew none of them would admit it, but someone knew something and he needed to find out who.

'OK, you might as well go,' he said.

The three men got up to go but Peter stopped Glynn. 'Can I have a word, Glynn?' he asked.

'Sure, go ahead,' said Glynn.

Peter watched the other two men leave the room and waited until he heard the sound of the latch clicking on the front door. 'Hang on a minute,' he said. Then he walked down the hall and peeped through his spyhole to check Sam and Mickey had walked away. He returned to the room and poured both Glynn and himself liberal measures of brandy into crystal tumblers.

'It's about David,' he said, sitting back down at the table.

Glynn nodded.

'I'm worried about him. He's getting a bit too fuckin''

trigger-happy for my liking. And cocky, too. It's ever since he started doing coke.'

'I know what you mean,' said Glynn. 'There was no need for him to use the gun on that last job.'

'I fuckin' know it. He's becoming a liability, and he's getting fuckin' worse. I might have to let him go. I can't risk having the cops breathing down my neck. But I know the shit will hit the fan once I do it. You saw what he was like.'

'Yeah, doesn't like being put on the spot, does he?'

'Dead right. But there's more,' said Peter, his voice dropping. 'I almost don't even want to say this but... I think it's him.'

'What, you mean...?'

'Double-crossing me, yeah.'

'Shit!'

'I know. I can't fuckin' believe it after everything we've been through together. I've known him since we were kids. I can't believe he'd betray me.'

But even as Peter spoke those words, he thought back to a time when David had betrayed him previously. It had been when they were kids. They'd been lifting lead from the roof of an abandoned factory with their friend Alan, and David had fallen through one of the skylights. His injuries were so bad that Peter and Alan had called an ambulance, then fled the scene once it arrived.

Peter had known there was no need for David to

have given his and Alan's names to the police. But, nevertheless, he had done so. Peter had shrugged it off at the time. They were only kids, after all, and David would have been shaken up by his injuries.

Glynn's voice broke him out of his reverie. 'That's the trouble once they're on the fuckin' coke,' he said. 'They lose all reason. I know what you mean, though, mate. You and him were good mates, weren't you?'

'Yeah. We were once,' said Peter, taking a comforting swig of his brandy.

'What makes you think it's him?' asked Glynn.

'Just intuition and the way he's been acting.'

'OK. Well, let's not jump the gun on this, Pete. You don't wanna miss summat while you're suspecting the wrong guy, do you?'

'Suppose not. But, I don't see who else could have done it.'

'I know, but it's best to make sure. I tell you what, why don't I do a bit of sniffing around; see what I can find out? Then we'll know for sure.'

'Good idea, mate,' said Peter.

'Do you mind if I ask the name of the firm that beat us to it?' said Glynn. Peter looked at him suspiciously until Glynn added, 'It might help me find something out.'

'Yeah, sure,' Peter said. 'It was the Millers.'

'Aah, makes sense,' said Glynn. 'It's their type of thing.'

'Yeah, they're fuckin' slimy enough to nick someone else's job, as well,' Peter replied. When Glynn shrugged, he added, 'Oh, and thanks,' leaning over to clink his glass against Glynn's.

'No probs, mate. It's for the good of the firm,' said Glynn.

Peter's disappointment in his friend David had made him drop his guard. Glynn was making all the right noises so he willingly put his trust in him. After all, Glynn hadn't given him a reason not to. Yet.

3

Adele returned to her cell ready for lockdown. Her cell mate, Anna, was already inside and looked as though she had been there a while. As usual, she was splayed out on the bottom bunk wearing only her ill-fitting underwear. It wasn't a pretty sight.

Adele averted her gaze from Anna's obese body as she walked into the cell. She didn't want to encourage her. Although Adele had made it obvious to Anna that she wasn't interested in any sexual encounters inside prison, it didn't stop Anna from flirting. Adele couldn't imagine anybody being attracted to Anna but it seemed that she remained ever hopeful.

'I see you've been with Caroline again,' she commented.

'So, what's the problem?' Adele replied.

She knew that Anna was jealous of her friendship with Caroline. Putting any sexual attraction aside, Anna was still drawn to Adele. Once she had found out about Adele's crime, she had spent the first couple of weeks of

Adele's sentence parading her around like a pet pony, proudly showing off her friendship with a violent killer.

Anna was one of those people who was always desperate to impress. For her, having a callous killer for a cell mate was exciting and gave her bragging rights amongst the other inmates.

Adele hadn't figured Anna out at first. She had appeared intimidating because of her size and her manliness, and it had taken Adele all her courage to stand up to her. But it soon became obvious that it was all a front. Deep down Anna wasn't tough at all.

When Anna had read about Adele's crime and found out that she was the sister of notorious gangster Peter Robinson, she held her in high esteem. Within no time most of the prison knew what Adele was inside for, thanks to Anna, and those who didn't know of her reputation soon found out when her brother turned up at visiting time.

'No problem,' Anna sniffed in response to Adele's question, pulling a newspaper up to cover her face.

Adele stepped over and pulled the top of the newspaper down, revealing the smirk on Anna's face. Anna knew something, that was obvious, but Adele realised that she wouldn't reveal what she knew straight away. Instead she'd enjoy the feeling of power at withholding the information.

This was one aspect of Anna's character that Adele didn't like. It was pitiful really. Anna wasn't too bright and didn't often get the chance to get one over on anyone. She therefore made the most of any chances that came her way. Adele, recognising this, was gradually learning how to play her.

Anna had her good points, too. She was fiercely loyal, and once you were a friend of Anna's you had a friend for life.

Adele decided to ignore Anna's remarks and feign disinterest. Anna would probably be so anxious to string her along that she wouldn't be able to resist feeding Adele a few more snippets. Adele had guessed right.

'Like two peas in a pod, you and Caroline, aren't you?' asked Anna after a while.

'Don't know what you mean,' Adele responded.

'Well, you've got a lot in common,' said Anna.

'Really?' asked Adele, taking care to keep her voice calm.

'Oh, yeah,' Anna added enthusiastically.

Adele grabbed a book and climbed onto the top bunk, smiling to herself as she waited for Anna to continue, confident that she would.

It was several minutes before Anna spoke again. 'Well, for a kick-off, you and Caroline are both brainy.'

'Yeah, and there's ten years between us.'

'Doesn't matter,' said Anna. 'You both don't do drugs.'

'She's got children, I haven't.'

Adele could hear Anna pant as she rushed to provide an alternative statement. 'You both dress nice,' she gushed.

'She's fair, I'm dark,' Adele countered straight away, stifling a giggle. She was enjoying playing with Anna.

There was a pause before Anna added her next morsel of information. 'You're both in for a long stretch.' This time there was a confident edge to her voice.

Aah, now we're getting there, thought Adele. It was obviously something to do with Caroline's sentence.

'I've got a temper, she hasn't,' said Adele.

'Ha-ha,' chuckled Anna. 'I hope for your sake that she never fuckin' turns on you, then.'

Now Adele was intrigued. 'Go on, what's she in for?'

'You mean you don't know?' asked Anna.

'It never seemed the right time to ask.'

Now Anna was winning the game and Adele could hear the glee in her voice as she said, 'Well, if she's not gonna tell yer, then it's not my business to.'

'Why not? You didn't mind telling everyone about me.'

Anna sniffed. 'Yours was common knowledge anyway. It's been all over the fuckin' papers.'

'Right. So, you're not going to tell me?' Adele asked, becoming a little irritated.

'No. It's none of my business who you choose to spend your time with.'

Although Adele felt a little annoyed with Anna, she

decided not to play along any more. She wouldn't give her the pleasure. Adele felt confident that if she left it long enough, Anna would tell her anyway. She wouldn't be able to help herself.

Instead Adele tried to focus on her book. As she lay on her bed one of the guards came and announced that it was time for lockdown. Adele heard the heavy metal cell door slam shut and she had a sinking feeling in the pit of her stomach. It always had that effect on her, even though she'd been inside for a few weeks now. As usual, she tried to rein in her anxiety and took deep breaths to steady her racing heart as she thought about being locked inside the tiny cell overnight.

Then her mind drifted back to the nights when as a child she had lain in bed, waiting for her father to come home from the pub. The feeling of fear that never left her throughout her childhood. The violent rows between her parents. Her mother's injuries the next day. Then the way in which his aggression had escalated over the years, leading to him viciously beating up her brother.

The vivid recollections were only making her anxiety worse so she tried to concentrate on something good instead: her grandma. She was the one who had always supported Adele and Peter, and encouraged her to make a better life for herself – until she died from cancer. Unfortunately, despite her grandmother's best attempts, Adele had still ended up in this place.

Soon after the guard had locked the cell door the night noise started. Prisoners were shouting to each other from cell to cell.

'You all right, Jen?' Adele could hear amongst other conversations. Then she heard the ear-splitting sound of a panicked scream and someone else screeching to be let out. Loud banging followed, as it did most nights. It was the cue for others to join in and a relentless din took over the prison. Inmates were yelling and screaming while the guards competed with an incessant metallic banging as they shouted for the prisoners to keep quiet. It was some time before the racket abated and Adele finally fell asleep.

Adele had been wrong about Anna. The next day Anna still refused to tell her what crime Caroline had committed: saying only that Adele should ask Caroline herself, but it would be best to choose her moment carefully. Adele knew that this was Anna's way of wielding power. Any advantage she had over others helped to mask her own insecurities.

Although Adele could have asked someone else, it didn't feel right to do so. Besides, she was still learning who she could trust and who she couldn't, and she didn't want to risk it getting back to Caroline that she had been asking questions about her.

Adele knew enough to realise that the rumour mill in

this place worked on overtime, and she wouldn't want Caroline to think she had been disloyal. It left her with no choice: she would have to ask Caroline herself but, like Anna said, she would have to choose her moment carefully.

4

Adele met Caroline on the corridor, which was full of excited chatter as hordes of prisoners made their way to classes. It was a rare treat in the prison and something Adele and most of the other inmates eagerly anticipated.

'You all right?' Caroline asked.

It was a typical question from Caroline, but it put Adele on guard. She felt as though Caroline had picked up on her unease following the conversation with Anna the previous day.

She tried to appear relaxed. 'Sure,' she said. 'Art class is always something to look forward to, isn't it?'

'Yeah, very therapeutic. And, God knows, we need that in this place.'

Adele recognised an opportunity to steer the conversation round to what she wanted to know but she avoided appearing too blatant.

'Yeah, you're right. But it's not only this place. It helps to take your mind off things on the outside.'

She noticed Caroline's expression change: a shifting of the eyebrows and a furrowing of her brow. Adele continued, knowing she had hit a nerve. 'Y'know, it helps you to deal with the demons,' she said.

She stared into Caroline's eyes, waiting for a response but, just then, Denise came bustling up with Louise in tow. Adele flinched as Denise held out her hand to her, worried about what Denise would do next.

Denise surprised her. 'I just wanna say, no hard feelings,' she gushed, grabbing Adele's hand and shaking it. 'I just got the wrong end of the stick… sorry… I should have known it's not your bag, anyway.'

Adele gazed back open-mouthed with shock before replying, 'N-no problem. Sorry if I was a bit rough. I forget at times, it's just automatic.'

'That's all right,' said Denise, forcing a grin.

'I'm sorry, too,' said Louise, following Denise's lead. 'I mean… that Denise thought something was going on. 'Cos there wasn't. Well, we both know that, don't we?'

Adele grinned back, amused at Louise's attempts to extricate herself from any suspicion, then watched them both hurry on up the corridor.

She turned to Caroline. 'Well, that's a relief,' she said. 'I was half expecting a bit more bother from them two.'

'Don't be so sure,' warned Caroline.

'What do you mean?' Adele felt a rush of fear.

Caroline sniffed. 'The whole thing looked a bit devious to me. Denise is either kowtowing to you because you've got the better of her or she's trying to lull you into a false sense of security.'

'Really?'

'Yes, you need to watch your back. She's a sly one and I wouldn't trust her as far as I could throw her.'

A cold chill shot through Adele and she didn't speak for a few seconds.

'Don't let it worry you,' said Caroline, seeing the concern painted across her friend's face. 'After all, you've got the better of her once so you can do it again. But watch for Louise siding with her, and try to make sure you're never alone.'

'OK, thanks,' said Adele.

They continued walking to their art class. Adele remembered their earlier conversation and was wondering how to get back on topic when there was a commotion a few metres ahead of them. The crowded corridor became even more packed as everyone rushed to see what was happening. Adele and Caroline followed.

Once they had reached the scene, Caroline broke through the crowd with Adele behind her. There, on the floor surrounded by inmates, was a woman. She was convulsing, and Adele watched, alarmed, as her arms and legs twitched uncontrollably. Caroline stepped forward and immediately took control.

'Step back!' she said. 'Give her space. Has anyone got a pillow?' When no one responded she turned to Adele. 'See what you can find, will you? Just something soft to put under her head.'

The woman continued thrashing around as the throng of women gasped, and Caroline struggled to undo the top button of her blouse. For a few seconds Adele watched, her mouth agape, until Caroline prompted her. 'Adele! A pillow?'

Adele snapped to and she was about to go in search of one when someone passed a rolled-up sweater to Caroline, who placed it beneath the woman's head.

'Help me hold them back,' Caroline said to Adele. 'She needs space.'

She followed Caroline's lead, spreading her arms out to hold back the masses of curious onlookers. Adele's heart beat rapidly as she watched the woman on the ground, her body jerking involuntarily. 'Will she be OK?' she asked Caroline, her voice full of concern.

'Yes, she'll come out of it soon. Don't worry.'

They continued to hold the prisoners back. Adele could feel the crowd of women pressing behind her as they tried to catch a glimpse of the woman on the ground.

'Keep back! Give her space,' Caroline kept repeating, and Adele could see the determination on her face.

Two prison officers arrived just as the woman was coming out of the epileptic fit.

'Get back!' one of them shouted.

Then they stepped forward, pushing Adele and Caroline out of the way while they attended to the woman and put her in the recovery position.

'Thanks, but no thanks,' Caroline muttered sarcastically as she and Adele walked away.

'Bloody hell! That was scary,' said Adele.

Caroline smiled. 'You'll get used to it.'

'What? You mean, it's happened before?'

'Oh, yeah. To her and a couple of others.'

Adele stared back at Caroline in shock.

'She's a druggie,' said Caroline. 'Withdrawal can do that to them.'

'Oh my God! I didn't realise. It was so scary.'

'Yeah, it is the first time you see it.'

'You were brilliant,' said Adele.

'Not really. You just know what to do once you've seen a few.'

'Can it harm them?'

'Not usually. Most fits are over in a few minutes. The main thing is to give them room so they don't bang themselves on anything and to cushion their heads and loosen any clothing around the throat so it's not restricting their breathing. The trouble is, most prisoners are too busy gawking to do what needs to be done.'

'I noticed,' said Adele, beginning to relax now it was over.

'Come on, we're late to class,' said Caroline, speeding up the corridor.

In all the furore Adele had forgotten what she had been about to ask Caroline.

It was a few days later when Glynn called at Peter's apartment again. Peter ignored the doorbell at first; he was too busy entertaining two fashion models he had picked up the previous night.

When the ringing of the doorbell became insistent he slung on the jeans that he'd dropped on the bedroom floor in his haste to bed the two beauties, and he went out to the hall to see who it was. Peter pulled open his front door and found Glynn standing outside, looking exasperated.

'You took your time,' Glynn said. Then, as he took in Peter's semi-undressed state despite the fact that it was mid-afternoon, he grinned before asking, 'You been busy?'

Peter smiled back and said, 'Hang on a minute.'

He left Glynn in the living room while he told the two girls to get dressed and go home. He couldn't risk anyone overhearing his conversation with Glynn. Once he'd seen the girls leave his apartment, Peter came back into the living room where three champagne glasses and two empty bottles still littered the coffee table.

'Got any news?' he asked Glynn as he poured them each a tumbler of brandy and sat down.

'Oh, yeah,' said Glynn. 'But I don't think you're gonna like it.'

'Go on,' said Peter, his nostrils flaring as he inhaled sharply.

'I saw Dave in the Sportsman's. He was having a long chat with Steve Miller.'

'Did he see you?'

'Don't think so. I was on the other side of the bar. I peeped through a couple of times. He must have been talking to him for a good fifteen minutes from what I saw.'

'I never knew they were friends,' said Peter, gripping his brandy glass tightly till his knuckles turned white.

'Well, Pete, they looked pretty fuckin' cosy to me.'

'The double-crossing bastard!' Peter cursed.

'There's more,' said Glynn. 'I wanted to be sure so I checked with a mate of mine. He reckons Dave has been seeing Steve Miller a lot and they both score from the same supplier.'

'You're fuckin' joking!' said Peter, his face turning crimson.

'Wish I was, Pete.'

Peter got up and started pacing his apartment. 'Who is this mate? Is he kosher?' he demanded.

'Smithy? Yeah, course he is. I wouldn't have taken his word for it otherwise.'

'And can he be trusted not to let things go any further?'

'Sure. I've already put him straight on that.'

'The fuckin' bastard!' Peter cursed again. 'I can hardly believe it, but it must be Dave who betrayed me,' he continued. 'I can't see any other reason why he'd be getting so cosy with the Millers. And if he's scoring from the same fuckin' supplier, well, that says it all, doesn't it?'

'Looks that way… Sorry, Pete. I hate to be the one to break it to you. I know how close you and him were.'

'Yes, we were,' said Peter. 'But not any fuckin' more! He's been going downhill ever since he got hooked on the fuckin' coke. I think you and me need to pay Dave a visit and have a little chat.'

He emphasised the word 'chat' and they both knew what the implications were. This wasn't going to be a cosy chat. Peter wanted answers from David and if he didn't like the answers he gave, then he and Glynn would take whatever action was necessary.

'Sure. You know I'll back you up, mate. Any time,' said Glynn.

5

Adele had to wait until they had 'association' before she had a chance to speak to Caroline again. This was the period in the evening when inmates were free to mix with each other, and Adele often spent that time in Caroline's company. She found her in her cell alone, sitting on the bed reading a book. It always amazed Adele how Caroline managed to read effortlessly considering the clamour of prison life. Maybe it just took time to acclimatise to the noise.

'Hi, how's things?' Caroline asked.

'Not bad,' said Adele. 'What about you?'

'OK, yeah.'

Adele decided that if she wanted to find out what Caroline was in for then there was no sense in beating about the bush.

'Caroline, I've been wanting to ask you something,' she began, tentatively.

Caroline's expression changed straight away to one of sadness, perhaps tinged with guilt; it was difficult to tell. Her tone of voice changed too and it now had a hard edge to it. 'Let me guess,' she said. 'You want to know what I'm in here for.'

'Well, yeah. But if you'd rather not talk about it, that's OK.'

'No, it's all right.' Caroline sighed as she fidgeted nervously with the bedcover. 'I thought you might ask eventually. In fact, I'm surprised no one's told you. Anna's not usually one to keep a secret.'

It was as though Caroline was delaying the inevitable revelation. There was now a tone of irony in her voice – something Adele hadn't heard before – and she decided to tread carefully. She felt a pang of disquiet, which caused a prickle down her spine. It was obviously a sensitive subject.

'She wouldn't tell me,' said Adele. 'But you know Anna: knowledge is power, and all that.'

As soon as she said the words she realised how inappropriate they sounded and she quickly backtracked. 'I'm sure she didn't mean any harm, though.'

'It's OK,' said Caroline. 'It's probably best you hear it from me anyway.' She sighed again and there was a long pause before she continued. 'It's… for murder… my sentence… it's murder. But I expect you guessed that anyway.'

'Kind of, I suppose,' answered Adele, 'although I didn't know what to think really—'

Caroline quickly cut in as though she wanted to get this thing out of the way now that she had started. 'It was my husband.'

She looked up at Adele, seeking her approval before continuing. Adele nodded, and Caroline dropped her gaze to her lap.

'He'd been abusing me for years,' she said, as she continued to fidget with the bedcover, no longer able to meet Adele's eyes. 'I know,' she added, pre-empting Adele's response, 'I should have left him. That's what everyone says. But until you've been in that situation, you don't know. It happens gradually, over months or years. And you just get pulled along with it.

'It was his way of dealing with stress, unfortunately. A raised voice here, a slammed door there, if someone had upset him at work. Then sometimes he went too far and lashed out at me if I said a wrong word or even if I said something unintentional. He always took it the wrong way and it was difficult to calm him down, to make him see that I was on his side. Then, as time went on, his rages got worse.

'I suppose part of me wanted the man I married to come back. We were blissfully happy at first, and I wanted to relive those times so much... And there were still flashes of his old self from time to time, even at the end. That's what kept me going, I suppose, the thought that the man I loved would return to me.

'I used to make excuses for him, telling myself that it was because of the stress he was under, and that once things improved for him at work he'd go back to being his old self again. But as the years went by it was as though I didn't recognise him anymore. He changed so much.'

Her voice was now trembling and she looked at Adele again.

'It's OK, you don't have to,' said Adele. 'Not if it's too painful.'

'No, you need to hear it. Sooner or later someone will tell you and I'd rather you heard it from me.'

'OK, if you're sure,' said Adele.

Caroline took a deep breath and her gaze fell to her lap once more. 'It would affect our love making too. It often felt like he was seeking reassurance, wanting to know that someone still loved him. But he was never gentle when he was in one of those moods, not like he used to be. And I didn't dare say no, even though I knew it was going to be painful. Because if I did, he would accuse me of not caring, or even of having an affair.

'This particular night, he was home late. Thankfully the kids were stopping over at my mother's. It was obvious he'd been drinking and he started on me straight away. I tried to pacify him but he was having none of it. We were in the kitchen, arguing. I was fed up of trying to massage his ego and I started to retaliate. But he didn't take kindly to hearing a few home truths.'

She paused and took another deep breath, and Adele could see that her hands were shaking. Adele was about to say that she didn't need to hear any more when Caroline carried on, 'He was really hammering his fists into me. I didn't think he'd ever stop. And I was scared. But I was angry too.

'Eventually he did stop. I was on the kitchen floor. He'd just raped me... taken me there on the floor! I was bleeding from my nose and I was bashed and bruised. "That'll teach you," he said, walking away and, I don't know why, but for some reason I just flipped.

'He had his back to me as he walked away. I hated him for what he'd done. I was furious! I got up, rushed to the kitchen drawer and grabbed the first knife I could lay my hands on. I ran at him with it and stabbed him in the back of the neck. The blood was gushing and he yelled. Then I stabbed him again, and again. Until he was still. He fell to the floor and I kicked at him. Then I dropped to my knees, yelling at him. Calling him all the horrid names I could think of for what he'd put me through.

'I was still in a rage. As I stared at his evil face, memories of all the times he'd abused me flashed through my mind. I started to stab away at his clothes and his flesh. The blood seeped through. I cut a big hole in his trousers with the knife. I could see his penis poking through. I hated it! So I tore at his clothes until he was half naked.

'Then I cut it off,' Caroline said quickly. 'His testicles, too.'

Adele gulped. She pictured Caroline staring maniacally at her husband as she sawed through his private parts with a kitchen knife. A cold sweat trickled down her back as a rush of fear swept through her. She was sickened at the thought of how long it must have taken Caroline to cut off his penis and testicles, but she remained silent as Caroline continued.

'Then, when it was done, I was still raging. I don't know where it came from. It must have been building up for years. I just wanted rid of the bloody things. I hated them!' she cried. 'So I burnt them.'

'Oh my God!' cried Adele, and she then quickly swallowed down the bile that rose in her throat.

By this time Caroline was sobbing. 'I'm sorry,' said Caroline. 'I swear, to this day, I'll never know why I went that far. I don't know what possessed me.'

'It's all right,' said Adele, rushing to Caroline's side and putting her arms around her.

Adele felt tears cloud her own eyes. Although she was appalled by what Caroline had done, who was she to judge? After all, it wasn't that different from her own story. She too had been in that position. She had lost all control and hit her father repeatedly even as his skull cracked open and his brains spilt out.

They remained there for several minutes, Adele now also in tears and shaking. She didn't know what to say. What could she say? There were no words to explain why either she or Caroline had reacted so violently to their tormentors.

As she sat there silently, a rush of thoughts flashed through her mind. Everything made sense now. The way the other prisoners were wary of Caroline, even though she seemed such a caring person. And the way she and Caroline had been drawn to each other.

Eventually she spoke. 'Did you seek me out?' she asked.

Caroline looked up, her face red and blotchy and streaked with tears. 'I know what you're thinking,' she said. 'That perhaps I thought we would understand each other because of... our crimes. But no, not particularly. I mean, I knew what you were in for, and maybe I'd have judged you differently if it wasn't for my own experiences. But I didn't deliberately seek you out. I just liked you as a person.'

Adele nodded, unsure what to say next.

'Well, it's out in the open now,' said Caroline, with a sardonic smile.

'I won't hold it against you,' said Adele. 'How could I?'

And as she spoke those words Adele realised just how much her world had changed. At one time she'd have run a mile from someone who had committed such a heinous crime, no matter what the circumstances were. But inside these walls she saw Caroline as a best friend.

Their crimes were similar. They shared the guilt. And Adele knew that no one would ever understand Caroline in the same way that she did.

6

Adele was lying on the top bunk in her cell. She was having a good night's sleep; one of the best she'd had since starting her prison sentence.

It was the day after Caroline had made her revelation and their shared understanding had cemented their friendship. As Adele settled into prison life and made more friends, she was feeling more at ease and sleeping better.

She was currently dreaming about John, her exboyfriend. He was often in her thoughts and, even though she knew she would never see him again, occasional recollections of their happy times together could brighten an otherwise dull day.

Her dreams of him were often graphic in nature, too. They had shared a wonderful sex life and she often woke up with a smile following an explicit dream. Tonight was no exception. She murmured as his hands caressed her nipples softly. Then he drew her face towards his, meeting her lips.

As she awoke she could still feel a tingling sensation in her breasts and had a warm glow all over her body. Until she opened her eyes. There, leaning over her, was the pockmarked, manly face of Anna, accompanied by a faint smell of stale sweat. She had drawn her lips away but still had her hands inside Adele's nightshirt, resting on her breasts.

Adele shot up in the bed, her head colliding with Anna's. She was battling with a riot of emotions: her initial repugnance at the sight of Anna, disappointment that it wasn't John, then fury at Anna's audacity. There was a look of alarm on Anna's face as Adele pushed her ferociously away.

'What the fuck do you think you're playing at?' Adele yelled, giving Anna another angry shove.

Anna lost her balance and almost tumbled off the top bunk. She found the steps just in time before Adele could throw her off altogether. But Adele wasn't finished with her yet. She launched herself off the bunk, meeting Anna at ground level. Before Anna could react, Adele rammed into her, pinned her up against the cell wall and slammed her forearm across Anna's throat.

Adele's arm was pressed so tightly against Anna's throat that she gasped for air. She tried to prise Adele off her but failed. Anger was coursing through Adele's veins. She threw all her weight behind her forearm until it was wedged in place.

'You fuckin' cheeky bitch! How dare you?' Adele yelled as she slapped away Anna's hands.

Anna was going red in the face as she struggled to breathe, but Adele wouldn't let up. Her face was a mask of fury as she put more weight behind her forearm until it was even tighter against Anna's throat.

'You dirty, slimy fuckin' freak!' shouted Adele. 'Just what the fuck have you been doing while I've been asleep?'

Anna struggled to respond and Adele eased her arm away a little.

'Nothing,' Anna panted. 'It was the first time, I swear!'

'I don't fuckin' believe you. You dirty bitch!'

'It was! Honestly, I've never done that before, and I swear I'll never do it again.'

'You'd better fuckin' not!' said Adele, easing her arm a little more. 'Because if I ever fuckin' catch you doing anything like that again, I'll be straight off to the governor to demand a cell change. And I'll make sure she, and everybody else, knows why.'

As Adele released her grip, a look of relief flashed across Anna's face, which annoyed Adele even more. She jabbed her arm back tightly and spoke between clenched teeth. 'But before I go to see the governor, I'll give you the hiding of your fuckin' life! Do you understand?'

She jabbed her arm even harder to emphasise her point until Anna's eyes bulged. Then, feeling alarmed at how far she'd gone, she removed her arm and let Anna go.

Anna took a few sharp breaths before retreating to her own bunk and muttering something under her breath.

'What did you say?' demanded Adele, her adrenalin still pumping.

'You seemed to be enjoying it,' she murmured, more sure of herself now that Adele had let her go.

'Don't you fuckin' dare!' shouted Adele, stepping towards her again.

'All right, all right,' Anna babbled. 'Just saying.'

'Well, don't! You know very well that's not my bag and, even if it was, you'd be the last person on my list. So, in future, keep your fuckin' dirty hands to yourself!'

Anna grabbed at a magazine and held it in front of her face, pretending to read, but her shame was evident so Adele left her alone and busied herself tidying up the cell to take her mind off what had happened. She couldn't help feeling troubled, however, at the thought of what Anna got up to once she was asleep.

Denise and Louise were in the recreation area when Anna went over to join them. She was still recovering from the shock of Adele's recent attack.

'What's that mark on your neck?' Denise asked.

Anna fingered the red swelling around her throat, which felt tender to the touch. 'It's that Adele. She's a fuckin' lunatic!'

'What d'you mean?' asked Louise.

'She attacked me. She had me pinned up against the wall. I thought she was gonna fuckin' kill me!'

'You're joking!' said Denise. 'What did she do that for?'

'Nothing much,' sniffed Anna. Then, with her head hanging low, she muttered, 'I made a pass at her.'

'Aah, right,' said Denise, with a knowing smile. Then she added, 'So, what was wrong with just knocking you back like anyone else would have done?'

'Exactly!' Anna noticed that a small crowd had now gathered around them and she was enjoying playing to an audience. 'Instead, the mad bitch has to go and attack me. She's a fuckin' psycho! I tell you what, if either of you are thinking of making a play for her, I wouldn't bother, not if you value your life, anyway.'

'We wouldn't,' said Denise, giving Louise an evil stare.

'No, would we 'eck,' Louise quickly added.

'How come she got the better of you, anyway? You're bigger than her. I thought you would have fuckin' had her,' said Denise.

'She's stronger than you think,' said Anna. 'And she's a fuckin' kickboxing expert, isn't she? Haven't you seen her in the gym doing her stuff? She's good at it – fast, too. She had me up against that fuckin' cell wall before I even knew what was happening. Anyway, from what I heard you didn't do so well against her when she had a go at you.'

Denise sniffed. 'She just caught me by surprise, that's all. She looks like butter wouldn't melt but, you're right, she's a fuckin' lunatic when she loses it. Anyway, she'd better not fuckin' go for me like that again. 'Cos next time I'll be ready, and I'll fuckin' have her.'

Anna noticed the steely look of defiance on Denise's face as well as the concerned expressions on the faces of some of the other inmates. Anna realised that perhaps she had gone a bit too far. After all, Adele had good reason for doing what she had, although Anna wasn't about to admit that to anyone. And despite Adele attacking her, Anna still had a soft spot for her and wouldn't want her to come to any harm. Denise was a tough adversary and it wasn't good to get on the wrong side of her.

What Anna didn't realise was that Adele's reputation was gaining momentum. The other prisoners already knew what had happened between Adele and Denise, and this new revelation was further cementing Adele's status as someone who wasn't to be messed with.

'She's all right really. She's just got a bit of a temper, that's all,' Anna said.

'You've soon changed your fuckin' tune!' said Denise.

'Like I said, she's all right really. You've just gotta make sure you don't upset her.'

Denise scowled at Anna. 'We'll fuckin' see about that,' she murmured before walking away with Louise trailing behind.

Anna stared after them, worried that she might have stirred things up unintentionally. She only hoped that Adele wouldn't suffer because of her big mouth.

7

When David answered his front door, his hair was messy and his clothes creased. Peter smelt the faint odour of BO and guessed that David hadn't showered and was probably still wearing the same clothes as yesterday. He screwed up his face in disgust.

'Heavy night, was it?' Peter asked scathingly as he and Glynn stepped inside.

David looked down at his crumpled clothing. 'Yeah,' he laughed. 'Fuckin' great night. I crashed out on the sofa.'

They walked through to the lounge.

'D'you wanna drink?' David asked.

'No, thanks,' said Peter, his nostrils twitching at the stench of the place.

'This isn't a social visit anyway,' added Glynn.

A look of unease flashed across David's face. 'What's wrong?'

'Sit down!' ordered Peter. 'We need to talk.'

David did as he was told while Peter and Glynn remained standing.

'Right, for a start, do you wanna tell me why you've been seeing so much of Steve Miller?' Peter asked, his tone harsh.

'I haven't. What you on about?'

'You've been meeting him in the Sportsman's. And from what I've been told, you've been getting pretty fuckin' cosy.'

'No, I haven't. That's a lie,' David protested. Then he looked up at Glynn. 'Did he tell you this?'

'Never mind who fuckin' told me!' Peter snapped. 'I've heard it from more than one person. And, from what I've heard, you've met him a few times.'

'That's bullshit! I don't have owt to do with him.'

'You sure?' asked Peter, 'Only, from what I've been told, you and him even use the same fuckin' supplier!'

'I don't know what you're talking about. I don't even know who he scores from. I don't have anything to do with the guy.'

David's voice had taken on an alarmed tone now as he watched Glynn alternately balling his hands into fists then cracking his knuckles. Peter nodded to Glynn, who walked over to the sofa and dragged David off it by the scruff of his neck.

'Get your fuckin' hands off me!' David yelled.

Peter nodded again and Glynn responded by belting David while keeping a grip on him with his other hand.

The punch landed squarely on David's jaw and he pulled back, clutching his face. He tried to wriggle free but Glynn kept hold of him, his large hands crushing David's flesh.

'Get your fuckin' hands off me!' David repeated, his arms flailing wildly about as he tried to break free of Glynn's grasp.

Glynn landed another sharp punch to his nose. Blood spurted from David's nostrils, and Glynn wiped his knuckles in disgust.

'They're lying!' David shouted. 'Whoever told you is lying.'

Glynn hit him again repeatedly until Peter signalled for him to stop and Glynn stood aside. 'Tell the fuckin' truth, David, or he'll carry on hitting you!'

'I'm not fuckin' lying!' David squealed, his face now blood soaked and contorted with pain.

Peter stepped up to David so their faces were only centimetres apart.

'I know what you've been up to so don't keep telling me fuckin' lies!' he hissed.

David opened his mouth to speak again but the sight of his former friend's angry face silenced him. Peter's face was blood red, and the veins in his throat were taut.

'I can't fuckin' trust you anymore! You're a loose cannon, Dave,' he said, his voice now a mix of anger and bitter disappointment.

Peter quickly checked himself, not wanting to show any sign of weakness, and his voice took on a more menacing tone. 'I should have known by the way you've been acting lately. Getting too big for your fuckin' boots!'

As Peter spoke the last words he aimed a sharp blow to David's gut. David doubled over, squealing in agony. While Glynn held David from behind, Peter continued to rain punches. His aggressive onslaught helped him release his fury and disappointment in his one-time friend. When David begged for mercy and screamed out in pain, Peter became even angrier, belting him repeatedly as the blood spattered around them.

He didn't stop until his fists were sore. Then he stood back, eyeing David's bloody, swollen face. 'You're a fuckin' disaster, Dave,' he cursed. 'Get back to your coke-head mates. You're no fuckin' use to me now.'

Peter walked away and signalled for Glynn to follow. As Glynn let go of David, he slumped to the ground.

'What a fuckin' loser,' Peter muttered as they made their way out.

Peter was upset as well as angry. He felt bad having to punish David. He'd been his friend for a long time and they'd been through a lot together. Doling out punishments was one thing, but doing it to a former mate was another matter. But he couldn't afford not to. David had to be taught a lesson. No one took the piss out of Peter Robinson and got away with it.

As he made his way out of David's home, Peter was already feeling remorseful. He knew it was the drugs that had turned his friend. Once they got a grip, you lost all logic. But he couldn't carry someone like that. He'd be forever watching his back. He couldn't trust someone who had lied and deceived him. So, he walked away to the sound of David still protesting his innocence.

Caroline wished she hadn't let Adele rope her into her kickboxing session again. Despite Caroline's criminal history, all that wanton aggression just wasn't her scene at all. But Adele needed someone to partner her while she practised her moves and Caroline didn't like to refuse a good friend.

They were in the gym and Caroline was clutching a long kickboxing pad, which covered most of her torso. While Adele jabbed at the pad, Caroline threw her weight behind it to stop her feet from shifting. As Adele continued to jab, she seemed to be working herself up into such a fury that Caroline had to push harder to maintain her position.

Something seemed to have upset Adele recently but Caroline wasn't sure what. Maybe it was the incident with Anna that had shaken her. Caroline had tried to help her laugh it off but Adele was having none of it. Although Caroline had tried to play it down, she could understand why Adele was so freaked out. It can't have been nice to think that someone was mauling you while you were asleep.

Caroline also found the kickboxing sessions boring. While she held onto the pad her mind drifted and she gazed around the gym. She could see a small group of women, a few metres behind Adele. They had taken a break from their workouts and were now watching Adele practising, and whispering amongst themselves.

All of a sudden Adele took a mighty front kick off the back leg, striking the pad with some force. It took Caroline by surprise and she rocked backwards, almost toppling over. While Caroline tried to recover her balance, Adele continued to jab rapidly at the pad.

'Steady on, Adele. Bloody hell!' said Caroline. 'You nearly had me on the floor then.'

Adele paused on hearing Caroline's words and she seemed to take a few seconds to come back into focus.

'Bloody hell!' Caroline repeated. 'I don't know who you thought this bloody pad was then but I hope it wasn't me.'

'Sorry,' said Adele, standing with her hands on her hips and breathing heavily. 'I just got a bit carried away, that's all.'

Caroline stepped forward and tapped lightly on Adele's shoulder, the kickboxing pad now hanging loosely from her other hand. 'No worries,' she smiled, 'but I think it might be time to take a break. My bloody arms are killing me from holding onto this thing.'

Adele smiled back and both women walked over to the side of the gym to have a rest. Caroline noticed that the crowd of prisoners continued watching her and Adele until they reached the far wall, then they dispersed and carried on with what they were doing.

'I think you're attracting a bit of attention,' whispered Caroline.

'What do you mean?' asked Adele.

'A few people were watching you work out.'

'Who?'

Adele didn't know most of the inmates but there were two whose names she would be familiar with because of their reputations for being tough. When Caroline told her who they were, Adele raised her eyebrows in surprise.

'Why would they be watching me?' she asked.

'Because... you're getting a bit of a reputation as a fighter.'

'What? Just because I do kickboxing?'

'No,' Caroline sighed. 'A few of the hard nuts have found out what happened between you and Anna.'

Adele cringed with embarrassment.

'No, not that,' Caroline quickly continued. 'She won't have told them what she did to you. She'd be too ashamed of that. But, you know what Anna's like for being dramatic. Apparently, word is going around that you're a bit of a lunatic when you're riled.'

Adele laughed. 'Really?'

'Yeah. In fact, some are saying you're the new number one. Since Shazza was released nobody has taken her place. There are a few who would like to but they're all biding their time. Denise is one of them, and since you took Denise on as well as Anna, your name is now right up there.'

'You're joking!' grinned Adele.

'No, I'm not. But don't take it as a compliment. You need to tread carefully. Once you're seen as the number one, there are plenty of people who want to bring you down and take your place.'

Adele's grin was quickly replaced by a frown. 'Shit! I didn't realise. I was just trying to defend myself.'

Her brother's warning words to her before she went inside rang in her head. *Whatever you do, don't show any sign of weakness or they'll fuckin' have you.* She'd taken his advice but was beginning to wonder whether that was a mistake. She didn't realise it would elevate her to top-dog status, and the last thing she needed was a bunch of hard cases having a go at her. Looking at some of the women around the gym, with their muscular physiques and hardened expressions, it made Adele wonder about the former 'number one'.

'What was she like, this Shazza?' she asked.

'Shush,' whispered Caroline. 'She's still got plenty of friends in here.' Caroline checked to make sure no one was watching before dropping her voice and continuing, 'Not very nice. Ruthless, in fact. A lot of us were relieved to see the back of her. But, of course, there were those that sucked up to her. Can't say I blame them. It's all about self-preservation in here.'

'I'm glad I wasn't around to meet her then,' said Adele. 'Come on, let's go back to the cells. I think I've had enough for one day.'

Caroline waited for Adele while she showered and got changed, then they made their way back to the wing together. When they reached Caroline's cell, Adele turned down her offer of a coffee. 'No, thanks, I've just remembered that I'm due to pay the governor a visit,' she said.

'Oh, yeah?' said Caroline, raising her eyebrows inquisitively.

'Yeah, nothing bad,' said Adele. 'I'll tell you about it later but I need to dash now.'

8

Two officers called to collect Adele and take her to see the governor. Adele was disheartened to see that one of them was Prison Officer Fox. They walked in silence with Sly occasionally leading Adele by the arm to display her authority.

As Sly's nails dug into her forearm Adele looked at her, the contempt evident in her expression, but she didn't say anything. It didn't do to upset Sly. Adele had been warned about the woman's spiteful ways. It seemed that she could make your life a misery just as much as some of the prisoners.

'Come in,' called Governor Jones when Sly knocked on her office door.

'Prisoner Robinson here to see you, ma'am,' said Sly.

'Very well,' Governor Jones replied. 'Bring her in.'

Prison Officer Fox stepped inside the office, followed by Adele and the other prison officer. Straight away Adele noticed the lovely fresh scent inside the room. It reminded her of a stroll in the park and was in sharp contrast to the clinical smell of disinfectant in the rest of the prison.

The two officers stood to either side of Adele while she waited for the governor to address her. Adele hadn't seen much of the governor to date, but now she took in her appearance. She was slightly larger than average, aged around fiftyish and smartly dressed. Her hair was platinum blonde and neatly coiffured into an old-fashioned hairstyle. It reminded Adele of the shampoo and set her grandma used to have.

In terms of her features, the governor had one of those faces that was difficult to read. This was exacerbated by the fact that she looked over her glasses at Adele with her head bent forwards and her expression hidden. The governor's eyes flitted between Adele and the open file on the desk in front of her.

Governor Jones remained dispassionate as she addressed her, and Adele guessed that she would be able to discern the governor's personality through her words rather than anything else. While Adele was being addressed, the two officers remained standing on either side of her, watching keenly.

'You arranged to see me?' the governor prompted Adele, her voice lacking any warmth.

'Yes,' said Adele, suddenly feeling intimidated by the formal procedure, the vast desk and impassive demeanour of the governor. 'I w-wanted to ask you about educational opportunities,' she stammered.

'Information about our regular classes is readily available...' the governor began, her voice taking on a hint of irritation, which made Adele feel like a time-waster.

'It's not a regular class,' Adele cut in. 'I wanted to ask you whether I could do a distance-learning course in accountancy.' While Sly tutted, Governor Jones stared over her glasses at Adele. Again, Adele couldn't read her expression but she felt the governor wanted more information. 'I've already got bookkeeping qualifications,' she continued.

'And what do you expect to gain from accountancy qualifications?' asked the governor.

'I thought they might enhance my employment prospects when I'm released,' Adele replied. The governor didn't respond straight away. Instead she carried on staring dispassionately until Adele added, 'I thought it might make good use of my time in here as well, Governor.'

'Really?' asked the governor, assessing Adele for a few seconds before turning her attention to the file in front of her and flicking through its pages. After what seemed like an age the governor spoke again. 'Yes, I see from your file that you've done quite a bit of study. Did you do this during your time at Scott and Palmer solicitors?'

'Yes,' said Adele.

'Was that on day release or did you study in your own time?'

'In my own time,' Adele replied, her voice sounding small and shaky compared to the assertiveness of the governor.

'Well, in that case I suppose you're to be commended,' said Governor Jones, and as she stared over her glasses, Adele thought she detected the hint of a smile.

Adele could feel the weight of Prison Officer Fox's stare and she glanced quickly across at her. Sly's face was like thunder. She obviously wasn't impressed that Adele seemed to have found favour with the governor.

After another pause, the governor said, 'You'll have to leave it with me. There are procedures to be followed for courses outside of our normal curriculum, and then, of course, there are restrictions when it comes to budget. We'll have to justify the cost so I'll take another look at your file and see what we can do.'

'Thank you,' said Adele.

'Not too hasty,' the governor cut in. 'I can't promise anything but we'll let you know in due course.'

'Thank you,' Adele repeated before the governor instructed the two prison officers to lead Adele back to her cell.

★

Caroline was standing outside her cell chatting with Anna and a new prisoner called Cheryl. The prisoners had finished their work for the day and the strong smell of bleach filled Caroline's nostrils and stung the back of her throat. As she looked up the corridor, Caroline saw a well-built guard leading another new prisoner through the crowds of inmates. The prospect of a new arrival always made their time more interesting and they paused in their conversation as the newcomer drew nearer.

Caroline watched her approach. It was difficult to see her fully amongst the hordes of prisoners, especially since a large group of women was standing between them. But as the new inmate passed the group, Caroline noticed that the women fell silent until the new prisoner was out of hearing range. Then their conversation continued as a low murmur.

By this time Caroline and her friends were curious to catch a glimpse of the new inmate, too. It wasn't until she was around two metres away that Anna and Caroline recognised her. Caroline's breath caught in her throat when she realised who it was... Sharon Bamford.

Her height, her broad, toned frame and her frizzy brown ponytail gave her away first. Then, as she became nearer, Caroline noticed those painfully familiar features that bore an all-round look of imperfection. Her face was too flat, her nose too wide and her vivid turquoise eyes were small and beady, and seemed to pierce right through you. Caroline had often thought, sardonically, that Sharon's imbalanced face suited her imbalanced personality.

Oh no! Caroline thought, and her face must have registered her alarm, bringing her to Sharon's attention.

'Hi, Caroline. Hi, Anna,' Sharon greeted them over-enthusiastically as she drew level and flashed Caroline a fake smile.

Caroline could only manage a grimace in return, but Anna returned Sharon's greeting. 'Hi, Shazza. How are you? Didn't expect to see you back so soon.' Her tone was false and obsequious, and Caroline knew it was masking an inner fear.

'Ha-ha, I was missing you lot,' Shazza laughed. Then, as she passed them, she turned and added, 'Have you lot had your lovely prison dinner yet? What was it, Caroline, barbecued sausage and meatballs, as usual?'

She let out a raucous laugh and Caroline looked down at the floor in disgust. The prison officer tugged at Sharon's arm. 'Come on, Bamford. Let's get you settled in,' she ordered. Sharon turned face forward and carried on walking.

When Caroline raised her head again there was a look of astonishment on Anna's face. But neither of them spoke. They didn't want to risk being overheard.

'What's the matter?' asked Cheryl. 'Who is she?'

'That's Shazza,' whispered Anna. 'She's been in before.'

'So, what's the big deal?' asked Cheryl, picking up on their unease.

Anna didn't reply. Caroline knew she was too scared to say anything negative about Shazza, so it was up to her to respond.

'You'll find out soon enough,' she sighed, then turned and headed back to her cell.

Shazza was one of those people for whom prison was a way of life and it didn't seem to bother her in the least. She had already served several sentences for various crimes ranging from shoplifting to possession.

Caroline thought with bitterness about Shazza's previous sojourn. Of all the women Caroline had met inside, Shazza had been the most difficult. The woman was dominant, cruel and sadistic, and she always got her own way. She would put others down to make her look bigger and liked to gather allies in order to strengthen her position within the prison.

All the other prisoners were in no doubt as to who was top dog whenever Shazza was inside. And most were frightened of her. Although she enjoyed abusing Caroline verbally, she had stopped short of handing out some of the treatment that she reserved for the weaker prisoners. She homed in on them, and made their lives a misery.

As Caroline watched Shazza being led to her cell, a feeling of dread came over her. She knew that Shazza's arrival spelt trouble. And one thing was for sure: now that Shazza was among them, things were about to take a turn for the worst.

9

By the time Adele had finished seeing the governor it was visiting time so she was led straight to the visitors' room by the two guards. She spotted her brother straight away. It was difficult to miss him as several pairs of eyes were also pointed in his direction. As soon as he saw her, a big grin broke out on his handsome face. Adele strode purposefully in his direction while other prisoners and visitors whispered amongst themselves. Peter's visits always drew this reaction because of his reputation as a gangster.

He was dressed smartly in a tight-fitting polo shirt, which emphasised his toned physique, and he had placed his expensive-looking leather jacket on the back of the chair. His dark hair was cut short and neatly styled in the latest fashion.

'Hi, sis, how's things?' he greeted.

Adele took her seat opposite him. 'Not too bad,' she replied.

'Anyone been giving you grief?' he asked, and she noticed how he raised his voice and looked around the room; a veiled threat to anyone who might be considering it.

'Nothing I can't handle,' she laughed.

'Maybe they're getting the message then,' he grinned back, checking around the room once more.

'I dunno. One or two have tried it on.'

Peter raised his chin and his eyes locked on hers. 'I hope you sorted 'em out,' he said. 'Don't want anyone taking fuckin' liberties.'

'No problems. It was fine.' Then she paused before continuing, 'Let's just say the black belt in kickboxing has come in handy.'

'Glad to hear it. Looks like that was a good move, then.'

'Yeah, it's helped me to look after myself, but apparently some of the hard nuts are seeing me as a bit of a threat,' she whispered. 'Some are even calling me top dog.'

'Whoa!' he said loudly, holding his hand up, palm outwards. 'Be fuckin' careful.'

'Why?' asked Adele, his words reminding her of Caroline's previous warning.

Peter lowered his voice again. 'Because there's always someone else who wants to be top dog. And if they want it badly enough, they'll make sure they fuckin' get it, so you watch yourself.'

'Shit!' Adele gulped. 'But what if it's too late?'

'What do you mean?'

'Well,' she whispered, 'what if someone already wants to bring me down?'

'Then that's even more reason why you need to fuckin' watch yourself. Why? Has someone tried it?'

Adele kept her voice low. 'No, but there's an inmate called Denise. I had some trouble with her and I'm a bit worried about reprisals. She's got a reputation for being a hard case.'

'Be very careful, Adele,' he said. 'You can't trust anyone inside. Even those who you think are your friends can turn on you.'

Adele stared blankly at him before speaking again. 'I don't get it,' she said.

'What?'

'Well, first you tell me to look after myself and not let anyone take any liberties then, when I do, you tell me I've done the wrong thing.'

'Sorry, I didn't mean it to sound like that. It's just that it's a fine line,' he said. 'You've gotta look after yourself. You don't wanna be one of the weaklings who's everybody's dogsbody. But, at the same time, you don't wanna draw attention to yerself. Know what I mean?'

'Not really,' she replied, more confused than ever.

He put his hand on top of hers in a rare display of affection. 'Don't worry,' he said. 'You'll be OK. You seem to be managing up to now, anyway.'

She smiled back at him, hiding the unease that gnawed away inside her.

Adele hadn't been back from visiting long when Anna dashed into the cell. Her eyes were wide and her movements animated; something had obviously got her worked up.

'You'll never guess what!' she announced.

'What?' Adele asked, humouring her. Since Adele had threatened her, Anna was going out of her way to be nice. Adele felt a stab of guilt. Perhaps she had gone too far in pinning her up against the wall but Anna's behaviour had shocked her and Adele knew she couldn't afford to let anyone take liberties like that.

'There's a new inmate.'

'Oh, I know. She's sharing with Caroline. I've seen her about. The pretty, blonde girl? Cheryl, isn't it?'

'No, not her, you daft cow. Shazza!'

Anna spoke the last word with an air of menace, her eyelids twitching, and Adele suddenly realised that Anna was quite agitated. This new inmate must be really intimidating.

'Who's Shazza? Is she the one who's been in here before?' Adele asked, recalling her last conversation with Caroline.

Anna lowered her voice even though she had shut the

cell door behind her. 'A right fuckin' hard case. That's who.'

'Oh, right. I'll try to stay out of her way then,' said Adele.

Anna moved nearer to Adele and leant forward, her body language appearing conspiratorial. 'She was the top dog,' she whispered.

'So I've been told,' said Adele.

'She'll knock you off your fuckin' perch if you're not careful,' Anna continued.

'She's welcome to the "top dog" title. I don't want it.'

Anna stayed silent for several seconds, observing Adele with a puzzled expression on her face.

'Look, as long as she doesn't bother me, I won't bother her,' said Adele, but when Anna continued to stare she asked, 'What?'

Anna shrugged. 'That's not the way Shazza works.'

It was Adele's turn to look puzzled until Anna added, 'If she's got it in for someone, she's got it in for them. I just hope nobody tells her that you're the number one.'

'I'm not!' snapped Adele. 'Where on earth did you get that idea?'

Anna shrugged again. 'It's what everyone's saying.'

'Well, do me a favour, Anna, and put them straight, will you?'

'Sure, I'll try. After all, you wouldn't want Shazza for an enemy.'

'OK, thanks,' said Adele, but Anna wasn't finished.

'She's in for GBH this time, y'know. Can't say I'm surprised. Not after she bit someone's ear off last time she was in here.'

'You're joking!' said Adele, raising her eyebrows in shock.

'Wish I fuckin' was,' said Anna.

Adele stared at Anna, noting her facial expression. It was one of fear. Adele knew that look only too well. She had seen it on the faces of her family when she was a child. It happened whenever her father came back from the pub in one of his rages. And, just as it had when she was a child, that fear sparked a feeling of dread that tore through her insides like a razor blade.

10

Caroline was ready for Adele when she walked into her cell. 'You've heard the news then?' she asked.

'Yes,' said Adele, glancing over at Caroline's cell mate, Cheryl, who was tidying the top of her small bedside cabinet.

Cheryl took the hint and left the cell while the two of them talked.

'Is it true what Anna tells me: that Shazza bit someone's ear off last time she was in here?'

'So they say,' said Caroline. 'I didn't see the incident myself, but it wouldn't surprise me.'

'Is she really that bad?'

'Oh, yeah. Like I told you before, she's ruthless. I've never known anyone as bad as her.'

Adele gulped. 'Anna seems to think she'll challenge me,' she said.

Caroline had a look of resignation. 'She might well do. It depends whether word gets back to her about you.'

'I've told Anna to set the record straight. I don't want her to think I'm in competition with her. I'd rather just serve my time quietly.' Adele rushed her words, becoming anxious.

'Unfortunately, that might not be an option,' Caroline sighed. 'Don't forget about your fight with Denise. Like I told you before, that might not be forgotten and there were plenty of people who knew about it.'

'Shit!' said Adele.

Caroline strode across to her and put a comforting arm around her shoulder. 'It's OK. Try not to worry,' she said. 'It might not come to anything. But if it does, I'll be right behind you.'

Adele smiled nervously. 'Thanks,' she said, but despite Caroline's reassuring words, the unease that had been festering inside her since Peter's visit was growing and she was seriously worried.

Denise watched Shazza saunter across to her and Louise in the recreation room. She was their friend. Despite what others said about Shazza, Denise found her all right although even she was wary of getting on the wrong side of her. Shazza was always up for a laugh and, as long as you didn't wind her up, she was fine. They greeted her effusively.

'What the fuck are you doing back so soon?' Denise laughed, hugging Shazza tightly.

'Got into a bit of bother, didn't I?' Shazza sniffed.

Denise smiled and raised an inquisitive eyebrow.

'Wasn't my fault,' said Shazza. 'I was just in a pub with my fella minding my own fuckin' business when this tart walks in and starts playing up to him. And that docile bastard starts flirting back at her. I told him to pack it in but he took no fuckin' notice. So I warned her, and the silly cow laughed in my face then walked off. I wasn't gonna stand there and let them make a fuckin' mug of me, was I? So I went after her.'

'Don't fuckin' blame you,' said Denise.

'So what did you do?' asked Louise, staring at Shazza with wide-eyed admiration.

'I let her fuckin' have it, didn't I? Teach her to fuckin' flirt with my fella!'

'What did he do?' gushed Louise.

'Mike? He tried to stop me, but not straight away. I think he was enjoying it too much, ha-ha. Gets his rocks off from seeing two birds scrapping. I'd already broken the cow's nose and had her screaming before he got hold of me. You know me; I'm like fuckin' lightning when I get pissed off. Then some other blokes stepped in. Mike tried to drag me away from the pub before the coppers got there but I was fuckin' blazin' and wanted to have a go at him too for giving that tart the come-on.'

'So did the coppers get you?' asked Louise.

'Well, I wouldn't fuckin' be in here if they hadn't, would I?' asked Shazza.

Denise could see that Shazza was starting to become a bit irritated by Louise's questions so she gave her a nudge.

'Shut the fuck up, Louise,' Denise said. 'What is this, twenty fuckin' questions, or what?'

But Louise was too foolish to take Denise's warning seriously. 'Are you still seeing Mike?' she asked.

'Am I fuck! I dumped the bastard. I was sick of him messing me around. That tosser couldn't keep his dick in his pants if you paid him! What kind of a fuckin' mug do you think I am?'

Denise could tell that Shazza was getting rattled so she nudged Louise again.

'So, what's the news in here?' Shazza asked.

'Not much to tell really,' said Denise. 'We've got a few newbies. She's one of them; that fit blonde bird over there,' she said, nodding towards Cheryl, who was standing chatting with a large group of women several metres away. 'And then there's her, Adele fuckin' Robinson,' she said, pointing her finger at Adele, who was standing on the other side of the recreation area with Caroline.

'Gather you don't like her then?' asked Shazza, chuckling.

Denise spat on the ground in response.

'Like that, is it?' said Shazza. 'So, who's been top dog while I've been away?'

Before Denise had chance to reply, Louise cut in, 'She is. Adele.'

Shazza sized Adele up. 'You must be fuckin' joking! She doesn't look handy to me.'

'Well, she is,' said Louise. 'She's a kickboxing expert.'

'What's she in for?'

'Killing her dad,' Louise replied while Denise stared contemptuously. 'She bashed his head in.'

A look of realisation flashed across Shazza's face. 'Aah, I thought the name rang a bell,' she said. 'That's the sick fuck who hit him with a brass ornament, isn't it?'

'That's the one,' said Denise, with a grimace on her face. 'She's Peter Robinson's sister.'

'No wonder she fancies her fuckin' chances,' said Shazza, looking across at Adele once more.

'Not only that,' said Louise, who had now become quite animated, 'she beat Anna up. Nearly killed her. Anna's throat was a mess.'

'Did she fuck!' snarled Denise.

'Well, she hurt her, anyway,' said Louise. 'And what about what she did to you?'

Denise sneered at Louise. Her girlfriend's admiration for Adele was beginning to get on her nerves. 'That was nowt!' she snapped. 'She just caught me off guard, that's all. She thinks she's tough but, don't worry, I'll fuckin' have her. I'm just biding my time.'

'Anna's no big deal anyway,' said Shazza. 'Everyone

knows her bark's worse than her bite. She might be a fat cunt, but she's as soft as shit. How long's this Adele been in?' she asked.

'Only a few weeks,' Denise replied. 'But she got a seven-year stretch.'

'That's not much for what she did, is it?'

'They gave her manslaughter. It was self-defence. Apparently her dad was a right twat. He'd been abusing her mam for years.'

Shazza nodded her head, a look of steely determination painted on her face. 'So, she thinks that bumping off her old man makes her a hard case, does she?'

'It's not just Anna who calls her top dog,' said Louise. 'A lot of the other prisoners are saying it, too.'

Again Shazza stared across at Adele, her eyes lingering for longer this time. 'We'll have to fuckin' see about that, won't we, girls?' she said.

For a few seconds nobody spoke. Then Shazza said, 'Anyway, girls, I'm off to the gym. Thanks for giving me the heads-up.'

Once she had walked away, Denise turned to Louise. 'Why don't you learn to keep your fuckin' trap shut?' she said.

'What do you mean?' asked Louise.

'Adele this, Adele that, Adele the fuckin' other. Anyone would think you were in love with her or summat. Don't forget what she did to me!'

'I haven't. I was just trying to warn Shazza, that's all.'

'Yeah, well, Shazza knows what she's dealing with now, doesn't she?' Then a smirk played across Denise's lips before she spoke again. 'Let's see how fuckin' tough Robinson is when Shazza's finished with her.'

11

Adele glanced nervously across at the group of women who were standing on the other side of the recreation area. So, that was what Shazza looked like! Adele took in her height and frame, and suppressed a shudder. The woman was big, and mean-looking. She noticed Shazza glaring at her and quickly looked away.

'What do you think's going on over there?' she asked Caroline.

'Dunno, but whatever it is, you can be sure they're up to no good.'

'She keeps giving me evils,' said Adele.

'Try not to worry about it. Shazza nearly always wears a scowl anyway. Don't look at her.'

'They seem to get on,' Adele persisted.

'Yeah, they did last time she was in here. Denise isn't stupid. She knows it's best to stay on the right side of

Shazza. Denise might be tough but she wouldn't dare take on a nutcase like Shazza so she stays well in with her. On their own they're trouble but the two of them together are a force to be reckoned with.'

Adele's eyes opened wide in alarm.

Caroline covered her hand with her own. 'Like I say, try not to worry,' she said. Then she sighed before continuing, 'It's as well to be prepared, though, just in case she tries anything on.'

Shazza then walked away from Denise and Louise and headed in their direction. But before she reached them she stopped and spoke to Anna, who was halfway across the room. It was obvious from Anna's body language that she was on her guard and had been keeping her head down, hoping Shazza wouldn't notice her.

After they had spoken a few words Shazza grabbed the front of Anna's T-shirt and twisted it between her clenched fingers. Then she rammed her fist up against Anna's chin and said something that Adele couldn't hear from where she was standing. But her body language told Adele that it wasn't friendly.

Anna's head flew back and she took a step backwards. Then Shazza let go of Anna's T-shirt and Anna passed her something out of her pocket. Anna's movement was slow, her shoulders slumped, as though she had given up the item reluctantly.

'What the hell d'you think she's up to?' Adele asked

Caroline, lowering her voice so that Shazza couldn't hear her.

'She'll be stealing cigs or something off her,' Caroline whispered.

'She can't do that!' said Adele, affronted.

'Oh yes she can,' said Caroline quietly. 'She's Shazza. She can do what the bloody hell she wants, and she gets away with it.' Adele stared back at Caroline, the resentment written all over her face. 'Don't even think about it!' Caroline advised.

'What?' asked Adele.

'Saying anything to her about Anna,' Caroline whispered. 'You'd be a fool to mess with her. It's best to leave it alone.'

Then Shazza left Anna and continued in their direction. Adele noticed that as she walked across the room the other inmates either kept their heads down or greeted her enthusiastically. It was obvious to Adele that they were trying to ingratiate themselves. Shazza had a confident strut. It was as though she was enjoying the attention.

As Shazza drew closer to Adele and Caroline, she stared directly at Adele. Despite Caroline's advice not to look at her, Adele couldn't resist taking a curious peek. Shazza's features were rigid and unflinching, and as their eyes locked, Adele could feel her piercing glare through vivid turquoise, beady eyes. It seemed to cut right through her.

Then Shazza sauntered by, nodding and grinning at Caroline as she passed them. She didn't say anything. But Adele knew in that moment that Shazza had made her an enemy and a cold shiver of fear ran through her.

Peter rang his contact Spikey. 'Right, I'm ready to take stock,' he said, making sure he gave nothing away on the phone.

Within minutes Spikey had arrived, bringing with him four guns. Peter handed over the cash and led him out of the flat. Then he made another call, this time to Glynn.

'Round the gang up. We need to make plans,' he said. A voice sounded at the other end of the phone and Peter replied, 'Yeah, don't worry. Now that nasty business with Dave is sorted we can concentrate on the next job. Make sure they're here in the next hour.'

He cut the call and waited for his gang to arrive.

As soon as Peter had them all seated around his dining table he said, 'Right, lads, first up you need to know that I've had to let Dave go.'

Mickey let out a gasp as he and Sam stared at Peter, open-mouthed.

Peter swallowed. 'He's let me down... badly. We can't carry him any more so he had to go.'

He noticed Mickey and Sam exchange surprised

glances but he wasn't prepared to go into any more detail. It was done and there was no point harping on about it. He had to focus on the future.

'Let's move on,' he said quickly, letting them know that the subject of David was now closed. 'We're stepping things up a bit. The next job we do, we'll all be tooled up. I'm taking no fuckin' chances.'

He handed out the guns to Glynn, Mickey and Sam, and put the fourth one to one side. He already had his own gun, which was hidden somewhere safe where no one would find it.

Mickey whistled. 'Nice one,' he said. 'These'll do the job.'

'Yeah, but don't forget,' said Peter, 'no fuckin' shooting unless you have to.'

Although Peter had closed the subject of David, his mind was still on him as he briefly remembered how David had shot a security guard dead during a previous job. He could tell that his men knew what he was thinking, too.

'These are just frighteners,' he continued. 'Maybe the next have-a-go hero will think twice if we're all tooled up. Right, now down to business,' he said.

He walked over to the sideboard and took out some plans. 'Follow me, lads,' he said, leading them through to the dining room where he unfolded several sheets of paper and placed them on the dining table.

The men crowded round to take a look. 'I told you we were stepping it up,' he said. 'This firm takes loads of cash. It's well worth a go.'

The men stared at the plans, which had been drawn up with meticulous attention to detail. They showed Smart and Sons' cash and carry, together with the street where it was situated in Trafford Park and the various other buildings near to the firm.

'We need to track what happens to the cash they take,' said Peter. 'Does a firm collect it? Or does one of the directors take it to the bank? How often is it taken to the bank, and whereabouts in the building is it stored in the meantime? Let's find out their pattern. But don't make it fuckin' obvious.

'You see that?' he asked, pointing to a diagram of a pub, which was situated across the road from their target. 'That's where we're gonna start. They rent out rooms. So, Mickey, you're gonna book yourself in under an alias and then keep a lookout, see what goes on.'

A grin flashed across Mickey's face. 'Sounds good. I'm up for that,' he said.

'Don't worry, it is good,' said Peter. 'I told you we were stepping it up.'

He then continued to detail their surveillance operation, giving out instructions for each of his men to follow. When he had finished, he stood up, stretching himself to his full height and asked, 'Any questions?'

'Yeah, just one,' said Sam, tapping on the dining table nervously. 'Did you tell Dave about the job before you got rid of him?'

'No!' Peter replied hastily. 'Don't worry about him. He knows fuck all, and it's best that way... Now, is everyone clear about what's involved?'

They all muttered their understanding and Peter strode over to his drinks cabinet. He took out the brandy and poured each of them a generous measure into a crystal tumbler. While he was pouring he heard the sound of the doorbell ringing. 'About fuckin' time!' he said.

'I'll go,' said Glynn.

While Glynn went to answer the door, Peter pulled a fifth tumbler out of the drinks cabinet and poured brandy into it.

He looked up as Glynn returned to the room with another man. Peter nodded at them, then turned to Mickey and Sam. 'Guys, meet Mike Shaftesbury, the new fifth member of the gang,' he said. 'He's a sound guy and comes highly recommended. Isn't that right, Glynn?' He smiled at Glynn, who patted Mike on the back. 'Mike, meet Sam and Mickey,' he added, nodding at each of them in turn.

Peter sauntered over to the dining table carrying two of the glasses while Glynn and Mike grabbed the remainder. They handed the drinks round, then Peter picked up the gun he had left on the table earlier. Once the men had a glass each, Peter held his up in a toast. 'To bigger and better things,' he said before handing Mike the gun. 'Welcome to the gang.'

12

Anna had been trying to avoid Shazza or, at the very least, make sure she was with Adele and Caroline when Shazza was around. Maybe Shazza wouldn't try it on when they were there. But it wasn't always possible to have them with her as she didn't work in the kitchens with them.

She was on her way to her cleaning work with Cheryl, the new girl, when she caught sight of Shazza walking towards them along the corridor. Anna could feel a tremor in her stomach as she took in Shazza's harsh features and tall, broad frame. And, even worse, Shazza had Denise and Louise with her. Anna decided to play nice and hope Shazza would be OK with her.

'All right?' she greeted when Shazza was within hearing distance. She smiled at Shazza, Denise and Louise in turn.

The other women returned her smile but Shazza just nodded. 'What have you got for me?' she asked.

'Nothing,' said Anna.

Shazza took a swift look around, checking for guards, then stepped up to Anna. Denise and Louise closed in to shield them from view.

'I said what have you got for me?' Shazza repeated, glaring at Anna and prodding her with her forefinger.

'Nowt, honest,' said Anna.

Although Anna had decided that she wouldn't give in to Shazza again, she could feel the fear coursing through her veins as Shazza's vivid turquoise eyes bored into her. Meanwhile, Denise and Louise were also staring menacingly, and Cheryl's pretty face wore a panicked expression. She had turned pale and her pupils were dilated.

Within no time, Shazza was behind Anna, and had her arm up her back. Denise stepped behind Shazza so she wouldn't be seen if any prison officers happened to pass by.

'I fuckin' know you got some stuff this morning, you fat cunt! So you'd better hand it over.'

Anna thought about resisting but Shazza winched her arm up her back until a sharp pain shot through her.

'Well?' demanded Shazza.

When Anna didn't answer straight away she pulled her arm even tighter. Anna could feel the sting of tears in her eyes as her shoulder screamed out in agony. She was frightened it might become dislocated if Shazza pulled any tighter.

'OK,' she said, and relief flooded through her as Shazza released her grip on her arm. 'Come to my cell later and I'll give you some.'

'That's better,' said Shazza, stepping back in front of her as a guard appeared. 'See you later,' she sang merrily for the guard's benefit.

When Shazza walked away Cheryl looked at her and asked, 'You all right?'

Anna shrugged but her blood was pumping ferociously. 'Some fuckin' use you were,' she said, trying to mask her humiliation.

'I'm new,' said Cheryl. 'I didn't know what to do. Sorry, but I don't wanna get on the wrong side of her.'

Anna shrugged again. She felt a stab of guilt. It was wrong to take it out on Cheryl. She couldn't blame her for being frightened of Shazza; the woman was terrifying!

'What did she want, anyway?' asked Cheryl.

'Shush, don't let the screws hear you.' Then she whispered, 'Weed.'

When Cheryl didn't reply Anna sighed and said, 'Come on, let's get going.'

Shazza's vicious treatment had shaken Anna. But she was frustrated too, knowing that there was no point trying to stand up to Shazza. It would only make matters worse. It was common knowledge how ruthless Shazza could be, and Anna was convinced that if she hadn't agreed to Shazza's wishes she would have dislocated her shoulder and got Denise and Louise to say it was an accident. She shuddered at the thought.

While Shazza had Denise and Louise on side, Anna knew that she couldn't win. No, the best thing she could do would be to accede to Shazza's wishes and treat her as nicely as possible.

Adele was reading a book in the cell that she shared with Anna but it was difficult to concentrate. The prison was noisy but, apart from that, something about Anna just wasn't right today. Ever since she had returned from her work she had been on edge. It was impossible to read while Anna kept disturbing her with trivialities. When she wasn't fiddling about with her things on the top of the cupboard, she was asking stupid questions.

'This is nice, isn't it? Where did you get it?' Anna asked, lifting one of Adele's sweaters out of the cupboard.

'For God's sake, Anna!' said Adele. 'Will you leave things alone and stop fidgeting?'

Anna stuck out her bottom lip before replying. 'All right, be like that. I was only making conversation.'

Adele felt a twinge of guilt for snapping. Anna might

have been a nuisance but a part of Adele felt sorry for her, especially when she had seen how Shazza treated her. 'Sorry,' she said. 'But I'm trying to read and this book's really good. Can't you find something to do?'

'Suppose,' Anna shrugged before grabbing a magazine and throwing herself onto the bottom bunk.

Adele felt the bunks shake and cursed under her breath, but thankfully Anna then left her alone. She was just beginning to enjoy her book when Shazza arrived with Denise and Louise in tow. Anna shot out of her bunk and stood to the side while the other three women walked into the cell. Adele felt a shudder of fear.

Without any preamble, Shazza walked up to Anna and said, 'I've come to collect that stuff.'

Adele put her book to one side while she anxiously watched the scene from the top bunk where she lay. She saw Anna turn towards the cupboard, then rummage about in a drawer before pulling something out and handing it to Shazza without speaking.

'Is that all?' asked Shazza, staring scornfully at the small packet in her hand.

Anna looked back at her with fear in her eyes, then shrugged.

'I know you've got more so hand it out,' demanded Shazza, moving menacingly towards Anna.

As Anna turned back towards the cupboard, Adele asked, 'What's going on? Why are you giving things away, Anna? And what is it?' She had a feeling she knew what was in the packet but she wasn't sure.

'She fuckin' owes me!' snarled Shazza before Anna had a chance to reply.

'Is that right, Anna?' Adele asked.

'What fuckin' business is it of yours anyway?' asked Shazza.

'It's OK,' Anna quickly interrupted. 'Shazza's right. I owe her.'

She then handed another packet to Shazza, but Adele could tell by the look of disappointment on Anna's face that she was doing so unwillingly.

'Are you OK with this, Anna?' Adele asked again.

Anna looked up at her. 'Yeah, course I am,' she said, but her eyes told a different story as did the imperceptible shake of her head. She was pleading with Adele to drop the subject.

'So there you go,' said Shazza, looking up at Adele, who was trying to avoid the frightening glare of Shazza's evil eyes. 'Aren't you Peter Robinson's sister?' she asked, now giving Adele her full attention.

'That's right,' Adele replied.

'I believe he thinks he's a bit of a hot shot but from what I've been told he ain't all that.'

'I wouldn't know,' said Adele, trying to hide her fear.

'Seems like you might take after each other, seeing as how you seem to fancy your chances as well,' Shazza continued.

'No, I don't,' said Adele. She sat up in the bed. 'Look, I just want to serve my time in peace. I'm not here to cause trouble.'

'That right? Only, from what I've been told, you've already stirred things up a bit.'

Denise nodded. 'Yeah, fucking bitch!' she cursed.

Shazza didn't speak for several seconds but she carried on staring at Adele, her eyes piercing through her once more. This time Adele didn't look away. Instead she bravely held Shazza's gaze.

Then Shazza spoke again. 'My ex knows your brother,' she said. 'In fact, there's a rumour that he's working with him now.'

'Who's your ex?' Adele asked automatically although she didn't know many of the people Peter associated with nowadays.

'Mike Shaftesbury,' said Shazza.

'No, I don't know him.'

'It's no biggie, anyway. He's a tosser and he always was a poor fuckin' judge of character as well.'

'Apparently so,' said Adele, but Shazza didn't pick up on the irony of her words.

Instead Shazza mimicked her childishly. Then she turned on her heel and left the cell with Denise and Louise following behind. Denise flashed Adele a look of contempt before she went. Adele was relieved to see them go.

'Are you OK, Anna?' she asked.

'Yeah, course I am. Why shouldn't I be?'

'I just don't understand why you're giving your stuff away to Shazza, that's all.'

'You heard what she said,' said Anna defensively. 'I owe her. We're mates. We do each other favours.'

'Funny, but she didn't look too matey to me,' said Adele.

'Course she is.'

'So why did you owe her the stuff?' Adele asked. 'And what is it, anyway? Is it drugs?'

'She gave me a cig the other day,' said Anna, ignoring Adele's last question.

'Two packets for one cigarette? That's a bit expensive, isn't it?'

'It's obvious you don't fuckin' smoke,' said Anna whose voice had now adopted a defensive tone. 'Otherwise you'd know how fuckin' dear cigs are.'

'OK,' said Adele. 'But I hope you haven't got any more drugs in the cell. I don't want to get in trouble if the guards do a search.'

'I haven't,' snapped Anna. 'It's all fuckin' gone now, isn't it?'

Adele remained silent. The incident had troubled her, not only because Anna was doing drugs but also because she was so petrified of Shazza. It said a lot about the sort of person Shazza was. And now it seemed that Shazza had taken against her, too.

The few words that Denise had spoken had also made

it obvious that her previous fight with Adele was not forgotten. There were bound to be repercussions and as Adele lay struggling to sleep that night she became seriously worried about what those might be.

13

Peter and three members of his gang were sitting inside a souped-up Ford Escort, a few metres away from Smart and Sons, and tucked behind a Volvo. Sam was in the driving seat, with Peter in the front passenger seat and Glynn and Mike sitting in the back.

'Right, according to Mickey they should be coming out any minute now so keep your eyes peeled,' Peter said.

They all looked across the road at the doorway of Smart and Sons cash and carry where a stream of people was beginning to emerge.

'OK, here they are,' said Peter, watching most of the people cross the road and file into the Commercial pub. 'Regular as fuckin' clockwork, just like Mickey said.' They continued to watch the procession of staff go into the Commercial.

'Those two look promising,' said Glynn, with a smile painted on his handsome face as he eyed two attractive young women.

'Yeah, I've already spotted them,' said Peter.

'Mike, I think you should stick to the old crones,' said Glynn. 'Sorry, mate, but I don't fancy your chances with those birds.'

'Thanks a fuckin' million,' said Mike. 'You saying I'm an ugly bastard or summat?'

The other men in the car laughed. It was commonly accepted amongst them that Mike wasn't the best looking; Peter and Glynn were the ones with the looks. As an elderly worker walked into the pub, Glynn said, 'There y'are, mate. You never know. Your luck might be in.'

When their laughter had subsided, Peter glanced at Glynn and Mike in the back seat and asked, 'Right, lads, are we ready?'

They nodded in response and Peter eased open the car door and bid a quiet farewell to Sam. Glynn and Mike joined Peter on the pavement and the car sped off down the road.

'Right,' said Peter, as they walked towards the pub. 'Remember what I said. Don't be too fuckin' obvious. We don't want to give the game away.'

By the time they were inside the Commercial, the place was heaving, mostly with the staff from Smart and Sons. There was an obvious camaraderie amongst them as they stood in groups around the bar area, chatting and sharing banter.

Peter and his accomplices approached the bar, bought

their drinks and took them to a table that commanded a good view of the bar.

'OK,' whispered Peter. 'Let's just watch for now before we make a move. And steady with the fuckin' drink. We wanna keep our wits about us. They're the ones that need to get pissed, not us.'

For over an hour Peter and his cohorts sat drinking slowly while they watched what was going on around them. They noticed that as time went on some of the older staff began to leave the pub. Most of them were middle-aged and Peter guessed that they were probably family men and women stopping for a drink or two before going home to the spouse and kids. Of the remaining staff he surmised that most of them were those with no ties, who could stay out as long as they wanted without going home to grief.

As the space around the bar opened up, Peter spotted the two girls they had seen entering the pub earlier. They were now standing on their own, gazing around the pub's interior. He nodded at Glynn, who had already noticed them. There was also a group of older women, sitting a few tables away, who he had seen leaving Smart and Sons.

'Right, here's the plan,' Peter whispered. 'Mike, you go and chat to that lot.'

'Cheers,' said Mike, sarcastically. 'What am I supposed to say? Do you come here often? What's the nightlife like?'

'I dunno, you'll think of something,' said Peter, grinning. 'Ask them about the area or summat. Say you're new around here.'

Mike stood up then picked up his pint with a frown on his face and ambled across the room.

Peter looked at Glynn. 'Right, those two it is, then,' he said.

They walked across to the two girls they had seen earlier and Glynn opened up the conversation. 'Hello, ladies,' he greeted. 'How are you? I'm Glynn and this is Pete.'

The two girls smiled back, flattered to be receiving attention from two smartly dressed, good-looking guys.

Peter found out that the two girls were called Kath and Janice. After they had spent a few minutes talking to both girls, it seemed obvious to Peter that Kath had her eye on Glynn so he concentrated on Janice.

'Can I buy you a drink?' he asked. When she nodded, Peter quickly made his way to the bar and came back with a double, hoping she wouldn't notice.

'So, what do you do for a living?' asked Janice.

Bloody hell, thought Peter. *This one doesn't waste any time.*

He knew the type. It wouldn't be long before she asked him what kind of car he drove and whether he owned his own home.

'I work for a security firm,' he said.

'Ooh, are you one of those guys in uniforms?' asked Janice, flirtatiously.

'No,' grinned Peter. 'I work in the offices. Why, what do you do?' he asked, although he already knew where she worked.

'I work over the road,' she said.

'Where's that then?' asked Peter, keeping up the pretence.

'Smart and Sons. It's that cash and carry opposite.'

'Didn't notice it. The name rings a bell, though. I think we might collect the cash from them.'

'Why, what's the name of your firm?' she asked.

'Translucre Security,' said Peter.

'No, we don't use them,' said Janice. 'We use another one.'

Janice didn't divulge the name of the firm and Peter guessed that she wasn't yet drunk enough to give too much away. Hopefully that would change once he had bought a few more drinks.

'Yeah, it's always best to have a firm collecting the cash these days. It's too risky otherwise,' said Peter.

Janice shrugged and Peter knew the onus was on him to keep the conversation going. 'What do you do at Smart and Sons then?' he asked.

'I work in the cash office,' said Janice. 'That's how I know that Translucre aren't our security firm.'

Bingo, thought Peter, but he hid his delight. 'Ah, right,' he said. 'Perhaps I was mistaken. Maybe it's another firm with a similar name. Anyway, no worries. Can I get you another drink?' he asked.

Janice eagerly held out her empty glass and Peter went to the bar, suppressing a smirk. He couldn't believe his luck! Now all he had to do was ply Janice with a few more doubles before getting her to tell him all about her very interesting job in the cash office of Smart and Sons cash and carry.

'Do you wanna cuppa?' asked Anna, who had been restless for the last fifteen minutes, fiddling with things and jumping from one thing to another as though there was something on her mind.

'No, thanks,' said Adele.

'You sure?' Anna asked.

'Yes,' said Adele, trying to stifle her irritation with Anna. It seemed that every time she got a chance to read a book, Anna started making a nuisance of herself.

'I've got some nice biscuits we can have with it,' said Anna, lowering her voice. 'Only, it's probably best not to tell anyone else.'

'Go on then,' smiled Adele.

When Anna had got the drinks ready, Adele jumped down from her bunk and joined Anna, who was sitting on the edge of her bed sipping at her cup of tea. Adele was careful not to get too close, though. They may have made up but Adele still didn't want to encourage any amorous advances.

'Nice, these biscuits, aren't they?' asked Anna. 'Don't let anyone see them, though,' she added cradling hers in her hand so it wouldn't be visible to anyone entering their cell.

'What is it, Anna?' Adele asked.

'What d'you mean?' Anna responded, defensively.

'There's something on your mind, isn't there?' Adele thought it might be something to do with Shazza picking on her.

'No, course there isn't,' said Anna.

'Well, why are you so restless then?'

'Dunno. That's just me, I suppose.'

They ate and drank in silence for a few minutes until Anna said, 'There is kind of something.'

'Oh, yeah?' said Adele, raising her eyebrows.

'It's Shazza.'

'Go on,' said Adele, half expecting Anna to confide in her about how Shazza had been bullying her.

Anna spoke hesitantly. 'Well... you know she was the number one last time she was in here, don't you?'

'Yes, I believe so,' said Adele.

'Only, she doesn't like anyone treading on her toes, y'know.'

'Yes, I got that impression,' said Adele.

'Well, don't say I've said owt,' Anna continued, and Adele detected a tremble in her voice. 'But she'll stop anyone who gets in her way.'

'OK, I think I gathered that as well.'

'Yeah, but what I'm trying to say is... well... she thinks you're the one to stop.'

'Why?' asked Adele. 'I told her I don't want any trouble. If she wants to be the number one then she's welcome to it.'

'Yeah, but...'

'Go on,' Adele urged when Anna paused.

'Well, it's just that Shazza doesn't work like that,' said Anna, who then rushed to defend her words. 'Don't get me wrong, she's a mate and all that. We get on, y'know... we do each other favours... so don't think I'm calling her. I wouldn't do that.'

Adele noticed a slight twitch of Anna's lip when she stopped speaking. She nodded for her to continue. 'But the trouble is,' Anna said, 'other people are telling her you're top dog, and it's pissing her off. You need to be careful, Adele, that's all I'm saying... oh, but I didn't tell you that, OK?'

'Don't worry, Anna,' said Adele. 'It won't go any further.' Although she spoke confidently to Anna, the adrenalin was pumping. Shazza was trouble and she wanted to bring her down.

Adele stared into Anna's eyes and asked, 'You're frightened of her, aren't you?'

'No. Course not,' Anna replied hastily. 'I told you, she's a mate. And I'm not calling her. Don't tell anyone I was calling her.'

'Don't worry, I won't,' Adele said, wondering how Anna could regard Shazza as a mate when all she seemed to do was talk down to her and take things from her. Adele didn't say anything further but Anna's words had shaken her. The last thing she needed was to have to watch her back every minute of the day.

14

It was visiting time and Adele was sitting at a table with her brother, Peter, across from her.

'So, you said on the phone that you wanted me to find out about Shazza,' he said.

'Shush, keep your voice down,' said Adele, checking around her to make sure no one had overheard.

'OK,' said Peter. 'Well,' he whispered, 'as you know, her ex-boyfriend is a mate of mine, Mike Shaftesbury. So, I casually mentioned to him that you were in here and he told me that's where his ex is, serving time for GBH.'

Adele nodded for Peter to continue.

'I asked him who she was, pretending it was in case you might know her. Then he started telling me what she was in for and it just went on from there. From what he tells me, she's a right fuckin' head case. You'd do well to stay away from her.'

'I believe so,' said Adele, the anxiety showing in the taut lines on her face. 'How bad is she?'

'Well, Mike didn't have a fuckin' good word to say about her, that's for sure. When he was with her they used to fight. But he said it was 'cos she provoked him. He only had to look at another woman and she'd give him a slap right there and then in the pub, in front of everyone. I think it was a power thing with her, letting everyone know that he was her property.

'Then, one night, he woke up feeling something stinging his chest and the mad bitch was putting her cig out on him. They'd had a row the night before but he thought they'd smoothed it over till she started again the next day. In the end he ditched her; he didn't want any more of her aggravation, especially after she beat up a woman in the pub. That's why she's in here now.'

'Really?' asked Adele. 'She's been telling people she finished with him. I knew she was in for GBH but I didn't know the details.'

'Yeah, she broke the poor cow's nose just because Mike was talking to her.'

'Jesus!' said Adele, her eyes wide with shock.

'You look worried,' said Peter. 'Has she been giving you any trouble?'

'Not exactly, but she hasn't been too friendly either.'

'Best keep out of her way then.'

'I wish it was that easy,' said Adele, pursing her lips. 'From what my cellmate tells me, some people have been calling me top dog and it's winding her up. She's got people on her side too, like that Denise, who I had a bit of trouble with.'

'Fuckin' hell!' said Peter. 'I thought I told you to keep a low profile.'

'It's not my fault,' said Adele, exasperated. 'I was just looking after myself like you told me to.'

'Right, you listen to me,' he mumbled to her across the table. 'I know her fuckin' sort and if she thinks you're a threat she'll be after you. It sounds like it's too late to avoid her. What you need now is a bit of fuckin' damage limitation. What are your mates like?'

'What do you mean?' Adele's words were rushed, her face now pale and her breathing harried.

'Are they the sort who will have your back? When I was inside I always knew who I could rely on whenever I needed back-up.'

'Well, yeah. A couple of them are,' she said, 'but they're no match for Shazza and Denise.'

'Doesn't matter. You need to make sure you're never on your own; safety in numbers and all that. If Shazza and her mates catch you on your own they'll probably jump you. And I don't think that mad cow would stop at just a slap.'

'Jesus, Peter. You're scaring me,' she whispered.

'I just want you to be prepared, that's all. Besides, you're a fuckin' kickboxing expert, aren't you? She probably knows that so she won't try anything when she's on her own. But if she's got people on her side then you need to have mates on your side, too.'

Adele gulped. 'OK,' she said. 'Thanks for the warning,' but, although she was thanking him, at that moment she didn't feel as though she had much to be grateful for.

'Bloody hell, Adele. You look as if you've lost a pound and found a penny,' said Caroline as Adele sloped into her cell with her shoulders slumped, and plonked herself down on Caroline's bunk. 'A bad visit was it?'

'No, it's not that,' said Adele, looking across at Caroline's cell mate, Cheryl, and giving her a feeble smile.

Cheryl left the cell so that Adele and Caroline could talk.

'I'm seriously fuckin' worried,' said Adele, once Cheryl had gone.

'Why, what's happened?'

'Shazza,' Adele whispered. 'That's what. According to our Peter she's a bit of a head case. He's got a mate that used to go out with her.'

'I told you she was bad news,' said Caroline.

'But not only that,' said Adele, 'I had a warning from Anna, but I promised her I wouldn't tell anyone, so please don't let it go further.'

'No, I wouldn't. Why, what did she say?'

'Well, she went all round the houses first, as though she was frightened of warning me off, but the gist of it was that Shazza's gunning for me.'

'Shit!' said Caroline.

'Peter's told me to make sure I'm never on my own. He reckons Shazza and her friends will jump me as soon as they get a chance.'

'OK,' said Caroline, adopting a reassuring tone. 'Well, I'll be with you as much as possible. You know that, but I can't be with you all the time.'

'I know that,' said Adele.

'What about Anna? Won't she have your back?'

'I think Anna's frightened, Caroline. She's been on edge for days. It's weird. She keeps telling me Shazza's her friend and yet Shazza's taking stuff off her: cigs and drugs. Anna tries to pretend that they're doing each other favours when it's obvious she doesn't want to part with the stuff. But, at the same time, she's being really creepy with me; trying to do me favours all the time. It doesn't make sense.'

'It does to me,' said Caroline, confidently. 'Can't you see? Anna's hedging her bets. She's waiting to see who comes out on top.'

'Bloody hell! She's not as daft as I thought.'

'No, she isn't,' Caroline said. 'It's like I've told you before, it's all about self-preservation in here.'

Adele's face dropped.

'What's wrong?' asked Caroline.

'I suppose I'm a bit disappointed with Anna really. It feels like she's playing me.'

'She's not a bad sort, to be honest. But it's fear, Adele. That's what's motivating Anna at the moment. She'd probably love to be on your side. It's obvious how much she looks up to you, but she's frightened of what Shazza would do to her. So, instead, she's trying to keep you both sweet.'

'That doesn't leave me a lot of allies then, does it?' said Adele.

'Well, that new kid, Cheryl, isn't so bad, y'know. Like Anna, she's frightened. There aren't many who aren't frightened of Shazza. But she's not kowtowing to her like Anna seems to be doing. At least, not yet, anyway. I think perhaps we should bring her in; let her know the score.'

'OK, as long as you think we can trust her.'

'I think we can although it's not always possible to be sure, especially in this place. We'll try to get her to stick with you when I'm not around. Maybe that will help.'

'OK, Caroline. Thanks,' said Adele. But she left

Caroline's cell feeling only marginally less ill at ease than when she had entered.

Adele knew it was only a matter of time before Shazza and Denise made their move. Peter had told her to stick with her allies but there were very few people she could rely on. Most of the prison was frightened of Shazza and Denise, which meant that when they did strike, there was a good chance she'd be on her own. And she was terrified at the thought of what they would do to her.

15

Mickey looked at his watch again. 'Are we ready to go yet?' he asked Peter.

'Not yet,' whispered Peter. 'Give it a couple more minutes.'

They were in a store room at Smart and Sons cash and carry. It was late-night opening and Peter planned to wait until at least fifteen minutes after closing time before they made the hit. That should be sufficient time for the store to be clear of customers. He wanted as few people as possible inside the building.

While he waited he felt a buzz as the adrenalin pumped around his body. He'd been planning this job for weeks and now it was finally here. This was the part he enjoyed; when all those weeks of planning came together in a hit that would hopefully land them a good pay-out. Like Mickey he couldn't wait to get moving but he didn't want to take any chances.

Through information he and his gang had gathered,

Peter knew that on late-night opening the takings from Smart and Sons weren't banked until the following day. Instead the staff totalled it up in the first-floor cash office, then put it into the safe overnight.

After a few more moments of waiting, he heard the sound of someone approaching. 'Shit!' he said to Mickey. 'Quick, hide.'

They were prepared for the possibility of someone checking the storeroom after closing time. Peter and Mickey had entered the store a few days previously using a business card from Mickey's uncle's plumbing business as ID. Then they'd carried out a recce.

The store room had several large plastic containers on wheels, which were used to take the goods into the store. Peter realised straight away that these could prove useful. Now, as the footsteps drew closer, they each found one that was almost empty and hid inside it, placing some empty cardboard boxes over themselves so they couldn't be seen.

They heard someone breeze into the room whistling to the tune of 'Karma Chameleon', badly. For some seconds nothing happened but Peter could sense a presence. He held his breath as he waited for the person to leave, hoping he or she wouldn't spot that the two containers now looked almost full.

Fortunately whoever it was didn't notice and soon Peter heard the store-room door slam shut. Then there was silence.

'Fuck! That was close,' muttered Mickey.

'You can say that again,' said Peter, letting out a loud breath before easing himself gently out of his hiding place.

Peter looked at his watch. 'Not long now,' he whispered. 'Then we can go.'

He waited a short while longer before switching on his walkie-talkie so he could speak to Glynn, who was hidden in another area of the store with Mike. 'Everything all right your end?' he asked once he had made contact.

'Yeah,' whispered Glynn.

'Right, you ready to go then?' Peter continued.

'Yeah.'

'OK. Go now!' said Peter, putting his walkie-talkie inside his jacket, slipping on a mask and pulling out his gun.

After checking that Mickey also had his mask on and his gun ready, Peter gave him the nod and they dashed out of the store room.

They headed to the front of the store as planned. As they ran, the only sounds Peter could hear were his and Mickey's footsteps dashing up the aisle, and his own harried breathing.

When they neared the store front, he heard voices. Quietly chatting at first. But then raised in alarm.

The staff had twigged something was wrong.

Peter reached the top of the aisle. The store front tills

came into view. Three members of staff were bagging up cash. Two women and a man. They stopped what they were doing, mouths agape, bodies immobile with shock. But before they could react, Peter and Mickey drew near and levelled their guns.

The eldest member of staff, a middle-aged woman with steely grey hair, let out a screech and covered her mouth with her hand.

'Not a fuckin' word!' said Peter, pointing his gun at her. 'Do as you're told and everything will be OK.'

The younger woman began to cry. Her tears were accompanied by a distraught whimper. Peter nodded towards the door and Mickey stepped up to it and checked it was locked. Meanwhile Peter kept watch over the staff. While Mickey stood guard at the exit, Peter levelled his gun at the man.

'You the manager?' asked Peter. The man nodded sombrely. 'OK,' Peter responded. 'How many staff are in the building?'

'Just us and two in the cash office,' said the manager.

'OK, carry on what you're doing,' ordered Peter. 'And get a fuckin' move on!'

He nodded at Mickey again. Mickey pulled out his walkie-talkie and spoke to Glynn.

'They're ready as soon as we are,' he said, and Peter knew that meant Glynn and Mike were in the cash office.

'How many are with them?' asked Peter, while keeping an eye on the staff.

'Two.'

Peter then addressed the manager again. 'OK, sounds like you were right. But you better not be telling me fuckin' lies,' he added, looking from the manager to the barrel of his gun and back again.

'No, there's definitely no more,' said the manager, with a tremble in his voice.

Peter noticed that the young girl had become jittery and had slowed down bagging up the money. 'Come on, get a fuckin' move on!' he shouted. She jumped. Then, spotting Peter's eyes on her, she scooped up the cash with shaking hands and piled it haphazardly into bags. 'I want every fuckin' till emptied,' demanded Peter.

While Peter kept watch, the adrenalin continued to course fiercely around his body causing a surge of mixed emotions. Apprehension. Excitement. Exhilaration! That familiar high that powered him.

'You finished?' he demanded when the staff came to a standstill.

'Yes,' nodded the manager.

'Right, take them upstairs. To the cash office,' Peter instructed. 'And no fuckin' funny business!'

He followed the staff through the store while Mickey stayed on the ground floor.

Up the stairs. To the left. No surprises so far. Peter knew the score. He'd added details to his plan of Smart and Sons as he and his gang had built up a fuller picture. Two doors down and they were in the cash office. Glynn and Mike were already waiting. They, too, were wearing masks.

Inside the office were a further two members of staff who were already tied up. Peter recognised Janice, the girl he had plied with drinks till she spilled the beans on the day-to-day operations of Smart and Sons.

He didn't recognise the other girl, but he had anticipated Janice would be there. And he was prepared. He and Glynn had already decided that Mike would do the talking once they were in the cash office.

'It's all there,' said Mike, pointing to two bags laden with cash.

Peter nodded his instructions to his accomplices. Then Glynn and Mike stepped up to the three members of staff who were not yet tied up. They were each grasping a coil of rope in one hand and a gun in the other. While Peter continued to cover the staff with his gun, Glynn tied up the manager. Mike grabbed roughly at the young girl. When his hands groped viciously at her breasts, she screamed and tried to pull away.

'Shut the fuck up!' yelled Mike, swiping her across the face with the butt of his gun.

Peter heard a loud crack as the gun smashed against

the bridge of her nose. She let out an agonised screech and Peter sprang forward. As blood gushed from the girl's broken nose, Peter gave Mike a sharp nudge and shook his head frantically from side to side. Mike spun the girl around, gripping her arms and forcing her hands together. 'I said shut the fuck up!' he shouted at her again.

'Please, Jenny. Keep quiet!' begged the older woman, in tears. 'You heard what he said.' She nodded at Peter as she spoke. 'Do as you're told and everything will be all right.'

When the older woman's pleading eyes met with Peter's he quickly shifted his gaze. He preferred to remain detached.

Jenny's screams subsided into a distraught whimper. When Mike tied the rope tightly around Jenny's wrists, her eyes were wide with fear as they stared in terror at her attacker. While tears sprang from her tormented eyes, blood pumped from her busted nose and her whole body trembled.

Peter was glad when they had finished tying the staff up. He didn't like the way this was going; Mike was a bit too fuckin' free with his hands for his liking. Peter and his gang grabbed the bags of cash between them, then fled through the first-floor corridor and down the stairs. Mickey was now waiting for them at the back door. He eased it open and they dashed out to the waiting car where Sam was seated behind the wheel ready to speed off.

As he took his seat in the front of the car Peter heaved a sigh of relief. At last! They'd done it. He was elated to have got away with the cash, but disturbed by Mike's behaviour. While they congratulated each other, Peter went along with it, thrilled with their haul. But he hadn't overlooked the vicious way Mike had handled the young girl. The recriminations would follow later.

16

When Adele and Caroline walked into the recreation area Shazza and her friends were gathered in one corner. While Denise and Louise glanced in Adele's direction, Shazza whispered something to them. Adele saw Shazza look at her and she felt a sharp pang of fear before the three of them approached.

'Oh, no, here's trouble,' warned Caroline.

Adele took a deep steadying breath as she watched the three women make their way over. Shazza strode purposefully, nudging other inmates out of her way while keeping her eye on Adele.

As Shazza neared her, Adele could feel her heart racing. Then Shazza's eyes locked with hers, sending a shiver down Adele's spine as the intense turquoise of Shazza's irises shot through her like a laser beam.

Shazza's thin lips formed into a smirk as she swung at her. Shazza's fist dug sharply into Adele's stomach, making her gasp and stoop forwards clutching her abdomen. Adele straightened up, trying to regain her breath as she watched Shazza walk past with an evil grin on her face.

Hardly giving herself a chance to recover, Adele sped after her. She shoved into Shazza's back sending her hurtling forwards. Shazza screeched, then spun around and launched herself at Adele.

The other prisoners stood back while Shazza clawed at Adele's face and yanked at her hair. Denise and Louise held onto Caroline, stopping her from going to help her friend. Adele felt a sharp pain as Shazza pulled out a tuft of hair. Her eyes smarted. A brief flashback to another era: Jessie Lomas, the school bully. Taunts and humiliation. The feeling of helplessness. The sting of defeat.

Determined not to be beaten this time, Adele fought back. At close range she swung a right hook at Shazza, landing the punch hard on her temple. Then she swiftly followed that with an uppercut. Shazza stumbled backwards. Trying hard to stay upright, she stared at Adele in stunned silence, her mouth agape.

Adele was about to follow through with a kick from long range when three prison guards swarmed them; Sly and two others. Sly threw herself at Adele, her bulky frame forcing Adele back. But Adele was fired up. She could taste victory and wanted to finish the job.

While Sly yelled at her, Adele pushed back, trying to

get to Shazza. Her adversary had recovered her footing and was now yelling at Adele.

'Come on then, you bitch! I'll fuckin' have you,' she yelled.

For a few ferocious seconds the guards battled to contain the two irate women. Adele tried to tug herself free from Sly's clutches and dart around her. But Sly held her firm. Adele fought until she had loosened her grip. She was pulling away when Sly snatched at her blouse, tearing the material and exposing the mound of her breasts.

Then Sly pulled her roughly back, sinking her nails into the soft flesh of Adele's upper arm. Another guard rushed to Sly's aid and they pinned Adele up against the wall. Still Adele fought to break free, powered by anger and hatred.

'You stay where you are, Robinson, or you're in big trouble!' Sly shouted.

Adele glared at her. Their eyes met: Adele's full of anger, Sly's full of contempt. Adele continued to struggle. She felt the sting where Sly's nails had dug into her flesh. For a brief moment, she was tempted to hit back. But then she thought about the futility of it all and her muscles relaxed against the pressure of the guards' strong hold.

'Right, Robinson! You've done it now, my girl. Just wait till the governor hears about this,' barked Sly.

Adele stared back at her, incredulous. 'But she started it!' she said. 'I was just defending myself.'

'Try telling that to the governor,' said Sly, her tone scornful.

Adele could tell from the sneer on Sly's face and the contemptuous way she looked at her that this was about more than just doing her job. She had taken against her and had now become yet another one on Adele's growing list of enemies.

'Get back to your cell!' ordered Sly. 'You can wait there till we come and take you to see the governor.'

The two prison guards released Adele and she walked towards the door. As she turned to go, she noticed Shazza now hovering in the background. Adele tried to ignore the glowering expression on Shazza's face, which told her this wasn't over. She turned away and went to join Caroline, who was waiting to walk with her.

'You all right?' asked Caroline.

'Yeah,' said Adele, trying to cover herself up by adjusting her blouse.

'Here, put this on,' said Caroline, passing her her cardigan.

'Thanks,' said Adele. She did her best to smile while fighting tears and trying to control her shaking limbs.

'Come on,' said Caroline. 'Let's get back. I know it's easier said than done, but try not to worry. We'll have a chat later in my cell where no one can hear us.'

Adele gave a weak smile then bowed her head, battling

silently with a raging fear that threatened to overwhelm her. She knew Caroline's heart was in the right place but it didn't matter what Caroline might have to say. They both knew that Adele was in the firing line, from both Shazza and Sly. And there was nothing Caroline could do or say that would make things any easier for her.

Peter and his gang arrived at his apartment and placed the bags full of cash onto the dining table. Before they began splitting it up, Peter turned to Mike, his face stern. 'What the fuck happened there?' he asked.

'What do you mean?' Mike retaliated.

'The girl. Was there any fuckin' need for that?'

'I had to shut the screaming bitch up, didn't I?'

'But you didn't shut her up, did you? You made her fuckin' worse!'

'What's the big deal? She's nowt to you, is she?'

'I'll tell you what the big deal is,' Peter hissed, his face now flushed with rage. 'We don't fuckin' operate like that! No violence unless necessary. That's the rule.'

Mike shrugged and Peter glared at Glynn, waiting for his response.

'Pete's right,' Glynn said. 'It's not how we do business, Mike. It makes the coppers even keener if we've done someone over.'

'Fair enough,' Mike shrugged again. 'If that's how you want it.'

'It's how we do things,' said Peter. 'And anyone who doesn't want to do things my way has no fuckin' place in this gang.'

'All right, keep your hair on,' spat Mike. 'For fuck's sake! I've already said I'm all right with it, haven't I?'

'Well, just make sure you fuckin' are!' added Peter.

Mike stared back at him, then snatched his share of the takings and fled out of the apartment. Then Sam and Mickey each took their share and said goodbye to Peter and Glynn.

'Can I have a word, Glynn?' asked Peter before he had a chance to leave.

'Sure,' said Glynn, and he hung back until Sam and Mickey had gone.

'I'm not impressed with your mate,' said Peter.

'You've no worries, Pete. He's all right. He's just used to doing things a different way, that's all. He'll soon come round to our way of thinking.'

'I fuckin' hope so,' said Peter, "cos I've no room for loose cannons in this firm. I've just got rid of one and I don't fuckin' want another.'

'No worries. Like I said, Mike's all right. And he's a different kettle of fish from dickhead Dave.'

'Well, I suppose I'll have to take your word for it for now. But he's gonna have to fuckin' prove himself. Let's hope he comes up to scratch on the next job.'

'He will,' replied Glynn. He then drained the dregs from his celebratory glass of brandy and picked up his share of the cash. 'Right, Pete. I'm off. I've gotta decide what I'm gonna do with this little lot.'

He flashed a charming smile at Peter before going.

Once they had all left, Peter sat swirling brandy around in a crystal tumbler and thinking back to what had happened with Mike. He wasn't happy with him at all. Rough handling the girl was bad enough but Peter didn't like his attitude either. It irked him to think that he'd got rid of Dave only to replace him with more trouble.

He tried to console himself. Perhaps Glynn was right. Maybe Mike would toe the line now he knew the score. He hoped so, because he didn't need more grief from his men. What he did was high risk enough without his men acting out of line. But, apart from Mike being a bit too eager, the job had gone well.

He glanced over again at the stash of money on his dining table. As leader of the gang and chief planner, Peter had taken the biggest share from the job. Yes, it had definitely been a good earner. He was now building up a tidy sum of money, which would come in very useful in the future. Peter already had plans of how he wanted to spend it. Big plans. He was going places, and nothing and nobody was going to stand in his way.

17

Governor Jones looked over the rim of her glasses at the three guards standing in front of her.

'Perhaps you'd like to start by telling me exactly what happened,' she said to none of them in particular.

'Well,' began Prison Officer Fox, 'we rushed in when we saw a fight taking place. I went straight to prisoner Robinson. I could tell she was getting out of hand. The woman was like a banshee but I held her back before she could inflict any more damage.'

'And exactly what damage did she inflict?' asked Governor Jones.

'The other girl's face was scarlet where she'd punched her. Vicious, it was. And it wouldn't have stopped there. She was going mad to get at her—'

'Who was the other prisoner involved?' Governor Jones cut in.

'That new one, erm... what's her name?'

'Sharon Bamford,' replied Prison Officer Roberts.

Governor Jones raised her eyebrows and pursed her lips on hearing Shazza's name. 'I see. Yes, we had a lot of trouble with that prisoner last time she was in here, didn't we?'

'The pair of them are nothing but trouble, if you ask me,' said Officer Fox, scowling and folding her arms beneath her voluminous breasts.

'I didn't ask you,' said Governor Jones, her tone measured and firm.

'Well, I was just saying so you know—'

Governor Jones cut in again. 'Officer Roberts, would you like to tell me your version of events?'

Her patience with Prison Officer Fox was wearing thin and she wasn't in the mood for her negative opinions of the prisoners. What she needed was a fair, objective account and it seemed that, yet again, Prison Officer Fox was incapable of giving it.

Governor Jones surveyed her over the rim of her glasses, noticing how she had puffed herself up and her scowl had developed into a grimace. She was obviously affronted that her version of events wasn't sufficient. The woman was a menace! With her biased point of view, it was no wonder the women called her Sly.

She was just as bad with the other staff. Governor Jones was all too familiar with her sort: the type who would do anyone a bad turn if they thought it would further their own ambitions.

Judy Roberts was a different kettle of fish altogether.

Governor Jones had taken to her from the moment she had employed her, six years ago. Fair and honest, with the prisoners' best interests always at heart, she was just the sort of officer that Governor Jones liked on her staff.

The other officer, Alice, was new to the job and Governor Jones didn't have much knowledge of her up to now. Nevertheless, she would listen to each officer's version of events before she decided how to handle the situation.

'We were across from them when it all started,' said Prison Officer Roberts. 'So, the two women were already fighting before we could react. However, listening to what the prisoners had to say, it seems that Bamford deliberately attacked Robinson.'

'You can't trust what they have to say,' Sly cut in. 'Liars and thieves, the lot of them.'

'Prison Officer Fox, could you please let Officer Roberts finish telling her version of events?' said the Governor, her voice now taking on a sterner tone.

Sly sniffed in response, then puffed up her breasts and shook her shoulders.

'Robinson retaliated,' Officer Roberts continued, 'then Bamford attacked Robinson again, who hit back.'

'Hit back? She was like a lunatic!' said Sly.

The governor ignored her and turned to the third officer. 'Do you agree with Prison Officer Roberts' version of events?' she asked.

'Yes,' said Alice. 'That sounds about right.'

'Very well. Thank you, ladies,' said Governor Jones, dismissing the officers, who then filed out of her office.

It seemed clear to her that prisoner Robinson had a temper, which had obviously landed her in here in the first place. It was a pity that it should spoil her because, from what she had seen of Robinson, she seemed to be an otherwise sensible, intelligent woman.

Governor Jones mulled over matters while scanning the files of the two prisoners involved. She would have to have a good think before deciding what form of punishment was appropriate for each of them.

It wasn't long after lunch before Sly and another prison officer came into Adele's cell ready to accompany her to see the governor. As Adele walked along the prison corridors, led by Sly, she could feel her heart beating erratically. She was dreading finding out what her punishment would be. The last thing she needed was to have time added onto her sentence. It was bad enough as it was.

When they arrived outside the governor's office, Shazza was being led away by another two guards. She glared at Adele as she passed and then hissed. Adele quickly broke eye contact, not wishing to be pinned down by the intense gaze of Shazza's vivid turquoise eyes.

'Wait here!' ordered Sly, leaving Adele with the other

guard as she stepped up to the office door and knocked on it in an exaggerated, officious manner.

When the governor shouted for her to enter, Sly grabbed hold of Adele's arm tightly and dragged her towards the door. 'Right, come on!' she ordered.

Once inside the governor's office, Sly and the other guard took their place at either side of Adele in the centre of the room. Sly surveyed her while the governor peered above her glasses. Her eyes switched from the file on her desk to Adele and back again, as they had during the previous meeting.

For several seconds Adele felt exposed under the scrutiny of both the governor and the prison officers. She could feel her knees shaking and her face was flushed.

'Now then,' said the governor. 'I'm afraid I'm very disappointed in you, prisoner Robinson. I was surprised when my officers told me you had been involved in a fight. It's difficult to believe that you're the same young lady that wanted to study in order to make good use of your time here.'

'I'm sorry, but it was self-defence,' said Adele. 'I was—'

'Yes, I'm aware of what happened,' said the governor. 'My officers have given me a full account.'

Adele saw Sly puff out her chest and raise herself to her full height, obviously overjoyed that Adele was getting a telling-off. Adele wasn't sure whether the governor wanted a response, and she stood awkwardly for several seconds, as the governor studiously examined her.

Adele felt exactly like she had as a child when the local gossips would scrutinise her as she went in the corner shop, displaying their blatant disapproval. She was self-conscious. Ashamed. Inadequate. She was bad. Her family was bad. And she deserved all she got.

Before she could get too carried away in her thoughts, the governor looked up from her file again and, without preamble, she said, 'Two weeks' loss of canteen.'

Two weeks without any treats. That was bad. But although Adele was disappointed, she was also relieved. At least the governor hadn't added any time onto her sentence so the punishment was relatively mild.

'Thank you, ma'am,' said Adele, not really sure what words were appropriate under the circumstances.

As Adele spoke, she noticed the expression on Sly's face, which conveyed her disappointment that Adele hadn't been punished more severely.

Adele waited for the governor to dismiss her, but instead she said, 'I've received some information about your studies.' She looked up at Adele. 'I've found a suitable course of study, which can be taken on a distance-learning basis.'

Adele's face broke into a smile despite her punishment and the hostile look on Sly's face.

'It's fortunate for you that I had already put you

forward for the course,' continued the governor. 'But before I let you go ahead, I want your assurance that there won't be a repeat of today's behaviour.'

'No, there won't,' said Adele. 'I promise... Oh, and thank you so much, I really appreciate it.'

'Very well, I'll send the study materials down to your cell as soon as we receive them.'

'Thank you,' Adele gushed. Then she felt Sly grasp her arm tightly and, together with the other guard, they led her out of the office.

Once they were well away from the governor's office, Sly said to the other guard, 'It's OK, I can handle her from here.'

Sly waited till the other guard had walked away, then she said to Adele, 'Don't think you're anything special, Robinson. You're just like the rest of them in here. Scum!'

Then she grabbed Adele's arm even tighter and dragged her along the corridors and back to her cell.

Adele didn't say anything in retaliation. She knew that it would only make matters worse for her. With Shazza and Sly both against her, things were already bad enough.

18

When Adele returned to her cell, Anna was lying on her bunk facing the wall with her back to her. Adele noticed Anna roll down her sleeve quickly and hide something in her other hand. She couldn't tell what the item was as Anna had her fingers clenched tightly around it.

'Anna, are you all right?' asked Adele.

Anna rolled over and Adele could tell by her sluggishness that she was reluctant to face her. Straight away Adele noticed that Anna's face was blotchy and tear-stained.

'What's happened?' asked Adele.

'Nothing,' said Anna, running her finger across the swallow tattoo on her cheekbone as she wiped away a stray tear. Her other hand was still closed around the item she was concealing.

'But you've been crying,' said Adele.

'No, I haven't. I've just got a bit of a cold. That's all.'

Adele wasn't convinced, 'Come on, Anna. Out with it,' she said.

'I've told you... I'm all right,' Anna bit back, turning round to face the wall again.

'What's that in your hand?' asked Adele. 'I hope it isn't drugs.'

'No, it's nothing,' Anna snapped.

Adele sighed, knowing there was no way she'd stop Anna from taking drugs even though she didn't approve. Like most of the women in here, Anna was an addict, and she depended on a regular supply of drugs to get her through the day.

'Shazza can't keep taking things from you. You've got to tell her no!' said Adele.

Anna didn't reply at first but Adele could hear her stifle a sob. Then Anna asked, 'How did you get on, anyway?'

'Two weeks' loss of canteen.'

'Not bad considering.'

'That's what I thought. It's gonna kill me going without chocolate for a fortnight, though, and I'm running out of toiletries.'

'Don't worry, you can borrow some of mine.'

'Thanks, Anna,' said Adele.

As Adele thought about the way Shazza had been treating Anna, she decided to try tackling her again. 'Y'know, Anna, you don't have to keep giving Shazza your things. If you stand up to her then she can't get away with it.'

'Oh, yeah, and a fat lot of good that did you.'

'Well... OK. I've lost a fortnight's canteen but it could have been worse.'

'I don't mean that,' said Anna, her tone now timid. Then she whispered, 'Repercussions.'

'Oh, I see,' said Adele, the thought making her shudder. 'Well, maybe it's best if we all stick together. Caroline's already said she'll stick with me so we could do the same for you.'

Anna turned and looked at her again. 'Yeah, if you want,' she said. 'Might not help, though.'

Then Anna turned away once more. It was obvious to Adele that she was frightened. Her sentences were clipped, her facial muscles taut, and she lay on the bed in a foetal position.

Anna was still hiding something in her hand. At first Adele thought it was weed but now she suspected that Anna had been injecting herself with drugs and didn't want Adele to see the marks on her arms. Recently, she had noticed that Anna had started wearing long-sleeved tops rather than parading around in her underwear like she used to. Maybe that was why.

Anna wasn't the only one who was scared. Adele knew that standing up to Shazza may have been a big mistake. Now that she had come to blows with her, she dreaded what Shazza was going to do next.

But as she had made a stand, she had no alternative other than to see it through. Looking at Anna's frightened form, she knew that she couldn't let things carry on as they were.

True to her word, Anna had tried her best to stick with Adele and Caroline whenever they ventured outside the cell. They were standing having a chat in the recreation room – Adele, Anna, Caroline and Cheryl.

Straight away Adele had noticed the bruising around Cheryl's right eye. 'What the hell happened to you?' she asked.

'Nothing, I fell,' said Cheryl.

'She won't say,' Caroline chipped in. 'But I've got a good idea what really happened.' Her gaze wandered over to Shazza, who was playing pool with Denise while Louise watched, and Adele's jaw dropped in alarm.

Cheryl rushed to defend herself. 'I told you, I tripped.'

Adele knew they'd get nothing further out of Cheryl, who looked terrified. They grew silent and Adele glanced at what was taking place between Shazza and Denise. Although they were several metres away, Adele could hear them talking and laughing as they played. Adele tried not to watch but their loud banter drew her attention.

Shazza was just about to take a shot. She was leaning over the pool table, gazing at the striped ball on the green baize. But Adele sensed Shazza's gaze drifting in her direction. She noticed a brief upward movement when the whites of Shazza's eyes were replaced by vivid turquoise and black pools of hatred.

Then Shazza raised her head and her eyes met Adele's, sending a stab of anxiety through her. She noticed the familiar smirk on Shazza's narrow lips as she carried on feeding the cue through the fingers of her left hand. But the cue was no longer on the ball. Shazza had tilted it slightly so it was now aiming at Adele. She sneered at Adele as she continued to point the cue and thrust it backwards and forwards menacingly.

There was no doubt in Adele's mind about the message Shazza was sending. Caroline had spotted it too and was tutting and scowling.

'What's the matter?' asked Anna, seeing Caroline's reaction.

'Nothing,' said Caroline, quickly turning away but flashing Adele a look of concern before she did so.

Adele tried to look away too but her eyes were drawn to Shazza. She had that effect. It was the way she acted; the implicit threat displayed by her body language, which put Adele on her guard. She felt a constant need to check what was happening; to steel herself for whatever Shazza was going to do next.

Shazza and Denise played on for several minutes. Then Shazza potted the black and let out a roar. 'Fuckin' told you I'd win!' she shouted.

They shared a hug. Then, just as Denise was breaking away, Shazza whispered something in her ear. Denise smiled back and followed Shazza as she strode across the room, heading towards Adele and her friends. Louise quickly ran behind, trying to keep pace with the two larger women. Adele could feel her heartbeat speed up.

As soon as she was standing next to them Shazza asked Anna, 'What've you got for me?' Her tone was aggressive and she stood hand on hip and shoulders pulled back as she waited for a reply. Although her words were directed at Anna, her eyes settled on Adele, gauging her, and waiting for her reaction.

Adele could feel her dread turning to annoyance at Shazza's brazen attitude. Then Anna put her hand inside her pocket.

'Don't!' warned Adele, reaching across and blocking Anna's arm. 'You don't have to, Anna!' she said, sounding bolder than she felt.

Anna stared back at Adele, her face a mask of fear. 'No, it's OK,' she said, dragging her arm away. 'Shazza's a mate. I owe her one.'

All eyes were now on Adele, waiting to see what she would do next. The grimace on Shazza's face and the cocky way Denise was standing made Adele even angrier.

'You don't owe her anything!' she yelled.

Shazza's eyes switched from Adele to Anna, her

eyebrows now raised inquisitively. 'Is that right, Anna?' she asked, her tone full of menace.

'No, course it isn't,' said Anna, and she quickly wrenched her arm from Adele's grasp.

Adele could see the cigarettes that she had pulled from her pocket.

'Here,' Anna said, thrusting them at Shazza.

'That's better,' said Shazza, grasping the cigarettes.

Then she flicked her head back, locking eyes with Adele once more.

'At least Anna knows what's good for her,' she said. 'It's a pity you don't. You fuckin' will do, though, before much longer.'

Before Adele had a chance to reply, Shazza walked away. Denise sneered at Adele before she and Louise rushed to catch up with their friend.

Caroline turned to Adele. 'Take no notice,' she said. 'We'll make sure no harm comes to you. Won't we, girls?' she asked Anna and Cheryl, but although they nodded their agreement, their expressions said something else.

Adele couldn't fail to see the fear on the faces of her friends. It wasn't over between her and Shazza. Adele had no doubt that she was just biding her time. Sooner or later she would make a move and, when she did, Adele would have to make sure she was ready.

19

Adele was thrilled to receive a parcel a few days later and had a feeling she knew what was inside. The brown wrapping paper had already been opened then resealed by the guards, but it didn't spoil Adele's enjoyment. As she tore excitedly at the paper, Anna looked on despondently.

'Oh, wow!' said Adele, holding up her pristine study booklets and fingering them as though they were precious jewels. 'I can't wait to get started on this lot.'

'What are they?' asked Anna.

'They're the study booklets for my accountancy course,' said Adele, flicking through the pages of one of them. 'I told you about it. Remember?'

Anna shrugged, her lips set in a grim line and her eyes downcast. 'Whatever turns you on, I suppose,' she muttered.

Adele smiled at her reaction but didn't say anything. She couldn't expect Anna to understand her excitement, not when education didn't mean anything to her. She knew someone who would understand, though – Caroline – and she was anxious to share her news with her. In her haste Adele rushed from the cell leaving Anna alone.

'Guess what?' she announced when she caught sight of Caroline inside her cell, thumbing through the pages of a magazine. Caroline looked up expectantly.

'I've received my study materials,' said Adele, holding out one of the booklets for Caroline to examine.

'Excellent,' said Caroline, putting the magazine down on the bed. 'Let's have a look.'

Adele passed her the booklet and Caroline flicked through the pages, stopping at one of them. 'Bloody hell, Adele. This is all a bit over my head.'

'It will be, seeing as how you studied English,' Adele laughed.

Caroline grinned back, 'Well, I hope you're up for the challenge.'

'Oh, yeah,' said Adele. 'In fact, I can't wait to get started. It'll help to pass the days more quickly in here, that's for sure.'

Cheryl, who had been watching them, now tried to share their enthusiasm. 'What is it?' she asked.

'An accountancy course,' said Adele.

'Oh…' said Cheryl.

When she didn't say anything more, Adele continued, 'I used to do bookkeeping and accounts work before I came in here so I thought it would be good to get some more qualifications.'

Cheryl stared back blankly so Adele added, 'It should help to pass the time as well as increasing my chances of work when I'm released.'

'Good for you,' said Cheryl. 'I wish I was that brainy.'

Adele smiled at her.

'You never know until you try,' Caroline said to Cheryl. 'You're not doing so bad with your classes, are you?'

'Not really, but I've only just started them and I was rubbish at English and Maths at school,' said Cheryl.

'Well, a lot can depend on the teacher,' added Caroline. 'And it's different when you're at school, too. A lot of people go on to study after they've left school, and they find they get along a lot better when they're a bit more mature. Just keep trying and you never know what it might lead to.'

'Thanks,' said Cheryl, a radiant smile lighting up her pretty features.

Adele was glad Caroline had stepped in. She hadn't been sure what to say to Cheryl but Caroline had a way of speaking to people that spurred them on without sounding too patronising.

'You stopping for a cuppa?' Caroline asked Adele.

Adele raised her eyes and drew her lips back. 'I shouldn't really. I've left Anna on her own.'

'We'll only be a few minutes,' said Caroline. 'Anyway,

Shazza takes from her whether we're there or not. I think you're the one we need to protect more than Anna.'

'Thanks. Cheer me up, why don't you?' laughed Adele. 'Still, I think it's best to keep an eye on things. I don't trust Shazza with her.'

'Sorry, I was being a bit insensitive,' said Caroline. 'I know what you mean. It's just so bloody restrictive having to keep an eye out all the time, isn't it? Anyway, do you fancy that cuppa?'

When Adele hesitated, Caroline persisted: 'Go on, just a quick one.'

'Oh, all right then,' said Adele. 'You've twisted my arm. We can make it a celebratory one now I've received my course booklets.'

Once they got chatting, the time soon passed and it was another twenty minutes before Adele headed back to her own cell.

'Wait a minute,' said Caroline. 'I'll walk back with you.' She turned to Cheryl. 'You'll be OK for a minute, won't you?'

Cheryl nodded but Adele noticed the way her eyes darted nervously from Caroline to her, then back again.

'You sure?' Caroline asked.

'Yeah, course I am,' said Cheryl.

As soon as they were outside the cell Caroline whispered to Adele, 'I won't leave her long but I needed to have a quick word with you.'

'OK,' said Adele, raising her eyebrows inquisitively.

As Caroline walked along the corridor with Adele, she continued, 'I think Shazza might have got to Cheryl, too. Apart from the black eye, she's been a bit troubled lately. I've tried raising the subject but she denies there's a problem.'

'Um, not much you can do if she won't talk about it,' said Adele.

'I know, but I think we're best to keep an eye on her, even so.'

'Yeah, sure,' Adele replied.

They neared Adele's cell door, and Caroline added, 'Anyway, I must dash back now. I don't like to leave her on her own but I wanted you to know.'

'Thanks for telling me,' said Adele. 'I suppose it's best if we all stick together as much as possible.'

'Yeah, and you were right about Anna before. We should keep an eye on her, too. I don't trust Shazza as far as I can throw her.'

'Tell me about it,' said Adele. She was now only a metre from her cell door and Caroline had stopped, ready to turn round and head back to her own cell. 'See you later,' Adele added.

Caroline gave her a tiny wave and Adele stepped forward pushing her cell door open. With her mind still on Caroline and her new study booklets, she was totally unprepared for the sight that met her.

'Oh my God!' she yelled, spotting Anna lying on the bed, her clothing soaked with blood.

She ran over to the bed, screaming Caroline's name as a frisson of fear scurried through her, leaving a dry tingle in her mouth. But Caroline had already heard her and was soon inside the cell.

'Jesus Christ!' shouted Adele as her eyes scanned Anna's body, trying to locate the source of the blood.

Anna was lying on her back, her right arm down by her side, a discarded razor blade next to her fingers. Her other arm was draped across her body, the blood pooling beneath her left hand. Adele lifted Anna's hand and screamed as she saw the laceration across her wrist, which was still spurting blood. She also noticed numerous tiny cuts and scars along Anna's forearm.

'Leave me,' muttered Anna.

'Not a fuckin' chance, you silly cow!' cried Adele.

'Pinch the cut!' shouted Caroline. 'We need to stem the bleeding.'

Adele grabbed Anna's fleshy wrist and squeezed at either side of the laceration. Blood squelched beneath her fingers. Anna screamed in pain. But Adele kept a tight grip.

Caroline grabbed the bloody razor blade and ripped at Anna's bedding. She held out a strip of cloth. 'Quick, let me bind it,' she ordered Adele. 'You get help.'

Adele ran to the cell door. A crowd of inmates had started to gather. She spotted a guard on the opposite corridor. 'Help!' she shouted. 'Quick! We need help.'

The guard dashed towards the cell. It was Judy

Roberts. Two others seemed to appear from out of nowhere. They raced behind her. Judy reached the cell door and pushed her way through the throng of inmates.

'OK, I'll take over from here,' Judy said to Caroline as she rushed up to the bed.

Then two other guards hurried into the cell. One of them was Sly, who viciously tugged Caroline away. 'Stand back. Everybody get back!' she shouted.

Another two guards appeared and Adele could feel herself being forced back. Between them, the guards shoved the other inmates out of the way and slammed the cell door shut.

Adele peered anxiously through the cell window to see if Anna was all right. But a guard had covered it with her jacket. Adele stared desperately at the deep blue of the prison officer's uniform. Then she rocked back on her heels. Her feet were wired with the hum of adrenalin. She paced backwards and forwards until the crowd blocked her way.

The animated buzz of morbid fascination surrounded her. Prisoners jostled her as they fought their way to the cell door, full of frenzied chatter. Vying for their place at the front. Trying to catch a glimpse.

Of Anna. Of blood. Of death!

And their eagerness sickened Adele.

'What's happened?' inmates demanded excitedly as more of them arrived at the scene.

Caroline put her arm around Adele's shoulders and drew her aside.

'It's OK. The guards are on it,' she said and, as Caroline's words penetrated Adele's brain, she felt her eyes flood with tears.

'Oh God, I hope so!' she replied, shaking. 'I knew I shouldn't have left her.'

'Shush,' said Caroline, taking Adele into her arms. 'Don't blame yourself. You weren't to know she'd do something stupid.'

Adele tried to respond but then she caught sight of her hands. A recollection crowded her brain. Crimson hands. The brass cat. Covered in blood. Viscous and sticky. Hammering the cat against her father's head...

The reason she was in here in the first place.

'Oh God!' she yelled, the breath catching in her throat. Then her breath seemed to come in short gasps, accompanied by a wave of dizziness, as panic took over.

'Adele, it's OK,' Caroline reassured her, releasing her hold on Adele. 'Breathe! Come on, deep breaths,' she urged. Then, glancing behind her, she shouted, 'Back off! Give her some space.'

The other prisoners took a step back, staring fixedly at this new spectacle.

'I said back off!' shouted Caroline, but the women didn't move any further. Their curious eyes were watching Adele's every move.

'Come on, Adele. Take some deep breaths,' Caroline encouraged.

Adele tried to follow her instructions. She could feel her breath juddering inside her as it fed her lungs.

'That's it, nice and slowly,' Caroline continued.

After taking a few deep breaths Adele could feel the dizziness subside. But tears flooded her eyes again.

'It's OK,' said Caroline. 'Anna will be OK. She was still conscious when we found her. That's a good sign.'

'Did you see the other marks on her arms?' Adele sobbed.

'Yes,' said Caroline. 'I think she's been cutting herself for a while, by the looks of it.'

'Jesus! Why didn't I notice?' Adele cried. 'I should have known there was something wrong. She's been covering her arms up so I can't see them. I even saw her pull her sleeve down one day and hide something. I thought she was injecting drugs. Why didn't I challenge her more? I might have been able to stop her doing this!'

'Shush,' said Caroline. 'Don't go blaming yourself. We both know what's driven her to this.'

Eventually Adele became calmer and the inmates switched their attention to the cell once more. Three more guards arrived with a doctor. Two of them were carrying a stretcher. They cleared the inmates away from the cell door.

Caroline turned Adele away. 'They're going to fetch

her out,' she said. 'Come on, we can watch from over there.'

Although Adele was eager to make sure Anna was all right, she followed Caroline's instructions. She wasn't sure whether she could face the gruesome sight of Anna covered in blood again. And she knew Caroline was trying to protect her.

As they watched from the opposite corridor, the cell door inched open. The guards held the prisoners back while two of them carried the stretcher on which Anna was lying. Caroline turned Adele round again so she couldn't see.

Then Adele heard a prisoner announce, 'She's still alive!' and relief surged through her.

As Adele collapsed, sobbing, into Caroline's arms, she caught sight of Shazza over Caroline's shoulder. Her features were strained, the worry lines visible. It was obvious to Adele that Shazza knew Anna's suicide attempt was down to her.

There would be questions asked over this. And if the governor found out that Shazza was responsible, she would be in deep shit. But would that be enough to stop her? Adele hoped so because somebody would have to put a stop to Shazza. And if no one else could do it then Adele feared that the onus might be on her.

20

It had been two days since Anna's suicide attempt and she still wasn't back from the hospital. But at least Adele knew she was OK as Judy Roberts had kept her informed. According to Judy, Anna was receiving psychiatric assessment and the guards were keeping a close watch over her to make sure there weren't any further attempts.

During the last two days, many of the prisoners had been called in to the governor for questioning, including Adele. But she didn't give anything away. There was an unwritten rule in prison that you didn't grass. Adele knew, deep down, that Anna's suicide attempt was down to the torment she had received at Shazza's hands. She wasn't going to tell the governor that, though. She was already on the wrong side of Shazza as it was, and she didn't want to make matters worse.

Adele was on her way back from the kitchens where she worked and as she walked back to her cell she mulled the events over in her mind. She felt guilty for leaving Anna alone for so long that day, and for not spotting just how much turmoil Anna was going through. Perhaps she could have protected her more or found out from her exactly what was going on.

As Adele approached her cell she was alarmed to see Shazza leaving it. Adele wondered what she was doing there and hoped she hadn't stolen anything of hers. She dashed up to the cell and pushed the door open. Sitting on the bottom bunk was Anna, her left wrist covered with a dressing.

'Anna!' Adele cried. 'It's good to see you back.' Then she walked over to Anna, and despite the repugnance that the sight of Anna always elicited, she threw her arms around her. 'How are you?'

Anna shrugged. 'Not bad, I suppose.'

'Jesus, Anna! I've been worried sick about you,' said Adele, quickly releasing Anna as she caught a whiff of body odour. She looked into her sad eyes. 'Don't you ever do anything like that again!'

Anna didn't reply. Instead she dropped her head and gazed at the cell floor.

Adele took hold of Anna's hands, trying to ignore the dressing covering her wrist. 'I haven't told the governor or guards anything,' she said.

'Me neither,' sniffed Anna. 'Or the shrink.'

'But there's a reason you did what you did, isn't there?' Adele asked.

Anna shrugged again.

'Anna, don't keep it from me!' said Adele, her tone now stern. 'I can't help you if you don't tell me, can I? It's Shazza, isn't it? It's because of her?'

When Anna still didn't say anything, Adele persisted. 'What was she doing in here?' she asked. 'Was she having a go at you again?'

'Not really,' said Anna.

'Well, what did she want?'

Anna raised her head again and pulled her shoulders back. Then, with a look of resignation on her face, she said, 'She wanted to know what I'd told the governor. So I told her I'd not said anything.'

'OK, go on,' Adele encouraged.

'She asked me if anyone else had said anything but I told her I didn't know 'cos I hadn't seen anyone since I'd been back.'

Adele nodded for Anna to continue.

'I think she'll be all right with me now,' said Anna.

'What makes you think that?'

''Cos she said that if I keep my gob shut everything will be all right.'

Adele nodded again, this time satisfied with Anna's response. It was obvious to her that Anna's suicide attempt had shaken Shazza. In the past two days she had been acting differently towards all of them. Her attitude had been uncharacteristically friendly to the point of almost ingratiating. Caroline had also told her that Cheryl seemed a lot happier and she thought it was because Shazza was now leaving her alone.

Although Anna's suicide attempt had both frightened and upset Adele, at least it had put paid to Shazza's nasty behaviour. Adele hoped that things would continue as they were because, now that Shazza was behaving herself, it would make prison life a lot easier for all of them.

Two weeks later Adele was in the visitors' room with her brother, Peter, sitting across from her. The problem was that he was paying more attention to the attractive visitor behind her than he was to her. He was currently leaning to the side so he could see beyond Adele and was flashing a wide, welcoming smile to the female visitor at the next table.

'For God's sake! Will you behave yourself?' said Adele, exasperated.

'Gotta give 'em what they want, haven't I?' he grinned, winking at the girl before straightening back up and focusing on Adele.

'OK, I'm all yours,' he laughed.

'About bloody time, too,' said Adele who couldn't help but join in with his cheeky laughter. 'How are you, anyway? What have you been up to since I last saw you?'

'I've only gone and got myself a sunbed salon, haven't I? Good little earner it is, too.'

'And how did you manage that?' she asked.

'What d'you mean?'

'I mean, where did you get the money from?'

'Oh, y'know. Borrowed a bit, called in a few favours. The beds aren't too expensive if you know where to get them. It's all about having the right contacts, sis.' He winked again as he spoke the last few words.

Adele raised her eyebrows in disapproval. 'Is it?' she asked, knowing that she would never find out fully how Peter had come by the money to kit out a tanning salon.

'Anyway, what about you?' Peter asked. 'How are things on the inside?'

'Well, since that...' Adele lowered her voice, '... attempted suicide a couple of weeks ago, things have been a lot better.'

'That's good.'

'Yeah, I think it gave a few people a fright. Nobody's told the screws what really happened but I think a certain someone was worried about what would have happened if Anna had died. Since then she's been fine with all of us, and she's stopped picking on Anna and Cheryl.'

'Glad to hear it.'

Adele smiled across at him. 'Yeah, it makes life a lot easier when you don't feel as though you've got to watch your back all the time.'

'Careful not to take your eye off the ball, though, sis. I've told you before, you can't trust anyone inside. You might think things are going OK but you never know who's scheming behind your back.'

'Thanks for the warning,' said Adele, but she was only half listening, still preoccupied with how Peter had obtained the money to set up a tanning salon.

21

'Y'know,' said Adele, looking over the rim of her cup of tea at her friend, Caroline, 'after all these weeks, Anna's only just told me how bad it got with Shazza. It's no wonder she did what she did.'

'Really?' said Caroline.

'Oh, yeah. Shazza was worse with her than anyone. She was taking nearly all her cigs and drugs as well. Apart from that, there was the verbal and physical abuse. She used to do sly things like pinch her stomach while making nasty comments about her weight. Then, when they were on their own, she'd thump her in the stomach until she was winded, and laugh at her.

'But what really pushed Anna over the edge was that Shazza was going to get her to smuggle heroin in.'

'That's terrible,' said Caroline, her face full of concern. 'She didn't do it, did she?'

'No, that's why she tried to commit suicide – so she wouldn't have to do it.'

'Shazza was a bit like that with me,' said Cheryl. 'Only she didn't take my stuff as often and she only hit me once... She just threatened to do it again if I didn't give her what she wanted.'

Caroline tutted. 'Some people are just born bloody evil, if you ask me, and I think she's one of them.'

'Yeah, you can say that again,' Adele responded. 'I don't know whether she gave Anna such a hard time because she looks so intimidating. Maybe it gave Shazza a kick to have control over someone like Anna.'

'Who knows how the mind of someone like Shazza works?' said Caroline. 'She doesn't think like the rest of us. Anyway, I'm just glad for Anna's sake and everybody else's that it's over now, and at least we can go about our business without having to watch our backs all the time.'

'Me too,' Adele and Cheryl chorused.

The following day Caroline was in the association area with Adele, Cheryl and Anna when Shazza and her friends passed them on their way out. Shazza and Denise made a show of saying hello to them, as they had been doing since Anna's suicide attempt. They all returned their greeting but something about Shazza's face alerted Caroline. Her eyes seemed to hover over Adele and there was a slight sneer, which hadn't been there during the past few weeks.

Nobody else noticed, but Caroline was perceptive. She was also used to Shazza's ways from being in prison with her previously. Caroline instinctively felt that something wasn't right. Curious, she turned her head and her eyes followed Shazza as she passed them.

When Shazza thought no one was watching, she tapped Denise on the arm and said something. Caroline couldn't hear what it was, but she noticed the hard lines around Shazza's mouth and the way her brow furrowed. She and Denise exchanged knowing looks. Then Denise nodded back at Shazza and her face broke out into a sly grin. They didn't spot Caroline watching them but Adele did.

'What's the matter?' she asked.

'Nothing,' said Caroline. 'I'm just checking what that lot are up to, that's all.'

'They seemed OK,' said Anna, and Adele and Cheryl nodded their agreement.

'Yeah, it's probably just my imagination,' said Caroline.

'What is?' asked Adele.

'Oh, nothing. I suppose I'm just finding it a bit too good to be true since they've started being nice again.'

The deliberate lie tripped off Caroline's tongue but she knew it wasn't her imagination. It looked to her as though Shazza and Denise were scheming.

But there was nothing that Caroline could actually pinpoint. It was just a bad feeling and one that she wasn't ready to share with her friends yet. She didn't want to worry them unduly. Besides, with nothing concrete to tell them, they might just think she was being paranoid. So, she decided to wait until she found out a little more.

Peter, Glynn and Mike arrived at the George and Dragon pub in the city centre half an hour after closing time. The brakes of Peter's flash BMW screeched to a halt as they pulled up outside the building. He took his keys from the ignition and they got out of the car.

They were dressed casual but smart. Peter wore an expensive leather jacket, and Glynn and Mike wore tailored jackets with T-shirts underneath, a look made fashionable by the TV show *Miami Vice*.

Most of the customers had gone. There were just a few stragglers still clutching their pints while the bar staff walked around collecting glasses and encouraging them to drink up.

As Peter and his men crossed the pub, the landlord, Pat, looked at them from behind the bar. He greeted them but couldn't hide his fear; his shoulders were scrunched a little too high, his eyes were wide and his muscles tensed.

'All right, Pat?' Peter greeted as they approached the bar. 'Shall we go through?'

The landlord put down the cloth he had been using to wipe the bar and led the way through to the back room.

'You got the cash?' asked Peter as soon as they were in the back room.

'No,' said the landlord. As Peter glared at him, Pat took a deep breath and said, 'I can't do it anymore. It's eating into my profits too much.'

Glynn walked behind the landlord and grasped his arms from the back. 'Just give me the nod, Pete,' said Mike, ready to lay into Pat while Glynn held him back, cutting off his defences.

On this occasion Peter was glad to have Glynn and Mike with him. Since his previous disagreement with Mike, Glynn had had a word with him and he seemed to be towing the line. He was still a vicious bastard but there were times when that came in handy.

'Hang on a minute,' said Peter, and Glynn released his hold on Pat.

'How much does this place take?' Peter demanded.

'Don't know,' said Pat. 'It varies.'

'Don't tell me you don't fuckin' know! How much does it take in a typical week?' asked Peter.

'Dunno, a few thousand, I suppose. But I've got loads of overheads. Staff. Heating. Lighting. And the brewery's just put up the cost of the beer again.'

'Don't get fuckin' smart with me! I know how much the brewery's charging and it isn't gonna eat into your profits that much. All I'm asking is a few poxy hundred quid a month to keep people off your back, and you can't even manage that!'

'I'll take my chances,' said Pat. 'I'm sorry, Pete, but I'm not doing it anymore. You can't do this to me!'

'Can't we?' asked Peter, striding over to the landlord and grabbing him viciously by the chin until he could smell the fear coming from him. 'When everything goes fuckin' pear-shaped, and people start muscling in, just remember that I gave you a chance. We're a lot more reasonable than some of the firms round here but that doesn't mean I'm gonna let you take the piss. Now, are you gonna pay up or do I have to get my men to *persuade* you?'

Glynn was now holding Pat from behind again, and he and Mike were waiting for their orders.

Peter stepped back. 'Well, Pat, what's it gonna be?' he asked, walking over to the door.

Pat shook his head but his facial expression belied the brave front he was putting on. 'No,' he said, his voice sounding small and timid.

'Right, Mike, he's all yours,' said Peter, who then blocked the door so none of the staff could enter.

Mike stepped eagerly up to Pat. Then, once he was sure he had made eye contact, he launched his fist into the pit of his stomach. Pat gasped and let out a guttural moan. His instinct was to clutch his aching gut and he tried to wrench his arms from Glynn's grip. But Glynn held him tight while Mike quickly followed up with another punch to the stomach, then another. Pat winced and gasped as Mike's ferocious blows winded him.

After several sharp punches, Peter ordered Mike to stop. 'Right, Pat. What's it gonna be?' he asked.

Pat stood panting for a few seconds, bending forward from the waist, his arms still pinned back by Glynn.

'Well?' demanded Peter when Pat didn't reply.

'No,' muttered Pat, and Mike immediately started thumping him again, this time aiming his fists at Pat's face.

Pat's head pivoted from side to side with the force of each vicious blow. Then Peter heard a woman's voice coming from the other side of the door.

'Pat, Pat. What's going on? Are you all right?' she shouted.

The door handle turned and Peter could feel someone pushing at the door, trying to get in. He put his weight behind it to keep it shut tight. Then he had an idea.

'Stop a minute!' he ordered Mike.

While Mike paused, Peter quickly opened the door, clamped his hand over the woman's mouth and dragged her into the room. She gasped when she caught sight of her husband's bloodied face. His shirt was torn and his hair was matted with blood.

'Right,' said Peter. 'It seems that we're having trouble getting you to pay up,' he continued. 'So maybe your wife can be persuaded.'

The woman let out a small scream, which was suppressed by the might of his hand. He looked across at Pat.

'No, not Mary!' Pat pleaded as he stared back at Peter through terror-filled eyes. 'I'll pay it!' he gushed. 'But please don't hurt Mary.'

Peter could feel a reluctant sense of achievement envelop him. 'OK, but you've put us to a lot of trouble today, Pat,' he said. 'I don't enjoy having to put my men on to you but you didn't give me any fuckin' choice. You've wasted a lot of our time and effort so I'm putting the price up by a hundred quid.'

'No!' said Pat, his eyes wide open in alarm.

'OK, do I have to set my men on Mary then?'

Again she let out a suppressed scream. Peter had no intentions of setting his men on Mary but he wasn't going to let Pat know that. He knew that the threat of it alone would be enough.

'No! No, don't do that,' yelled Pat. Then he hung his head, resigned in defeat. 'I'll pay it,' he muttered.

'Glad you've seen sense at last,' said Peter. 'Right, here's what we're gonna do. Mary, I'm gonna take my hand away from your squealing gob, and when I do, I don't wanna hear a fuckin' peep from you. OK?'

He switched his eyes to Mary and she nodded at him.

'Good,' he said, taking his hand away, which was streaked with Mary's saliva. 'Now you and me are gonna go into the bar, Mary, and make sure all the customers and staff have gone home. Then you can get the money for me from the till… and not a fuckin' word to anyone, OK?'

'OK,' Mary murmured, her voice trembling.

'Excellent,' said Peter, now calm and business like. 'I'm sure you two will look after Pat for me while we're away,' he grinned to Glynn and Mike.

Then he looked at his spit-sodden hand in disgust, wiped it on Mary's sleeve and led her through to the bar. Relief surged through him but he wasn't going to let it show to anyone in this room. It had been a bad night's work but at least he'd got a result in the end.

22

Caroline had a bad feeling. It had been niggling her for days. There was something disingenuous about the way Shazza and Denise had been greeting her and her friends. Although they had been over-friendly since Anna's suicide attempt, something else had changed recently. Caroline could sense it but she couldn't quite make out what it was.

While Adele was away at the gym and Cheryl was playing pool with Anna, Caroline decided to slip away and see what she could find out. She crept up to Shazza's cell and listened outside, trying her best to appear casual in case anyone was watching.

She could hear the sound of Shazza, Denise and Louise talking. But their voices were faint from outside the cell and she had to strain to decipher what they were saying. She managed to catch snippets of their conversation.

'Today,' said Shazza, 'while... her own.'

Then Caroline heard Denise say something back but the only word she caught was, 'Anna'.

'Yeah, no problems,' said Shazza, followed by, 'We've got time... lock-down.'

Then they changed the subject and Caroline walked away from the cell, her blood pumping frantically. She needed to warn Anna!

It seemed to Caroline that they were planning to do something to Anna before lockdown. So, her instincts had been right after all...

'Anna, I need a word,' she whispered, once she had caught up with her at the pool table. 'Cheryl, you, too.'

Anna and Cheryl crowded around Caroline. 'I think Shazza and Denise are planning something,' she whispered, checking around her to make sure no one was listening in.

'Like what?' asked Anna.

'I'm not sure. I didn't catch all of their conversation but it involves you, Anna. And they're going to do it today. So I think you'd best be vigilant.'

'Shit!' said Anna, and the colour drained from her face.

'Try not to worry. It might be nothing. I didn't hear everything they said but I've just got a feeling they're up to no good.'

'So, what do we do?' asked Anna, her voice edged with panic.

'We stick together and hope I'm wrong,' said Caroline, tapping Anna affectionately on the shoulder.

★

Adele was in the gym practising her kickboxing. She often came alone now she wasn't worried about Shazza any more. It was usually quieter than the rest of the prison and she enjoyed the relative peace.

After she had finished doing an aerobic warm-up she did a quick kickboxing combination. Using an imaginary target she threw a jab first, then a cross punch followed by a right hook and an uppercut. Then she swapped sides, leading from the right foot this time and repeating the moves with opposite hands. She increased the intensity of each combination, building up a good sweat.

When she had finished delivering punches against her imaginary target, she practised a few kicks. Adele was just completing a back kick and knee strike combination. As she kicked her left leg backwards, she thought she spotted something in her rear peripheral vision. She had an eerie sensation of being watched, which made the hairs stand up on the back of her neck.

She finished the combination, raising her right knee forcefully then lowering it back to the ground. Then she paused, leaning forwards with her hands on her hips, trying to get her breath back.

'Very impressive, Miss Kickboxing Queen,' she heard. The sarcastic tone was unmistakable; it was Shazza.

Adele swivelled back, spotting the sneers on the faces of Shazza, Denise and Louise as they watched her.

'Now let's see what you can do to a real target, shall we?' Shazza asked.

The three of them stepped forward. They had obviously been planning this. Other inmates stood aside, not wishing to get involved. Within no time Shazza and her friends had surrounded Adele. Adrenalin pulsed through her as fear took a hold.

'Come on then,' said Shazza. 'Let's see what you can do, smart arse!'

Adele could feel the first stirrings of panic and she drew in a sharp breath that hit the back of her throat in a fierce blast of air. But she wasn't going to give in without a fight. She adopted a defensive stance, ready for the attack.

'Is that all you've fuckin' got?' said Shazza, scowling.

Their eyes locked and for a few tense seconds nobody spoke. Then Shazza grinned and said, 'Ooh, I see. You're waiting for us to make the first move, are you?'

She nodded at Denise, who charged at Adele, aiming her fist at Adele's face. But Adele was ready for her. She deflected Denise's fist, then countered with a sharp blow. It caught Denise full on the bridge of her nose.

Before Adele could follow up the punch she caught sight of Louise stepping around her. Straight away she felt her hair being tugged sharply from behind. Then Louise's arm was around her throat. Shazza had also closed in from the side. While Denise punched Adele around the head and torso, Shazza clawed at her face.

Adele tried her best to deflect Denise's punches. But she couldn't stop Shazza too, especially with Louise choking her from behind. Another sharp tug of her hair from Louise brought tears to Adele's eyes. It forced her chin upwards, leaving her face exposed and vulnerable. And her vision was no longer at eye level.

Unable to see her attackers clearly, Adele flailed around helplessly. But it was no use. As her punches missed their target, those of her enemies landed spot on.

Adele felt each stinging blow to her face and each bruising kick in her shins. She also heard the heavy pounding of each thump. Then someone dug her sharp nails into the delicate flesh of Adele's cheek and scored several lines down her face. Tears sprang to her eyes again.

'Get the bitch on the floor!' Shazza yelled.

As they tried to drag her down, Adele fought to stay upright. She knew they would inflict more damage once she was on the ground. Louise let go of Adele's hair while she tried to press down on her shoulders. Now they were back in her line of vision. Adele aimed a few jabs at Shazza and Denise, forcing them back. Beyond them other prisoners stood watching but nobody interfered.

Then Adele spotted Caroline rushing through the door and relief surged through her.

'Get your bloody hands off her!' Caroline yelled, running over.

Anna and Cheryl came through the door too and were also heading in Adele's direction. Then two prison officers appeared.

One of the other inmates spoke out when she saw the prison officers. 'Yeah, come on, Shazza,' said one of them. 'I think you've gone too far now.'

Before Adele's friends had a chance to get involved, Shazza stepped back from Adele and stood glaring at her. 'Come on, let's go,' she said to Denise and Louise, and they began walking away.

'Not so fast!' said Prison Officer Roberts. 'I saw what was going on. You three aren't going anywhere, apart from the governor's office.' Then the two guards led Shazza and her friends away.

'Go and get that seen to,' Judy Roberts said, turning round to look at Adele as she led Shazza and her friends through the door.

Adele took her eyes off them and looked instead at Caroline. 'Thanks,' she muttered, breathlessly, as she tried to force a smile and her eyes took in Anna and Cheryl, too.

'Bloody hell! Look what they've done to you. The nasty bitches!' said Caroline, examining Adele's face while Anna stared open-mouthed and Cheryl tutted.

Adele instinctively put her hand to her cheek where it was smarting. Then she brought her fingers away, noticing that they were daubed in blood.

'Ouch, that really bloody hurts!' she said.

'It will do, it's deep,' said Caroline, narrowing her eyes and wrinkling her brow.

'How did you know what they were going to do?' asked Adele, looking at her three friends.

'Caroline sussed them,' said Anna. 'She thought they were after me but when we couldn't see them in the rec room we thought we'd better make sure you were OK.'

'Yes, I overheard them scheming,' Caroline said. 'I'd had an uneasy feeling for days. It was the way they were being a bit too over-friendly. So I listened in to one of their conversations. I couldn't hear much from outside the cell but I heard Anna's name mentioned.

'They must have been discussing her in relation to you, maybe planning to get you when we weren't around. Then someone told us they saw them heading to the gym so I got her to send the guards while we ran ahead.'

'Thank God you got here,' said Adele. 'Otherwise, I don't know what the hell they would have done.'

Caroline smiled at her and put her arms around Adele's shoulders in her usual motherly fashion. Adele was thankful that it was all over, but she knew it was only a temporary reprieve. Shazza was back to her usual vindictive self. And Adele knew that, from now on, Shazza would make all their lives a living hell once more.

23

Peter walked into the Golden Bell nightclub. The owner, Max Bell, had asked him to come alone, but Peter was taking no chances. Max seemed an OK sort of bloke but you could never be sure so Peter parked a couple of his men inside the door while he strode up to the bar.

It was still early. There were only two customers at the bar nursing pint pots brimming with watered-down beer, and a few staff arranging tables and beer-mats, ready for the evening's onslaught. Behind the bar was a camp barman, delicately polishing glasses till they shone.

'Is Max upstairs?' asked Peter.

'I'll see if he's available,' said the barman, making a show of looking Peter up and down, with his lips pursed, then throwing down his tea towel onto the bar.

'He's expecting me,' snapped Peter.

Peter stood at the bar, tapping his fingers in irritation

while he waited for the barman to return. When he did, he pursed his lips again, nodded, then flicked his head back before turning on his heel and going back in the direction he had come from. Peter followed him closely behind, making a mental note to do something about the barman's attitude in the near future.

He led Peter up some stairs and along a corridor to Max's office. The barman knocked on the door.

'Yes,' called Max.

Then the barman pushed the door open and nodded before sashaying off down the corridor. Max was sitting behind a large desk, his features strained as he looked across at Peter. Within a few seconds he was out of his seat and shaking Peter's hand agitatedly.

'Please, have a seat,' he urged as he retreated to his own seat and entrenched himself behind the sturdy old desk. Then he pulled a decanter of whisky from one of the desk drawers and two glasses. 'Drink?' he asked.

'Not for me, thanks,' said Peter. 'I'd rather get down to business.'

He watched as Max poured himself a liberal measure of whisky then placed the decanter back inside the desk drawer. Peter noticed his shaking hands. Max had the face of a drinker; his complexion ruddy, his nose bulbous and a sheen of sweat on his skin.

Now in his mid-sixties, Max was looking every bit his age. Once he'd been a big, handsome man with a good physique, but now most of Max's muscle had turned to flab and his features were marred by heavy porcine jowls. *Sad really,* thought Peter. Max used to be pretty handy in his day but now he looked as though he couldn't even handle a bunch of nursery kids. He was also sporting a black eye.

'Well?' asked Peter when Max didn't speak.

Max took the glass away from his lips and seemed to hesitate a moment longer while he gulped his whisky. He was still clenching the glass so tightly that his knuckles were white.

'It's about the payments,' said Max. Then he took another swig of his drink before carrying on. 'It's getting more difficult to meet them. And... and... I'm still having trouble so I don't really see the point.'

Peter stared fixedly at him. 'Don't give me that bullshit! You've got plenty of ready cash. And what d'you mean, you don't see the fuckin' point? What sort of trouble are you having?' he asked.

'Like last Saturday. It kicked off big time; it was like bleedin' bedlam in here. I had to wade in to give the bouncers a hand. That's how I got this,' Max said, pointing at his black eye.

'I think you're missing the point, Max. The money you pay us is to stop other firms muscling in,' said Peter. 'We're not a fuckin' babysitting service! You've got your own bouncers to sort out any run-of-the-mill problems. If you don't pay us what you owe us, you'll have even bigger problems than you could ever fuckin' imagine!'

'I don't know,' Max sighed, looking dejected. 'I think I'm just getting too bleedin' old for all this aggro. Maybe it's time I packed it in and sold the place.'

Peter's eyes opened wide in alarm. That was the last thing he wanted. Max Bell's place was one of his biggest earners and he couldn't risk any new owners having their own protection.

'Let's not be hasty, Max,' he said. 'Who are you thinking of selling to?'

'I haven't got that far yet. It's just a thought but I don't know how much longer I can go on like this. I'm not as young as I used to be, y'know, Pete.' He took another gulp of his whisky, his hand trembling as he raised the glass.

Peter sniffed. 'It's a pity I haven't got the cash,' he said. 'I wouldn't mind running a place like this myself. I know of a few handy fellas I could put on the doors. They'd soon fuckin' sort things out.'

Max looked at him for a few seconds. He appeared to be mulling something over. Just when Peter was about to tell him to come out with it, he said, 'There might be a way round things.'

'What d'you mean?' demanded Peter.

'Well, what about a percentage? You could buy into it and put a stop to all the aggro while you're at it.'

Max had become more animated, as though he was warming to the idea now he had thought of it. Peter also liked the sound of it. His own nightclub, brilliant!

Why hadn't he thought of that? A buzz of excitement zipped through him but he put on his poker face. He'd play it cool, tell Max he was thinking about it. That way he'd be able to drive a harder bargain.

'What sort of percentage were you thinking?' he asked, impassively.

'Depends what you can afford,' said Max.

Peter noticed the strain on Max's face again. The man was desperate! It was obvious. He'd had his day and he couldn't wait to jack it in.

'Well, I've got a bit of a cash-flow problem at the moment. I've just forked out for a sunbed salon. But I should be getting some cash in soon. How about we start small and see how it goes? Then I could buy a bigger share as time goes on. How much would a 10 per cent share cost to start with?'

Max went all contemplative again as he ruminated over the figures. Then he said, '£20K.'

'Fuckin' hell! That's a bit steep, innit?'

'The club's worth over £200K, easily. And that's not just for the business. I own the building as well, and it's a bleedin' goldmine, as you know.'

'Yeah, but don't forget,' said Peter, 'I'll be adding value. Once you take care of the aggro, the classy punters will be flocking in. Then you can put your prices up... Tell you what, cut the price in half and I'll put a couple of my men inside as well. How's that sound?'

'Ooh, I don't know,' said Max. 'I'd be making a big loss.'

'OK,' said Peter, getting up from his seat. 'Forget it, business as usual then. So when I send my men round, you'd better fuckin' have what you owe me.'

'Hang on,' said Max, putting out his free hand while still gripping his glass tightly with the other. 'Let's not be hasty. Maybe there's a bit of room for manoeuvre.'

'All right, tell you what,' said Peter. 'I'll let you have a little think about it. But don't take too long. Oh, and I'll want an option to extend my share in the future whenever you choose to retire altogether. You've got till next Tuesday; otherwise we'll be here for your protection money.'

Then Peter paused momentarily and scrutinised Max's black eye as well as the empty glass in front of him, before adding, 'And, if you decide not to go in with me, I'll be doubling the fee, seeing as how the place has become a bit of a liability now under your sole ownership.'

Peter walked to the door and pulled it open with a confident swing. He now had his back to Max, but he could picture him visibly squirming in his seat, and he suppressed a smile.

Before Max had a chance to say anything further, Peter made his way along the corridor and down the stairs, then sauntered out of the place. He knew it wouldn't be long until Max came grovelling back to him, anxious to cut a deal that would work in Peter's favour.

While Peter was joining his men at the door, he heard the barman mutter under his breath, 'Thank God for that.'

But Peter didn't say anything to him. He didn't have to; he'd sort the barman out in his own good time. He chuckled to himself as he pictured the barman's face once he had given him his marching orders. *Don't worry, sunshine,* he thought. *Your days are fuckin' numbered.*

Adele and Caroline were on their way to the kitchens where they worked. Up ahead they could see Shazza, Denise and Louise heading towards them. As they watched, Shazza stepped in front of one of the other inmates and blocked her way. Adele saw Shazza take something from the inmate. Then she pushed her viciously aside and carried on walking, her face full of glee.

It was obvious that the other inmate had parted with the item reluctantly. Even from the back Adele could see her shrug then drag her feet. A few moments later Shazza drew level with Adele and smiled smugly at her while she walked past.

'Did you see what she did?' Adele said to Caroline, affronted. 'She's just taken something from that girl!'

'I know, I saw it,' said Caroline with a resigned air.

'It's not on!' said Adele. 'I can't believe she's still

taking advantage of people after she's already been punished for attacking me. She shouldn't be allowed to get away with it. I've a good mind to have a word with her, or to tell one of the guards.'

Caroline glared at her. 'Don't you dare!' she said. 'You've had enough trouble with that lot as it is. Do you want them to set about you again?'

'No,' said Adele, fingering the faint mark that was still on her cheek weeks after the attack. 'But someone's got to stop her. She's been getting worse lately. The whole bloody prison's frightened to death of her and Denise. And as for Anna! I can't bloody go anywhere without taking her with me. It's like having a limpet stuck to my side.'

'I know,' said Caroline, trying to stifle a grin at Adele's choice of words. 'It's the same with Cheryl. She's really shaken by what they did to you.'

'I'm fed up of having no freedom either,' Adele added, building herself up into a fury. 'It's been going on for bloody weeks now and I'm sick to death of it! Tell me, Caroline, why should one woman rule the entire bloody prison? It isn't right!'

'I know, Adele. I'm not exactly thrilled about it either. But sometimes in prison, it's about self-preservation, as I've said before. You do what you have to do to get through your time as easily as possible.'

Adele shrugged but didn't say anything more. There was no point taking things out on Caroline; it wasn't her fault they all had to go about mob-handed to protect themselves. It was really starting to get her down, though. Even Peter had advised her not to get involved, and he and Caroline knew a lot more about prison life than she did.

But Adele was finding it difficult to follow Caroline and Peter's advice. Caroline was a different person from her and she viewed things differently. Adele wondered how Peter had dealt with people like Shazza when he'd been inside. She felt sure that he wouldn't have taken any shit from Shazza if he had been in her situation. After all, he'd stood up to their tyrant of a father when he was only a kid.

After they had finished their work, Adele and Caroline made their way back to their cells. Caroline tried to make conversation but Adele was unresponsive; she was still troubled by Shazza's behaviour.

When Adele walked into her cell, she found Anna lying on her bunk. Anna quickly pulled down her sleeve and sprung to her feet as soon as she saw Adele.

'Where have you been?' she demanded. 'I thought you and Caroline would have met me. I had to walk back on my own.'

Adele noticed her bottom lip jut out as she finished speaking.

'Sorry,' said Adele. 'We were chatting to someone in

the kitchens… Anyway, Shazza doesn't bother you any more, does she? Not since you… well, you know.'

'Since I tried to top myself, you mean?' said Anna with tears in her eyes. 'She didn't for a while… but it's started again.'

'You're joking!' said Adele, outraged. Then she recalled the way Anna had been acting when she had entered the cell. She walked over to her and wrenched up the sleeve of her top. Amongst the scars was a fresh wound, the vermilion blood still moist and glimmering under the harsh glare of the cell light.

'Jesus, Anna! I can't fuckin' believe you're doing that again.'

Anna quickly withdrew her arm and pulled down the sleeve. Then she stared down at the floor, ashamed.

Adele was troubled. If Anna was self-harming again then Shazza must be really giving her a hard time. Adele had hoped that Anna's suicide attempt would have been enough to make Shazza leave her alone, but it seemed that Shazza was becoming cocky once more. And Adele's biggest fear was that Anna might try to kill herself again.

'What exactly has Shazza done?' she asked.

'Just taken a few cigs, that's all. But I don't want it to get as bad as it was before.'

Adele noticed the tremble in Anna's voice. She tutted loudly and said, 'She's a cheeky bitch!'

Then Adele climbed up onto the top bunk. She had

intended to do some studying but was too wired. For a while she lay there silently, the thoughts whirling around in her head. Adele had had enough of Shazza and Denise. She was sick to death of watching her back and seeing grown women reduced to terrified wrecks because of Shazza. Something needed to be done about them.

Adele considered reporting Shazza to the governor but that would only create more problems. Nobody liked a grass.

She pictured Anna on the day when she had found her with her wrist slit. Why were they letting Shazza do this to them?

No, something had to be done. And, if no one else would do it, then she'd have to take action herself.

Then an idea formed in her mind. There was only one way to put a stop to Shazza. Now she knew what she had to do. After all, she had the tools at her disposal. It was just a matter of biding her time and waiting for the right moment.

24

Peter lined up the staff of the Golden Bell ready to address them. Max had taken a seat off to one side and was nursing a tumbler of whisky while Glynn was standing next to Peter.

As Peter had predicted, Max had soon come back to him, anxious to cut a deal for Peter to have part-ownership. Not only that, but Max had also agreed to let him run the place; he would merely provide advice and back-up when needed.

Peter looked at each of the bar staff in turn, making them wait to hear what he had to say. It was important to exert his influence right from the outset and it gave him a buzz knowing they were all answerable to him now. Max had already given him the lowdown so he knew who were the shirkers, the slackers and the shady as well as who was reliable.

Most of the barmaids were pretty girls in their twenties with the odd exception. There was Paula, for example, who was a bit rough around the edges but, according to Max, an absolute diamond. Peter would need staff like her.

Then his eyes settled on the camp barman, Julian, not the best worker, from what Max had told him. And he definitely had an attitude problem. Noticing Peter surveying him, Julian began to roll his eyes and toss his head in mock annoyance.

'Right!' said Peter after some minutes. 'I'm Pete and this here is Glynn.' He nodded at Glynn, who remained impassive. 'You're probably wondering why Max has asked me to speak to you,' Peter continued. 'Well, I've got some news for you all. From now on I'll be running this place and you lot will be answerable to me.'

Peter turned to Max for affirmation and he responded with a nod of his head. As he turned back towards the staff, Peter noted the look of astonishment on Julian's face and he suppressed an amused smile. Some of the staff let out shocked whimpers and they began to mutter amongst themselves.

'Quiet, I haven't finished yet!' Peter commanded and he felt a glow of satisfaction when the staff became silent. Then he continued, 'From what I've seen up to now it seems to me that you lot have been slackening off a bit. So now there are gonna be a few changes.'

He delighted in the startled expressions on the faces of the people in front of him. 'For a start,' he continued, 'I want everyone to turn up to work on time. If you're a minute late, your pay will be docked. Secondly, I want smart dress – black trousers and white shirts for the men.' He looked intently at one of the barmen who was wearing faded jeans. 'Those won't fuckin' cut it, mate, so I'm sending you home to get changed as soon as I've finished speaking to you all.'

Peter noted the sulky expression on the barman's face but he carried on speaking. 'For the women, smart black skirts and white tops, no trousers. I don't mind how short you want to wear your skirts. It is a nightclub, when all's said and done.'

He flashed an appreciative look at the legs of one of the younger barmaids, who was wearing a very short skirt.

'Thirdly, no dipping the till. If I catch anyone at it then you'll be out on your arse, no questions asked. OK?'

He waited for the staff to indicate their understanding. Most of them did so but one or two said nothing so he raised his voice. 'I said, OK?' he demanded, scrutinising those who had failed to reply until they responded.

Peter noticed that throughout the time that he had been addressing the staff, Julian had been acting bored, gazing around the room and yawning in an exaggerated fashion. But Peter didn't say anything, not yet. He wanted to make Julian listen to everything he had to say first. Then he would make him squirm.

Eventually his speech drew to a close. 'I think that's about it for now but if anyone has any problems, make sure you come and see me, OK? If I'm not around then come and see Glynn.'

The staff relaxed and some of them began to walk away. Peter timed it until they had only taken a step or two before he spoke again. 'Oh, one last thing,' he shouted, waiting until they had all turned to face him. Then his eyes flitted to Julian. 'You at the end – Julian, isn't it?'

Julian nodded, his lips pursed in indignation.

'You're an ignorant little twat!'

Peter felt a sharp thrill as he noticed the look of shock on the faces of the staff, including Julian, who was stuck for words. 'In future, if someone is speaking to you, don't fuckin' ignore them. Right?'

'I wasn't,' protested Julian.

'OK, so if I ask you to repeat everything I've just said, you'll be able to remember, will you?'

A look of panic crossed Julian's face and Peter noticed Glynn flash an amused smile. 'I thought not,' he said. 'In any case, it doesn't matter. Because you're fuckin' fired!'

'You what? How dare you? You can't do that,' protested Julian, looking to Max for support.

Max looked as shocked as the rest of the staff but he didn't say anything.

'I'll take you to a tribunal,' Julian threatened, turning to go, then muttering 'bastard' under his breath as he walked away.

'Eh!' called Glynn, racing up to Julian, then pulling his arm up his back and marching him to the back door.

Peter laughed as Julian squealed at the vicious way in which Glynn kept a tight hold of him. 'Let that be a lesson to you all,' he said, before dismissing the staff and heading to the bar where he helped himself to a double brandy.

Glynn opened the back door of the Golden Bell and thrust Julian out into the street where he landed on the ground with a heavy thud.

'Ouch!' Julian screeched. 'That bloody well hurt.'

'It was fuckin' meant to!' said Glynn. 'Think yourself lucky I've not given you a fuckin' good hiding. Maybe in future you'll learn not to disrespect the people who pay your wages.'

Glynn eyed Julian as he lay on the ground pouting sulkily and rubbing his knees, but he noted that Julian was wary of making eye contact.

He was just about to lock the back door when he heard Julian speak.

'Fuckin' thug!' he cursed in a low voice.

Glynn wrenched the back door open again and dashed outside, standing over Julian, threateningly. 'What did you just say?' he demanded.

'Nothing,' mumbled Julian, his eyes now full of fear as he looked up at Glynn.

'Get up!' ordered Glynn, grabbing hold of the back of Julian's shirt collar and hauling him off the ground. Then he shifted his hands around to the front of Julian's shirt, bunching it up as his fists pressed tightly against Julian's throat.

'You fuckin' queer bastard!' he bawled. 'Your sort makes me fuckin' sick. You're a cowardly little shit, too. Waiting till I'd gone inside before you said owt. Did you think I wouldn't fuckin' hear you?' he asked.

Julian just shook his head. The cocky pout had now disappeared, replaced by a trembling bottom lip. He looked desperately at Glynn's face, which was now contorted with rage, and Julian's tear-filled eyes pleaded for leniency. But that only made Glynn more angry.

Looking at the ridiculous expression on the man's face, Glynn unleashed a barrage of brutal kicks and punches. Julian crumpled to the ground, curling himself into a ball and screaming out in pain.

When Glynn had finished he gazed down at Julian and let him have one last hard kick before warning him, 'In future, have more fuckin' respect for those in charge. And don't even think of reporting me to the cops if you know what's good for you,' he finally hissed before locking the door.

Julian remained silent as he lay battered and weeping on the street outside. But Glynn wasn't bothered. As far as he was concerned, that pathetic excuse for a man had disrespected him and he got what he deserved. Glynn was a ruthless operator and he did whatever needed to be done without any remorse. And if he had to do the same again, or even worse, he wouldn't hesitate.

25

Adele had been watching Shazza for days. Now, as she saw her leave Denise and Louise, then walk across the recreation area, she tailed her. It had been difficult for Adele to break away from Anna but she'd managed it. Adele didn't want anybody else involved in what she was about to do. She needed to do this alone.

As she watched Shazza confidently strut along the prison corridors, greeting other prisoners with an effusive high five and habitual insults, Adele could feel the rage building within her. Who did Shazza think she was, tormenting and goading the other prisoners as though it was her right?

Eventually Shazza reached her cell and went inside. Adele sped up until she was outside Shazza's cell. She peeked through the small window in the door. Yes! Shazza was alone.

Without hesitation, Adele turned the handle and pushed the door open. She dashed inside, noting Shazza's momentary look of shock, which she soon replaced with a smug grin. It was obvious bravado but Adele didn't give her a chance to gloat. She launched herself at Shazza, using the rapid kickboxing combination she had practised so well.

Shazza reeled from the stinging blows but then came back at her. She got in close, making it difficult for Adele to aim punches and kicks. Shazza latched onto Adele's hair with both hands, pulling her head forward.

But Adele didn't let Shazza drag her head down. Instead she brought her arms up through the centre and prised them in between Shazza's arms. Then she thrust them sideways in a speedy defensive move.

Shazza's arms flew outwards, forcing her to let go of Adele's hair. Before Shazza could recover, Adele stepped back and started aiming kicks at her. A powerful kick to Shazza's legs made them collapse beneath her. She crashed to the ground.

Without waiting for Shazza to get up, Adele rushed towards her. She quickly crouched down on one knee next to Shazza who remained dazed on the floor. Adele's other foot stayed firmly on the ground. But her knee was bent so she could use her thigh for leverage.

Adele grabbed Shazza's arm with both hands. She swiftly wrenched the arm over her thigh, bending it against the joint. The sudden movement took Shazza by surprise. Adele applied pressure. Then she heard a satisfying snap as the arm fractured.

Shazza let out an agonised scream. As Adele released Shazza's arm it flopped down to the ground, distorted and unnatural.

Adele got to her feet, just in time as Denise and Louise rushed through the door. She was primed for action, her defensive kickboxing stance automatic.

'You fuckin' want some?' she yelled at them.

Denise took a quick glance at Shazza, writhing and screaming on the floor. She shook her head frantically. But Adele was still raging. She stepped towards both of them and aimed a sharp punch at Louise, who backed away.

'No, please!' yelled Louise, and her frightened peal brought Adele to her senses.

She stepped over and slammed the cell door shut, then glared at Denise and Louise.

'Right, this fuckin' ends here! Do you hear me?' she fumed.

'Yes,' they both replied.

'I said, do you hear me?' she yelled again, staring at Shazza on the floor.

'Yes,' Shazza wept.

'Right, you saw nothing. OK?' she demanded.

'Yes, we just walked in and found her like this,' Denise gushed. 'We don't know fuck all about how it happened.'

Adele didn't press Shazza any further for an answer. She knew Shazza followed the code and wouldn't grass on a fellow inmate. Besides, her pride probably wouldn't let her admit how she had sustained her injuries. But Adele wasn't finished yet. There was something else she needed to say to all of them.

'From now on, you leave Anna alone, and Cheryl, and anyone else you've been picking on,' she said. 'If I ever hear of you tormenting anyone else ever again, I'll be back to finish the fuckin' job off!'

'OK,' groaned Shazza, and Denise and Louise nodded in agreement.

Satisfied that she'd done what she had to do, Adele then left them and made her way back to her own cell.

'Oh my God! What's happened to you?' asked Anna when she took in Adele's dishevelled clothing and tatty hair.

'Let me get tidied up first,' snapped Adele, the adrenalin still pulsing through her veins.

Anna did as she was told. Then, once Adele had calmed down, Anna asked her again what had happened.

'Let's just say you won't have to worry about Shazza and co. any more,' said Adele. 'But if you do have any problems, make sure I fuckin' know about it!'

'What have you done?' asked Anna, staring wide-eyed at Adele.

Adele smiled enigmatically. 'Enough,' she said.

'You've not killed her, have you?'

'No, Anna. I just hurt her enough to make her see sense, that's all.'

Anna continued to stare at her open-mouthed and Adele knew she had gone up even more in her estimation. But that hadn't been her intention. Adele was satisfied, however, that word of what had happened would quickly get around the prison. Now that Anna knew, she'd soon put everyone in the picture, especially when she saw Shazza's injuries.

Adele had known that she had the tools at her disposal. But she had been afraid to use them ever since she had killed her father in a violent rage. When she attended kickboxing classes, years ago, she had been taught that she was in possession of lethal weapons. And her instructor had warned her that she wasn't to use her skills unless absolutely necessary.

But today had been an exception. She didn't like doing what she had done. But she knew that it had been *absolutely* necessary. It was the only way that she and her friends would find any peace within the prison.

And now that she had sorted out the prison top dog there was no one else left to challenge her. She could finally serve out the rest of her prison sentence in relative harmony.

PART TWO

1989–1990

26

When Adele stepped out of the prison doors and into the outside world, it was a complete culture shock. She gazed in awe at the trees, the grass, even the roads. It was ironic that such a place had been built slap-bang in the middle of the idyllic Cheshire countryside. Adele had never had an appreciation for the countryside before, but more than five years behind bars had changed her view of things.

She glanced over at the high-spec car that was waiting. When she heard a toot of the horn, she looked more intently at the driver. It was her brother, Peter. A smile graced her lips; he certainly knew how to arrive in style.

Adele dashed over to the car and opened the passenger door. 'Bloody hell! This is a bit flash, isn't it?' she said.

'Jaguar XJ6, 1986 model; air con, anti-lock braking system, six-speaker sound system and stainless-steel window frames,' he bragged, flicking a switch on the car's dashboard. Dire Straits' 'Brothers in Arms' popped out of the car's CD player. He put it back inside its case and inserted a Tracy Chapman album.

'Wow! What's that?' she asked.

'Part of the sound system; it takes CDs,' he said.

Adele was amazed. CD players in cars! She'd never seen that before. All the cars she had been inside had cassette players.

'I bet this car cost you a bloody fortune, didn't it?' she asked.

'Enough,' he said. Then he grinned before adding, 'It's nice to be able to afford it, though.'

Adele kept quiet. Since she had been inside she had learned about Peter's burgeoning empire: the sunbed salons, the bookies and the nightclub. It still troubled her how he had been able to afford them in the first place. When she'd asked him he'd always been very vague, either tapping the side of his nose or telling her about having contacts and one thing leading to another.

Adele hadn't pressed him for more information about where he got his money from although she suspected he'd obtained it through illegal dealings. Nothing she said would change him so what was the point in giving him grief? Instead she decided to keep quiet and try not to get too involved. Still, she hoped that now he was a businessman, he might have left his life of crime behind him.

They swept along the country lanes, soon arriving

in Manchester. Adele gazed in wonder out of the car window, just as riveted by city life as she was by the Cheshire countryside. How things had changed in five years!

The cars were different; she spotted several models that hadn't been around before she went inside. The buses looked different, too. Peter said it was because they now operated through private companies. And even the phone boxes were different. She thought back with nostalgia to the traditional red phone boxes of her youth. They had been replaced by steely grey and glass structures, and had a silly picture of a man with a bugle etched into the glass.

As she commented on things around her, Peter filled her in on what had been happening in the outside world, laughing at her naivety. Eventually they arrived at his apartment. Despite his success in the business world, that was one thing at least that hadn't changed, or so she thought, until they got inside.

'Bloody hell! It's a bit plush, isn't it?' she asked, gazing around at the new furniture and trendy appliances.

Peter just smiled in response and she guessed that perhaps her ceaseless questions were starting to get on his nerves. He walked through to the kitchen and came back with a bottle of Bollinger champagne. Then he popped the cork and poured each of them a drink.

'Get that down you,' he said, passing her a glass. 'This is a celebration. You're free, at last! And when you've drunk that you can get your glad rags on. I'm taking you for a slap-up meal and then me and you are gonna hit the town.'

'But I've got nothing to wear,' she said.

'Oh yes you have,' said Peter. 'Follow me.' They walked through to one of the bedrooms and he showed her a wardrobe full of women's clothing. 'A girl I know helped me get some stuff ready for you coming out,' he continued. 'You might not like them all but I bought plenty. There's bound to be something there that takes your fancy.'

'Th-thanks,' she stuttered, taken aback.

Adele rifled through the clothes, many of which had designer labels. She didn't know what to say. It seemed her brother had thought of everything. 'Thanks,' she repeated. 'You didn't have to.'

'No worries,' he said casually.

But Adele was concerned. He'd already been good in offering to put her up until she found her feet. She felt bad as it was because she couldn't afford to pay for her keep. And he'd done so much for her in the past, risking his own freedom in trying to cover up the killing of their father.

'Anyway,' he said. 'Take your time, there's no rush. I've had an en suite shower room added to this bedroom. It's through there, if you want to freshen up before we go out.'

'Thanks,' said Adele. 'I think we'll have that drink first before I get myself ready.'

They went back into the living room where they polished off the champagne between them. While they drank they chatted. There was a lot to catch up on and plenty of things Adele hadn't told Peter during her time inside. Something else was also on her mind.

'How is Mam?' she asked.

'Oh, you know her: same old, same old.'

But Adele didn't know her mother any more. She hadn't seen her for over five years. Not since she had turned her back on Adele because she had taken her husband from her. Adele tried not to dwell on the thought and focused instead on enjoying her catch-up with her brother. But Peter wanted to continue the conversation.

'She's missed you, y'know,' he said.

'D'you think so?'

'I know so.'

'Why, has she said?'

'Not in so many words, but it's fuckin' obvious. Every time I mention your name I can see it in her face. She even filled up a few times… Why don't you go and see her?'

'I don't know. What if she doesn't want to see me?'

'Well, you'll never know until you try, will you?'

Adele sniffed and looked away until Peter took the hint and changed the subject. By the time they had finished the bottle, Adele was feeling a little light-headed. Bollinger champagne was a bit different from the occasional mug of moonshine that she indulged in while inside prison.

'I think I'll just have a lie down,' she said.

'OK, go for it. But don't forget,' said Peter, 'I'll be waking you up later so we can hit the town.'

By the time they returned to Peter's apartment in the early hours of the morning, they were both drunk, especially Adele. Peter headed to the drinks cabinet and pulled out two glasses and a bottle of brandy.

'Ooh, not for me thanksss,' slurred Adele. 'I've had enough.'

While Peter poured himself a drink she stared around at the apartment again, still amazed at how Peter had managed to afford all the modern gadgets and high-end furniture.

'Fuckin' brill night, that, wasn't it?' he said, plonking himself down on the settee next to her.

Adele smiled back but didn't respond. She was still thinking about how he could afford all this. Her mind drifted to earlier in the night and to some of the people they had met while they were out. Peter had a lot of acquaintances and some of them seemed a bit shady to her.

He had taken her to the nightclub that he co-owned and introduced her to a lot of the staff. Although she'd enjoyed herself while she was there, she felt a little uneasy. She'd picked up on some of the conversations with his contacts. There was all the usual talk about jobs, which took her back to the days when he had started out on his life of crime and made her think that he was still perhaps involved.

'Fuckin' hell, sis, you're miles away,' he said.

'I know... Actually, I'm tired. I think I'll go to bed,' she said.

'OK, see you in the morning,' he said, picking up the TV remote control and flicking the television on.

Once Adele was in bed she found she couldn't sleep. Troubled thoughts whirled around inside her head. She thought about the friends she'd left behind in prison: Caroline and Anna. She was missing them already and hoped they'd be all right without her. Caroline was one of the most genuine, caring and likeable people she had met, and Adele had even developed a fondness for Anna, despite her faults.

Her mind switched to Peter and his life of crime. She was determined to get herself a job and move out as soon as possible. While she was here she couldn't settle; she preferred to detach herself from his shady dealings.

But she was already worried about finding herself a job. Despite her qualifications and her previous work experience, she knew her prison record would go against her. Still, she could only try her best and hope things worked out.

And there was something else that was bothering her:

her damaged relationship with her mother. While Adele had been inside, she had tried to put all thoughts of her mother out of her head. After all, if her mother had chosen not to visit her, there wasn't much she could do to persuade her otherwise from within the prison walls.

As the time for her release had got nearer, though, thoughts of her mother had occupied her mind more and more. She'd been tempted to ring her many times but knew that it would be difficult to repair their relationship over the phone. So she'd decided that once she was released, visiting her mother would be high on her agenda.

But the prospect of that was daunting. Would she ever find it in her heart to forgive Adele? And if she rejected her once more, how would Adele cope with that?

The only way to find out would be to go to her as soon as possible. Then she'd know for sure instead of spending endless nights fretting about it. And, if her mother didn't want anything to do with her, she would just have to put her out of her mind once and for all.

27

Adele arrived in the street where she used to live in a run-down part of the city. The houses here had survived the slum clearance of sixties and seventies Manchester, which had made way for poorly planned high-rise blocks.

In many ways the street looked the same as it always had, with its weathered red-brick houses standing proudly side by side. The old concrete road still had a line of pitch running across it, which they'd used as a starting line for races when she was a child. And there was still a trace of paint spillage that had been there for years.

She remembered Peter prodding at the paint with a stick when it had blistered and softened in the sun, and the hiding he'd got from his father when the paint had stuck to his trousers.

Flagstone pavements ran either side of the narrow concrete road, with random holes between the slabs, which she and her brother used to roll their marbles into. Nowadays there were more cracks in the slabs. There were other differences, too. Children no longer played outside since the proliferation of cars that raced up and down the street had made it too dangerous. Gone was the corner shop of yesteryear and housewives no longer stood chatting at doorways.

Adele approached her mother's front door hesitantly, noticing that it had also been subject to change. It had been painted, but as she drew nearer she realised that it was a bad paint job. The surface was lumpy and uneven as though someone had painted over the loose flakes of old paint without sanding down the door first. The dint two-thirds of the way up the front door was still there, too, although it had been painted over.

She recalled the night when her father had made that dint. They'd all been in bed when he returned from the pub without his key. He'd hammered away at the door until her mother woke up and rushed downstairs to answer it.

Ignoring the painful memories of her tormented childhood she lifted the knocker and tapped repeatedly. She could feel her heart pounding in her chest while she waited for her mother to answer.

The sight of her mother shocked her. In the last five years she had aged a lot; she now looked much older than her forty-five years. She had put on weight, and the buttons of her shabby, stained blouse were straining against her ample breasts and rotund stomach.

The weight gain showed in her face, too. She now had jowls, as well as crow's feet around her eyes and deep lines on her forehead. The flesh on her face seemed to sag and her complexion was pallid. Adele noticed that her mother's hair was still lank and hung limply about her shoulders but it was now streaked with grey.

Shirley visibly flinched when she saw her daughter. 'Adele!' was all she could say. Her reaction threw Adele and for a moment they both stood there speechless. Eventually Shirley swung the front door back. 'I suppose you'd better come in,' she said and Adele followed her into the house.

As she walked through the hall the second thing Adele noticed was the familiar stench; cloying and unclean. But now it was suffused with the smell of cat urine. She felt herself gag as she walked into the living room, and quickly swallowed down the bile that rose in her throat.

Adele had mentally prepared herself for this moment. It was the room where she had killed her father over five years previously. She gazed over at the fireplace. The old rug on the hearth had been replaced with another tatty one, which was being occupied by a large ginger cat. Adele took a deep breath, trying not to think about her father's battered head and the blood that had soaked through the old rug.

She caught her mother's gaze and knew that she was thinking about what had happened, too. 'Sit down. I–I'll put the kettle on,' she said.

'Not for me, thanks,' said Adele, 'but you go ahead.'

Her mother dashed from the room and Adele guessed that she was finding it difficult being with her. While Adele waited for her to return, she looked around. Things hadn't changed much with the exception of the large television, which sat in the corner of the room. It was ostentatious and looked out of place.

Aside from that, the furniture was still the same, and the cracked mirror still hung on the wall. A mangy tabby cat pawed at her legs then jumped on her knee. She quickly put it down on the floor. It purred and went to join the ginger cat on the rug.

Shirley stepped back into the room, mug in hand, and sat across from Adele.

'How are you?' Adele asked perfunctorily.

'Not too bad, y'know,' said Shirley, failing to meet Adele's eyes. The tabby cat jumped on her knee and she stroked it affectionately. 'It's not easy being on yer own,' she said, and Adele felt a pang of guilt. 'But Tabby and Ginger keep me company, and the neighbours are good.'

The tabby cat purred on hearing its name and Shirley gave it her full attention. 'Yes, you do, don't you?' she said, rubbing its stomach. 'You little beauty.' Ginger purred and joined Tabby on her knee. 'Yes, you too.' She then laughed falsely. 'Oh, don't go getting jealous now, Ginger. You know I love you just as much.'

Adele could feel her eyes cloud with tears as she

watched the sad scene. Her mother was talking to the cats almost as though they were human. Is this what she had been reduced to?

She took a deep breath and blinked away her tears before addressing her mother.

'Mam, I just want you to know how sorry I am for everything,' she said. 'I would have rung you but I didn't know how you'd be.'

'I know,' said Shirley, looking over at her momentarily before switching her focus back to her beloved cats. 'Well, you're here now.'

It was obvious to Adele that her mother wasn't going to allow an emotional reunion. Although she had let Adele come inside, her defences were still up. Patching up their fragile relationship was going to be a long-drawn-out process.

But Adele was willing to try. Her mother might have rejected her when she killed her father in self-defence, after he had put them all through years of torment. But, at the end of the day, she was still her mother.

'Is there anything I can do for you?' asked Adele.

'No, I'm OK. I manage all right,' said her mother but, looking around the room, Adele was sure that her mother didn't manage very well at all. The furniture was covered in dust, the sofa full of cat hair and the sideboard stacked high with old newspapers, clothing, handbags and other items. Two mugs stained with tea, sat on the coffee table.

As she sat there, Adele could feel herself itching. She was tempted to scratch but didn't want to offend her mother when they were only just attempting to get back on track.

Adele tried to think of something else to say. 'That's a nice TV,' she commented.

Her mother bristled with pride. 'Thanks. Our Peter got it for me,' she said.

Adele was struggling once more for something to say so she enquired after her mother's neighbours. Then she listened patiently for half an hour while her mother waffled on about the local gossip.

Adele watched the clock, desperate to leave. This visit had been harder than she'd thought it would be. When sufficient time had elapsed, she made her excuses and got up to go. Her mother got up, too, putting the cats down on the rug.

'I'll walk you to the door,' she said.

At the front door, Adele gave her mother a tentative hug but soon withdrew when her mother remained stiff and unresponsive.

'I'll come again,' Adele said.

'Yes, that would be nice,' said her mother formally, almost as though she was a stranger, but Adele noticed the half-smile on her face. It was the first sign of emotion she had shown towards Adele during her visit. But it was a start.

Adele walked away with a heavy heart. Once she had

gone a few metres she stopped to scratch the itch that had been troubling her for the last half-hour. She rolled up her trousers, exposing the flesh of her legs.

There were tiny black dots along the top of her socks and she gazed at them, confused. Then she reached down with her hand. The black dots began to move and she drew back her hand in alarm before realising what they were. Cat fleas, loads of them, nestled into the tops of her socks. The place must be overrun with them!

Adele tried to suppress her repulsion. It was difficult seeing how low her mother had sunk. As a child, Adele had been used to the acrid stench and the mess, but it seemed to have got worse.

Adele could tell that her mother wasn't totally ready to forgive what had happened. But she knew that her mother still needed her, and she felt a tremendous responsibility towards her. She had done so even when she was little because her mother had always seemed so incapable. In view of everything that had happened, she felt that responsibility even more now, and it weighed down on her.

In the past few years an enormous chasm had formed between Adele and her mother. But, nevertheless, she was determined to visit again. She vowed she would do her best to help her mother and try to make things better between them.

28

Peter walked into the Sportsman's and scanned the room. It was a Wednesday night so it wasn't too busy. Along the ceiling ran wooden beams painted black from which hung assorted brass ornaments. The white walls were textured and the furniture was old but tasteful. A jukebox churned out hits from the late seventies. Peter noticed a faintly musty smell in the air only partly disguised by the vanilla-scented candles placed in alcoves.

There were few people in the pub and he focused on a couple of possibilities: men around his own age. He wasn't sure whether any of them fitted the bill; it had been ten years since he'd seen Alan and he didn't know whether he'd recognise him.

Then a guy in the corner stood up and waved. He was about Peter's own age but slightly taller. Peter eyed him up as he made his way over. Yes, it was definitely Alan. Peter noticed the honed biceps and the taut chest muscles protruding beneath his fitted T-shirt. Bloody hell! He'd certainly filled out during his time inside.

Alan greeted him with a broad smile and they shared a man hug, patting each other effusively on the back.

'Hiya, mate. How are you?' asked Peter.

'Not too bad. What about you?'

'Good,' said Peter. 'What you having?'

'No, it's OK. I'll get these,' Alan insisted.

As Alan walked back from the bar, Peter studied him again. Yeah, he'd definitely filled out although he was still lean as well as muscular. He'd shot up, too, and now stood at around five eleven.

'You're looking well, mate. What you been up to?' asked Peter.

'Oh, this?' said Alan, patting each of his biceps in turn while puffing out his chest. 'Fuck all else to do inside, is there?'

'True. So, what've you been up to since you got out?'

'Not much really. The odd house job, you know. But I'm looking for summat more lucrative, if you know what I mean.' He winked as he said the word 'lucrative' and had a quick look round to check no one was listening before leaning towards Peter and lowering his voice. 'I believe you're doing plenty now.'

'Oh, yeah,' said Peter. 'Got meself a good little firm going as well.'

'Anyone I know?'

'Mickey and Sam. They're still with me. Unfortunately

I had to let Dave go a few years back. Bit of a loose cannon.'

'Yeah, I heard about that. Word is that he didn't stitch you up, though.'

Peter shrugged. 'That's not what I heard, mate. But you know how it goes: once you've lost that trust you can't take any fuckin' chances.'

'Suppose so,' said Alan. 'Anyone else I might know?'

'Well, the other two main players are Glynn and Mike. In fact, Glynn's my right-hand man. He's a sound guy – smart, too.'

'What's his surname?' asked Alan.

'Mason, Glynn Mason.'

'Rings a bell but I can't say I know him. What about the other guy, Mike?'

'Shaftesbury's his surname.'

Alan pursed his lips and inhaled sharply. 'Ooh! I know him,' he said.

His reaction was unnerving and Peter looked at him with raised his eyebrows. 'And?' he asked.

'He's bad news, Pete. I knew him inside. Bit of a sly one. I'd watch your fuckin' back if I were you.'

'Really?' asked Peter. 'Can't say he's given me too much trouble up to now. He can get a bit cocky now and again but once me and Glynn let him know the score he usually toes the line. Besides, he's fuckin' good at what he does.'

'OK, mate. Just sayin'. It's up to you who you take

on,' said Alan, but Peter didn't like the way his lips curled and his facial muscles tensed.

Alan's expression was one of disdain. Alan had always been smart and if he thought Mike was a bit dodgy then maybe he'd best heed his advice. Peter had no intentions of sacking Mike – he'd given him no reason to – but maybe he'd keep a sharper eye on him in the future.

'Thanks for the warning,' said Peter. 'I'll bear it in mind. Anyway, let's get down to business. I've got a lot on at the moment and I could do with a few more members of the firm. I wondered if you fancied joining us. You could come in useful, especially with the security side of things. You look well handy,' he said, eyeing Alan's toned physique again.

Alan stayed silent for a few seconds, his face now fixed in concentration as though he was going over the details in his mind. Eventually he asked, 'Where exactly would I fit into things?'

'Well, Glynn's my number two, like I say. But, other than that, it would depend on who steps up to the plate. We're really going places, Alan, and there'll be loads happening in the future. We're gonna be the best fuckin' firm in town!'

'OK, I'll have a think about it,' said Alan. He then picked up his glass and drained the rest of his drink slowly before placing it smoothly back on the table. His expression was blank, his body language giving nothing away.

Peter, on the other hand, was a bit taken aback. Fresh out of prison with only a couple of house jobs behind him? He'd have thought Alan would have snatched his hand off. 'OK, suit yourself,' he said, 'but you won't get a better offer.'

Alan stood up and shook his hand. 'I'm off now, mate,' he said, 'but, like I say, I'll definitely have a think about it.'

'OK,' said Peter, 'but don't take too long.'

Peter watched him walk away. He was bemused. Alan had always been a smart operator, even when they were kids. In fact, he'd been surprised when Alan had stabbed a guy to death during a house break-in. Peter figured he must have panicked when he came face to face with the householder. They were only young at the time, when all was said and done.

Alan had got a long stretch for that, too, because he'd gone to the house carrying a knife. So the courts decided it was premeditated and it had gone against him.

When Peter had known Alan years ago he was the cool, calculating type who always wanted to plan the best way to do things. As Peter reflected on their meeting he figured that Alan had probably become even smarter with age. There weren't many guys who would have the front to keep him dangling. Yes, Alan would definitely be an asset to the firm. He just had to wait now and see what he decided.

*

Adele folded the application form and tucked it inside the envelope she was holding in her other hand. Over the past few years she had forgotten how much of a drag it was applying for jobs. She was already fed up of visiting job agencies, filling in application forms and sending CVs to companies, and she had only been at it for a couple of weeks.

During that time she hadn't had a single reply to any of her letters, let alone the offer of an interview. She tried to reassure herself that it was early days, but deep inside she was filled with self-doubt. After all, who would want to employ an ex-convict, especially one who had viciously killed her father?

She wasn't happy living at Peter's apartment either. Although he had made her welcome, she couldn't help but feel that she was in the way. He had brought girls back with him a couple of times after a night out, and there was always a bit of awkwardness when he greeted her in a morning with his latest squeeze in tow.

Then there were the telephone conversations and visits by people who he called his employees. Those conversations were always guarded or spoken in whispers and she knew they didn't want her to hear what was being said.

She had accepted that Peter was still involved in criminal activities and knew that, after all these years, she wasn't going to change him. But that didn't mean she was comfortable with the situation. And the sooner she could distance herself from it, the better.

Adele also wanted to help her mother and she would be better placed to do that if she was earning. It would be her way of trying to make things up to her. Adele had no doubt, from the flash TV sitting in her mother's living room, that Peter helped her in his own way. But she would help her with the more practical things, like providing decent food and taking her shopping for some new clothes.

She collected the envelopes that were lying on the table, then got herself ready to go out to the post box. Despite her growing self-doubt, she would send her applications off and continue to hope that, sooner or later, she would strike lucky and land herself a much-needed job. And if she didn't, well, she'd do whatever had to be done when the time came.

29

David was having a drink with his old friend Alan in the Lord Nelson, which was situated at the end of a row of over-populated houses. It was in one of the less salubrious areas of Manchester, surrounded by cut-price supermarkets, second-hand furniture and white goods stores, and a market selling cheap goods of dubious origins.

'So, what have we got lined up next?' asked David. 'Are we doing another house break-in?'

'Not sure,' said Alan.

'What d'you mean?'

'I mean, I think it's time for us to step things up a bit.'

'What are you thinking?' asked David.

'Well, I went to see our old mate the other day. Pete.'

'No fuckin' chance!' stormed David. 'I ain't working with that tosser. Not after he sold me out on fuckin' big-shot Glynn's say-so.'

David had told Alan all about his falling-out with

Peter a few years previously, and Alan hadn't been impressed with Peter's actions. What David hadn't told him, however, was that he had spent most of the weeks prior to the falling-out high on drugs. This had affected his behaviour and hadn't helped with Peter's judgement of him.

But the split with Peter had shaken David up a bit. For the next few weeks he had carried on taking cocaine. Then he had realised that all he was doing was robbing to pay for his drugs and that part of the reason Peter would never have trusted him was because he was taking drugs. He finally came to his senses and booked himself into a programme to get clean.

David hadn't taken drugs since, although he still liked a drink and he hadn't lost his impulsive personality or his lust for adventure. He had guessed that Glynn was the one who had put him in the frame when Peter sacked him, and he still hadn't forgiven either of them.

'Wait your fuckin' sweat!' said Alan. 'I haven't finished telling you yet.'

'OK,' said David, jumping back in an exaggerated fashion.

'Right, well, I won't lie,' Alan began. 'I went to see if he would give me work. I know you don't like what he did to you but I prefer to keep an open mind about these things, Dave. Besides, if I got my foot in I might have persuaded him to take you back on. And I did hope I might soon be running the show.'

David didn't say anything but he had a feeling Alan knew there was more to his parting from Pete than he had admitted. That was the thing about Alan, he was smart. And Alan always had a way of knowing.

'Anyway,' Alan continued. 'I didn't like the fuckin' set-up. That bloke called Glynn that you told me about has got his size nines right under the fuckin' table. And Pete's taken another bloke on as well. Mike fuckin' Shaftesbury. Right slimy bastard he is. I know him from inside. There's no way I could work with a twat like him. I'd be watching my fuckin' back all the time.

'That fuckin' Glynn's well in favour, too. Pete reckons he's his number two. He even had the cheek to tell me I might get on in his firm if I step up to the plate. Cheeky bastard! I think he's forgotten who was the brains when we worked together.'

'I told you how it is,' said David, relieved now that Alan was on his side. 'I think he's forgotten who his fuckin' friends are, too.'

'Yeah, but I don't forget anything, do I? Like when he did a fuckin' runner at that house break-in and left me to carry the can. He could have helped me tackle that bloke and we could both have got away. Instead I ended up doing a long stretch while he's building up his fuckin' empire.'

'So, what are you gonna do?' asked David, eager to hear Alan's plans.

'Well, I've been thinking, haven't I? I know a couple

of decent blokes. We could team up with them to do bigger jobs. And we'll take over some of the fuckin' security, for a start. Let Pete know he's not the only fuckin' firm in town. I'll teach him to dangle me on a piece of string.'

'Brilliant,' gushed David, delighted at this turn of events. 'So, when do I get to meet the other lads?'

'Give me a few days. I need to see 'em myself first, see if they're interested. Then, once they give me the go-ahead, we can arrange our first meeting.'

'Great.'

'OK, well, there's something else I want you to do,' said Alan.

'What's that?'

'Pete mentioned a couple of blokes who've worked with him for years. I wondered if you knew them.'

'Sam and Mickey? Yeah, course I do. We all used to work together on the bank jobs before Glynn big bollocks joined the firm.'

'Well, surely they're not happy about this Glynn being the number two seeing as how they've been around longer.' When David shrugged, Alan continued, 'You need to arrange to have a word with them, see if you can persuade them to join us. Imagine the inside info they'll have about Pete's operation.'

David stared wide-eyed as the realisation dawned on him.

'If we're gonna take over security,' said Alan, 'then

we need to do it the easy way. Why waste our time finding new fuckin' businesses to hit when we can just take over the ones they've got.'

David chuckled, then clinked his glass against Alan's. 'Fuckin' well smart,' he laughed. 'You always was a brainy twat.'

Alan laughed with him. 'Yeah, a brainy twat that won't be fuckin' messed with,' he said.

Adele put down her pen and sighed. She had just completed another job application but she doubted that this one would be any more successful than the numerous others she had filled in over the past few weeks.

'What's wrong?' asked Peter as he walked into the room. 'You look as though you've lost a quid and found a fuckin' penny.'

'It's these bloody job applications,' she complained. 'I'm sick to death of filling them in. I'm sure most of the firms just put them in the bin as soon as they see I've got a prison record.'

'Don't tell them then.'

'I can't do that. They have ways of finding out. Besides, how do I explain what I've been doing for the last few years?'

'Suit yourself,' he said. Then he pulled up a chair next to her and flicked through a couple of the application forms. 'Admin Assistant?' he asked. 'I thought you were a qualified accountant.'

'I am, but needs must.'

'You don't have to go through this shit, y'know,' he said.

Adele braced herself; she knew what he was about to say. 'I know, you've said before. There's a job for me in your firm. But, to be honest, I don't want to be there just because I'm your sister.'

It was a weak argument, she knew, but up to now she had hidden the real reason. The truth was she didn't fancy working with a load of criminals. But how could she tell Peter that without alienating him? And she had no room to talk, when all was said and done. But she had put that life behind her now and she didn't want to go back to it.

'I know the real reason you don't want to work for me, Adele. I'm not stupid!'

She felt her face flush. It was as though he had read her mind. 'S–sorry,' she began, hesitantly. 'I–I can't afford to get involved in anything illegal again. I don't want to go back to prison, Peter. I couldn't go through that again.'

'Who mentioned fuckin' prison? Look, you wouldn't be involved in anything illegal. The nightclub, the bookmaker's and the sunbed salons are all kosher. And you wouldn't be doing the job just because you're my sister. I need help with the accounts.

'Max has got the nightclub books in a right fuckin' mess and I'm a 50 per cent shareholder in the club now so I don't want to leave it to chance any more. Max has become more of a sleeping partner these days so I need to step up to the plate. And I haven't got a fuckin' clue about accounts or bookkeeping. I need someone who knows about all that shit; someone I can trust.'

He was putting up a very convincing argument and Adele felt herself smiling, listening to him. No wonder he was doing so well; he certainly had a way of persuading people round to his way of thinking.

'OK,' she conceded. 'I'll think about it.'

'Thank fuck for that!' he said.

'Hang on a minute. Before you get too carried away, I'll only do it on the condition that I don't get involved in anything illegal. And I want you to promise me that, Peter.'

'Course you won't. I've already told you, haven't I? Those businesses are all kosher and I worked fuckin' hard to build them up.'

'OK, OK, I'll take your word for it, then.'

'Good, so that's that. Now are we having a fuckin' drink to celebrate, or what?'

Adele went along with him, grateful that at least she had found work. But at what cost, she wasn't sure. As she sipped at the brandy Peter had poured she couldn't help but wonder just what trouble she was letting herself in for.

30

They'd arrived at the nightclub during the day so it wasn't yet full of punters.

'Come on, I'll show you the offices,' said Peter as he led Adele through the main room.

Before they reached the door that led up the back stairs, two men walked through it and towards them.

'All right, how's things?' greeted Peter, patting one of the men on the shoulder as they drew level.

Adele hadn't seen the two men before; they hadn't been there last time she visited the club with Peter. She noticed the size of them straight away but, as one of them smiled back at Peter then glanced over to her, she noticed something else. He was one hell of a looker! He kept his eyes locked on her for several seconds too long and she could feel herself blush under his intense examination. The other man she hardly noticed; she just registered that he was also big built but not particularly good-looking.

'Adele, this is Glynn,' said Peter, 'and this here is Mike,' he added, nodding towards the other man. 'This is Adele, my sister,' he said to the two men.

Adele's eyes shifted to Mike, glad of a chance to break her gaze away from Glynn. The heat of her face soon spread to her neck, and she tried to ignore the way Glynn made her so flustered. Feeling like a foolish teenager, she smiled self-consciously at the men as they each shook her hand.

But Glynn didn't let go of her hand straight away, and she looked up at him inquisitively. It was there again: that intense stare that seemed to penetrate through her body. She felt exposed, as though he was peeling off her clothing in his mind. She tried not to let her eyes linger on his for too long this time, but she still noticed his chiselled features and the cheeky smile that glided effortlessly across his face. The guy oozed charisma!

She dropped her gaze, still conscious of her burning cheeks. Then her eyes settled on his toned physique. His fitted black polo shirt did nothing to hide his rippling muscles. The sleeves stopped a short way down his upper arms, exposing the flesh of his bulging biceps. Adele felt a strange sensation zip through her, a hidden thrill.

She quickly brushed past, too embarrassed at her own reaction to hang around. Adele couldn't remember the last time anyone had had that effect on her. Maybe she had gone too long without a man. She stopped behind them, and out of their line of vision, while they spoke to Peter.

'We've just put the latest takings away,' said Glynn. 'Just till the banks are open tomorrow.'

His deep, baritone voice emphasised his masculinity, unsettling Adele even more.

'OK. Cheers, mate,' said Peter, before joining Adele as the men walked by.

'Glynn's my number two,' he said to Adele. 'He helps me with a lot of stuff, especially the security business.'

'What did he mean about takings?' asked Adele, her voice sounding self-conscious and out of place, even to her own ears.

'The banks aren't always open when we do the collections for the security business so we put them in the safe upstairs.'

'Ah, right,' said Adele. She was just about to ask what exactly was involved in the security business when Peter spoke again.

'Don't even fuckin' think about it, sis,' he said.

'What?' she asked.

'Glynn, that's what.'

'I don't know what you're talking about,' she said, but even as she spoke, she could feel her cheeks flushing again.

'It's fuckin' obvious you fancy the arse off him but he's not for you. I know he's a mate and all that, but you deserve better.'

'What d'you mean?'

Peter paused and seemed to be choosing his next words carefully. 'Let's just say he can be pretty fuckin' ruthless when he wants to be, especially where the women are concerned.'

'I'm not interested anyway,' said Adele, trying to appear blasé.

'Well, you've been warned,' said Peter. 'You'd do best to keep away from Mike as well.'

'I'm not interested in him,' she snapped. This time her vehemence was more apparent; Mike held no attraction for her at all. Then, she recalled the name. 'Is he the one that used to go out with Shazza?' she asked.

'That's right,' he said.

'Bloody hell, I didn't fancy him in the first place but, even if I did, I wouldn't have Shazza's leftovers,' she laughed, relieved that the focus of the conversation had shifted from Glynn.

Peter stopped at the door to an office and changed the subject. 'This one's mine,' he said, pushing the door open.

Adele peered inside, noticing the large, old-fashioned desk and leather captain's chair that dominated the room. While she looked, Peter dashed into the room, plonked himself behind the desk and took a cigar out of the desk drawer. He put it between his lips, still in the wrapper and pretended to draw on it, squaring his shoulders.

'A quick impersonation of Max,' he laughed.

'Is that the guy who owns the business with you?'

'Yeah, but he doesn't come in much nowadays. He's getting a bit past it. Like I told you before, he's more of a sleeping partner now. I'm hoping that he'll let me have an even bigger share sooner or later.'

Adele just nodded, taking everything in.

Next they walked down the corridor to another office. 'This one's yours,' said Peter, opening the door and leading her inside. 'It's the cash office. There's the safe I told you about,' he added, nodding towards a safe that stood on the floor against one of the walls.

The desk inside this office was more modern and had a PC on it. Around the office were shelves full of files. Adele switched the computer on. 'Let's have a look where we are with things,' she said.

'Oh, the books aren't all on the computer,' said Peter. 'Max was in the middle of transferring those for the nightclub but he only got about halfway then he seemed to give up altogether. I don't think computers are his strong point.'

'You're joking!' said Adele. 'How do you manage to keep on top of things then?'

'With these,' said Peter, handing her some ledgers off the shelves.

Adele took a look inside the ledgers. She saw that all the nightclub takings had been recorded but the outgoings were only recorded up to two months ago.

After that there was nothing. 'What's happened to the latest expenditure?' she asked.

Peter handed her another file. 'Like I said, Max got a bit bogged down with trying to computerise everything,' he said. 'All the receipts are in here. They'll need writing up into the ledgers.'

Adele sighed. 'Bloody hell, Peter. You didn't tell me things were in such a mess.'

'Why d'you think we need an accounts whizz?' said Peter, laughing.

But Adele didn't find it funny. 'What about the other businesses? What have you got for them?' she asked, frowning.

'The files are all on that shelf over there,' he said. 'They've all got the names on the front of the file so you know which business they're for.'

Adele stared with dismay at the files he was referring to. There was a ledger for each of the businesses but also a series of A4 folders. She opened one and peered inside. It was full of receipts dating back several months.

'Has nobody entered these into the ledgers?' she asked, the disgust apparent from her tone of voice.

'Don't think so. None of us knew what to do with 'em. We've had a few temps who sorted some of it out but none of them stayed long.'

'Bloody hell, Peter! You've set me a right task here.'

'Yeah, but you're up to it, aren't you, sis?' He flashed her one of his charming smiles.

'I've got no bloody choice, have I?' she said. 'It's not as if employers are banging on my door to give me a job.'

'Cheer up, sis. You'll soon have it all sorted. And, anyway, it'll be a challenge. Better than sitting at home filling in loads of shitty job applications, isn't it?'

Adele thought about her frustration during the last few weeks when she hadn't been able to find work. Not only had she felt frustrated, she'd also felt dejected. The longer she went without a job, the more it got to her.

A job would get her out of the apartment, too. She was getting fed up of her own company. The only friends she had were those still in prison; any others had steered clear of her as soon as they found out about her crime. It would be good to mix with people again.

Her mind flitted to Glynn. Yes, she would also see more of him. Just the thought of him sent her pulse racing and she tried to put him out of her mind and to focus on other things instead. His kind of trouble she could do without.

She took another look around the office while she thought things over. It was more than a challenge; it was a mammoth task. But it was doable, just. And it was better than the alternative.

'OK, how much will you be paying me and when d'you want me to start?' she asked.

31

Glynn and Mike walked into the George and Dragon. The landlord, Pat, stiffened as soon as he saw them approach the bar.

'In the back,' said Glynn, lifting the latch on the end of the bar, then following Pat through to the living quarters.

'Well?' asked Glynn once they were standing with Pat in his living room.

Pat gazed back at them, confused. 'What?' he asked.

'Don't get fuckin' smart,' said Glynn. 'You know what we're here for.'

Mike stepped up to Pat and grabbed him by the throat. 'Don't fuckin' take the piss!' he stormed. 'Get the fuckin' money. Now!'

Mike then pushed Pat viciously, forcing him to step back.

When he had regained his footing, Pat still had a confused expression on his face but it was now tainted with fear. 'B–but I've already paid this month's money,' he said.

'What d'you mean, you've paid? We haven't fuckin' had it,' said Glynn.

'He's a piss taker,' Mike chipped in. 'It's not the first time he's tried to get out of paying.'

'No, I'm not lying,' Pat pleaded as Mike hovered menacingly close to him. 'One of your guys came with another two blokes yesterday.'

Mike took a step closer to Pat.

'Hang on a minute,' said Glynn. 'What d'you mean, one of our guys? Who was it?'

'I don't know his name but he was definitely one of your lot. He's been before with Pete.'

Mike flashed a look of incredulity at Glynn, who then asked. 'What's he look like?'

'Red hair, about five foot nine, average build. That's about all. Just an average-looking bloke.'

'Sam,' said Glynn, exchanging a look of concern with Mike. 'Why the fuck would he have been here yesterday? He doesn't do this pub now, except when we can't make it.'

Then the realisation dawned on him. They hadn't seen Sam around much lately. He'd told them he was taking a few days away with his wife and kids, and Peter had OK'd it, knowing how hard Sam had worked for them in the past. But what if he hadn't really gone on holiday?

'What about the other two guys? Do you know them?' Glynn demanded.

'No, I've never seen them before. But one of them was a tough-looking bastard, almost six foot, I'd say, and he had a good build on him.'

Not wishing to lose face in front of the customer, Glynn said, 'Right, well, Sam doesn't work for us anymore. I don't know what fuckin' firm you've paid but it wasn't us. So, it's business as usual, Pat. Get the money.'

'But that means I've paid twice.'

'I don't give a shit. That's your own fault for falling for it. You should have rung me or Pete to check them out.'

'But, he was one of yours.'

'*Was* one of ours!' said Glynn. 'He fuckin' isn't any more. Now, we're going to collect what we came for. I suggest you chalk yesterday's payment down to your own stupidity. And in future, you pay us and only us. OK?'

Pat looked at Mike as though he was weighing up his chances if he had the nerve to refuse. 'But what if they put the screws on me?' he asked.

'Don't worry, we'll fuckin' sort that lot out,' said Glynn. 'I doubt if they'll come round here again once we've finished with them. But if they do, you or the missus needs to get straight on the phone to us. OK?'

Pat nodded reluctantly and walked over to the safe where the takings were kept.

'Good man,' said Glynn as he took the money and walked away.

'Fuckin' hell!' said Mike, once they were outside the pub. 'I can't believe Sam's stitched us up.'

'Me neither,' said Glynn, spitting on the ground. 'What we gonna do?'

'Well, first thing is to tell Pete. Then we're gonna find out just who Sam is fuckin' working with. But don't worry, we'll sort him and his crew out! No one fuckin' messes with us and gets away with it.'

Adele was working late. It was a few days since she had started work for Peter and she was beginning to realise just how much effort it entailed. She'd spent the first two days looking over all the paperwork so she could assess exactly what was involved.

The highest earner by far was the nightclub. Then there were three sunbed salons and a bookmaker's. To her relief the ledgers had been kept fairly up to date for the sunbed salons and the bookmaker's, but Max had fallen behind with the accounts for the Golden Bell.

Bringing the accounts for the nightclub up to date was going to be her biggest challenge. She decided the best thing to do was to transfer all the information onto the computer. It was a mammoth task but at least it would make things easier to maintain once everything was on there. She was already working extra hours each evening to bring it all up to date.

As she tapped away at the computer keyboard,

Glynn and Mike sauntered into the office. Adele looked up and immediately felt herself blush as she took in Glynn's powerful frame and chiselled features. She quickly looked back down at her keyboard to disguise her embarrassment.

'Hiya, sweetheart. You not saying hello then?' asked Glynn.

She reluctantly raised her flushed face to see Glynn looking her over appreciatively. The cheeky smile was there again, as well as the twinkle in his eye and the confident air.

'Sorry, I was busy,' she babbled. 'I wasn't deliberately ignoring you.' She inwardly cursed her choice of words. Why was she defending herself?

'That's all right, sweetheart,' he said, winking at her. 'We won't keep you long, just wanted to bank this cash.'

He held up a bag of money, then crossed the office and put it in the safe while Mike waited in the doorway. Adele could feel her face cooling now Glynn's eyes were no longer on her. Once the money was tucked inside and the safe door locked, he turned around to face her again. 'Is Pete still in?' he asked.

'No, he went home early tonight. Said he had a bit of business to attend to there.'

'Aah, we all know what kind of business that is,' said Mike, with a lewd grin on his face. 'The dirty bastard will have taken a bird back with him. I bet he's—'

'All right, Mike,' Glynn cut in. 'Can't you see there's

a lady present?' He flashed Adele a very becoming smile and she felt the colour return to her cheeks as his eyes explored her. 'Has anyone ever told you what a lovely complexion you've got?' he asked her.

'Fuckin' hell, Mr Smarm strikes again,' said Mike.

'I'm not being smarmy,' Glynn responded. 'It's just that some of us know how to treat a lady.' He eyed Adele again before smiling and addressing her. 'Isn't that right, sweetheart?'

Lost for words, she returned his smile but willed him to leave her office. The guy was too much!

'Come on, Glynn. Save your fuckin' flirting for another time. You know we've got important stuff to sort with Pete,' Mike complained.

'OK, I'm coming,' said Glynn. 'I just wanted to make our new member of staff welcome, that's all.'

He walked to the door but before he went he turned back to face Adele. 'If there's anything you need, and Pete's not around, just give me a shout and I'll look after you,' he said.

'Thanks,' said Adele, feeling conscious of her scarlet cheeks under Glynn's keen gaze.

Adele was glad when they had gone. She didn't like the effect Glynn had on her. Her face was still flushed and she could feel her pulse racing. She took a deep breath and tried to focus on her work but she couldn't help analysing what had just happened.

Mike was right; Glynn was smarmy. But there was

something about him that drew her in. She wished it didn't. He was a textbook charmer, a man who probably came on to all the women. And she couldn't help but feel flattered even though she should know better than to fall for his patter.

Adele thought about her brother's warning. She knew it was only a matter of time before Glynn made a move on her. But, despite the thrill that she felt when she saw him, Adele had a bad feeling about Glynn. So, she decided that she would do everything in her power to resist his advances. Deep down she knew that a man like Glynn would only bring her trouble and she'd already had more than her share of that in her life.

32

Peter was having a night in with a good-looking blonde who worked behind the make-up counter of Lewis's in Manchester. It was the third time he'd seen the girl. Her sex appeal was undeniable and he'd greeted her with a passionate kiss as he grasped her buttocks before letting his hands roam up to her breasts.

'Steady on, randy,' she giggled but they both knew her protests were half-hearted.

They went through to the lounge and as he slipped one hand down her tight-fitting jeans, she sighed with pleasure. Then she eased her legs apart, allowing him to slip one finger inside her. He took her there and then on the sofa. After it was over, they put their clothes back on, he poured them both a drink and switched on the TV.

They were currently sitting watching a film but he'd missed half the story while she yattered away. The truth was, once the sex was over, she bored him. He had no interest whatsoever in the latest cosmetic products or shop-floor gossip, and her fake posh, department-store voice was starting to get on his nerves.

He was thinking up what excuse he could use to get rid of her when the doorbell rang. *Thank God for that!* he thought as he dashed to answer it.

'All right?' he greeted Glynn and Mike, but he could see by their faces that things weren't all right.

He led them into the dining room. 'Wait in there for me. I'll be with you in a minute,' he said.

Peter then went into the living room.

'Everything all right, babe?' the blonde asked.

'No, it's not. I'm afraid I've got a bit of business to attend to so you'll have to go.'

'Oh,' she said, sounding put out. For a few seconds she sat there gaping at him.

'Come on, I haven't got all day. It's important,' he said.

'Oh, be like that, then,' she said, getting up and grabbing her coat.

She walked up to him and pouted, waiting for him to respond. He quickly planted a kiss on her lips, hoping it would get rid of her.

'When will I see you again?' she asked.

Peter cringed at the cliché. 'I'll call you,' he said. But, of course, he knew he wouldn't.

He was glad when he finally let her out of the front door so he could go and find out what was troubling Glynn and Mike.

'What is it?' he asked once he had joined them in the dining room.

Glynn came straight to the point. 'Sam's done the shit on us.'

When Peter gazed at him, incredulous, Glynn and Mike filled him in on what had happened at the George and Dragon pub.

'So much for his fuckin' family holiday,' said Peter, cynically. 'Jesus Christ! I can't believe it. Not Sam. I never thought he'd do anything like this.'

'Well, he fuckin' has,' said Mike.

'Who's he working for? Do you know?' Peter asked, ignoring Mike's caustic comment.

Glynn and Mike both shook their heads.

'Right,' said Peter. 'I want you both to do some sniffing around. I need to know who he's working with and what the fuck's going on.'

'What d'you want us to do about Sam?' asked Glynn.

'Find out what you can first,' Peter replied. 'Then we'll deal with Sam. Don't worry; he isn't gonna fuckin' get away with this.'

It was Friday night and Adele was having a well-earned drink after work in the club. She'd been doing the books for two weeks now and, although there was still a hell of a lot to do before she got the accounts fully in order, at least she was starting to make some progress. She'd worked late nearly every night this week so she welcomed the chance to unwind with a glass of wine.

Peter had been sitting with her chatting at the bar but he'd been called away to tend to something so she was currently on her own. It didn't bother her, though; in the couple of weeks that she'd worked there Adele was getting to know the bar staff. She felt quite at home as she sat sipping her wine, people watching and tapping her foot to 'Pump Up the Jam'.

There wasn't anything interesting going on at the bar so she swivelled her stool and looked around. The interior of the club was dark, the combination of blue strobe lights and artificial fog creating a cerulean haze. Adele squinted as she gazed towards the dance floor. If she was honest with herself, she was secretly hoping she'd catch sight of Glynn, and it wasn't long before she spotted his chiselled features and honed physique as he strutted across the room.

On his way to the bar Glynn stopped to chat to a couple of people. The first conversation seemed amicable and there was a lot of laughter and back-patting as they parted. But the second time he stopped to talk to someone, the conversation didn't seem so friendly. Glynn's handsome features had formed hard lines and the way he nodded his head towards the man as he spoke told her that he was having a go at him about something.

The man seemed to shrivel as Glynn chastised him, then he skulked away. Glynn looked up as the man walked away, then drew his shoulders back and changed his facial expression as he mixed with the punters again.

As she watched, Adele also noticed the girls. She was amused by their reactions as Glynn walked past them. Some were more subtle than others, simply raising their eyebrows or sharpening their gaze as they admired him. Others were blatant: either staring openly, then whispering and giggling with their friends, or shouting flirtatious greetings to him.

Adele also noticed Glynn's reaction. He was all too aware of his appeal and was lapping it up as he strode cockily towards the bar. She smiled to herself as she thought, *Peter was right. This one is definitely to be avoided. He's got nearly every woman in the club swooning over him and he knows it.*

This time when Glynn approached her, she didn't turn into a gibbering wreck. While she'd watched him, she'd prepared herself, and the wine had given her some courage.

'Hiya, sweetheart!' he greeted. 'What's a gorgeous girl like you doing sitting here all on her own?'

Jesus, she thought. *He might have the body and looks of an Adonis but his lines are yesterday's clichés.*

She smiled, amused. 'Peter's busy,' she said casually. 'Besides, I'm fine on my own.'

He smiled broadly and lowered his head towards hers while he whispered in her ear, 'You sure you don't want a bit of company, love? Male company. Only, your eyes are telling a different story than that gorgeous mouth of yours.'

She laughed at his audacity. 'Oh, yes. I'm sure,' she said. 'I'm perfectly all right on my own.'

He turned towards the barmaid. 'Can you give me a bottle of Pils, Cindy, love, and whatever this lovely young lady is having?' he asked, flashing a beaming smile at Adele when he referred to her.

'I'm fine, thank you,' said Adele, holding up her glass of wine to show him how full it was.

'OK, maybe next time,' he said.

Then he took his drink and winked at her as he left the bar. Adele turned her stool back around, resisting the temptation to watch him walk through the club again. A self-satisfied smile was painted on her face, pleased with herself that she'd managed to play it cool.

But, although she had stayed cool on the outside, her pulse was racing. It always did when Glynn was around, and a buzz of excitement shot through her. God, she wanted him!

Adele might have resisted Glynn for now but she felt as though he was pulling her into his lair. She knew

ll22222222222222222

it was dangerous but she felt herself being dragged there as though against her will. She didn't know how much longer she could resist the mighty attraction that drew her. And watching the effect that he had on other women only made her want him more.

33

Peter swung open the door to his apartment, allowing Glynn and Mike to enter. Their faces were grave and he guessed that whatever they had found out wasn't good. He tried to prepare himself for bad news while they sat down at his dining table and he fixed them all a drink.

'So, what's the score with Sam?' he asked.

'You're not gonna like it,' said Glynn.

'Go on,' Peter urged.

'The new outfit he's with have been operating a few weeks but he's only just joined them, as you know. Now, here's one of the things you won't like.' Glynn paused dramatically before continuing. 'The George and Dragon isn't the only one of our pubs they've muscled in on. There are two others, plus another that sussed them out and made an excuse to delay payment.'

Glynn then gave Peter details of the pubs affected.

'Fuckin' hell!' Peter cursed. 'Well, whoever this firm is, they're a bunch of cheeky bastards,' he said.

'I know,' said Glynn. He held up his hand, adding, 'But don't worry, we've made the licensees pay us and told them not to pay Sam's firm any more. Trouble is, we'll have to turf up whenever they're having trouble with this new outfit.'

Peter sighed, 'Yeah, looks like we're gonna have to fuckin' earn our protection money now.' He then paused before asking, 'What's the other thing?'

'Oh yeah,' said Glynn. 'I was coming to that. You're not gonna believe this! One of the blokes Sam's working with is Dave.'

'You're fuckin' joking!' said Peter, almost choking as he swallowed his brandy. 'Who the fuck are they?' he demanded.

'There's about half a dozen of 'em. They all hang out at the Sportsman's. The one in charge seems to be a guy called Alan. Mike knows him; he was inside at the same time as he was.'

'Yeah,' said Mike. 'Never did like the tosser.'

'Hang on,' said Peter, incredulous. 'Alan who?'

'Palmer,' Glynn answered. 'Big bastard, apparently, and a bit handy, too.'

Peter just stared at him, open-mouthed. He couldn't believe what he was hearing. One of his trusted employees and his two childhood friends had teamed up against him. It was hard to take in!

'You all right, mate?' asked Glynn when Peter didn't respond.

Peter just stared back and gulped. He'd been betrayed! And not only that, by the very people he'd trusted. In his mind he replayed the words he'd just heard, trying to make sense of it all.

David he could understand. He'd already let him down years ago and they'd parted on bad terms, although it didn't make his treachery any easier. But he still hadn't come to terms with Sam's betrayal. And now Alan! He just couldn't get his head round it. Why on earth would Alan start a rival firm? It wasn't so long ago that he was considering joining Pete's gang. And they'd always stayed mates. It just didn't make sense!

'D'you know him?' asked Glynn.

'Yeah,' said Peter, his voice almost a whisper. 'We used to knock about as kids: him, me and Dave. Did some of my first jobs with them two 'till Alan got arrested for knifing a bloke. I was on a job with him when it happened.'

'Shit!' said Mike. 'I heard about that when I was inside.'

'Yeah. The owner walked in on him,' said Peter. 'I was in the other room. I scarpered as soon as I heard the owner come downstairs. I panicked. I was only a kid. Didn't think about Alan till I'd got away. Then I found out what he'd done the next day.'

He was rambling now, going through everything in his head, trying to explain it. Maybe that's what it was.

Maybe Alan had never forgiven him for leaving him to it when they were kids! The thought that Alan might be on some sort of revenge mission sent a cold chill down Peter's spine.

Having a firm working against him was bad enough. But having a firm that was hellbent on revenge was fuckin' scary. He couldn't let it get to him, though. He wouldn't. How dare they have the nerve to try to take over his fuckin' territory?

No, he wasn't having it. If that's the game they wanted to play then he'd make sure he was the fuckin' winner. Nobody tried to take over his turf and got away with it, no matter what warped justification they had.

'You sure you're all right, mate?' asked Glynn.

'Whatever happened when you were kids, it doesn't give them the fuckin' right to muscle in on our turf!' said Mike.

'No, it doesn't,' said Peter, aware that he'd allowed Glynn and Mike to catch a brief glimpse of his vulnerable side. *That won't do*, he thought, straightening himself up and taking a swig of his brandy before adding, 'And they're not gonna fuckin' get away with it!'

Peter looked at Glynn, his mind now strategizing. Then another thought occurred to him.

'What about Mickey? Have they poached him, too?' he asked.

'No, as far as I'm aware he's still one of ours,' said Glynn.

Peter pursed his lips and let out a sharp puff of air, relieved. He didn't think Mickey would have done the dirty on him but after what Sam had done, he couldn't be too sure.

Now he was over the initial shock of Sam and Alan's betrayal, he had to think of a way to deal with it. And he was going to make sure he never again showed any sign of vulnerability to either his men or his enemies. He couldn't afford to.

Peter had learnt the hard way that no one could be trusted. If you didn't stand strong they tried to take the piss. Well, they might try, but they wouldn't fuckin' win! He was determined of that.

'What else are they up to?' he asked, knowing that Glynn would have unearthed as much information as possible.

'A few warehouse jobs, but that's about it. Seems like their main focus is taking over our fuckin' customers. And Sam's giving them the tip-off about who we deal with. If you ask me, he's become the biggest fuckin' liability. We need to stop him.'

'Yeah, we do,' said Peter, draining the last of his brandy. 'I want you two to sort it. Do whatever it fuckin' takes. The more dramatic, the better. I want to send a message, loud and clear, to anyone who thinks they can take us on. Mess with me and you pay the fuckin' price.'

34

A few days later Alan's new crew, David, Sam and three others, were sitting in the Sportsman's. Alan had given the landlord a backhander to make sure they had a small side room to themselves. Alan had just outlined their forthcoming plans and they were all now relaxing with a few drinks.

At around nine o'clock Sam stood up. 'I'm off now,' he said.

'You sure, mate?' asked David. 'It's a bit early, innit?'

'Yeah. I've promised the missus I wouldn't get too pissed tonight.'

The men let out a loud jeer.

'Some fuckin' gangster you are if you can't even stand up to your missus,' teased David.

'It pays to keep her sweet,' said Sam with a lascivious smirk. 'And I need to get home while she's still awake if I want my fuckin' payback.'

The men jeered again and David added, 'No wonder

she wants you fuckin' sober, mate. She's probably frightened you'll get brewer's droop.'

'Not me, mate,' Sam laughed. 'I'm always up for it.'

'Hang on!' said Alan. 'Before you go, I just wanna check; are you clear about what you have to do with that next job?'

'Yeah, sure I am. No problems.'

'OK, see you soon, mate,' said Alan.

'Give her one for me,' shouted David, and Sam left the Sportsman's to the sound of laughter and loud, excited chatter coming from the side room that the gang had now earmarked as their own.

Glynn and Mike were sitting in a black BMW a few doors down from the Sportsman's, watching.

'D'you know,' said Mike, 'Pete never seems to do any of the dirty work, does he?'

'Suppose not,' said Glynn. Then he laughed. 'That's what he's got us for.'

Mike's lips turned up at the corners. 'Makes me wonder, though, has he got the bottle for it?'

'Oh, yeah, course he has.'

'Well, I hope so 'cos he'd be a piss-poor leader if he hasn't.'

Glynn looked pointedly at Mike. 'What you suggesting?' he asked.

'Nowt, just saying. In my opinion you'd run the

show better than him. You've got the bottle for it. I'm not sure Pete has, that's all.'

Glynn was about to respond when something caught his eye. 'Here he is now,' he said, on spotting Sam's unmistakable shock of red hair. 'Quick, get down. We don't want him to see us straight away.'

'I can't believe he's on his own,' said Mike, who was bent forward so he couldn't be seen through the windscreen. 'This'll be easier than I thought.'

'Shush,' whispered Glynn, who also had his body bent forward but his head turned to the side so he could watch Sam as he passed the car.

It wasn't long before Sam drew level. 'Here he is now. Let's go!' ordered Glynn.

He shoved open the passenger door of the BMW, hitting Sam full on and almost knocking him off his feet. Momentarily registering the look of shock on Sam's face, Glynn charged at him, gripping him in a bear hug and dragging him towards the car.

By the time Sam realised what was happening, Mike had run round the car and approached him from behind. He thrust his hand over Sam's mouth while they both shunted him along the pavement. Sam put up a struggle but they were too strong for him. As soon as they reached the boot of the car they tossed him inside and locked it.

'Right. Fuckin' move it!' ordered Glynn.

Mike started the engine and they took off at speed.

Glynn could hear Sam yelling from the boot, 'Help, help! Let me out,' so he flicked a switch on the dashboard until the sound of Dire Straits blasted through the stereo, drowning out Sam's screams. Then he pulled out a roll of adhesive tape and a pair of scissors from the glove compartment.

'As soon as we get there, we'll tape his fuckin' gob up,' he said. 'We don't want anyone to hear him screaming.'

Mike continued to drive for several minutes until they were out of the city centre and had reached a run-down part of Ancoats. It was an area to the north of the city centre, formerly an industrial hub served by the Rochdale and Ashton canals. Nowadays many of the mills and warehouses had shut and the buildings were falling into decay. Mike pulled up at an abandoned warehouse and they both got out of the car. Glynn had the tape and scissors in his hand, ready.

As soon as Mike opened the boot, Sam shot up and tried to climb out. But Mike blocked him, using his full bodyweight to pin him down while Glynn taped his mouth. Then they heaved him from the car, yanked his arms behind him and taped those together, too.

'You can keep your fuckin' eyes open,' said Glynn. 'We want you to see what happens to traitors.'

To the sound of Sam's muffled yells, they dragged him towards the warehouse then hustled him inside. In the vast, dark interior was a series of corroding metal pillars as well as metal girders running along the length and breadth of the ceiling. They were lime green in colour but the paint was now peeling and spotted with rust. The place smelt musty after years of abandonment and decay.

Sam fought against Glynn and Mike as they hauled him along the rubble-strewn ground, stopping at one of the metal pillars. They'd already prepared the scene. Near to the pillar was a coil of rope and a pair of scissors. Another length of rope hung menacingly from one of the metal girders. Sam became frantic when he spotted it; the implication too horrific to bear.

As Sam struggled to break free, Glynn kept a tight hold of him while Mike smacked him hard across the face, temporarily stunning him into inaction. Then they thrust him towards the pillar and quickly tied him to it. Within seconds they had him restrained. They cut the tape from his wrists then secured his arms behind the pillar.

Sam's eyes flitted around him in wide-eyed terror. But there was no escape. Again he tried to yell but the tape across his mouth prevented it. As he let out a stifled, desperate squeal his eyes told of the dread that his voice couldn't express.

When Glynn and Mike withdrew their knives, Sam's body writhed around but the rope held him fast. His breath was now coming in short bursts as panic overwhelmed him.

'Right, let's start with his fingers,' said Glynn, and Mike was only too happy to comply.

'Yes, let's have one finger for each of our pubs that him and his gang have tried to muscle in on.'

Sam's squeal intensified, his eyes now pleading. But there was no sympathy from Mike. He stepped behind Sam and lifted his hand. Sam squealed again and let out a stream of urine just as Mike hacked into his finger. Mike scowled, showing his distaste as the smell of urine permeated his nostrils.

Without giving Sam chance to recover, Mike severed another finger. Then another. Until he had cut off four of Sam's fingers. Then he released Sam's hand, which bounced back against the pillar, coating the decayed paint with a crimson sheen.

Glynn wore a satisfied smirk. 'Now we need to make sure he can't tell everyone which fuckin' pubs we run,' he said.

'Yeah,' said Mike, as realisation dawned on him. 'It'll stop him fuckin' snivelling as well.'

Glynn's face now became hard set as he watched Mike remove the tape and heard Sam scream. Then all went silent as the blood gushed from Sam's mouth where Mike had sliced off his tongue.

'Ooh, it looks like he's lost his balls as well,' said Glynn.

'Good idea,' said Mike, eagerly lowering the knife towards Sam's genitals.

Glynn wasn't sure whether Sam heard their last words. He had already passed out.

When they had finished, they tied him onto the length of rope that hung from the ceiling. Then they hoisted him up until he was suspended, his lifeless head lolling forward. Blood gushed from his mouth and dripped from his body forming a viscous scarlet pool on the stony ground below.

They left him; mutilated, unconscious and close to death.

On their way home, they stopped at a call box. After giving Peter an update, Glynn rang the Sportsman's. 'Make sure Alan gets this message,' he said to the barman. 'Tell him he can find his fuckin' Judas at the Byson Street warehouse but there's not much left of him. And tell him, that's what happens when you betray someone.'

He put down the receiver then they got back into the car and sped away. While he drove, Glynn began to think. Mike's earlier words came back to him. Maybe Mike had a point. Perhaps he would make a better leader than Pete. It was something he hadn't given much thought to previously.

But now that Mike had mentioned it, the idea took root in his mind. One day, when the time was right, he might just do something about it.

35

Adele smiled as she looked at the figure on her computer screen. Yes! At last she'd managed to get it to agree with the total in the ledger. She was thrilled to have finally balanced this account, which had been a particularly tricky one.

As she switched off her computer, she looked at her watch – 6.45 p.m. That late? She started packing away her paperwork, intending to go down to the club and say goodbye to Peter before she left. If she was honest with herself, she was also hoping to catch a glimpse of Glynn, who was currently downstairs with Peter checking the stock before the staff and customers arrived. They were the only two other people in the building.

While she packed her things away, she began thinking about Glynn again, trying to picture him in her mind. She replayed his words when he'd called her 'sweetheart' and 'gorgeous', and a frisson of pleasure flowed through her. Then she checked herself; she was behaving like a love-struck teenager. Glynn would never be any good for her so it was best to try and put all thoughts of him out of her mind.

She was putting her files away in the cabinet when she heard a noise in the corridor. It sounded like footsteps coming from more than one person and they were coming fast. Her first thought was that it was Peter and Glynn, and the thrill of anticipation zipped through her at the thought of seeing her brother's sidekick.

But then she realised that the sound was coming from the opposite end of the corridor. Neither Peter nor Glynn would come that way. If they came upstairs they would enter the corridor from the other end, passing Peter's office before reaching the cash office where Adele worked. So it must be someone who had come through the back door and up the back stairs.

The sound of footsteps drew closer. She raised her head, staring at the office door, confused. Who would enter the building from the back door? Within no time she could hear them outside.

Then the door burst open. In ran a man. A complete stranger. Dark hair and skin. The image of Starsky from the TV cop show, but more menacing. Behind him was another stranger with a hefty physique. A third man sprinted up the corridor.

Adele felt the cold hand of fear grip her insides. She knew she was in trouble. Nobody would hear her screams from here.

'Where's the fuckin' cash box?' demanded Starsky.

He sped towards her and Adele saw a glint of metal as he pulled out a knife. He was now only a metre away, the knife pointing threateningly towards her. Adele's autodefence mechanism kicked in. With a swift two-handed movement, she smacked her right hand into his forearm and her left into the back of his hand, disarming him. The knife catapulted across the room.

Without pausing to pick up the knife, Starsky launched himself at her, his hands aiming for her throat. But Adele was too fast. She attacked his head and body using rapid martial arts moves. He staggered backwards, leaving room for his friend to lunge at her.

Then the hefty man was upon her. Adele felt a sharp punch in her face. Quickly recovering, she came back at him. They traded blows: her swift kickboxing moves against his heavy fists and bulky frame. A roundhouse kick sent him scudding backwards. But before she could advance, Starsky recovered. This time he came straight at her with the knife.

Then everything happened at once. The sound of running feet in the corridor. The shadow of a man speeding past the door. A gunshot. The knife at her throat.

As Starsky gripped her from behind, his knife grazing her throat, his friend sped out of the office and up the corridor. Adele felt a sharp prick as Starsky held the knife closer, nicking her flesh till a trickle of blood ran down her neck. She heard another two shots. Then Glynn was at the door, gun in hand, with Peter behind.

'Drop the fuckin' knife!' Glynn demanded, but Starsky resisted.

Glynn's gun was pointing at the man, who was using Adele as a shield.

'No fuckin' way!' said Starsky. 'Stand back so I can get out.'

'Please, Glynn,' begged Adele, her voice shaking. 'He'll stab me if you don't let him past.'

Glynn and Peter stood to one side but Glynn's eyes never left the man. His hard stare was intimidating even to Adele, who he was trying to protect. There was now a clear path through to the office door.

'Move!' Starsky ordered Adele, pushing her from behind.

They edged slowly to the door. As they passed Glynn and Peter, the man swivelled Adele around to give him cover. Then he stepped backwards still holding tightly onto her until he reached the door. Adele could feel his harried breath on the back of her neck. She was trembling now, her legs shaking as she took each terrifying step.

When he released her Adele slumped to the floor, her legs giving way beneath her. The man flew up the corridor. She felt Glynn push past her. Then Peter was by her side.

'You OK, sis?' he asked, his voice full of concern.

The sound of gunshot rang out again. Three shots. Then silence. Peter helped her to her feet while shouting out, 'Glynn. Are you OK?'

But there was no reply. Adele heard the sound of someone running up the corridor again. This time there was only one set of footsteps.

'Come on, let's get you sat down,' said Peter, putting his arm around her and steering her to the chair.

She could feel her heart pounding, partly with shock, partly with fear over Glynn.

'Glynn, are you OK?' shouted Peter again, rushing to the office door and pulling out his own gun.

Glynn appeared at the door just as Peter reached it. The gun was still in his hand. 'Yeah. I got the bastard!' he said. 'But the other two have scarpered. The back door was wide open but I've bolted it so they can't get back in.'

Adele stared at the gun in alarm and noticed the look on Glynn's face. Was it relief, or satisfaction? It was hard to tell.

'Is he dead?' asked Peter.

'Think so, yeah.'

'Shit!' said Peter. Then he seemed to spend a second in thought before saying. 'Adele needs something for the shock. You stay here. I'll grab a drink from the bar. Then we can decide what to do.'

He disappeared. Adele wanted to shout at him to

come back but she was too late. Her reactions were delayed by panic. As soon as he was gone, she started to take in what had just happened. As the harsh reality hit her she sobbed uncontrollably till she felt she couldn't breathe. Her whole body was shaking with the shock.

Within no time Glynn had crossed the office and was with her, taking her in his big muscular arms and holding her tightly till the sobbing subsided. Reassuring her. Calming her.

'It's OK,' he said, gently stroking her back. 'It's over.'

He took a tissue from the box on her desk and dried her tears. Then he smoothed back her tear-sodden hair.

'Adele, listen to me,' he said. 'It's over now. They're gone.'

She rested her head on his shoulder and drew comfort from his strong embrace. By the time Peter returned she was a lot calmer.

'Here, get that down you,' said Peter, pouring a glass of brandy and handing it to her. Then he turned to Glynn and said, 'I've rung Mike.'

Glynn nodded and for a few seconds they watched Adele down the brandy. Then Peter asked Glynn to follow him into the corridor to talk. She could hear them whispering and caught snippets of the conversation, which filled her with terror. The gist was that the man was dead and they needed to dispose of the body and clean up.

Peter came back inside the office. 'Right, sis, finish your drink. I'm taking you home,' he said.

'But, won't we need to call the police?' she asked.

'No, we can't chance it.'

'But what will we do?'

'Don't worry about it. Glynn and Mike will sort it out. I'll explain it all when we get back to mine.'

Everything was still a bit of a blur for Adele. It had all happened so fast and she was traumatised. Although she wasn't sure whether they were doing the right thing, her mind was in turmoil. So she relied on Peter's guidance. Just like she had done on a previous occasion, years before. On the night when she killed her father.

They stepped outside the office. In her dazed state she registered everything that was happening. But it felt surreal; as though she wasn't a part of it. Glynn was standing further up the corridor, trying to block her view of the body. Peter steered her quickly away but not before she had caught sight of the blood spatter. She shuddered as he led her towards the stairs and out of the building.

Mike arrived just as they were getting into Peter's car.

'He's upstairs,' said Peter. 'Make sure you get rid of every trace.'

'Don't worry. We will do,' Mike said.

Then Peter sped off and Adele sat in the passenger seat, numb with shock. Something devastating had taken place tonight. And she had been a party to it.

As a result, things would never be the same again. Just like the night when she killed her father, the after-effects of this crime would surely mar her life for years to come.

36

It was just before nine in the evening. Adele was sitting in the living room of Peter's apartment downing more brandy. She had taken a shower and cleaned up the small wound on her neck, and now it was time to talk.

'What will happen when the police find out?' she asked Peter.

'They won't.'

'But the men that escaped – won't they report it?'

'They wouldn't dare. They know they'd be nicked for attempted burglary.'

'But, surely, they're going to realise their friend is missing. What if they *do* report it to the police? They might do it anonymously. Then we'll be in trouble for not informing the cops in the first place.'

'The police won't take them seriously, especially if they come to the club, because they'll find nothing. Glynn and Mike will scrub the place clean. There'll be no trace that the man was ever there.'

'But what about the body?'

'Don't worry about that. Glynn and Mike will take care of it.'

Adele stared blankly at him for some minutes. He seemed so calm when she was in turmoil! She couldn't understand how he could be so matter-of-fact about Glynn killing a man. Her head was in a whirl, going over everything that had happened. She still had questions and was just about to speak again, but Peter beat her to it. She felt as though he knew what she was thinking.

'Look, Adele, I need you to keep this to yourself or we'll all be in the shit and Glynn could get nicked for murder. The guy deserved what he got. He had a fuckin' knife at your throat, for God's sake! Glynn just did what was necessary. He did it for you and he took a big risk in doing it. And you wouldn't want the guy who'd nearly killed you walking the streets, would you?'

'But why were you and Glynn carrying guns?' she asked.

Peter let out a long, slow breath, as though he was running out of patience with her. Then he spoke as if he was explaining something to a child, his words slow and over-emphasised.

'Self-protection,' he said. He looked down his nose and puckered his lips before continuing. 'Look,' he said. 'The nightclub business can be pretty fuckin' ruthless at times. There are all kinds of people trying to muscle in all the time. I run a clean ship but that's only because I won't take no shit off anyone.'

'What do you mean?' she asked.

'Druggies, protection rackets, all sorts of low life. Those sorts of people don't piss about. So we carry the guns for protection. We don't normally use them but tonight Glynn had to. And, believe me, Adele, Glynn comes in pretty fuckin' handy at times. With the game we're in it pays to have someone watching your back.

'If you land Glynn in the shit then we'll all suffer for it. We're all accessories: you, me and Mike. Think about it. And Glynn was only trying to help you, when all's said and done.'

Adele thought about how Glynn had comforted her when she fell to pieces. About his touch. The way he'd protected her. And she thought about her loyalty to her brother. She wouldn't report Glynn's crime. How could she after everything Peter had said tonight?

'OK,' she said. 'I'll keep my mouth shut.'

'Good,' said Peter. 'And don't worry; we'll make sure that place is watertight. Nobody will get inside again. We'll put someone on the back door and have better locks, and we'll make sure the door through from the club has a keyless entry system. No fucker will be able to get in unless they know the code.'

'OK,' Adele said again.

She felt anything but OK, but Peter's words had been

very persuasive. She knew that if she reported Glynn's crime, it wouldn't solve anything. In fact, it would just make matters worse.

'Take a couple of weeks off while you get over the shock,' said Peter. 'By the time you come back we'll have everything sorted.'

The following day Adele went to stay with her mother. Although she had agreed to Peter's suggestion, she couldn't quite face being at his apartment at the moment. She hoped that staying with her mother would take her mind off things. It wasn't going to be easy, though, with her mother's home being the place where Adele had killed her father.

In the weeks since she had left prison, Adele had visited her mother regularly. She'd got rid of the cat fleas and cleaned the place up, and now it wasn't so bad. There was still a bit of a smell but it wasn't quite as pungent as previously.

Adele was also getting more used to going into the living room. The first couple of times she had found it harrowing looking at the hearth: the scene of her crime. But now, although she would always feel guilty and repulsed by what she had done, she could face it without feeling distraught every time she walked into the room.

Her mother was mellowing towards her too, and actually seemed grateful that Adele had helped her clean the place up. When she'd asked to stay for a while, her mother had seemed glad of the company. Adele knew, though, that she couldn't afford to let her mother get too used to it. She must continue to stand on her own two feet. With this thought in mind, Adele decided that she would get her own place and move out as soon as possible.

'It's only for a couple of weeks,' said Adele when she arrived at her mother's door and walked down the hallway.

'How come you're not staying at Peter's anymore?' her mother asked.

'Oh, y'know, I feel like I'm cramping his style a bit.'

'Aah. Women, you mean?' her mother asked, flashing Adele a knowing look.

'Something like that.'

'He never introduces me to his girlfriends, y'know,' said her mother.

'Maybe he hasn't found the right one yet.' Then Adele quickly changed the subject. 'D'you mind if I take my case upstairs?'

'No, you go on. Help yourself.'

Adele went up the stairs and into her old bedroom. It hadn't changed much. The décor was now outdated and there was a tiny rip in the wallpaper, which Peter had done when they were children. Her books were still on a shelf along one wall and the head of her old bed stood facing the window. It had been stripped bare.

She went into her mother's room and searched for some bedding but it was all old and shabby. Adele decided she'd take her mother to the shops and treat herself to some new bedding. She'd need some for her own new home anyway so she might as well take her mother shopping with her.

Adele plonked herself down on the bed and looked around the room. Memories of her troubled childhood crowded her mind and tears filled her eyes. She'd spent so many sleepless hours in this room, fretting and trembling while her parents fought downstairs.

A lot had happened in the last few years and she wished she could roll the clock back and start again. But she couldn't. And now she had these latest troubles to add to her misery.

She needed space to come to terms with what had happened in the club, and whilst her childhood home wasn't ideal, she didn't have much choice at the moment. So she'd seek refuge here for a couple of weeks till she could get her head around things. And she seriously hoped that by the time she returned to work, she'd find a way to cope with the fallout.

37

Glynn arrived at Peter's apartment not long after Adele had left. The cheeky smile and glint in his eye were absent; instead his chiselled features were strained.

'How did it go?' asked Peter once they were sitting down in the lounge.

'It was fuckin' hard work,' said Glynn, 'But don't worry; no one will find anything in the club. We've got rid of every trace.'

'What about the body?'

'We've taken care of that, too; it's been disposed of.'

Peter raised his eyebrows inquisitively until Glynn continued.

'Let's just say our friend Mike is pretty handy with an electric saw. It makes it easier to get rid of a body if it's in pieces.'

'OK, I get the picture,' Peter said. 'You sure no one will find it?'

'Oh, yeah, I'm sure,' said Glynn. 'What about your Adele? Did you have a word with her and tell her to keep schtum?'

'Yeah. It won't be a problem. Adele knows when it's best to keep quiet; don't worry about that.'

'Good, as long as she does,' said Glynn. ''Cos if she spouts, we're all in the shit.'

'She knows that. She's not gonna do anything stupid, don't worry. I've told her; we're all accessories. And she knows you were only trying to protect her.'

Glynn smiled at this last comment and Peter silently cursed himself. He shouldn't have said that; he didn't want to encourage Glynn where his sister was concerned.

'What did she say about the guns?' asked Glynn.

'She was surprised, I must admit. So I told her how fuckin' ruthless the nightclub business is and that we need them for self-protection. She swallowed it and she knows fuck all about us offering protection to other pubs and clubs. She just thinks we're in the security business but she doesn't know the details. I'd like to keep it that way, too.'

'Well, I'm hardly gonna fuckin' tell her, am I?' said Glynn.

'Who do you think they were?' asked Peter.

'What, the men who broke into the club?' Glynn said.

Peter nodded.

'Small time, I think. No one I recognise, anyway, so I don't think we've got any worries.'

'Maybe not,' said Peter.

'Think about it,' Glynn added. 'If they'd have been a rival firm they'd have been carrying guns or machetes or summat, not poxy little knives... Nah, if you ask me they're just a bunch of chancers. And when they realise their friend has disappeared without a trace, we won't hear fuck all from them. They've probably shit themselves.'

'OK,' said Peter. 'I've given Adele a couple of weeks off. She's a bit shaken so she's gone to stay at my mam's. I've told her we'll get the place secured by the time she's back. I want better locks on the back door, someone posted there when Adele's working and a key-coded lock on the door from the club. D'you think you could sort that, mate?'

'Sure. Leave it with me.'

Glynn then got up to go but Peter stopped him. 'Hang on a minute. What about Sam? Has there been any comeback?'

'No, we left a message at the Sportsman's for Alan, as I told you, but I've heard nothing since. I would imagine they've seen his body by now, though. I'm wondering whether they'll get rid of it themselves or whether they'll leave it for the police.'

'Well, I've not heard anything in the news yet so we'll wait and see,' said Peter. 'How bad was it, anyway?'

'Oh, it was bad. Mike's a bit of a sick fuck. Kept chopping little bits off him. Then we strung him up from the girders. They'll get one hell of a fuckin' shock when they see him.'

Peter stared at Glynn for a few seconds, trying to hide his astonishment that Glynn and Mike had gone so far.

Glynn broke the silence. 'Look, you said you wanted to send a message, so we didn't piss about.'

'No, that's OK,' said Peter, feigning acceptance. 'But we've got to expect repercussions. I know Alan of old, and him and his crew are not gonna fuckin' take this lying down.'

'No problems,' said Glynn, confidently. 'We'll be well ready for them.'

Adele was sitting in her mother's front room, trying to brush aside her harrowing memories of killing her father in front of the fireplace where the cats were now snuggled up. She was watching the news with her mother when a headline caught her attention.

It was about a murder in Manchester. The police had found the mutilated body of a man in an abandoned warehouse. They suspected that he had been tortured to death, and were now looking for the perpetrators.

'Bloody hell! Who'd do a horrible thing like that?' her mother remarked. 'And so close to home, too.' She looked across at Adele, then seemed to check herself, and Adele knew that the memory of what she had done to her father had flashed through her mother's mind.

Even though they were now getting along together, their relationship would never be quite the same as before. Adele's brutal killing of her father would always stand between them and the recollection would crop up at unexpected moments.

Adele tried to shake all thoughts of her father from her mind as she watched the TV. When the reporter mentioned the name of the victim, she felt a jolt. It seemed familiar although she wasn't sure why. Sam Sutton? She replayed it over in her head. Where had she heard that name?

Then it came to her. She thought that Peter may have mentioned him when he had shown her around the club that first time. He'd quickly run through a list of the main members of staff. Then he'd mentioned someone who was on holiday but would regularly call in at the office to deposit takings in the safe. That was a Sam; she was sure of it. And she thought the name he'd mentioned was Sam Sutton.

Her skin prickled at this sudden realisation. Coming on top of the killing in the club, it put her senses on alert. Something wasn't quite right. But, knowing how highly strung her mother was, it wouldn't pay to mention it to her.

Neither would she mention what had taken place in the club. There was no way she could let her mother know that she and Peter had helped to cover up Glynn's shooting of the man who attacked her. She'd never cope with that news, not on top of all the other bad things that had happened in the past. Although her mother wasn't taking as much medication since she no longer had an abusive husband to put up with, nevertheless, she still wasn't the strongest person in the world.

But Adele's curiosity had been piqued. She wanted to know whether Sam Sutton was the same person who had worked for Peter. So she decided to wait until her mother had gone to bed; then she would phone Peter and find out.

38

Peter was in the club, keeping an eye on things, when the phone rang. It was late. But that didn't necessarily mean it was bad news. His men regularly called him with reports when they were out on a job or collecting protection money from the businesses they looked after.

He was surprised to hear his sister's voice, though. His first thought was that he hoped to Christ she hadn't got cold feet about the club killing. But as soon as she spoke that fear was allayed.

'Peter. Do you know the name Sam Sutton?' she asked.

As soon as she said Sam's name Peter knew what was coming but he calmed himself and tried to act normal.

'Yeah, he used to work for me,' he said.

'I thought I'd heard you mention him,' said Adele.

'Why are you asking?'

'He's been killed,' said Adele. 'It's just been on the news.'

'You're joking!' Peter said. He tried to sound surprised. 'Why, what's happened?'

'The police had a report of a body in an abandoned warehouse and when they went to investigate they found him. Apparently he's been mutilated and tortured.'

'Shit! That sounds bad. Poor Sam!'

'I know. And what about his family?' asked Adele. 'It must be awful for them.'

'Yeah,' said Peter, feeling a pang of guilt. 'Don't worry, I'll go round to see his missus tomorrow, see if there's anything I can do.'

'What do you think happened?' asked Adele.

'I don't know. He didn't work for me anymore and I'd not seen him for a couple of weeks.'

'Why did he leave?'

'Just said he'd had a better offer and that was that.'

'Bloody hell! It's terrible, isn't it? And I expect the police will be round asking questions.'

'Probably. I hope they find the bastards. What a shit thing to happen!'

'Well, I just thought you should know, seeing as how he used to work for you.'

'Yeah, appreciate it, sis, even if it is bad news… Fuckin' hell, that's knocked me for six, that has.'

'I bet it has,' said Adele. 'Sorry to be the one to break it to you.'

'No worries. Thanks anyway,' he said before finishing the call.

Shit! So the news was out. Although Peter was aware of what had happened to Sam, hearing his sister relate the facts still got to him. After all, Sam had once been a friend, even if he had done the shit on him. So, when the police came calling, he wouldn't need to act very much to show his regret. But, as for his men, they'd never know how upset he was about Sam. It didn't pay to show weakness.

He took a few minutes to compose himself, ordered another brandy from the barmaid, then went in search of Glynn and Mike to prepare them for the imminent arrival of the police.

Glynn and Mike were sitting in a corner of the club chatting to two attractive young women whose eyes lit up when Peter came to join them.

'I need a word, upstairs,' Peter said to his men, and the two women's faces dropped.

Once they were in the privacy of Peter's office he came straight to the point. 'Cat's out of the bag about Sam. It's been on the news. Our Adele told me.'

Glynn and Mike nodded for him to continue.

'The police found him in the warehouse so it looks like Alan's crew left the police to sort it out. They'll have seen the body first, though, so we need to be ready for them when they hit. They'll probably go for the club so we need to make sure our security's tight.'

'Sure,' said Glynn. 'I'll get right on it.'

'The police will be round asking questions, too, so we need to make sure our stories match. Here's the gist of it – he worked for me but he left a couple of weeks ago, said he had a better offer. He used to help in the nightclub, carrying stock in and stuff, and he collected money from my businesses and put it in the safe.'

There was a confused look on Mike's face. 'You don't wanna go telling the coppers that,' he said.

'I'm talking about my legal businesses,' Peter responded. 'The bookies and sunbed salons. I'm not gonna fuckin' tell the coppers about our protection, am I? You numpty!'

Mike glared at Peter but didn't comment further.

'Right, are we all clear on that then?' Peter asked.

'Sure,' said Glynn. 'What about Adele? Does she suspect anything?'

'No. She didn't sound like she did, anyway.'

'OK, that's good,' said Glynn, and he and Mike left the office.

Peter sat down at his desk. He needed a few moments alone to go over things in his head. He wished to God that Mike and Glynn hadn't gone so far when they had killed Sam. Sure, he wanted to send a message. But he was seriously worried about reprisals. He knew Alan and David would want revenge.

Glynn and Mike had been gone only a couple of minutes when Peter received a call from reception to let him know that the police were here to see him.

'Bring 'em up,' he instructed, and then he took a deep steadying breath as he prepared himself for the worst.

39

It was Adele's first day back at work and she was nervous. She hadn't previously realised just how cut off her office was from the rest of the club. It was OK when Peter and some of the other staff were around but when they weren't there it was scary.

As she sat there going over some of the figures she found it difficult to concentrate. Every little noise set her on edge; the central heating rattling around in the pipes or the wind blowing through the corridor. And even though Peter had tried to reassure her about the increased security, she still felt exposed.

Now, as she looked up from her desk, she began to relive the night when she had been attacked. A sliver of fear ran down her spine as she recalled the way her attacker had held a knife to her throat till he drew blood.

Things could have ended very differently for her if Peter and Glynn hadn't appeared when they did. She shuddered as she imagined the man plunging the knife deeper into her throat.

Her overactive imagination became grounded in reality when she heard the sound of footsteps in the corridor. She shot out of her seat, listening keenly, the blood pumping through her veins as she prepared to defend herself.

She wondered who it could be, but tried to reassure herself that it was just one of the staff. Whoever it was, they were coming from the direction of the back stairs; the same direction from which her attackers had approached that night.

When Glynn appeared at the door, Adele let out a slow breath, her shoulders slumping with relief.

'You OK?' he asked.

'Yeah, sure,' she said, feeling embarrassed by her over-reaction, and sitting back down at her desk.

'I've just been double-checking the back door to make sure it's locked. You've got no worries; I think we've finally got it through to the staff that they need to keep it locked.'

'I wasn't worried,' she said, 'just curious.'

'You sure?' Glynn asked, crossing the office and putting a reassuring hand on her arm.

She pulled away instinctively, the heat of his hand making her blush. Inside she was battling with conflicting emotions. After what had happened she felt vulnerable in this office on her own. Part of her wanted his protection, wanted him to take her in his arms and tell her everything would be OK. But another part of her railed against those feelings.

Adele didn't want to be a victim; not any more. She'd had enough of that as a child and had fought against it during her time inside. When she left prison she'd promised herself that she would never again be vulnerable, that she could stand up for herself and didn't need any man to protect her. Besides, her brother had warned her against Glynn and she knew he was bad news.

'Yes, I'm sure,' she said, willing him to leave. The thrill of his touch and the way he looked at her was too much.

But he remained where he was and gazed intently into her eyes. 'You don't need to act brave in front of me,' he said. 'No one would blame you for being a bit freaked out by what happened. After all, the bastard had a knife at your throat.'

'I told you, I'm OK,' Adele said. 'I can handle myself.'

'I've no doubt about that.' He smiled and she felt her insides turn to mush.

When she didn't respond he seemed to falter momentarily. Then he spoke her name hesitantly, as though he had something crucial to impart. 'Adele... I just want to say that what you saw that night... well, when I saw that guy hold a knife to your throat, I knew I had to stop him.'

'But he'd already let me go,' she said.

'I know, but something in me just snapped. I couldn't let him get away. Not after what he'd done, and not when I could see how terrified you were.'

She blinked. There was no point denying how frightened she had been that night. Anybody would have been shaken up when they'd had a knife held to their throat.

'I–I didn't mean to shoot him. Not really. The guns are just for protection. But, like I say, it was instinct.'

Despite herself, she was touched by his contrition, and the thought that he'd done it for her.

'It's OK,' she said. 'I understand.'

'How are you getting home tonight?' he asked.

'I'm on the bus. But it's OK; I'll be all right.'

'Have you moved into your new flat yet?'

'Yes, at the weekend.'

'Ah, right. So this'll be the first time you've had to go home to an empty place?'

'Yes, but I'll be fine,' she protested.

'Look, I can see you're a bit shaken. You've no need to go home alone; I'll take you home.'

'No, I'll be OK, honestly.'

'I wasn't asking; I was telling you,' said Glynn. 'What time are you finishing?'

'Don't know.' She shrugged. 'About six, I suppose.'

'OK,' said Glynn. 'I'll be here.'

Then he patted her on the shoulder and left her office before she could protest any further. She smiled to herself, secretly flattered at his attention. And the way he wouldn't take no for an answer made her glow all over.

She continued to work on her accounts, her attention still drifting. But this time she wasn't fretting over strange noises; she was thinking about Glynn and her excitement at the prospect of him taking her home.

The day dragged and Adele was willing the time to pass so that she could see Glynn again. She kept staring at the wall clock, concerned when it reached five past six. Irritated with herself for being so keen, she decided she would give it another five minutes before she gave up on him and set off for home alone. Then she heard him; his confident, masculine steps heading up the corridor. When his face appeared at the door she actually felt butterflies in her stomach.

'It's your very own Prince Charming, come to escort you home,' he joked, and she couldn't resist smiling at him.

'I'll just pack my files away,' she said.

'OK, fine.' He plonked himself on a corner of her desk and folded his arms.

While she packed, she could feel his eyes on her the whole time. Adele shuffled her papers about self-consciously, slipping them clumsily into the files. Under his intense gaze she seemed to have lost control of her fingers and could feel herself becoming flustered.

'Do you want any help?' he asked.

Adele noticed the wide grin on his face. He knew the effect he had on her and was enjoying it, she thought. In the end, she left some of the files out, grabbed her bag and headed to the door, anxious to be out of his line of vision.

Within no time she could feel him close behind her and as she opened the door into the corridor she could feel his hot breath on the back of her neck. It sent a quiver down her spine and she cursed herself for wearing her hair up today.

When they arrived downstairs, he took his car keys out of his pocket and they walked to his BMW. 'No buses for you tonight,' he said. 'You're travelling in style.'

She smiled again and got into the car. While he drove she stared out of the window, only turning her head occasionally to give directions. She was too embarrassed to meet his gaze.

'Here we are, your ladyship,' he joked as he pulled up outside her home in Chorlton.

The area differed from that of her childhood home. The streets were wider, the houses bigger and the roads lined by trees. Many of the Victorian houses were now occupied by students and graduates who had stayed in the area.

Her home was inside a large Victorian house, which

had been turned into flats. There was a narrow path, then three stone steps up to the main front door. On either side of the path was a low brick wall with tall hedging, which obscured the view of the front door from the road.

'Car park's at the back,' she said. 'I'll show you.' Then she indicated a driveway to one side of the brick wall.

When Glynn had parked the car she let them into the building and they climbed the stairs to her first-floor flat. While she walked up the stairs she could feel a protective hand on the small of her back. It sent a tingle throughout her body. She was deliberating what to do when they reached her flat. As she approached the front door, she became more and more aware of the situation till finally she turned and spoke to him.

'OK, I'll be fine now,' she babbled.

'You sure?' he asked.

Adele noted the raised eyebrow and the smirk on his face, and she was tempted. She wanted him yet she should resist. Then he moved into her, his lips seeking hers. She could feel her body yielding to him but her mouth stayed tightly clamped. Then she swiftly pulled away just as his lips grazed hers and a moment before it was too late.

'Like that, is it?' he asked as another sexy grin flashed across his handsome face.

Temporarily foiled but unperturbed, it seemed, he acknowledged her goodbye then walked away. Adele shut the door quickly before she changed her mind, and she willed her pounding heartbeat to slow down. Phew! She felt a rush of blood warm her face and neck when she realised just how close she'd come to giving in to him. And if she had done, who knows where she would have stopped?

She stood motionless next to her front door for a few seconds, recalling the lines of his handsome features and his masculine yet sensual gestures, and a warm glow lit her from within. Despite the temptation, she'd resisted him for now. But next time, she couldn't be sure that she'd have the power to do so again.

40

Sandra was the manageress of one of Peter's sunbed salons, Super Sol Tanning Salon. It was located in Heaton Moor, an area where people had a bit of extra money to splash out on little luxuries. Super Sol was also one of Peter's more profitable sunbed businesses. Sandra did a good job and, as the manageress of a sunbed salon, she looked the part.

In her late thirties, Sandra was one of those women who made desperate attempts to slow down the passage of time and tried to make the best of herself. Her blonde mid-length permed hair was always immaculate, her nails finely manicured and her make-up perfect. And she was permanently tanned, which made her an excellent advert for the business.

This particular evening she was the last one in the shop. As the day drew to a close, business slowed down so she let her assistant finish early. Her other assistant was away on holiday.

Although Sandra enjoyed her job, she still looked forward to the end of the day when she could finally shut up shop and go home to a restful evening. She was just tidying things away when three large men wearing hoodies walked through the door. She looked up in alarm, knowing that nobody was due to visit; Peter's men had already been to collect the takings.

'Sorry, but we're shut,' she said, although she somehow knew that these men weren't here to use the sunbeds, and a cold tremor of fear shot through her.

The last of the three to enter the shop turned the sign in the shop window from 'Open' to 'Closed'. Then he bolted the door and drew down the blinds. Sandra stared in terror as the other two men approached her.

'Get in the back!' one of the men ordered, grabbing her arm roughly and marching her through the shop.

Sandra tried to resist but she knew it was pointless. They were all bigger and stronger than she was. She let out a terrified screech but the man clamped his hand across her mouth.

Once they were in the back room he pushed her forcefully and she landed on the floor with a thump. Sandra was about to protest until the man spoke.

'You'll keep your fuckin' mouth shut if you know what's good for you!' he said.

She drew back from the men into a corner of the room and sat rubbing her knee where it had hit the floor. 'We haven't come for the takings,' said the first man. He nodded at the other two who stepped towards Sandra.

'No, please!' she screamed as one of the men lunged forward and aimed a fierce kick at her abdomen.

Sandra curled into a ball, covering her face with her arms, while the men laid into her. She sobbed and squealed as she felt every fierce blow from them. When they stopped Sandra remained in a ball, dreading that there might be worse to come. Then she felt her hair being yanked from behind while the first man pulled her head back till she was facing him.

'Please, no!' she begged, looking up at his savage features.

'I'm not here for you, you stupid bitch!' he spat. 'This is a message for your boss. Let him know that Alan has just fuckin' evened the score. You got that?' he yelled, smacking her across the face.

'Yes,' Sandra sobbed.

Then the man turned to the other two. 'OK, carry on,' he said.

Sandra didn't have a chance to cover her face this time. The two men dashed forward in a brutal attack, which left her lying bruised and battered in the secluded back room of the shop.

Peter dashed round to Super Sol Tanning Salon as soon as he received the distressed call from Sandra, stopping only to collect Glynn on the way. When he arrived, he saw that the door to the street was slightly ajar and he and Glynn ran in.

Peter could see that the reception area was empty. He and Glynn hurried through the shop, searching each of the tanning booths and calling out Sandra's name.

'In here,' came a small timid voice from the back room.

Peter and Glynn exchanged concerned glances and ran in search of Sandra. She was sitting down, her head bent forward. Peter could see that Sandra's usually immaculate blonde waves were streaked vermilion and matted, and there were blood stains in the corner of the room.

He walked up to her and gently whispered her name. She looked up; her blood-spattered, swollen face was streaked with tears and her eyes were darkened pools of fear. Peter had to stop himself from flinching at the sight of her bloody, bruised face.

'Who did this to you?' he asked.

'I don't know,' sobbed Sandra, 'but they sent a message. Something about Alan evening the score.'

'Shit!' Peter cursed, then he asked, 'What did they look like?'

As he had expected, the descriptions of two of the men fitted Alan and David to a T. How could they do this? Then he thought about what Glynn and Mike had done to Sam and it made sense.

'Come on, love. Let's get you home,' said Glynn.

Peter secured the shop as they left, and Glynn led a trembling Sandra to the car. Peter knew that Sandra would never set foot in the place again. It would be far too traumatic for her.

They deposited Sandra at home and made sure she had someone to stay with her. Before they left, Peter took a wad of notes out of his wallet.

'I'd prefer it if you kept all this quiet,' he said, handing Sandra the money. 'If there's anything you need, anything at all, just ask. OK?'

Sandra nodded. A few seconds later the doorbell rang. 'That'll be my sister,' she said.

'OK. We'll let her in on our way out,' said Peter. 'And don't forget what I told you.'

He and Glynn then turned and walked away.

'We can't fuckin' take this lying down,' said Glynn when they were inside the car.

'I know,' said Peter. 'It's a fuckin' liberty.'

'What you gonna do then?' Glynn demanded.

'I don't know. Let me have a think. It's no good rushing at this. I need to think carefully about it. But, at the moment, I need a fuckin' drink.'

'Me, too,' said Glynn. 'We'll chat about it in the club but we can't afford to let them get away with it. Otherwise who knows what other fuckin' liberties they're gonna take?'

'I said I'll think about it!' Peter snapped, the strain of the situation getting to him.

Glynn didn't reply so Peter left it at that for the time being. He tried to keep his mind on his driving rather than the violent acts of retaliation Glynn would expect him to carry out on Alan's gang. As his eyes studied the road, he didn't notice the steely look of fury on Glynn's face.

41

Adele wasn't looking her best when she answered the door that Saturday morning. She was busy unpacking boxes full of items she'd accumulated since starting work for Peter. Determined to put the flat into some sort of order as soon as possible, she'd grabbed a pair of old jeans and a tatty T-shirt and put them on without taking a shower. She'd do that later once the work was out of the way, then change into something more becoming. Her hair was also tied up chaotically in a bright orange scrunchy that she'd found lying around.

God, she hated moving home! It would be weeks before she could remember where she'd put all her things. While she worked, Adele toyed with the idea of going to the club that evening, depending on how tired she was. She might even accidentally bump into Glynn. On second thoughts, perhaps it wasn't a good idea.

When the doorbell rang Adele was in the middle of emptying a large box and placing her crockery and cutlery in her kitchen cupboards. She tutted as she raced to answer the door, leaving a pile of discarded plates on the kitchen surface.

'Glynn!' she said, surprised to find his handsome face beaming at her from the doorway. She patted her hair, conscious of what a mess she must look. 'I–I wasn't expecting visitors.'

'No worries,' he said.

'Erm, come in,' she said, pulling the door open. 'I'll make us a brew.'

He followed her through to the kitchen. 'Excuse the mess,' she said. 'I'm still trying to get the place in order.'

He smiled again. 'Will you stop fretting? Everything looks fine, and you look great. I thought you might need some help; that's why I called round.'

'Really?' she said, secretly suspecting it was just a pretext. 'But you might mess up those smart jeans.'

'Do I look as though I'd be bothered by a bit of dust on my jeans?' he asked.

This time she smiled. 'Suppose not,' she said.

When the kettle boiled she asked, 'Do you take sugar?'

'Yes, one spoonful,' he said.

'Damn,' she said. 'I can't remember if I've put the sugar away.'

She looked around the bottom shelf of the cupboard but couldn't spot it at first glance.

'It's there,' Glynn said, pointing to the shelf above.

Adele looked up and saw it behind some jars just as Glynn stepped behind her and reached up to the shelf. She turned round, leaving him to get the sugar. Then she became conscious of his close proximity and tried to step aside but his broad frame blocked her way. He smiled at her awkwardness. For a few moments they remained still, the atmosphere between them electric.

Glynn pulled out the bag of sugar and put it down. But he remained where he was. He kept smiling, his eyes lingering on her. It felt like a force field between them, drawing her in. She was growing weaker, finding him harder to resist. Adele could feel herself blush, knowing that he felt it too. She was about to ask him to let her pass. Then his lips came to meet hers.

As their lips touched, Adele felt herself being pulled in to his passionate embrace. The lure of his kiss and the heat of his masculine body felt so good, and she wanted more. As the kiss grew deeper and more intense, his hands began to explore her curves. Ripples of pleasure flowed through her skin, under her flesh and deep inside her.

His lips moved down to her throat, nuzzling it, and she could feel herself responding. When he slipped his hand under her bra and toyed with her nipple she thought she would explode with pleasure. Then he smoothed his hands under her buttocks, caressing them in a slow, gentle movement.

As she gasped with desire, he gripped her buttocks

tightly and lifted her. She gripped her arms around his neck as he walked her through to the bedroom and laid her down on the bed. He lifted her T-shirt from her and she loosened her hair, feeling it tumble wantonly about her shoulders as she watched him unbutton his jeans.

When he stripped off her jeans and slipped his fingers inside her, she gasped. His fingers explored her moist insides then he drew them out and entered her. She screamed with delight as he plunged himself deep inside her. Wave after wave of intense pleasure rose through her body, sending a thrill that reached every extremity till her head tingled and her legs grew weak.

Then it was over. She lay in his arms, their bodies slick with perspiration. His thick arms enfolded her, comforting and protective, and she sighed.

'You OK?' he asked.

'Mmm,' she hummed.

He laughed. 'Are we having that cuppa then?'

She giggled in response. 'In a minute,' she said. 'I just want to stay like this for a bit.'

It had been so long since she'd had a man. She'd forgotten how good it felt. And now that she'd given in to him, she wanted more. Her decision was made. She was powerless to resist him anymore. And now she was his.

It had been fast and furious; very different from her sexual experiences with her former lover, John. Glynn was a dominant lover but she'd found it strangely erotic, maybe because she'd gone such a long time without the feel of a man.

But, as she thought later about how rough he'd been with her, she felt slightly unnerved. She pushed the thought aside. Glynn had a way of setting her alight and she couldn't wait till the next time she saw him and he took her again.

'Come in,' shouted Peter when he heard the knock on his office door.

It was Max. Peter had been expecting him and was just about to utter a greeting but something about Max's bearing stopped him. He looked ill and years older than the last time Peter had seen him, only a few weeks ago. As Max walked into the office, he seemed to be finding it an effort to drag one foot in front of the other and he was panting from the walk upstairs.

The usual ruddiness in Max's cheeks had almost disappeared. Now his colouring was mostly pallid with a small dot of pink on the apple of each cheek. Peter guessed that the dot of colour must have been a result of the exertion on climbing the stairs. It was accompanied by the usual sheen of sweat, which covered Max's face.

'Have a seat, Max. What's the problem?' Peter asked, because it was obvious from his appearance that there was a problem.

'Thanks,' said Max, pulling out the seat opposite

Peter's. As he sat down he let out a weary breath and his shoulders sagged. 'Them bloody stairs will be the death of me,' he commented.

Peter waited for him to gather himself before he told him what he was here for. Max didn't often visit the club these days, preferring to leave things in Peter's hands, so whatever it was, it must be important.

'I'm not so good, Pete,' he said. 'My liver's buggered. I've been going through tests for a while but I didn't want to tell you anything till I knew for sure. Anyway, it's cirrhosis.'

'Jesus, Max, that's bad news, mate!' said Peter.

'I know. It's shit.'

'Is there anything they can do for it?'

'Not really, no. They keep hassling me to give up the drink but it's too bleeding late for that. The way I see it is, I won't be around that much longer so I might as well enjoy it while I'm here.'

'I'm really sorry to hear that, mate,' said Peter and, although he was genuinely sorry, he knew that Max's deteriorating health would also have an impact on the nightclub business so he waited to see what else Max had to say.

'Anyway, I'm giving up the nightclub altogether so if you want to buy the other 50 per cent I'm giving you first option.'

'Jesus!' said Peter, taken aback. 'Yeah, I'd love to.' Then he tried to curb his over-enthusiasm in view of

Max's poor health. 'I mean, I wouldn't want the club to get into the wrong hands and it would be much easier all round if I was the only one running the show. But I haven't got that kind of cash to stump up just now.'

'You don't need to pay it all at once,' said Max. 'I'm happy to sign the bloody lot over to you now. Then you can pay me back monthly out of the profits. Call it a loan.'

'I don't know what to say,' said Peter, genuinely taken aback. 'That's really generous of you.'

'Think nothing of it,' said Max. 'I'll still be around for a bit if you want any advice about anything but I'm too bloody ill to get involved. I like the way you run things, Pete, so I'd prefer you to take over ownership rather than any other bugger, if I'm honest. Besides, your loan repayments will give me some income to help me see out my days.'

'Don't talk like that, Max,' said Peter. He'd grown quite fond of the old guy since he'd become part-owner of the Golden Bell.

'Why not? It's the bloody truth,' Max replied. 'No point beating about the bush. It is what it is.' He paused for a moment, waiting for Peter's response, but when he didn't say anything, Max added, 'Well, that's that then. So, if we're agreed, let's sort out the figures and for Christ's sake let's have a drink to celebrate.'

Peter looked at Max and smiled. He was glad Max was being so matter-of-fact. He wasn't given to big emotional displays himself and had struggled with how to react to Max's sad news.

But Max had made it easy for him. Instead of being maudlin, Max had turned it into a celebration. And, in a way it was. Max was retiring and Peter was about to become 100 per cent owner of one of the most popular clubs in Manchester. That would help to cement his reputation on the Manchester nightclubbing scene as well as throughout the Manchester gangland fraternity.

42

After a few days Peter reached a decision about Alan. Retaliation was pointless. They would just go on targeting each other's businesses and employees, and where would that end? Nobody would come out as the winner. So Peter decided that the best way of dealing with things would be to have a meeting with Alan and see if they could sort things out, man to man. After all, he had once been a friend so maybe he could get him to see reason.

'You sure this is what you want to do?' asked Glynn as they drove to the Sportsman's with two heavies in the back of the car.

'Seems like the best way to sort it out,' said Peter. As he glanced over at Glynn he thought he detected a look of disdain. 'Don't you agree?'

'Yeah, sure. You're the boss and you know the guy so perhaps you can talk some fuckin' sense into him.'

When they arrived at the Sportsman's, Peter said to

Glynn, 'Leave the talking to me.' Then he turned to the two heavies. 'You two come in with us, but stay by the door. We don't want to wind anyone up unless we have to.'

Again Peter noticed that look of scorn on Glynn's face and, although he wasn't saying anything, Peter felt that Glynn would have handled things differently. He could appreciate his point of view but violence wasn't always the answer. Besides, he and Alan went back a long way so he was a bit perturbed at the way Alan had teamed up with David. He secretly hoped he could make him see sense.

They walked inside the Sportsman's and the two heavies stayed at the door as instructed. But the customers had noticed, and as Peter crossed the room with Glynn he could feel all eyes on them.

'That's him, the hard-looking one in the corner,' he whispered to Glynn, who stuck to him tightly.

Peter noticed David sitting next to Alan, with several others in the same corner of the room. As he drew nearer to the table where they were sitting, David's eyes locked with his. The look was hostile – venomous, even – and Peter tried to hide the disquiet that tugged at his insides.

'Hi, Alan, David,' he greeted, nodding at the others as well to let them know it was a friendly visit. 'Can we have a chat, Alan?' he asked.

'Fire away,' said Alan, leaning back confidently in his seat.

'In private,' added Peter.

'There's nowt you can say to me that you can't say in front of my friends.'

Peter noticed Alan's use of the word 'friends' rather than 'employees' or 'men'. 'OK,' he said. 'I'm here to ask you to back off our businesses.'

Alan sniffed. 'Don't know what you're talking about,' he responded casually.

'I think you do, Alan.' Peter then took a deep breath, trying to stay calm. 'Look, I'm not here for trouble,' he said. 'I'm asking you nicely to leave my businesses alone.'

'And what makes them yours, exactly?' asked Alan with a smug look on his face.

'Come on, Alan. You know how it works. Everyone knows we look after them. There are plenty of others you can collect from.'

'Well, you're not doing a very good job of looking after them, are you? When my men walked into the George and Dragon, Pat practically fuckin' begged us to take the money.'

Peter noticed the sly grin on David's face as Alan spoke. He sighed, then said, 'Look, Alan. What is it you want? I've offered you an in with the firm. There's still a place for you if you want it.'

'And what about Dave? Is there a place for him?' Alan snapped.

'You know the answer to that one,' Peter said, glancing across at David.

'Yeah, because that bastard stitched me up!' shouted David, nodding towards Glynn.

'You stitched your fuckin' self up, you loser,' Glynn retaliated.

David got up out of his chair. 'You know that's a fuckin' lie!' he shouted, pointing viciously at Glynn.

Glynn made a move towards David but Peter held him back. 'Leave it, Glynn,' he said. 'We've come here to sort things out, not to make more fuckin' aggro.' Then he turned to Alan again. 'What's your answer?'

'It's a no. I don't like the fuckin' company you keep. And did you really think I'd want to work with you after what those tossers did to Sam?' Alan said, eyeing Glynn.

Peter ignored Alan's reference to Sam, knowing that he couldn't find words to excuse what Glynn and Mike had done. He could have mentioned what Alan's gang had done to Sandra, but that would only inflame the situation. Instead he said, 'Right, if you don't wanna work for me then fair enough, but I'm asking you one last time to leave our businesses alone.'

'Or else?' asked David.

'Repercussions,' said Glynn, with a sinister air.

This time Alan stood up. 'Fuckin' bring it on!' he yelled.

Glynn lunged towards him but Peter managed to hold him back. He nodded to his men at the door who dashed over. 'Grab him,' he said, between gritted teeth.

The two heavies got hold of Glynn and pulled him towards the exit while Alan and David sprang forward menacingly. Peter held up a placatory hand. 'It's OK, we're going,' he said.

He waited till he was halfway across the room then, to save face, he turned round and added, 'This isn't the end of it, Alan. But don't forget, I tried to do things nicely and you wouldn't fuckin' have it.'

Glynn waited till they were outside before addressing Peter. 'What the fuck you playin' at?' he yelled, when the two heavies let go of him. He swiped his hands viciously down his suit, smoothing imaginary creases where the heavies had gripped him. 'You made yourself look a right fuckin' mug! And me, too.'

'Did I fuck!' said Peter. 'I told you to keep out of it. You've just wound Alan up more.'

'He needs to know the lie of the fuckin' land!' raged Glynn. 'They think you're a soft twat.'

'No they don't!' Peter retaliated. 'I told him that wasn't the fuckin' end of it.'

'So, what have you got planned then?' Glynn asked, sarcastically.

'I don't know,' said Peter, his frustration showing. 'I'll think of something. Don't worry; he ain't fuckin' getting away with it.'

'Well, you better fuckin' had do,' warned Glynn.

'What the fuck's that supposed to mean?' Peter countered, but Glynn kept quiet. 'Look,' continued Peter, 'just 'cos you're well in with our Adele, don't think you're running the show now.' There was a look of surprise on Glynn's face. 'Yeah, I fuckin' know,' Peter added, looking down his nose at Glynn.

'She's got fuck all to do with anything!' snapped Glynn. 'I know you don't like me seeing her 'cos of my past but, at the end of the day, Pete, she's just an ex-con like the rest of us.'

'No she fuckin' isn't!' Peter ranted. 'Our Adele's been through a lot so you better not shit on her.'

'I wasn't gonna. Anyway, she's not a kid, y'know; she's capable of making her own decisions. Why you being so fuckin' protective?'

Peter didn't respond. Glynn had hit a nerve. He didn't know everything about Adele and her past, and there was no way Peter was going to be the one to break it to him.

Thoughts began to flash through his mind about everything he and his sister had been through. The years of abuse at their father's hands. His drunken rages. The cruel way he had treated their mother, which finally culminated in Adele killing him in a violent frenzy. And as Peter recalled their troubled childhood, he capitulated. Maybe he had overreacted because of his over-protectiveness towards his sister.

'OK,' he said. 'Having a go at each other isn't gonna get us anywhere. I've given Alan the chance to back off. If he won't take a friendly warning then he'll have to fuckin' do it the hard way. Don't worry, he won't get away with taking over our businesses. I'll fuckin' fix him.'

That seemed to pacify Glynn, who stayed quiet for the journey back, but Peter glanced at him once or twice. His face was stern, his eyes alight from the fire within him, and Peter couldn't help but wonder what was going on inside his head.

David looked across at Alan and chuckled. 'I bet you're quaking in your fuckin' boots, aren't you?' he asked, sarcastically.

'What do you think?' said Alan.

'So, what's the upshot?' asked one of the other men.

Alan sniffed and looked at all the men seated around the table, then spoke loudly. 'The upshot is this…' When he had got everyone's attention he continued, 'We stick to the fuckin' plan.'

'Aren't you worried about repercussions?' asked the man.

'Do I look fuckin' worried?' asked Alan, the fury evident in his tone of voice.

'Alan doesn't scare easily,' sniggered David.

'If anyone's fuckin' worried, it's Pete,' Alan said.

'That's why he came here with his goons. Like that was gonna fuckin' scare me!' He looked around at his men again, holding the gaze of one or two of them until they shuffled uncomfortably in their seats. 'Anyway, he might try to hit back, especially if that prick that was with him has anything to do with it, so I want you all to be vigilant. Go around in pairs. Don't walk about alone; get taxis. You know the drill.'

The men nodded. 'I don't want another fuckin' repeat of Sam,' said Alan. 'But if they think they're gonna just walk in here and talk us round after what they did to him, then they're fuckin' mistaken. Like I said, we stick to the plan. Pete and his crew won't know what's fuckin' hit 'em.'

43

'So, how did it go?' Mike asked Glynn.

'It was a fuckin' joke!' Glynn replied. 'I don't know what's got into Pete but I think he's turned fuckin' soft. He was practically begging 'em to leave our businesses alone. That Alan's no fuckin' mug either. There's no way he'll take any notice of anything Pete says.'

'I thought they were mates.'

'Yeah, years ago, but there's no fuckin' way they're mates now. There's already bad blood between Pete and Dave ever since he fired him. But this Alan has definitely taken Dave's side. He didn't show an ounce of fuckin' respect for Pete.'

'I told you that Alan was a tosser,' said Mike. 'I couldn't fuckin' stand him when we were inside.'

'Yeah, but he's no mug either. He'll carry on doing what the fuck he likes unless we do something to stop him.'

'Why aren't we doing it, then?'

'We are. Pete says he's gonna come up with something.'

'And do you believe him?'

Glynn only shrugged.

'I told you before, Glynn, you'd make a better fuckin' leader than Pete. He's handling this all wrong.'

Glynn looked away, deep in thought. He agreed with what Mike was saying. He'd been feeling it for a while and this latest turn of events had made him doubt Peter's leadership skills even more. The guy was out of his depth.

But he was also the brother of his latest squeeze and, although Glynn didn't like to admit it to himself, he was a bit taken with her. He wasn't gonna let anyone else know that, though, especially Adele. It didn't pay to show his softer side to anyone, but she was getting under his skin. And there was no way he could keep things sweet with Adele if he stitched up her brother.

He looked back across at Mike. 'Let's see what he's gonna come up with. He said he'd fix this fuckin' Alan, so let's wait to find out what happens.'

'And what if he does fuck all?' asked Mike.

'Then me and you will have another little chat and decide where we take it from there,' said Glynn.

He stared at Mike for several seconds after speaking, his eyes fixed on him while the contours of his face were set in hard lines. It was his way of letting Mike know that he meant exactly what he said. Although he didn't want to upset things while he was with Adele, Glynn knew that he'd rather take action than see the firm go to shit. He'd just bide his time and, when the time was right, he'd make his move.

Peter had been mulling things over in his mind for a few days. He was in a predicament for sure and the pressure was on him to do something. In fact, he was under pressure from all sides.

Alan's reaction had surprised him when he had met him. Gone was their friendship and trust. Instead Alan had made it clear that he was now firmly set against him. For whatever reason, he had taken David's side. Not only that, he'd started his own crew and was out to prove himself.

Peter knew from experience that Alan was a sharp operator; intelligent, too. He had always been the smart one when they were kids, and was a natural leader. Alan was a great guy to have onside but it wouldn't pay to have him as an adversary. Peter couldn't just sit by and let Alan take over his businesses; he'd worked too hard for what he had.

But he didn't want their rivalry to escalate either. After Sam's death and what had happened to Sandra, things were already bad enough.

It would have been easy to retaliate, as Glynn

would have done. All he needed to do was give the order and he had plenty of willing men who would do whatever was necessary. But that would also have been dangerous.

Peter had learnt over the years that you had to put some thought behind your actions, and he wasn't stupid enough to keep sacrificing his people in a war that no one would win. And although Peter didn't like to think he was scared of repercussions, knowing Alan as he did, he feared that if he was pitched in a war with Alan then he might not come off the victor.

Peter was also worried about his own men. He knew Glynn was a threat, and that Glynn and Mike were tight. As their leader he had to demonstrate his authority. He had to let them know he wouldn't be made a mug of. He'd already made a mistake in trying to appeal to Alan's better nature. As a result he'd lost face in front of both Alan's men and his own.

He cursed himself for taking Glynn and his men to the meeting. It would have been better if he and Alan had met one to one in private. Then he wouldn't have had all those people witnessing his humiliation. And maybe, with no one around to impress, Alan might have been more reasonable.

Eventually, after a few days of deliberation, he did what he should have done in the first place, and approached Alan alone. They arranged a meeting, just the two of them, in a pub that none of their men frequented. As he took one last look at his watch and saw it was time to go, Peter tried to ignore the pang of disquiet that sat in the pit of his stomach.

When Peter arrived in the pub there was no sign of Alan so he bought himself a drink and sat and waited. And waited. Twenty minutes after their arranged time Alan finally breezed into the pub, appearing casual and unfazed. Peter knew it was an act, deliberately designed to throw him off kilter, but it still got to him.

Peter watched as Alan bought himself a drink then sauntered over to the table where he was sitting. He stood up to greet him but Alan slid into the chair opposite without any acknowledgement, then remained quiet and gazed around the room.

'How's things?' asked Peter when the silence threatened to engulf him.

Alan sighed deeply. 'Let's just cut the crap and get on with it, shall we?'

Peter was taken aback but tried to hide it. Part of him wanted things to be like old times. Planning jobs together. The rush of excitement. The thrill of escape. The banter between him, Alan and Dave.

But he knew those days were gone and any attempt at friendly chat would be taken as a sign of weakness. So, instead, he did what he had come here to do. He reached under the table and pulled out the bag holding the money.

'It's all there,' he said. 'You can go in the men's and count it if you like.'

'No, it's OK,' said Alan. 'I'll take your word for it, but you know what'll happen if it's short.'

Alan's eyes penetrated deep into him, but Peter held his gaze, refusing to be intimidated.

'OK,' said Peter. 'Well, like I said on the phone, it's a one-off payment. If any of our businesses get touched or any of my staff get harmed after this then it's all-out fuckin' war and none of us will win.'

'Yeah, I heard you,' said Alan, continuing to stare intently at Peter. Then he downed the remainder of his drink in one fast swig, slammed down his glass and waltzed out of the place.

Peter stared after him, hoping to God he had done the right thing. It had been a private arrangement between the two of them on the understanding that nobody else was to find out about it. Peter couldn't afford for anyone to know, especially Glynn.

While he was thinking about it, Peter decided that he'd break the news of their stand-off to Glynn next, without mentioning the money, so he left the pub and headed back to the club. He found Glynn there, standing at the bar with Adele by his side.

'Can I have a private word, Glynn?' he asked.

'Sure.' Glynn patted Adele on the knee. 'See you in a bit,' he said before he followed Peter to the upstairs office.

'It's sorted,' said Peter, once they were both sitting down.

'How d'you mean?' asked Glynn.

'Me and Alan have had a little chat,' said Peter. 'He knows the score. He daren't muck about with us anymore. He knows what will fuckin' happen if he does.'

Peter saw Glynn raise an eyebrow in surprise, and knew that he had risen in his estimation. But there was still a little doubt there. 'Fair enough, but he doesn't strike me as the type of bloke who scares easily,' Glynn said.

'He isn't but he's not fuckin' stupid either. He knows what happened to Sam, don't forget. So, I just explained to him that there'll be more of that unless he backs off. And, after all, we've got a much bigger firm. He knows they'd come off worst.'

Glynn nodded at Peter, a smile of admiration now lighting up his face. 'Nice one,' he said. 'Well done.' Then he stood up, patted Peter on the back and left him alone.

Peter heaved a sigh of relief once Glynn was gone. He'd pulled it off, and not only did it mean that Alan's crew would back off but it also meant he wouldn't lose face in front of his men. He just hoped to God that Glynn would never find out the real reason Alan had agreed to all this.

44

Adele had been seeing Glynn for a few weeks. She had spent the past few hours in the club with Glynn, drinking wine, dancing and having fun, and now she was tipsy. When Glynn suggested they went upstairs for a bit of privacy she went willingly.

Once they were inside her office, she shut the door and walked over to him. They began to kiss passionately, their hands exploring each other's bodies. Adele felt a tingle as Glynn put his hands inside her top and caressed her nipples through the flimsy material of her bra. Then he moved his hands round to her back, and slipped them down to her buttocks, which he clasped firmly.

When Adele responded with a low moan, Glynn slid his hands down her thighs, lifted her skirt and pulled down her underwear. He raised his hands to her buttocks once more then lifted her and placed her on the edge of the desk. Within no time, he had dropped his pants and flung her legs wide. Then he entered her. It was over in a matter of seconds, leaving Adele deflated.

During the few weeks since Adele had started seeing Glynn their relationship had changed and she had learnt a lot about him. Gone was the contrition he had shown after he had shot a man to death. Instead she was noticing that he had a menacing air about him when he was dealing with people in the club. It was carefully disguised but, nevertheless, it was there.

His threats were veiled, his intimidation manifested through a hard stare, narrowed eyes or a screwed-up face when things weren't going his way. Despite this, Adele was drawn to him, and in some ways, the fact that he was so powerful was a bit of a turn-on for her.

But she was beginning to realise that the relationship wasn't perfect. There was the love making, for example. She had thought that the urgency of their first time had been the result of the sexual tension that had built up over the preceding weeks. She expected him to slow down once they got together, to become more tender, but he hadn't done.

Every time had been the same. There was no delicate embrace, no thoughtful caress; it was just fast and frantic with an overriding urge to satisfy himself as soon as possible.

Nevertheless, they were growing closer in other ways. She was his woman and he was very protective towards her. Their conversations were also becoming more intimate as they found out more about each other.

Adele wanted to get closer to Glynn; perhaps to achieve something that was missing in their love making. As she felt the disappointing after-effects of their brief sexual encounter, she held him tightly to her, drawing comfort from the warmth of his body.

Adele decided she had reached the stage in a relationship where confidences were shared. She therefore thought the time was right to tell him about her past. But it was a hell of a thing to divulge. After a few drinks, though, in spite of her apprehension, she was feeling brave enough.

'Glynn, there's something I need to tell you,' she began.

'Oh, yeah?' he asked, seeming disinterested.

'Yes, I've been meaning to for a while. But... well... the time just never seemed right,' she said, sitting up and releasing her hold on him so she could look into his eyes. 'You see, it's about me. Something I did... You probably knew I'd been inside when I came to work for Peter.'

'He did mention it, yeah.'

'Did you know what I'd been inside for?'

'No, but I gather it was a long stretch so I'm assuming you weren't nicked for stealing a loaf of bread.' He smiled as he said these last few words.

His blasé attitude caught her off guard. She was

trying to tell him something serious – something life-changing – yet he was acting as though they were sharing a joke.

'I killed my dad!' she blurted out, her frustration getting the better of her.

'Shit! That is bad,' he said.

'Yes, and I've lived with the burden of it ever since. It was one night. He'd beaten my mother up something shocking...'

Glynn held up his hand to silence her. 'Adele, it's OK. I understand. I know what it's like, remember?'

Her mind went back to the night when he'd shot a man outside her office because he'd held a knife to her throat. 'Yes, but this was different,' she said. 'I went too far. I couldn't help myself. I just lost it. I started hitting him with something and I couldn't stop.'

As she relived the event, she could feel herself getting worked up. Her voice broke as tears threatened to overwhelm her.

Glynn moved forward and put a hand on her shoulder. 'Don't beat yourself up over it,' he said. 'You did what you had to do. From what you've just said, it sounds like the old bastard deserved it. I bet you were pushed, weren't you?'

She nodded.

'There you go, then. If it's any comfort, that guy at the club wasn't the only one I saw off. And sometimes you have to get pretty bloody callous to show people that you won't be fucked around with.'

'How d'you mean?' she asked, her voice almost a whisper. She was shocked at this unexpected change in the tone of the conversation.

'You just do what you have to do,' he said. 'Especially when someone betrays you or betrays the people you work for.'

Adele sat silently for some moments, taking in his words. She couldn't believe he was being so casual about killing people. Then a recollection flashed through her mind: the news report about Sam. She felt a jolt as anxiety flooded her body.

'Did Sam betray you?' she asked, fearing that she already knew the answer.

'He betrayed Pete, and I work for Pete.'

'So, Sam's death. Was that you?'

'I was involved, yeah. He betrayed us. Sometimes people do things and we have to punish them. It was the same for you, wasn't it? You're just like me, aren't you?'

Adele thought over what she'd heard in the news about Sam; the fact that he was cruelly tortured and died an agonising death. Could her brother really have condoned the violent murder of an ex-employee? A feeling of panic zipped through her and she had an overwhelming urge to vomit.

To think that Glynn claimed to have been involved in

Sam's brutal killing because he betrayed Peter was more than she could handle. This was the man she was going out with. The man she'd just had sex with! She put her hand over her mouth and tried to stifle her gagging reflex. The thought sickened her and she quickly drew herself away from him.

'No, I'm not like you. I'm not like you at all!' she yelled. 'It was one moment of madness and I've regretted it ever since. And I'll go on regretting it for every day of my stinking, miserable life! I was pushed. I didn't mean to do it but I was pushed. But you! You're callous and you're calculating... and, and... you're just fuckin' cruel!'

'Eh, come on,' he said, touching her arm.

'Don't you dare touch me!' she raged. 'You disgust me.'

Adele jumped down from the desk, knocking over the wastepaper bin in her haste to get away. Then she ran through the building and out of the door into the street. It was raining heavily but she didn't stop running till she was well away from the club.

She leant against a wall, her shoulders sagging and her head bowed. The rain drenched her clothing and dripped from the sodden locks of her hair. She was panting heavily and it took her some time before her breathing steadied.

As she stood there in the rain she thought about the

sort of person Glynn was, of the shocking things he had done. She retched and she continued retching until her stomach was empty.

When she had finished vomiting she straightened herself up. But it was some moments before she had recovered enough to move from that spot. Tears ran down her face. Sticky mucus and vomit were pasted around her lips, and her rain-soaked clothing clung to her body.

But her tears weren't just because she had lost Glynn. They were mainly for herself. And as she thought about what her life had come to, she sobbed so hard that her body juddered.

No matter how much she tried she could never escape from her tortured past. And although she was sickened at the thought of what Glynn had done, was she really any different? Because, no matter what her reasons, she had killed, too. And in the most brutal way.

Would she ever be able to move on or would her past actions affect the rest of her life? Maybe she would always attract men like Glynn: cold-bloodied killers who made it their business to kill. Perhaps she just wasn't good enough for anyone decent.

Eventually, she came to her senses. Realising what a sight she must look, she took a tissue out of her handbag and wiped her face. Then she went in search of a taxi to take her home. She needed to confront her brother about the things Glynn had told her. But at the moment she couldn't face going back into the club. All she wanted was to get away.

In the morning, when she had calmed down, she would have a good think about what to do. Things had changed for her now that she knew what Glynn really was. And the fact that her brother had employed somebody like that made things a whole lot worse.

But what Adele didn't know was that the man she had allowed into her bed was about to become a far bigger enemy to her and Peter than anybody she had ever had to stand up to during all her traumatic years behind bars.

45

It was Monday morning. Adele had spent the weekend going over what Glynn had told her on Friday night, when she had last seen him. Instead of rushing round to Peter's apartment to confront him the following day she had waited until now. She needed time to recover from the initial shock and to think about how to tackle Peter.

When she arrived at work, Peter was already there.

'All right, sis?' he greeted when he saw her walking into his office. Then he smiled. 'You're a bit late, aren't you?' he said. 'I was beginning to think you weren't bothering.'

'I wasn't in a rush,' she said, her face stern and her tone detached.

The smile slipped from his face, replaced by a look of concern as he picked up on her mood. 'What's wrong?'

She took a seat across the desk from him and took a deep, calming breath. 'It's about Glynn,' she began.

'Aah, I thought you'd had a barney when you

disappeared from the club on Friday night. But I decided to leave you to it. I'm not one to interfere in all that relationship shit.'

'It's more than just a barney,' she said.

He seemed to straighten himself up in his seat on hearing her words. Then he nodded. 'OK... What is it?'

'He told me something on Friday, and it changes everything.'

She paused again, watching the changing expressions on Peter's face: from affability, to curiosity, to apprehension.

'You knew what he did to Sam, didn't you?' she asked. Her voice had now taken on an accusatory tone and Peter's facial expression changed once more, to one of alarm.

'I–I...'

'Just fuckin' admit it, Peter!' she shrieked. 'You sent him to kill Sam. You sent him to torture and maim that poor man...'

'Hang on a minute,' Peter interrupted, leaning forward in his chair. 'I didn't know they were gonna go that far.'

'So there was more than one of them?'

'Yeah. Glynn and another one,' he said, disinclined to reveal Mike's name.

'What exactly did you think they were gonna fuckin' do? Did you tell them to kill him?'

'I... not really, no.'

'Then what the hell did you tell them to do, because Glynn told me he'd killed Sam for betraying you?'

'He did betray me.'

'But that's no reason to kill someone!'

'Look, Adele, just stay out of this, will you? You've no idea what's gone on.'

'Then why don't you fuckin' enlighten me?'

'You don't need to know.'

'I do need to know!' she yelled, standing up and plunging towards him. 'You let me go out with him. You knew what he was and yet you never tried to warn me. You let me go out with a fuckin' killer!'

Then she noticed the look on his face as she said the last word. There was a jolt of recognition and he visibly flinched. It hit her, too. Was that why Peter hadn't warned her about Glynn? Because she was a killer, too.

Peter seemed to take some seconds to recover before he spoke. 'I did warn you about him,' he said. 'But you wouldn't listen.'

'Well, you didn't fuckin' warn me enough!' she said, turning on her heel and stomping out of his office.

She dashed down the corridor and into her own office where she slung her personal belongings haphazardly into a plastic carrier bag. Thoughts raced around in her head. There was still so much she didn't know. How had Sam betrayed Peter? And just what sort of business was her brother in where people tortured and maimed someone as punishment?

But she'd been too angry to find the answers. And the way Peter had flinched had inflamed her even more. She saw now that no matter how much Peter had supported her in the past, it didn't change his perception of her. And his true feelings had all come out in his reaction to that one word. Killer!

All the way home on the bus Adele replayed things over in her head. The conversation with Peter, the way he had reacted and her previous confrontation with Glynn. There were still so many unanswered questions but for now she had found out enough. And what she had learnt told her that there was no way she could go on working for Peter.

Coupled with her aversion to being involved in anything illegal was anger at her brother. Why had he insisted she work for him? He knew the sort of activity some of his businesses were involved in and yet he hadn't bothered to tell her. Did he really think so little of her that he thought she deserved to be amongst people as callous and ruthless as Glynn?

When the bus arrived at her destination she almost missed her stop as she was so preoccupied. As well as anger and disgust at what she had been involved in, she was worried about her future. Her job with Peter was the only work she'd been able to find when she was released from prison and she doubted whether she'd have any better luck this time.

She walked briskly from the bus stop to her flat, her frenzied footsteps echoing her inner turmoil. As she drew nearer to her front door she thought about the bottle of red that was waiting on the wine rack, knowing she wouldn't be able to resist it tonight. In the meantime she'd watch something mundane on the TV to take her mind off things.

While she climbed the stone steps up to the front door Adele pulled the key out of her handbag. She struggled to keep hold of the plastic bag she was carrying and her other belongings while she set about opening the door.

She was just about to put her key in the lock when she heard movement behind her. She looked over her shoulder and her breath caught in her throat as she spotted the weasel features of David. He had another even meaner-looking man with him.

Before Adele could say anything, David clapped his hand over her mouth and brought his other hand around her body. He pulled her roughly towards him, his fingers lingering over her breasts. She heard a clinking sound as her key dropped to the ground, and she smelt the offensive stench of unwashed bodies.

Between them, David and the other man dragged her down the steps and into the small front garden so she was hidden from the road, behind the hedging. Adele could feel panic starting to take a hold of her as she worried about what they were about to do.

Then she spotted the knife in the man's hand and his hostile eyes piercing through her. Still holding her tightly from behind, David hissed into her ear, 'Keep your mouth shut and he won't touch you but if you squeal you've fuckin' had it!'

Adele was unable to speak. His hand was still covering her mouth. So she merely nodded in agreement.

'Right,' said David. 'This is a message for your brother and I want you to make sure he gets every fuckin' word. OK?'

Again she nodded.

'Tell him we've just taken over two of his clubs: Angels and Bramleys. Our men are on the fuckin' door now. Do you get that?'

He took his hand from Adele's mouth so she could speak. 'I don't work for him anymore,' she said, almost pleading.

'I don't give a fuck who you work for! Give your brother this message and tell him that we won't be fuckin' paid off any more. Do you understand?'

'Yes,' said Adele.

'Right, well make sure you take that fuckin' message to him. It's about time he knew how the land lies.'

'OK,' said Adele, her fear evident from the tremble in her voice.

'And tell him that we know where you fuckin' live

now, so he'd better back off if he knows what's good for him.'

He let go of Adele, and pushed her towards the steps where she landed face first, with her belongings scattered around her.

Once she had heard them dash off into the distance Adele struggled back to her feet, her legs shaking. Then she picked up her things. Her knees were bloody and smeared with dust and her hands were sore and dotted with tiny stones. She wiped her trembling hands down her clothing and set about finding the key.

As soon as she was back inside her flat she slid the bolt on the door, dropped down onto her knees and wept. The encounter had shaken her badly. And now, even more than before, she feared for her future.

46

Adele couldn't settle. The adrenalin coursed through her body as she kept reliving what had just happened. She couldn't understand how on earth David and that other man knew where she lived. They must have followed her from work. She got up to check the window locks for the third time since she had been home. Then she looked out over the street, making sure nobody was watching her.

It was no good. She couldn't go on like this. She thought about ringing the police but, after what Glynn had revealed previously, she was worried that it might land Peter in a whole heap of trouble. For some minutes she deliberated. Did he really deserve her protection, considering what he was involved in and the fact that it had put her at risk?

Then Adele thought about how he'd helped her out when she was in trouble some years ago. She decided to speak to him first; she owed him that much, at least. But she wasn't about to let him off lightly. She wanted to know what the hell was going on. But she couldn't do it by phone; this matter was far too delicate to be handled that way. No, the best way to find out would be to see him face to face.

Apart from being shaken, Adele was angry. She'd just been viciously man-handled and threatened because of something her brother was involved in. And now, thanks to him, she no longer felt safe in her own home.

In the end she decided to take a cab to the club. As soon as the cab came to pick her up she left her flat, double-checking that the door was securely locked. Then she dashed downstairs and out of the building, locking the main door behind her. She heaved a sigh of relief once she was tucked inside the taxi.

When she arrived at the club, Adele marched up to Peter's office, ready to confront him. To her dismay, Glynn was also there, standing to one side of Peter's desk. For a moment she balked, but then her anger took over and she slammed the door shut behind her. There was no way she was going to let Glynn stand in the way of what she had to say.

'I don't know what sort of shit you two are involved in but I've just been fuckin' threatened outside my flat!' she yelled. 'Just what the hell is going on?'

'Calm the fuck down,' said Peter while Glynn eyed her warily.

'Don't tell me to calm down when I've just been

dragged off my fuckin' front steps and threatened by that bastard David!'

Peter raised his eyebrows. 'David? What did he say?' he asked.

'Something about them having two of your clubs. Oh, and they won't be paid off any more.'

'Bastards!' cursed Glynn, and she noticed him exchange a brief look with Peter.

'What the hell was he talking about?' Adele continued. 'I thought you only had this one club.'

'OK, calm down and I'll explain,' said Peter.

Adele dragged out a chair, plonked herself on it and folded her arms across her chest. She glared across at Peter, who was sitting on the other side of the desk, then up at Glynn before her eyes settled back on her brother. 'Right, I'm calm,' she said, her face stern. 'Start explaining.'

'OK,' said Peter. 'I need to know more first. Which clubs was he talking about? Did he say?'

'Angels and summat beginning with B.'

'Angels and Bramleys?' asked Peter.

'Yeah, that's right.'

Peter took a deep breath before continuing. 'We look after them,' he said tentatively. 'You remember I told you before about the nightclub game being a bit ruthless?'

'Yeah, I remember,' said Adele, her tone still hostile.

'Well, part of our business is to offer security services

to pubs and clubs. Some of 'em were getting aggro from gangs so we offered to help them out.'

'How very kind of you,' said Adele, sarcastically. 'So, what did David mean?'

'Unfortunately people like David and his mates are part of the problem. Even though we've got our men on the door at these places, they still give them aggro.'

'So why didn't I know about this part of the business?' demanded Adele. 'And, presumably, these clubs pay you to help them out so why isn't it in the books?'

'I did tell you about the security side of the business. I just never got round to telling you the details,' said Peter. 'And the cash does get entered into the books. I keep a separate ledger for that side of the business.'

'Why?' asked Adele, still determined to find answers.

'Well, you had enough shit to sort out so I decided to leave it till you'd caught up with the rest of the bookkeeping.'

'Bet you did,' said Adele. 'I was wondering why you were banking so much money. Now it all makes fuckin' sense.'

Peter just stared back at her.

'Right, well, I'm out of here,' she fumed. 'There's no fuckin' way I'm ever coming back to work for you. And, I'll be letting the police know about David and that other thug as well.'

'No, don't do that!' warned Glynn. 'Don't go getting the fuckin' coppers involved.'

'Why not?' asked Adele. 'I think it's about time the police knew exactly what you two get up to.'

'Don't do it, Adele,' said Peter. 'It'll only provoke David and his mates even more.'

Adele wasn't convinced. 'Right, I'm going,' she said. 'But I will be phoning the police because I need to feel safe in my own fuckin' home.'

'No you're not!' said Glynn, stepping in front of her and blocking her way to the door. She noticed the air of menace about him as she stared into his eyes. 'You're not going anywhere,' he said.

'Hang on a minute, Glynn,' said Peter, getting out of his chair.

'Not till she's heard what I have to say,' said Glynn.

'Get out of my way!' she yelled, thumping his chest with her fists.

Glynn held her hands back while he continued to speak. 'You're in it as deep as us,' he said, 'so why don't you just fuckin' sit back down and listen to what I've got to say before you go off half-cocked and make a stupid decision you'll regret.'

She continued to glare at him but then Peter spoke up. 'It's best you listen, Adele. You don't wanna go landing us all in lumber if there's a way out of it.' Then he turned to Glynn. 'Let go of her.'

When Glynn released his hold on her hands she stared from him to Peter, then back again. The determined look on Glynn's face unnerved her and, despite her anger, she was starting to feel anxious. Did she really want to risk the consequences if she went to the police? After all, Glynn wasn't just someone who worked for Peter; he was a ruthless killer.

'OK, go on,' she said, sitting back down.

Adele could swear there was a slight smirk on Glynn's face as he began speaking. 'Well, it's like this,' he said. 'For starters, you witnessed a murder in the club and neglected to report it to the police. They could have you for that.'

'You wouldn't,' she said, wishing she felt that confident.

'Not deliberately, no. But if you start shooting your mouth off to the police then it'll all come out. Secondly, don't forget that I killed that man for you.'

'No you didn't!' she yelled. 'He'd already let go of me. He was running away.'

'And did you think I was gonna risk him coming back and doing more fuckin' damage?' Glynn spat. As he spoke she noticed the tendons tighten in his throat and the way he clenched his jaw. 'After all,' he continued, raising his voice, 'he did have a fuckin' knife at your throat!'

'Calm the fuck down, Glynn,' said Peter.

Glynn took a few moments to compose himself, his chest heaving as he took several deep breaths. 'So, like

I was saying, I did it to protect you. Thirdly, Dave and his goons now know where you live so you're gonna need protection.'

He glared at Adele and gave her a moment to digest this information.

'And lastly,' he added, 'the police will be very interested in you if they think you've been doing the accounts for a firm of crooks, especially when you've only just served a stretch. So, like I say, you're up to your fuckin' neck in it.'

'You bastard,' she cursed. Adele knew he had her, and in her desperation she looked to Peter, hoping he would counter what Glynn had said. 'Just what the hell are you involved with?' she asked her brother.

But Peter didn't answer her question. Instead he said, 'Glynn's right. I think it's best if you stick with us, Adele, and leave the cops out of it. I want to protect you; believe me, I do. If you agree to stay, I'll have someone watching over your place 24/7. Just say the word.'

'You mean you're fuckin' agreeing with him?' she asked, disgusted with her brother.

'It's the only way, Adele. I need you here. I'm fuckin' clueless with the books, like I've told you before, and I don't wanna get anyone else involved. I'm not having a stranger nosying in my fuckin' business. Besides, what else are you gonna do? You're best off here with us. I wanna fuckin' protect you.'

'No you don't! You're just looking out for your own

interests. You're as big a fuckin' crook as he is,' she shouted, her eyes switching to Glynn.

Then she stormed out of Peter's office for the second time that day, too infuriated to think straight about what had happened.

But that would come once she had calmed down and thought long and hard about her situation. And sooner or later she was going to have to reach a decision.

47

As soon as Adele had gone, Peter rounded on Glynn. 'What the fuck did you have to tell her all that for?' he demanded.

Glynn hit back. 'There was no fuckin' choice. She was going to the cops, for fuck's sake! We couldn't let her do that. If she got the coppers involved they'd soon find out about the protection money and maybe even find out it was us that killed Sam and that other guy. Then all our fuckin' necks would be on the line.

'Besides, she's no fuckin' innocent. She's been doing the books for long enough. She must have known there was summat going on.'

'She didn't know fuck all!' shouted Peter, 'because I kept all that from her. As far as Adele was concerned, I've got a nightclub, a few fuckin' sunbed salons and a bookies. That's all.'

'Well, it was the best way, as far as I'm concerned.'

'No it wasn't! She could still go to the fuckin' coppers, and now she knows all about the protection money.'

'Will she fuck go to the cops!' Glynn grinned before adding, 'She's too scared of the consequences.'

'Well, I just hope you're right,' said Peter.

'Course I am. No worries,' said Glynn. 'Anyway, what's this about you fuckin' paying off Alan's firm?'

Peter broke out in a sweat and loosened his shirt collar as he felt the heat rising through his body and up to his face. 'It was the only way,' he said.

'Well, it didn't fuckin' work, did it?' said Glynn. 'So now they've had your money and they're still doing us over. They must have thought you were a right fuckin' mug!'

'Shut the fuck up!' yelled Peter. 'I'm running this firm so you'll keep your fuckin' opinions to yourself if you wanna keep your job.'

Glynn glared at Peter, his face a mask of anger. Then he seemed to bite back his fury as he said, 'That doesn't mean you're always right, y'know. And, for the record, I think you've made a fuckin' big mistake. Alan's firm will think they can walk all—'

'All right, all right!' snapped Peter. 'Don't you think I know that?' Peter knew the row was getting out of hand so he took a step back and then said, 'I trusted him, OK? He used to be a mate. All right, we could have hit them again like we did with Sam but it didn't fuckin' get us anywhere last time so I thought I'd try summat else.'

'Look, Pete. You've got no fuckin' choice now. We've got to hit 'em hard. We can't afford to let 'em take the piss.'

'Don't you think I fuckin' know that?' said Peter. 'Don't worry, they're not gonna threaten my sister and get away with it.'

'OK, so what you gonna do?'

'I don't know, yet,' Peter said. 'But one way or another they're gonna fuckin' pay.'

'OK, let me know when you've made a decision,' said Glynn cynically, before strutting out of the office.

Once Glynn had gone, and Peter was on his own, he loosened his collar further then pursed his lips and let out a long gasp of air. He noticed how his hand trembled as he brought it back down.

Jesus! What a fuckin' mess. Now he was really up against it. Alan had double-crossed him, big time! There was no way he could let him get away with that, especially after he had threatened Adele.

But there was another reason he couldn't afford to let Alan's firm get away with it. Glynn had doubted his leadership and he couldn't allow that to happen. It was too easy for the fuckin' vultures to pounce if they thought you couldn't hack it any more. After all, that had been the reason why he'd acquired the Golden Bell in the first place. He'd known Max could no longer handle the nightclub business and he'd swooped.

Adele was so on edge that she couldn't settle in one place. David and his cronies knew where she lived, and that terrified her. What if he and the other guy turned up again? What if they did something even worse than threaten her this time?

Her limbs were twitchy and her chest was tight with panic. Every little sound alerted her and she kept checking to make sure the door and windows were locked, despite the fact that she lived on the first floor.

She'd been back at home for an hour, and when she wasn't worrying about someone bursting through the door at any minute, she was reliving her brother and Glynn's words. She didn't know what to do. If the circumstances had been different she would have gone straight to the police and no messing. But David and the other goon had threatened her because of something her brother was involved in. And she didn't want to risk getting Peter in trouble with the law.

Adele's mind was in a jumble. Glynn's words 'firm of crooks' kept coming back to her. So did the fact that Glynn had viciously murdered Sam for betraying Peter. She'd read in the papers about gangs taking over nightclubs and injuring and threatening the bouncers. In some instances even the customers had been attacked. Surely that couldn't be what Peter did! Could it?

Adele thought about her options. She really didn't want to go back to work for Peter, not if what she suspected was right. But what else could she do? And who else would protect her? She couldn't live in a place where she didn't feel safe.

Maybe she should get away. But she couldn't return to her mother's house; David knew where that was, too. And there was no way she could bring trouble to her mother's door after all she had already been through.

Perhaps she could get away altogether to somewhere no one would find her. But where would she go? If she stayed working for Peter, maybe David and his cronies would follow her home again. But if she moved to another part of the country, how would she manage? She couldn't get work without references. And she'd already struggled, as it was, with her prison record.

In the end she decided to phone Peter. She needed to know more before she decided what to do. Maybe she would catch him when Glynn wasn't there; she might get more sense out of him then.

Peter answered the phone on the third ring. 'It's Adele,' she said, and she heard him let out a heavy sigh. 'Peter, I've been going out of my fuckin' mind with worry here. Just what the hell is going on? And why did you go along with Glynn when you know what he is?'

'Look, Glynn had a point. I need you onside, Adele. I can't have you running to the police. It might lead to all kinds of problems.'

'Are you frightened they'll find out about the protection racket or about your men killing Sam?' she sniped.

'Who mentioned a protection racket?'

'It's fuckin' obvious, Peter. I'm not stupid. Or maybe you think I am; maybe that's why you had me working for you in the first place.'

'No, it's not like that at all, Adele.'

'What the fuckin' hell is it like, then?' she screeched. 'Did you think that working with a bunch of criminals was what I deserved after what I'd done?'

Adele knew she was becoming hysterical as well as irrational now, but she couldn't help it. Her brother had put her in an impossible predicament as well as placing her in danger and she rued the day she had ever gone to work for him.

'Now you're being fuckin' ridiculous!' he bit back. Then she heard another heavy sigh and he added, 'Look, Adele. I didn't know things would come to this. I tried to keep you out of it. If you must know, that's why I hid the ledgers for the security side of the business.'

'Well, you didn't do a very good job of protecting me, did you?' she barked.

'Look, sis, I didn't know what was gonna happen with David. But if you come back to work I swear I'll protect you. I'll make sure there's a car posted outside your flat all the time.'

'And if I don't?'

'That's up to you. But if you go to the cops, you could still be implicated. After all, you've been doing the books and you knew about the man who Glynn killed.'

'Thanks a fuckin' million!' she cursed.

'I'm sorry it's come to this, sis. But, like I say, I'll do my best to protect you if you come back.'

'And just what would I be getting involved with if I did come back?' she asked, becoming calmer as she realised the futility of losing her temper.

'It's best you don't know everything. There's a lot of heavy shit going down at the moment. I'd prefer it if you didn't know too many details.'

'Peter, I need to know just what the hell I'd be getting involved with if I come back,' she said, between gritted teeth as she fought to remain calm.

'I've told you, Adele, it's best you don't know. I can protect you more that way. The more you know, the more the coppers can get out of you if it comes to it.'

'So now we're getting to the bottom of it,' she said sardonically. 'You're not keeping me in the dark to protect me; you're doing it to protect yourself. Why is it so important that I come to work for you, anyway? Why won't you protect me if I don't work for you?'

''Cos for one thing, I have to fuckin' pay my men to protect you so I'd like to think that at least you're doing something to earn that protection. But for another thing, I need someone onside who I can trust.'

His last few words hit home. 'Are you saying you can't trust Glynn?' she asked.

'You can't fuckin' trust anyone in the nightclub business, Adele, no matter how sound they might seem. You don't know what it's like in my position. I'm under pressure from all fuckin' sides and I daren't show my men any signs of weakness. I've already had Dave and Sam do the shit on me. I don't want anyone else to do the same just because they think I can't fuckin' hack it.'

He sounded desperate, almost pleading for her support. And it was at that point Adele realised that her little brother had perhaps bitten off more than he could chew.

But how could she criticise him for his mistakes? She too had made mistakes in life. And who had stood by her when she'd made the biggest mistake of all? Peter. He had been there when she needed help. And now that things were the other way round, how could she turn her back on him?

Adele closed her eyes and took a deep breath. She was about to make a decision that she hoped she wouldn't regret.

'OK,' she said. 'I'll come back. But only if you protect me.'

48

It was the following day and Glynn and Mike were out collecting. As he sat behind the wheel of his BMW, Glynn turned to Mike, who was sitting across from him.

'We'll take the long way round; it'll give me a chance to fill you in on what's been going on.'

'Yeah, what is it?' asked Mike. 'You sounded pretty fuckin' serious on the phone.'

'Oh, it's serious all right,' said Glynn. 'Pete's only gone and shot himself in the fuckin' foot.'

'How d'you mean?'

'He tried to pay off his old mate Alan. But it's fuckin' backfired. So now, as well as trying to collect on our fuckin' patch, they're collecting from two of our biggest fuckin' nightclubs as well; Angels and Bramleys.'

'You're fuckin' joking!'

'Wish I was, mate. Tell you what, Mike, I bet that Alan thinks Pete's a right fuckin' mug!'

'He is a fuckin' mug! They're well taking the piss.'

'Dead right.'

'So what's Pete gonna do about it?' Mike asked.

Glynn shrugged. 'He seems fuckin' clueless to me. He's promised to do summat but he doesn't know what. So I've left it with him. He's supposed to be running this fuckin' firm, when all's said and done. But I'll tell you what, he'd better not take too fuckin' long deciding or I'm gonna take matters into my own hands.'

'Well, I'll be right behind you,' said Mike. 'I told you he can't fuckin' handle it. He's a soft cunt. You'd be better off running things.'

Glynn turned to Mike and smiled. 'Just biding my time, mate. Let's see what he comes up with, then we'll take it from there.'

One of the first things Adele did when she was back at work was to sneak into Peter's office when no one was around. Peter had told her he was out on business so she had a bit of time. He'd also trusted her with a spare set of keys in case she needed anything while he was away.

She slipped through the office door, closing it quietly behind her, then had a quick look around the room. His desk was the best place to start. Where else would she expect him to hide something he didn't want anyone else to see? She tried each of the drawers but to her consternation they were locked until she got to the pen tray concealed in the top of the desk.

Amongst the assortment of pens, pencils and rulers was a keyring with two keys on it; a silver one and another, which was small and bronze coloured. Adele quickly inserted the silver key into the top drawer of the desk with shaking hands. But she had no joy so she tried the bronze key, then each key in turn in the next drawer down.

Her heart sped up as she felt the bronze key ease its way into the lock and then catch when she turned it. She pulled the drawer open and flicked through the assortment of musty files. Nothing.

Next she went to the filing cabinet, which was also locked. Adele pushed the silver key into the lock and eased it open, then pulled the top drawer out. It was full of files. As she began to flick through them she heard the sound of footsteps in the corridor, and stopped dead. She glanced at the door, expecting it to swing open any moment. Her heart was pounding.

She stood still, her breath catching in her throat. It was too late to hide. She'd be caught in the act. Adele's eyes switched back to the row of files in the cabinet. She was about to slam the drawer shut. While she was frantically trying to think up an excuse for why she was in the office, she spotted it: the file she had been looking for.

She quickly grabbed the file and slid it under the desk.

She'd come back for it later. Then she shut the drawer and waited. But the footsteps faded. Whoever it was had walked past and were on their way up the corridor.

She grabbed the file from under the desk and placed another on top of it. If someone spotted her they'd think she'd come to collect the other file, which related to one of the sunbed salons. Then she left the office as quietly as she could and made her way back to her own office.

When Adele walked into her office she jumped in alarm. There was a man there, standing with his back to her. A large man. He was getting something from the safe. Then she realised it was Glynn and she felt a momentary anguish tinged with relief. At least it wasn't someone come to attack her again. As she stared at his back, she realised that he wasn't getting something from the safe; he was putting something inside.

Glynn turned round and glared at her, making her aware of the shocked expression on her face. 'What's wrong? It's only me,' he said. Then he smiled his usual disarming smile, but it no longer impressed Adele.

'I suppose you're banking your dirty money again, are you?' she asked.

He laughed at her as he shut the safe and made his way across the room. 'Pete told me you were back. I knew you'd see sense in the end.' Then he surveyed her through narrowed eyes. 'I think we need to get something straight, sweetheart,' he said in a low growl. 'It's not my dirty money; it belongs to your brother, which is why

I'm putting it inside *his* safe. So, while you're having a go, is there anything else you'd like to say?'

'I've got nothing to say to you, so I'd rather you left my office,' she snapped.

'Fair enough, but I think you need to remember that your brother is just as fuckin' crooked as I am. So don't blame me if you can't fuckin' handle what he does for a living.'

She didn't retaliate. What could she say? Deep down, she knew that she'd been threatened by David because of her brother's actions. 'Just go, will you?' she said, pulling out her chair and slapping the two files on the desk. While Glynn hovered near the door she looked down at her desk and pretended to be immersed in the contents of the first file, the one relating to the sunbed salon.

To her relief she heard the sound of the door shut. Then she looked up again, checking that he had definitely left the room. Once she was satisfied that he had gone, she slid the bottom file out from beneath the one for the sunbed business. It was marked 'Security' and inside it was a ledger.

Adele's rapid heartbeat turned to thunder as she scanned the ledger. It was all there in black and white: names of pubs and clubs, addresses, proprietors' names, collection dates, amounts, a paid column and even an end column headed 'Notes'. Most of the names had a tick in the paid column, but where they hadn't there was a coded message under the notes. Words such as 'revisit', 'action 1' or 'action 2' swam out from the page.

There was no doubt in Adele's mind what was going on here. Peter could dress things up as much as he liked by calling it security but this ledger confirmed what she had already suspected. Her brother was running a protection racket.

Despite having her suspicions confirmed, Adele knew that she would stick with her decision to work for Peter. After all, she had exhausted all other possibilities and this was the only viable option open to her.

And if Peter had promised to protect her from things as best he could then she would go along with that. So she shut the ledger and returned it to its hiding place. Now that she knew for sure about his illegal sideline, she would rather try to put it out of her mind and focus on the other businesses.

She knew that nothing she said would make Peter give up the protection business; he was already in too deep for that and, like he had said, he couldn't afford to show his men any sign of weakness. So she would try to forget that she had ever seen the ledger and hope that Peter's world was not about to come crashing down around them.

49

Adele was working late. There was still a lot of work to do so she tried to concentrate on that rather than her disturbing discovery. Work helped to take her mind off things: her fear of being attacked again, and the nagging worry about what Peter was involved in.

In the past couple of days she had also tried to repair her fractured relationship with her brother. If she had to work with him then she didn't want it to be in an unpleasant environment. So they kept their conversations strictly to the legal businesses and left other things unsaid.

Noticing how late it was, she put her files away and left her office. She still had one job to do before she left for home: she needed Peter to sign a cheque for supplies to the nightclub. He'd been out all day but had rung her to say he was back so she decided to go in search of him and see if she could get his signature before she went home.

When Adele saw that Peter wasn't in his office she decided to try the nightclub. There he was, sitting at the bar nursing a large measure of something alcoholic; she assumed it was his usual tipple of brandy. To her consternation, Glynn was also sitting at the bar alongside Peter.

Adele tried to ignore Glynn while she spoke to Peter. 'Hi, I thought I might find you here,' she said. Then she passed him the cheque. 'Can you sign this for me so I can put it in the post tomorrow?'

'Have you got a pen?' he asked.

'Shit, sorry. I forgot to bring one down with me.'

'It's OK,' Glynn interrupted. 'Cindy,' he shouted to the attractive young barmaid who was busy organising the glasses ready for that evening's custom. 'You got a pen, sweetheart?'

'Might have,' she said, flirtatiously. 'What's it worth?'

'You know I'll see you right,' said Glynn, laughing raucously. 'Don't I always?' He winked at Cindy lasciviously.

Then Cindy grabbed a pen from the back shelf and trotted across to Glynn with it. Her skirt was short and Glynn eyed her toned legs. She placed the pen in front of him, flashed him a smouldering look, then hovered, awaiting his response.

Glynn covered her hand with his own, then took up the pen. 'Thanks, love. You're a darling,' he said, winking again and flashing his well-rehearsed disarming smile.

'No problems, honey,' she said, turning round and walking away, her hips swaying provocatively.

Glynn turned towards Peter as he passed him the pen, and Adele noticed the smug expression on his face. She returned him a look of contempt then dropped her gaze. His flirtation bothered her but there was no way she was going to let him know that so she kept her mouth shut.

While she was waiting for Peter to sign the cheque another of the bar staff, Paula, arrived. She was a good ten years older than Cindy and hadn't aged well. Paula had the look of a woman who had too many of life's burdens to bear. It showed in the fine lines on her forehead, her strained features and the dullness of her hair.

'What the fuck time d'you call this?' shouted Glynn as Paula rushed to take her coat off.

'Sorry, I had to take my little boy to the doctor and it took longer than I thought. Then I had to give him his tea and get ready.'

'Couldn't you have got a morning appointment?' Glynn asked, his tone austere.

'No, I told Peter about it,' she said, gazing beseechingly at Peter.

'Yeah, it's OK,' said Peter, holding his hand up towards Glynn. 'I gave her permission. Her little lad's not well.'

Glynn nodded, his eyes full of venom as he continued

to stare at Paula. 'What the fuck d'you call that?' he asked as Paula finished removing her coat revealing a plain, knee-length skirt and buttoned-up blouse. 'That's not gonna fuckin' attract the punters, is it?' he asked. 'You wanna take a few lessons from Cindy here. She knows how to dress to impress.'

He smiled at Cindy, who revelled in the compliment, wiggling her shoulders enticingly while thrusting her breasts forward and shaking her hair back.

'Leave her alone!' said Adele.

'Who asked your opinion?' snapped Glynn.

'Leave it, Glynn,' said Peter. 'Paula's got a lot on her mind at the moment.'

Glynn glared across at Adele, then turned his attention to Cindy once more. 'You still up for that date I promised you?' he asked.

Adele quickly snatched up the cheque that Peter had signed and made her way to the door to the sound of Cindy giggling while Glynn continued to flirt with her. She didn't want to hang around while he rubbed her nose in it.

She was angry; at the way he had flirted so blatantly in front of her, and at his treatment of Paula, who was a good worker in obvious need of the meagre wages that her bar job paid. But most of all she was angry at herself because she hadn't seen what Glynn was really like. How could she have been foolish enough to be taken in by a man like him?

*

The sound of 'Ride on Time' by Black Box was blasting through the speakers in Angels nightclub. Alan and David were sitting at a darkened corner table while the strobe lighting cast neon-bright bursts of colour around them. There were two young women with them and the booze was flowing. It had become a regular haunt for Alan and his crew since they had muscled their way in, and the management were eager to supply them with free drinks to keep them onside.

'I need the loo,' one of the girls shouted over the sound of the music, then she extricated herself from David's over-amorous attentions. 'You coming?' she asked her friend, who was wrapped around Alan.

The two girls headed towards the ladies. David smiled across at Alan, and waited for a lull in the music before he spoke. 'Fuckin' brilliant this, innit?' he said.

Alan smiled back, not knowing whether David was referring to the club atmosphere, the girls' company or the free booze. Maybe it was a combination of the three.

'Perks of the job,' he said. Then he looked around him, making sure no one was listening before he added, 'Make sure you don't get too pissed, though. We've still gotta have our wits about us. I'm expecting retaliation any time. Pete will be well pissed off that we've taken over this place and Bramleys.'

'No probs,' said David.

When the first strains of 'Back to Life' by Soul II Soul started up over the speakers Alan knew it would be difficult to make himself heard without shouting so he switched topic.

'Where are you off to after here?' he asked David.

'Back to mine, innit.' David lowered his voice only marginally before continuing, 'She's fuckin' gagging for it, mate. What about you?'

'Hers or mine, not sure yet. Might get some bottles to take away.'

'Dead right. I hope they'll be freebies, too.'

'Course they will,' said Alan. 'They know I'm the fuckin' gaffer.'

He smiled confidently. Alan was enjoying having control of the two nightclubs and all the benefits that went with it. And he would continue to enjoy it because there was no way he was going to allow Peter's firm to regain control.

Mike spent the best part of five minutes queuing at the bar in Angels nightclub, and it had irritated the hell out of him. He was used to getting served straight away in the Golden Bell. But he knew it was important to look the part of an average punter so it was better if he had a drink in his hand.

Once Mike had been served, he threw some change

moodily at the barman and walked around the nightclub's interior until he spotted Alan and David sitting in a corner with two attractive young women.

Keeping a safe distance from them, Mike concealed himself behind a stone pillar. He didn't want to be recognised by Alan, who had known him while he was inside. The pillar provided perfect cover, giving him a good view of Alan's table while staying hidden.

Mike peered over. While he watched, a barmaid sauntered to the table with a tray laden with drinks. He noticed that there were already more than enough drinks for four people in front of them; they were obviously being greedy. David chatted with the barmaid as she passed the drinks around. Then, just as she was about to walk away, he grasped her buttocks. The barmaid squealed and quickly left the table while David and Alan laughed uproariously.

As he watched, Mike's face formed a scowl. Bastards! They were really living it large and acting as though they owned the fuckin' place. He noticed there was still a massive queue at the bar; it seemed that waitress service was only for the privileged few.

It was obvious to Mike that Alan and David were now firmly ensconced in Angels nightclub. There was something else, too: the bouncers had changed since the last time Mike had been here. He had an uneasy feeling that Alan's mob were now also controlling the doors. That meant they could decide who came into the club, including the dealers, and they would take a handy mark-up from any drugs sold. Mike knew enough people for him to check out whether that was the case.

Mike quickly downed his drink. He'd seen enough of Angels for one night. Now he was off to Bramleys to find out what was going on there. Then he'd have to report back to Glynn about what he'd seen. He knew for sure that Glynn would want to do something about it. And it would involve a lot more than pissing about trying to pay Alan off, like Pete had done.

50

The Golden Bell was heaving. Adele had let Peter persuade her to stop by for a few drinks. Even though she wasn't in the mood for a night out, she knew it was Peter's way of getting things back on track between them. Besides, it was Friday night and she had nothing else lined up other than sitting at home worrying every time she heard the floorboards creak.

She wasn't enjoying herself. Tonight the music seemed too loud, the lights too bright, and the crowds stifling. Plus, she no longer had the excitement of watching out for Glynn. Now that she had found out exactly what he was, he irritated her.

Adele had just fought her way back from the ladies to find that her bar stool was now occupied and Peter had disappeared.

'Where's Peter?' she shouted across to the barmaid, Paula, while dabbing her clammy cheeks with a tissue.

Paula shrugged and shouted back, 'One of the bouncers wanted him for something. Don't know what.'

'Can you get me another drink, please? Same again,' said Adele, who had decided to hang around for a bit longer to see if Peter returned.

Once she had her drink in hand, Adele turned round, her back to the bar, and watched what was going on in the club. Bored, she decided to leave if Peter hadn't returned by the time she had finished her drink. She was draining the last of her brandy and Coke when she noticed a disturbance on the other side of the dance floor.

Glynn was doing his rounds of the Golden Bell, checking everything was in order, when he spotted one of the bouncers, Barney, involved in an altercation with another man. He couldn't identify the other man at first; he was only small and a crowd were beginning to gather around them.

It was only as he drew closer that he realised it was Little Gaz. Jesus! That was all he needed. Barney was a good guy to have working for you but sometimes he was just too keen.

He sped towards them, calling out as he approached, 'What's going on?'

Barney had hold of Little Gaz by his shirt collar. 'I caught this little shit selling drugs and then he tried to do a runner,' he said.

Little Gaz looked up and was met with one of Glynn's piercing stares, which said, *Keep your mouth shut or you've had it!*

'Leave him to me,' said Glynn. Then he nodded at the crowd. 'You take care of this lot. Tell them to fuck off out of it or we'll chuck 'em out.'

Barney looked concerned for a moment, but the rough way Glynn handled Little Gaz and the size difference between them told him that Glynn was well capable of handling this situation.

Glynn marched Little Gaz across the floor, through the foyer and out into the street. Then he dragged him into the alleyway that ran down one side of the club. Once they were out of sight he let go of him.

'What the fuck d'you think you're playing at?' he fumed. 'I thought I told you to be fuckin' careful.'

'I was,' pleaded Gaz. 'I didn't know that big bastard was watching, did I?'

'Hand 'em over!' demanded Glynn, referring to the drugs that Gaz was carrying.

'Why? I'm gonna try to flog 'em somewhere else.'

'Oh no you're fuckin' not!' yelled Glynn, pinning Little Gaz up against the wall. 'You're gonna do as you're fuckin' told or I'll have to do something about it. I want your takings for tonight as well.'

'But that's not our deal,' Little Gaz protested. 'You only take a mark-up usually.'

'Yeah, and you don't go getting fuckin' caught usually,' said Glynn. 'Do I have to smack you around before you'll do as you're told, or what?'

Little Gaz slumped his shoulders resignedly and Glynn could see his hands shaking as he put them into his trouser pockets and pulled out a packet of cocaine and a wad of notes.

'Right, that's better,' Glynn said, grabbing the packet and the money from Little Gaz. 'Now, I want you to smack me one.' He held up his hand and pointed at his left cheek, saying 'Right here.'

'You what?' asked Little Gaz, dumbfounded.

'You heard!' growled Glynn. 'Do as you're fuckin' told.'

Little Gaz stood back nervously then stared at Glynn for a few moments before swinging his fist. It landed on the bridge of Glynn's nose with a loud thud, causing him to reel back.

A few seconds later, Glynn regained his footing. 'Fuckin' hell! You can't half punch for a little cunt,' he said.

Little Gaz grinned until Glynn's next words swiped the smile away. 'Right, now fuck off! And don't bother coming back.'

Little Gaz made as if to protest. 'You heard!' yelled Glynn, holding his fist back, ready to deliver.

Little Gaz's bottom lip jutted out and his shoulders

drooped as he hurried away. Then Glynn slipped the package into his pocket and went back into the club. He was gutted. The drugs mark-up had been a nice little earner but he daren't risk it after this, not for a while anyway. Maybe in the future he'd give it another go; he'd just have to bide his time till the heat died down.

Adele rushed across the dance floor, trying to see what the trouble was. But her progress was slow as she tried to push her way around drunken and perspiring revellers. As she drew nearer she spotted Glynn hauling somebody away. Despite Barney shouting at the crowd it was some time before Adele could break through.

At the door to the foyer she was met by Peter.

'What the hell's going on?' he asked.

'I don't know, but I saw Glynn pulling someone away.'

They rushed into the foyer just in time to see Glynn heading back into the club. Blood was pouring down his face from a busted nose and his left cheek was red.

'Oh my God!' said Adele, concerned despite her animosity towards Glynn. 'Are you OK?'

He grinned. 'Sure, nothing I can't handle.'

'What the fuck happened?' asked Peter.

'The bastard was trying to flog drugs in the club. I got 'em off him but the little shit smacked me one, then got away.'

'We'd best report it to the police and hand the drugs over to them,' said Adele.

Glynn flashed a smarmy smile. 'That's just what I was gonna do,' he said.

Little did Adele and Peter know that Glynn's intention was to be seen taking a hard stance against drug pushers. That way he could gain police trust.

51

It was a week since the incident with the drug dealer. Peter was sitting in his office going through some paperwork when Glynn walked in. He looked up at Glynn's handsome face, noticing that the bruising on his left cheek was beginning to fade and had turned yellow.

'We need to talk,' Glynn announced, his tone severe.

Peter knew what he was there for even before he spoke. Glynn would be pressing him to retaliate against Alan's mob. And Glynn wasn't the only one. Several members of his gang had asked what they were going to do. Peter knew that he had to be seen to be taking action otherwise he'd lose their respect. And if you were in charge, you had to have respect from your men.

For the past week or so Peter had been in turmoil. He knew the situation couldn't go on. It was bad enough that Alan's crew were muscling in on their businesses but when they had beaten up Sandra they had taken things to a whole new level. It was costing him a fortune, too; since Sandra had been beaten up he had to have people watching over all his sunbed salons and the bookies.

Then there was the threat to his sister. There was no way he could allow that to happen again. Nobody messed with his family and got away with it. So, although the thought of taking action against his old friends didn't sit well with him, he knew it was something he had to do.

The question was, what sort of action would he take? It had to be something forceful enough to send a clear message to Alan that they weren't to be messed with.

The incident with the drug dealer had bought Peter some time. While the police had been sniffing around, Glynn's mind had been on other things, giving Peter a chance to decide what he was going to do. And now it was time to push forward.

'It's about your old mate, Alan,' Glynn continued. 'It turns out his firm aren't just collecting from Angels, Bramleys and a lot of our pubs. They've taken over the doors of the two clubs as well.'

'I fuckin' know. I heard about it,' said Peter.

'They're lording it up, too,' Glynn continued. 'I had Mike do some sniffing around. He saw Alan and his mate in Angels acting like they own the fuckin' place.'

'Cheeky bastards!' Peter cursed.

'Yeah, they're really starting to take the piss. We need to put a stop to it, Pete. Our men are getting really fucked off about it.'

'I know,' said Peter. 'You've already told me.'

'So what are we gonna do? We can't just fuckin' let this go on!'

Peter took a deep breath, pulling his shoulders back and puffing out his chest. 'We're gonna raid them,' he said. 'And we're gonna hit them fuckin' hard!'

He noticed Glynn's facial muscles visibly relax and knew that this was what he had been waiting for.

'We'll take the two clubs at the same time,' said Peter. 'They won't know what's fuckin' hit 'em! And by the time we've finished, their bouncers will be doing a runner.'

Glynn's face broke out into a wide grin. 'Sounds good,' he said. 'So what's the plan?'

'I'll take a few of our men to one of the clubs and you take some to the other club at the same time. We'll give their bouncers a fuckin' good going-over.'

'Sounds good. Only thing is, we can't afford to leave ourselves exposed here,' said Glynn. 'Who'll look after this place while we're away?'

'Well, we'll have our usual guys on the doors and I can get Adele to take care of any admin in case the staff want petty cash or anything. I'll tell her we're both out on business.'

'Yeah, but I'm talking about security. How about we

leave Mike here with a couple of our hardest men to watch over things?'

'OK, I'm fine with that,' said Peter.

'How soon?' asked Glynn.

'As soon as possible. I don't think we can afford to wait much longer, the way things are going.'

'That's what I've been telling you,' said Glynn.

'Yeah, I know. But we got caught up with all that business about the drug dealer, didn't we?'

Glynn didn't reply and Peter got the feeling he wasn't convinced about his reason for the delay in taking action. 'Right, how about next weekend then?' he continued. 'Maybe Saturday.'

'Great. We just need to sort out some weapons now.'

'We can't go carrying guns,' Peter told him. 'It's too fuckin' risky. I don't want anyone getting killed. That's why me and you need to lead this, so we can make sure.'

'Yeah, but we still need to cause a fair bit of damage. They'll take no fuckin' notice otherwise.'

'I know that, Glynn. I was planning to take knives but I don't want any serious damage, just enough to make sure they get the fuckin' message.'

Although Peter was trying hard not to appear soft in front of Glynn, the thought of inflicting damage on his two old friends or anyone working for them still bothered him. But Alan had forced him into this so he had no alternative.

'Leave it with me,' said Glynn. 'I'll sort the fuckin' tools out, don't worry.'

'OK, let me know when you've got hold of them. In the meantime, I'll let our men know what we're gonna do and I'll sort out the finer details, like who's going to each of the clubs. We'll have to make sure that everyone keeps schtum, though. We want it to be a fuckin' big surprise to Alan and his gang.'

'Don't worry, it fuckin' will be,' said Glynn.

Adele had managed to avoid Glynn since the night when the drug dealer had escaped from the club. But now, as she sat at her desk entering some figures onto her computer screen, she could hear him talking to Peter in his office. The conversation sounded serious although it was difficult to hear exactly what they were saying.

Then they finished speaking and she heard the sound of footsteps approaching her office. Peter or Glynn? She wasn't sure. But as she thought about the possibility of it being Glynn, her heart rate increased. She silently cursed the fact that he still had that effect on her.

'What do *you* want?' she asked, when he appeared at the door.

'Ouch!' he mocked. 'Is that any way to speak to your former lover? It wasn't so long ago that you couldn't get enough of me.'

'That was before I found out what you were really

like,' she snapped. 'And the only reason I couldn't get enough was because it was usually all over before it had even bloody well started. So, for your information, you're crap in bed.'

He ignored her last scathing comment, focusing instead on the first. 'What makes me laugh about you, Adele, is that you think you're so much better than the rest of us. But when it comes down to it you're just the same. You know what goes down with your brother's businesses yet you didn't turn down the job when he offered it, did you?'

'I didn't bloody know then what was involved,' she said. 'And that's still far more than I want to know.' Thinking of the protection racket, she added, 'You just keep your illegal activities to yourself and leave me out of it. It's because of your bloody blackmail that I'm still here. Otherwise I'd be well away!'

She hated the fact that his goading was getting to her, but she couldn't help becoming angry. 'We're nothing alike!' she screamed. 'You're ruthless and callous, and you don't fuckin' give a shit about anybody but yourself.'

She glared at him for a few moments, watching the sly smirk on his face as he mocked, 'Ooh, temper, temper.'

'D'you know,' she asked, refusing to back down now she had started, 'I used to think you were respected by the staff, but now I realise that it isn't respect at all. It's fear. You actually bloody intimidate them. Well, apart from the ones that you play up to, like Cindy, that is.'

'Ooh, steady,' he said. 'Anyone would think you were a bit jealous.'

'You must be bloody joking! She's welcome to you and good luck to her. She'll need it.'

'You know your problem, Adele?' he asked, before answering his own question. 'You're still holding a torch for me.'

She laughed and, although it was more of a snigger, it still sounded strange in the hostile atmosphere. 'You're deluded as well as fuckin' nasty,' she sniped.

'Doesn't stop you from caring about me, though, does it? Like last week, when that druggie smacked me one. You were all worried about me then, weren't you?'

'No I bloody wasn't! I was just showing the same concern as I would have done for anybody.'

'OK,' he said, breezing out of her office to the sound of Peter in the corridor asking what was going on. As he passed through the door Glynn called over his shoulder, 'You keep telling yourself that, sweetheart, and you might actually start believing it.'

Once he had gone, Adele hammered her fists on the top of her desk. She could hear him talking in the corridor with Peter, his tone now conciliatory. As the rage consumed her she prepared herself to tackle her brother, too, if he came to see her. But then all went quiet and Adele was left alone once more, trying to calm her raging temper.

How foolish she'd been ever to be taken in by Glynn. But that was what he was like: a charmer. He took you in till you'd served your purpose. Then he stabbed you in the back.

52

Peter was pacing up and down his apartment, the muscles of his legs and feet powered by his nervous energy. Glynn was due to arrive any minute and Peter wasn't looking forward to his visit one bit. He approached the drinks cabinet, tempted to pour a copious measure of brandy. But it was too early for that; he needed to keep his wits about him.

Glynn had told him on the phone that he'd sourced some weapons and would be calling round to deliver them. They'd also be discussing the detailed plans for their forthcoming raids on Angels and Bramleys. A feeling of disquiet gnawed away at Peter every time he thought about the raids. But he'd have to hide his true feelings from Glynn.

He hated the way Glynn made him feel. As a career criminal Peter had never shied away from doing what had to be done. But there was something about Glynn that was beginning to unsettle him. He had a naturally dominant personality. In fact, his personality was so forceful that he could take over without you even realising it. And that was exactly what Peter wanted to avoid.

For the past few weeks Peter had felt as though things were slipping away from him. He could see it in the attitudes of his men whenever they were around him; particularly Glynn. He knew he was losing their trust, and the pressure was on him to win it back. And the way to do that would be to make sure his men, and everyone else, knew who was top dog.

Peter jumped when he heard the doorbell. That would be Glynn now, full of his usual charm and confidence. Peter straightened himself up and took several deep breaths, ready to show Glynn who was boss.

Glynn was calm and business-like as he walked through the door and gave a sharp nod of his head. His face bore a grave expression.

'I've got 'em,' he said, slinging a large hessian sack on the table, then rolling it down till its contents were exposed.

Peter tried to suppress a sharp intake of breath as he peered inside the sack. He stepped forward to get a better view. There was no doubt that Glynn had come prepared. An assortment of metal gleamed under the ceiling light. Peter did a quick mental inventory: machetes, meat cleavers, hunting knives and crow bars. He tried to act casual as he eyed the deadly arsenal.

'You've done well,' he said.

'Told you I'd sort it,' said Glynn. 'Take your pick. I'm taking a fuckin' machete. I'll make sure no bastard tries it on with me.'

Peter grabbed a crow bar, gripping it tightly in his right hand and running the fingers of his left hand smoothly along the length of it in mock admiration. 'This'll do for me,' he said, as he began to tap it against the palm of his left hand, disguising his growing unease. 'I tell you what,' he said, putting down the crow bar and grabbing a machete, then pulling it out of its sheath, 'I'll take this as well.'

Glynn looked at him, confused. 'Why d'you need both?' he asked.

'Crow bar to do the job and machete for back-up,' said Peter. 'Look, there's straps to tie it round your leg so it's easy to carry. No one will fuck about with you when you've got one of those in yer hand.'

Glynn grinned at him. 'Not fuckin' daft, are you?' he said.

Peter smiled, knowing he'd taken the first step in regaining Glynn's respect. He secretly thought Glynn's choice of weapons a bit extreme but he didn't want to lose face.

'OK, down to business,' he said. 'I'm hiring two vans so we can take plenty of men. I want Jonny and Rav to drive. You in one van, me in the other, and another six men in the back of each. Jonny and Rav can stay in the vans so we can make a quick getaway.'

'So there'll be seven of us raiding each of the clubs?' said Glynn. 'You sure that's enough?' he asked when Peter nodded.

'Oh, yeah,' said Peter. 'Don't forget, they won't be expecting us, and with the weapons we'll be carrying, they'll have no fuckin' chance.'

'OK, sounds good to me,' said Glynn.

'Right, so now we've just got to decide who's going to each club with us and what time we're gonna hit 'em,' said Peter, putting the weapons back inside the sack, then pulling out a chair and sitting down. 'Then we'll get the lads round and give 'em the drill.'

In front of him was a pad and pen, which he'd placed there earlier. He picked up the pen and began tapping the nib of it nervously on the pad.

Glynn pulled up a chair, too. 'OK, let's go for it,' he said, in eager anticipation.

53

Adele was sitting at the bar in the Golden Bell chatting to the barmaid, Paula. She liked this time of the evening, just before most of the customers arrived. Adele also enjoyed watching the customers make an entry. There was always a buzz of excitement as they eagerly anticipated their night of fun. The transformation of the club from an empty cavern to a thriving party zone within the space of an hour or so always intrigued her.

She'd struck up quite a friendship with Paula since she'd been working in the upstairs office. It was amazing what you could learn about someone when you took the trouble to find out.

Paula was a single mum who put in a lot of hours at the club so that she could provide a better life for her children. Abandoned by her kids' father, she relied on her parents to look after her children while she worked at the club. And when she wasn't working at the club or looking after her children, she also put in a few hours during the day at a café. Adele admired her work ethic and resented the way Glynn treated her just because she wasn't as young or glamorous as some of the other barmaids.

While they were chatting, the first of the evening's customers arrived. Spotting that Cindy and another barmaid were busy chatting to two of the bouncers, Paula went to serve them. Knowing that it would be some minutes before Paula finished serving, Adele swivelled her stool and had a look around the club.

On the other side of the dance floor she could see Glynn and Mike deep in conversation. They were too far away for her to tell what they were saying, but judging by their body language, it was something serious.

Glynn was standing very close to Mike and gesticulating a lot with his hands while Mike kept nodding his head in response to what Glynn was saying. Then Glynn took a quick look over his shoulder as if he was checking no one was listening. He didn't spot Adele watching them from a distance as he craned his neck even closer to Mike and whispered something into his ear.

Adele quickly swivelled her stool back till it was facing the bar. She had a feeling Glynn was up to no good and didn't want him to spot her watching them. She smiled at Paula, who came back to join her and they chatted again until Paula became too busy to talk. Peter wasn't in the club that night and Adele soon became restless once she didn't have Paula to chat to so she called a cab to take her home.

'Glad I've seen you, mate,' Glynn said to Mike when he bumped into him in the club.

'Why, what's up? Have you found someone else to deal with things?'

Glynn knew Mike was referring to the arrangement he had previously had with Little Gaz. As Glynn's close ally, Mike knew all the details and had received a share of the mark-up for agreeing to ignore the nefarious activity. He also knew about Glynn's intention to replace Little Gaz with another dealer as soon as he could.

'No, not that. I haven't found anyone yet but I've got other things to sort at the moment. It's to do with the raids on Angels and Bramleys that I told you about.'

'What is?' asked Mike.

'Opportunity fuckin' knocks, that's what,' said Glynn. When Mike stared back, nonplussed, he elaborated, moving closer to him and lowering his voice. 'Remember I told you I was waiting for the right chance before I made my move?'

Mike nodded.

'Well, when we do the raids next Saturday, that's when I'm gonna do it.'

'Nice one. And about fuckin' time too! So, how will you do it?' asked Mike.

'Pete's told me the plan for next Saturday,' Glynn responded, keeping his voice low. 'He's leading one team, I'm taking the other. The plan is for you to stay here and look after this place.'

'No fuckin' chance!' Mike fumed. 'I wanna be part of the action.'

'Hang on a minute,' said Glynn, placing a placatory hand on Mike's shoulder. 'I said that's the plan, but it's not what's gonna fuckin' happen if I've got anything to do with it.'

Mike grinned. 'OK, so what *is* gonna happen?'

'Well, to start with, Pete's gonna have a meeting with everyone to fill them in so I need you to pretend it's all news to you. We don't want him to suspect anything. Pretend to go along with it. Maybe even complain a bit about staying here, but don't fuckin' overdo it. We don't want him to change the plan, 'cos he's just played right into our fuckin' hands.'

'So come on, for fuck's sake, what we gonna do?'

Glynn took a quick look over his shoulder to make sure no one could hear. Then he leaned in towards Mike and dropped his voice still further while he outlined his treacherous scheme.

54

It wasn't until Adele was in the taxi that Glynn and Mike's cosy chat came back to her. The more she thought about it, the more she was convinced they were up to no good. Perhaps she should have a word with Peter and warn him. But what would she say? There was nothing to tell him other than the fact that she had a bad feeling.

Then she checked herself. Perhaps it was just her paranoia where Glynn was concerned. She didn't trust him but that didn't necessarily mean he was doing anything untoward. She smiled wryly at the absurdity of that thought; what he did for a living was untoward but she had come to recognise that as part of who he was.

Maybe they were just discussing the security business, which would explain why they looked a bit suspicious. After all, the very nature of the business was underhand. And Peter was in it as deep as them. She knew that her brother was no innocent and, as she had previously told him, she wanted no part in that side of his business.

Nevertheless, something was niggling away at her. It was perhaps a sixth sense, a bad feeling that Glynn and Mike were planning something. And if that was the case then perhaps Peter needed to know. With that in mind, she decided to ring him as soon as she got home.

Peter was taking the night off but he wasn't having a good time. Earlier in the evening he'd received a call from Max's wife, who was distraught. Apparently the old guy had popped his clogs. It had happened much sooner than Peter expected and he found himself feeling quite saddened by the news. Peter went to visit Max's widow straight away and offered to help out in any way he could, including financially.

Max had died before Peter had a chance to pay back everything he owed him, and his widow didn't seem to have a clue. She still thought Max was the majority owner of the Golden Bell until Peter put her in the picture.

It was ironic really. As a hardened criminal Peter could have taken advantage of the situation. But he couldn't do that. Instead he would stick to his arrangement with Max and carry on paying instalments to Max's wife until he was finally 100 per cent owner of the Golden Bell.

As he sat in Max's lounge, drinking strong tea with his upset widow, Peter felt consumed with pity for her.

Max's wife was having difficulty dealing with his death. She was an elderly lady, pale and feeble-looking. She wore smart, good-quality clothing although it seemed to hang loosely on her skeletal frame. It was obvious to Peter that she'd lost a bit of weight since the news of Max's ill health had hit her.

As Max's widow spoke to Peter she cried continually, pausing at intervals to dab her eyes with a tear-drenched tissue. Whenever Max's name was mentioned a fresh wave of sobs would come over her, making her body shudder involuntarily. It was painful to watch.

The fact was, Peter had become quite attached to Max since he'd moved into business with him. Despite his obvious failings, Max was a good guy and he'd helped Peter a lot with sound advice and business acumen. He'd become a bit of a father figure to him. It was probably the closest Peter had come to having a father figure, given how his own dad had mistreated him.

Peter was relieved to get away from Max's home. The emotional strain was getting to him, though he would be loath to admit it. There was no way he could face anyone tonight. So he rang Glynn, made up some excuse for not being at the club, then hit the brandy.

He'd be OK in the morning but he just wanted this one night to himself when he could drink to Max's memory. In the morning he would put on a brave face while he broke the news to Adele and Glynn.

When he had spent several hours drinking alone,

Peter fell into a heavy alcohol-induced sleep. He didn't hear the phone ringing.

Once Adele was inside her flat and had removed her coat and shoes, she picked up the phone and dialled Peter's number. The phone rang out several times. He was obviously not at home. Maybe he was visiting another of the clubs that he did business with. No wonder he hadn't let her know that he wouldn't be in the Golden Bell that night. Her mind began to wander and all thoughts of her intended conversation with Peter soon disappeared.

Adele quickly got ready for bed. It was late and she was tired. As soon as she hit the bed she drifted off to sleep. And by the time she awoke the next day she had forgotten all about her intention to tell Peter about Glynn and Mike's suspicious conversation.

55

It was Saturday, the night of the raids. As he looked around at the fifteen men crowded into his office Peter loosened his collar for the second time. He was feeling the heat but maybe that had as much to do with what they were about to do as it did with the number of people packed into a confined space.

He desperately wanted tonight to run smoothly. Not only did the future of his firm depend on it but he suspected that his leadership of the security business might do, too. He had to be seen to be taking a hard line with rival firms.

Peter had already briefed his men a few nights previously so everyone knew who the drivers were and who was accompanying him and Glynn. Currently they were all waiting for Glynn to come back into the office. There was a buzz of excitement as the men chatted amongst themselves.

Peter saw the office door open, then the crowd of

men made way as Glynn walked up to him. 'The coast's clear,' he said once he was standing by Peter's side.

Peter knew he was referring to Adele as he'd sent him to check whether she was in her office, knowing that she would notice if a large group of men passed by.

'Right, lads, listen up,' Peter called over the excited clamour. 'You're all going out the back way as planned. Me and Glynn will go out of the front door and meet you at the vans. As far as the staff are concerned, us two are out on business so we have to be seen to be leaving the club. Don't forget, Jonny is driving the van to Angels, which is the one I'll be getting in, and Rav is driving the van to Bramleys with Glynn. Now, before we leave, is everyone clear which van you're in?'

The men muttered their understanding.

'OK, now don't forget, keep the noise down as you leave. I don't want to raise any fuckin' suspicion. All right?'

Again the men murmured their agreement.

'Right, come on then. Let's go,' he said, and he and Glynn followed the men as they filed out of the office.

As Peter and Glynn walked down the stairway leading to the club, Peter's apprehension turned to abject fear. His stomach was fluttering and his hands were moist. He fought to contain it, telling himself not to be stupid. It wasn't the first time he'd done something like this, after all. He'd had to get heavy with people before so why was tonight any different?

But it *was* different. He'd had a bad feeling ever since he and Glynn had first discussed it. Maybe it was because he was targeting his one-time friends, or perhaps it was because he'd felt pressured to do it. He couldn't explain why but, whatever the reason, he tried to ignore the ominous feeling that nagged away at him.

They reached the foyer and Glynn spoke for the first time since they had left the office. 'Shit, the back door!' he said.

'What about it?' asked Peter.

'We need to make sure it's shut properly,' said Glynn. 'Don't forget, we can't afford to leave this place exposed while we're away.'

Glynn had already turned towards the back entrance. 'I'll do it,' he said. 'It won't take two mins.'

'OK, I'll hang on here for you,' said Peter.

'No, it's OK,' said Glynn. 'Don't forget, Angels is a bit further away so it won't matter if you set off a couple of minutes earlier than me. In fact, it'll mean there's more of a chance of us hitting them at the same time.'

Peter hovered for a few moments, uncertain but unable to come up with any other reason to stop Glynn going to the back door.

'Don't worry, it'll only take a couple of minutes,' said Glynn. He walked out of the foyer and into the darkened interior of the club on his way to the back door.

'OK,' said Peter, going towards the exit and trying to quell his growing sense of disquiet. 'I'll see you back here later.'

As soon as he had walked through the foyer and inside the nightclub, Glynn turned left, and secreted himself next to the glass door that partitioned the club interior from the foyer. He turned and watched Peter head out of the exit. Then, satisfied that Peter would be on his way to the van, he went in search of Mike.

As instructed, Mike was hovering around the bar area, ready. One flash of Glynn's eyes and Mike set off to the foyer, where they met up.

'Just give it a minute to make sure he's gone,' said Glynn. 'Then we'll go.'

By the time they reached the van, Peter's party had already departed. Glynn opened the back doors and six heads swivelled around in his direction. 'Right, guys, there's been a slight change of plan,' he said. 'Something urgent's cropped up that I've got to sort so Mike's gonna take my place.'

Without waiting for their response, he patted Mike on the back. Mike then jumped into the van. 'Make it quick, Rav,' Glynn called to the driver. 'Pete's lot will be well on the way by now.'

He shut the back doors of the van, then jumped into his own car and sped off up the street.

*

Adele was sitting on a bar stool, people watching as usual. In front of her was a glass of water. She'd decided not to drink wine tonight as she wanted to keep a clear head. Peter had left her and Mike in charge of the club and she wanted to make sure she had her wits about her. Although he had assured her that Mike would take care of any aggravation, she didn't really trust Mike.

Peter hadn't disclosed what was so important that it kept both him and Glynn away from the club on the same night. Even though she'd pressed him for details, he'd just said that they had important business to tend to and it was best if he didn't tell her any more than that. Then he'd reassured her that there was nothing for her to worry about.

She'd been watching Mike for the last half-hour. He seemed edgy, pacing about and constantly looking around. He was certainly taking his responsibility seriously, she thought. Maybe it was the first time he'd been left in charge of the club and he was a bit nervous about it.

The club was starting to fill out and a group of people made their way to the bar area, momentarily blocking her view of Mike. By the time they had moved out of the way she realised Mike was gone. Curious, she said to Paula, 'Where did Mike go?'

Paula shrugged. 'Not sure, but he was heading towards the foyer.'

Adele wasn't sure what had piqued her curiosity; maybe she was just worried about having to take charge of things on her own. But whatever it was, something made her go out into the foyer to see what Mike was up to. She arrived just in time to see Mike walk out of the club with Glynn.

'Mike, where are you going?' she shouted but they were on the other side of the large club foyer by then and neither of them seemed to hear her.

After a moment's hesitation Adele dashed after them. She opened the door, feeling a chill as the wind cut through the thin material of her top. Then her eyes scanned the street. It was difficult to pick out anyone from the crowd of people outside the club. Some were queuing to get in but others were hovering in small clusters, chatting and laughing.

A thought occurred to her. They could be round the back of the club, which was where most of the staff parked their cars, on a croft across the road. She fought her way through the crowd, then turned down the side street that led to the rear of the club.

A van was approaching as she turned into the back street. She caught a glimpse of Mike in the front passenger seat as it passed her. By the time she registered that it was him, the van had gone.

Adele peered across at the croft. She could see Glynn

getting into his car. Instinctively she ran towards him, shouting his name. But he was soon inside, slamming the door with a resounding crash. She watched, frustrated as he sped up the street in the opposite direction.

'What the hell...?' she said, giving voice to her confusion. What on earth was going on? Why had Mike left the club without telling her when he was supposed to be keeping an eye on things? And what were Peter and Glynn up to?

Adele stood on the pavement momentarily paralysed by indecision, gazing after Glynn's car but not seeing anything. She wished she had pressed Peter for more information when he told her about his plans for the night. Because now she really needed to know. And there was no point ringing his flat. He wouldn't be there. He was out doing God knows what.

Something was going on and she hadn't a clue what it was. But whatever it was, she was almost certain that it wasn't good.

56

Peter was on his way to Angels nightclub. The journey seemed to be taking ages, even though it had been only a few minutes since he'd set off.

The red Transit van wound its way through the nightclubbing throngs and Peter felt a familiar surge of adrenalin. His heartbeat increased, his vision and hearing grew keener and his hands were moist. He would normally associate those feelings with the buzz of excitement that always preceded a big job. But now they translated into fear.

Peter's ears hummed from a cacophony of sound: the animated chatter from the back of the van interspersed by the screech of laughter from eager revellers. The street lights seemed to dazzle his dilated pupils, causing him to blink incessantly. His heart was like a taut drum being hammered by an over zealous musician. And the flutter inside his stomach had become an insistent growl.

Peter tried to hold himself in check. Why was he

so frightened? He wasn't used to feeling like this. He decided to embrace it; treat it as though it was the usual adrenalin rush and nothing more. Then he'd concentrate on doing what had to be done.

Glynn was sitting inside his black, souped-up BMW. He'd made record time, taking all the shortcuts that a van would have trouble negotiating, and even jumping the lights once or twice. He'd parked within view of Angels, but not too near.

As he looked out at the club entrance he could tell he was still early, and a smile flitted across his lips. He took out his mobile phone, an expensive but worthwhile investment. New to the market, it was small and discreet, unlike the brick-type cellphones that were now being used by businesses. It also set him apart as a sharp and savvy operator.

Glynn had already made his first call to warn the management of Angels that they were about to be attacked. He just had one more call to make as soon as the van arrived. He flipped down the front of his phone, admiring the neat keypad. Then he waited.

As the van turned into Jasper Street Peter could feel his breath catch in his throat. They had arrived!

He looked at the hordes of people further up the

street, gathered around the entrance to Angels. His already pounding heart sped even faster but he quashed the feeling that enveloped him as he spoke to his men. Instead he channelled the rush of adrenalin that surged through him.

'Right, lads, don't forget we're jumping straight out as soon as Jonny stops the van. Then we charge through the crowd and go for the bouncers, OK?'

The men nodded and murmured in response.

'OK, don't forget, as quick as you can,' he repeated as the van drew nearer. 'We need to take the bastards by surprise!'

The van screeched to a halt and the men jumped out, led by Peter. He gripped the crowbar tightly, then sprinted across the pavement. The handle of the machete felt strange pressed up against his leg. But he ignored it, and focused, driven by a crazed burst of energy that pumped through his body.

Just like any other job he told himself. The buzz. The rush. The determination. Briefly noticing the crowd but fixed on the goal.

His sharpened vision zoomed in on the bouncers crowded around the door. Black suits, white shirts, enhanced physique and resolute bearing. He briefly registered his men by his side and heard the screech of the crowd.

Then he was on the bouncers; he and his men pushing them back and into the foyer. Loads of them. And more coming forward. Much more than he expected! Before long he and his gang were boxed in. But it was too late to turn back.

He swung the crowbar, smashing it down onto the nearest bouncer. The man fell back, blood pumping from a gaping gash to the side of his head. Peter's men fought alongside him, slashing their destructive weapons at the enemy, who were also tooled up.

Two other bouncers went for Peter. He felt their fists and a sharp blow to the head from something hard. Their hands grabbed viciously at his arm. Then the crowbar was gone. He saw yet more bouncers, heaving against him till he fell to the floor.

He was in a daze, the might of oversized feet striking his torso and head. Then a moment's reprieve as he saw a gap between their legs. He heard the sound of the crowd. Screaming. Shouting. Crying. A siren?

He had to get up! Peter rolled away from the bouncers, forcing himself unsteadily to his feet as the machete grazed against his leg and his heart pounded. A disturbing sight met him as he got off the floor. Carnage! A heaving mass of testosterone and blood.

He tried to pick out his men from the crowd. Where were they? Then he spotted one or two. Surrounded by bouncers, they were trying to fight their way through, but failing. Peter briefly took in the sight of blood on the face of one of them and the look of desperation on the face of the other.

The siren had stopped. Bright lights dazzled in a sea of black suits. Where were the rest of his men? He could only spot the same two who were bedraggled and bleeding. Without hesitation he lifted the machete and ran forward. Slicing it into the black suits. Ripping off strips, puncturing flesh and leaving a crimson trail.

Then Peter heard the heavy tread of footsteps from behind. And voices, lots of voices. Before he could turn round, he felt his arms being wrenched backwards and the machete tugged from his hand. There was the feel of something restraining his wrists just as he saw a horde of police officers. The booming voice of authority: 'Come on, men. Get this lot in the van!'

Then a voice addressed him: 'I'm placing you under arrest.'

Peter turned and looked at the staunch features of the police officer who gripped him by the arm and, together with a colleague, led him out of the building.

Then he saw what had happened to his men. They were also being led away. Expressions of defeat were pasted on their battered faces as they shuffled miserably out of the building.

Shit! thought Peter. He was done for.

Glynn was still inside his BMW watching Angels. He saw the red Transit van speed off up the street, with Jonny behind the wheel, just as the police arrived. Jonny obviously wasn't waiting around for the outcome. A smirk formed on Glynn's face as he thought about Jonny's disloyalty. You definitely couldn't trust anyone in this game!

The police swarmed into Angels. It was a few minutes before they re-emerged, leading several bloodied and beaten men to the police van. The first of the officers opened the back of the van and pushed his captive inside.

Then Glynn's face lit up as he saw Peter being led outside by two burly police officers. What a result! He couldn't have timed things better. Glynn couldn't read Peter's expression from this distance but his bitter disappointment showed in the way he hung his head and dragged his feet.

It looked like the police had arrived just in time, too. Peter had obviously been heavily involved in the fighting. His jacket hung off one shoulder at an odd angle and was heavily blood-stained.

Glynn started his engine. There was no point hanging around any longer. The job was done. He just hoped Peter ended up serving time. With him out of the picture he'd soon have Adele doing as she was told. Then he'd be running things his way at last.

57

Adele was worried. She'd been managing the club herself for the past hour and hadn't seen any sign of Peter, Glynn or Mike. Fortunately, nothing of any magnitude had occurred inside the Golden Bell and the staff seemed to have everything under control.

But that wasn't the main source of her worry. Her concern was for her brother. She knew something bad was going on; she just didn't know what. She'd tried ringing Peter's flat a few times, even though she doubted that he'd be there. As she'd predicted, the phone just rang out, unanswered. And the longer she waited, the more anxious she became.

Eventually she spotted Glynn walking into the Golden Bell. Despite her feelings about Glynn, she was relieved to see him. Perhaps he could tell her what had happened to her brother.

She rushed up to him. 'Glynn, what the hell's going on?' she asked.

'What d'you mean?' he countered, brusquely.

'You know very well what I mean!' she said. 'Where the hell is Peter? And why did you all leave the club at the same time when Mike was supposed to be looking after things here?'

'Too much for you to handle, was it?'

'No, it bloody well wasn't!' she snapped, annoyed that he was being so offhand with her. 'I wasn't worried about the club but I am worried about Peter.'

'There's nowt to worry about. He's out on business,' he said.

'What business? Where is he?'

'Ask your brother. Let him decide how much he wants you to know.'

He turned to walk away from her but she grabbed his arm. He stopped, glared at her and wrenched his arm free from her grasp. Then he dusted down his sleeve where she had held it, as though her hand was contaminated.

'I can't ask him when he's not here, can I?' she yelled. 'You're all I've got at the moment and I need to fuckin' know what's happened to my brother!'

Glynn grinned. 'Feisty one, aren't you?' he said.

Her anger wasn't helping so she tried pleading with him instead. 'Glynn, please tell me where Peter is.'

'Stop worrying. There's nowt to worry about.'

'Well, why won't you tell me then? And why did Mike leave the club?'

'He's out on business too. He had to take my place,

if you must know. I've had to visit my sick aunty in hospital. That's why there was a change of plan.'

'Then why didn't you tell me?'

'Because it all happened in a bit of a rush,' he said through clenched teeth. 'I got a call to say my aunty had taken a turn for the worst.'

She looked at Glynn, unsure whether to believe him, and examining his face for any signs. But he was difficult to read. Maybe there was some truth in what he was saying. She wasn't sure.

Adele was just about to ask him more questions when Mike arrived. Without saying anything further, Glynn rushed off, and he and Mike both went through the door that led to the upstairs offices, leaving Adele anxious and frustrated.

The following morning Adele awoke from a fitful sleep. Despite the cool weather she was sweat-drenched. Peter was the first thing on her mind and she wondered if he had returned home yet. She rang his apartment straight away but again the phone went unanswered. So she rang Glynn, but there was no answer from him either, or from the offices above the Golden Bell.

Adele showered and dressed quickly, then left without eating, hoping she might find out more once she arrived at the club. But neither Peter nor Glynn nor Mike was at the Golden Bell when she arrived.

Although it was a Sunday, she spent an anxious few hours poring over her bookkeeping to take her mind off things. It didn't work. When lunchtime arrived she left her office and went downstairs, intending to go outside for some fresh air. But there inside the club were Glynn and Mike, deep in conversation.

She rushed up to them but Mike walked away as soon as he spotted her, leaving her alone with Glynn.

'Have you seen anything of Peter?' she asked.

'No, but Mike's just brought me some news,' he replied.

She looked at him, curious, until he spoke again. 'He's been arrested.'

'W—what for?'

'He was out on a raid last night.'

'A raid? What do you mean?'

'Oh, come on, Adele. You're not that fuckin' naïve,' he snarled. Then she thought she spotted the faint sign of a smirk as he added, 'The coppers caught him attacking the bouncers at Angels.'

'What? Why?'

'Why d'you fuckin' think? You know what game we're in, surely. The security business is no fuckin' walk in the park, y'know.'

He started to move away but she stopped him again, grabbing hold of his arm.

'What?' he yelled, pulling his arm away.

'What did he do?' she asked.

'They caught him with a machete. He made a bit of a mess of the bouncers, apparently.'

'You knew what was going on last night and you wouldn't tell me!' she accused. When Glynn just shrugged, she asked, 'Where is he? I need to go and see him.'

'Ha, you've got no fuckin' chance. The police are holding him. And, if you ask me, they'll be charging him, that's if they haven't done already. He'll probably get GBH.'

'GBH? You're joking!' she said as the shock registered. Then she asked, 'How long will they hold him for?'

'Depends if he gets bail or not. But if he doesn't get bail they'll hold him till the trial.'

'No!' she yelled.

This time there was a definite smirk on Glynn's face when he responded, 'I've sent a solicitor down there. I'll let you know when I hear anything further. But, even if he doesn't get bail, don't worry, you'll still be able to go and visit him.'

Then Glynn walked away, leaving Adele distraught. She stared after him, open mouthed with astonishment. Just what sort of world did Glynn inhabit where he seemed to think she'd be comforted by the fact that she could still visit Peter in prison if he didn't get bail? Memories of her time in prison were only too fresh in her mind. She wouldn't wish that life on anyone, especially her own brother, even if it wouldn't be the first time he'd been inside.

Adele couldn't believe her brother would do something so foolish. OK, so he'd been no angel in the past. But he was a businessman now. Why would he want to go getting involved in something like this? She couldn't understand any of it. And she wasn't happy that he'd kept her in the dark.

If she had known what he was involved in then maybe she could have talked him out of it. Adele silently cursed herself for ignoring what was going on around her. She should have made it her business to know.

As she stood in the middle of the Golden Bell, recovering from the shock and trying to make sense of what had happened, she came to a decision. From now on she would make sure she knew what went on in Peter's business world. After all, if the police didn't release him, she would be at the mercy of Glynn and Mike. And she didn't trust those two at all.

58

It was a week later and Adele was visiting her brother in Strangeways where he was being held on remand. As she peered across the prison visiting room a memory flitted through her mind. It was of the first time Peter had been locked up when he was only a boy. And how that had changed him! Thrown out by their father on his return from the detention centre, he'd spent his teenage years living in a squat; surviving on his wits and the wrong side of the law.

Now he was awaiting trial for GBH following his attack on the bouncers at Angels nightclub. She had chosen to visit him alone, even though her mother had pleaded with Adele to take her too. Adele knew her mother wouldn't visit him without her. The strain would be too much, but Adele could take her another day. Right now she had important matters to discuss with Peter and there was no way she could do that in front of their mother.

Catching sight of her brother's handsome face, Adele rushed up to the table where he was sitting. He stood up to greet her and Adele fought back the tears as they embraced.

'Oh, Peter,' she said, pulling away and holding him at arm's length. 'How are you?'

He shrugged. 'All right, y'know.'

They sat down, Peter on one side of the desk and Adele on the other. She took a deep breath, ready to speak to him. There were things she needed to know and she'd make damn sure she found them out before she left this place.

'Right, Peter,' she began. 'I think it's about time we spoke about everything. I've been burying my head in the sand up to now but I need to know exactly what's been going on,' she said.

He shrugged again. 'I thought you preferred not to know the details.'

'I did, but that was before. I think we've reached the stage now where I need to find out. After all, you're not gonna be around, are you? And I need to know what I'll be dealing with.'

'Glynn will look after the security business,' said Peter. 'He's already been in touch.'

'I bet he has,' she snapped, and her face fell into a frown. 'I bet he couldn't wait to get his bloody hands on it.'

'No, it's not like that. Glynn's a good guy.'

'Is he? Is that apart from the fact that he's a cold-blooded killer?'

'Shush,' he whispered. 'We don't want everyone to know, do we?'

Adele took no notice of Peter's warning and continued to demand answers. 'If he's so bloody loyal then tell me why he didn't go with you when you raided Angels?'

It was difficult to read the expression that now formed on Peter's face. Was it a look of resignation at having to divulge the details or was it shame at what he was involved in? Either way, his voice was barely audible when he said, 'Because he was supposed to go to Bramleys. We decided to hit them both at the same time.'

'But he didn't go, did he?' she asked.

'No, something cropped up. Mike had to take his place.'

Adele ignored his response for now. She was more concerned about what had driven her brother to do something so foolish. 'Why did you do it, Peter? Why?' she demanded.

'Because I had no bloody choice,' he grumbled. 'Alan Palmer is trying to take over the security in a lot of my pubs and clubs. He's even got his own fuckin' men on the doors of Angels and Bramleys. So we had to send him a message not to fuck with us.'

'Alan Palmer?' she asked. She hadn't heard his name for a long time.

'Yeah, Dave works with him,' said Peter.

Adele's mouth dropped open in shock. No wonder David and that other guy had threatened her. 'Jesus, Peter!' she said. 'Why do you get involved with these people? Those two have always been bad news!'

Peter hung his head in shame but didn't say anything.

'Was it really worth doing something so stupid just to stop them from taking over?' she persisted. 'Why don't you just give up the security business if those are the sort of people you're dealing with? Surely you've got enough with the Golden Bell and your other businesses.'

'Because I can't,' he said. 'You don't understand, Adele. If I backed away everyone would think I was a right fuckin' mug. They'd take the door of the Golden Bell and might even go for my other fuckin' businesses, too.'

He hesitated a moment before continuing, 'Besides, I don't want to walk away. Can't you see? It's what I do. It gives me a buzz. I'm a fuckin' big name and I get respect because of it.'

Adele stared at him, incredulous. After all this time she still didn't really understand her brother and what made him tick. For a short while she was stuck for something to say; then a thought occurred to her.

'Is that where the van was going that night?' she asked. 'To attack one of the nightclubs?'

'What van?'

'The white van that Mike was inside.'

'Yeah,' he said. 'That one was going to Bramleys.'

'And why did Glynn decide not to go?' Even though Glynn had already told her, she wanted to check that his story was consistent.

'He had to go and see his sick aunty in hospital,' said Peter. 'She'd taken a turn for the worst.'

'And you believe him?'

'Yeah, course I do. I already knew about his sick aunty.'

'And it just so happens that she took a turn for the worst on the very night that he was due to raid Bramleys,' she said sarcastically.

Adele watched as Peter's eyes narrowed and a deep furrow formed between them. She knew she'd sown a seed of doubt in his mind.

'Look, Glynn's a good guy,' he said, but his words seemed to belie what he must be feeling inside. 'Just because you don't trust him any more doesn't mean I shouldn't.'

'It's nothing to do with how I feel about him, Peter. Just look at the facts.'

'OK, OK. Maybe it was a coincidence.'

'Yeah, a bloody big coincidence. Have you checked whether he actually went to see his aunty that night?'

'Oh, come off it, Adele. I can't do that. Glynn's my number two. I've got to have some trust in him.

He's helped me a lot, y'know. He's even sorted out the solicitor for me while I've been in here. And he's the only one who can run the security side of things. He's the only other person who knows exactly what's involved.'

His words weren't convincing. To Adele he sounded as though he was trying to reassure himself about Glynn's loyalty. 'Are you really sure you can trust him to run your businesses for you while you're inside?' she asked.

'I didn't say he was going to look after my businesses, just the security side of things.'

'Well, what about your other businesses: The Golden Bell, the bookies and—'

'I was coming to that,' he cut in before inhaling sharply. 'I want you to look after them. They're all kosher. It's only the security business that's a bit dodgy.'

'Hang on a minute,' she protested, pulling herself back in her chair, and subconsciously creating a physical distance between them.

Peter cut in again before she could continue. 'I need you to look after them for me, Adele. You're the best person to do it. You know the accounting side of things and how the businesses run.'

Then he sighed before adding, 'The truth is, you're right. I don't really know who I can trust in my business. Dave and Alan have already betrayed me. And Glynn can be a bit ruthless at times. I need someone who I can depend on to keep an eye on things. That's why I'm asking you.'

'No way!' she said. 'It's too risky. I've already had David and his sidekick threatening me as it is.'

Peter reached out and took hold of her hand. 'Please, Adele. I'm begging you. I don't want to come out of here and find it's all been pissed away. I know you'll take care of things for me. Besides, what else will you do? Work for Glynn?'

Adele hadn't thought that far into the future. Her head had been full of concerns for her brother and the circumstances surrounding his imprisonment. She realised now that she had been relying on him to come up with the answers. But he was shifting the responsibility onto her and it had become terrifying.

'No, I'll get a job somewhere else. I don't know what I'll do. I'll think of something,' she said, uncertainly.

'Do you really think it'll be that easy?' he asked. 'I mean, you did struggle to find work last time.'

After watching her reaction for a second, Peter added, 'Please do this for me, Adele. It's taken me years to build things up and I don't want to lose it all.' Then he hesitated before he spoke his next words: 'I'd do it for you. You know I would.'

As soon as he said that Adele knew he had her. After all, he'd taken a big risk in trying to cover up her killing of their father. And he'd done it without question; out of loyalty to his sister. Now things had turned around. It was him asking her for help. How could she let him down after all he had done for her?

'Jesus, Peter!' she said. 'You're asking a lot. I hope you'll let Glynn know who's going to be in charge.'

'I was hoping you'd do that,' said Peter. 'Do I take it that's a yes, then?'

'Looks like I've got no bloody choice, have I?' she said, smiling wryly.

An impish grin lit up his face, reminding her of their childhood. It was the sort of grin he wore whenever he was up to mischief. 'Thanks, sis,' he said. 'I knew I could rely on you.'

They chatted for a few more minutes before Adele left. She was glad to get away from the large, imposing walls of Strangeways prison. That eerie old building was intimidating.

But Adele didn't go straight home. She needed time to reconcile the enormity of what she had just taken on. So she found a small café tucked away in the industrial back streets of Manchester, near Victoria Station, and ordered a cup of tea.

Adele sat gazing out of the café window, deep in thought, long after she had finished her drink. There was no doubt in her mind that Glynn was somehow behind Peter's arrest. She had known by the smug way in which he'd told her about it. Glynn probably thought he would have the perfect opportunity to take over Peter's empire once he was behind bars. And she was the only person who could stop him doing so.

As Adele nervously rubbed her finger around the rim of her empty tea cup, she vowed that somehow or other she would put a stop to Glynn. After all, she owed it to her brother to protect his empire and pay him back for everything he had done for her in the past.

59

It was a few days later and Adele was in Peter's office. She was waiting for all the staff to arrive for the special meeting she had called. It was something she had been putting off for the last couple of days. Just the thought of it made her heart rate escalate. But she knew she had to do it.

If she was to command the respect of the staff then she had to get things off on the right footing. And it had to be in Peter's office. It was a psychological move. This was the office where the boss had always been based, regardless of the fact that Glynn had been making himself at home there since Peter had been behind bars.

Glynn was the first to arrive and he automatically stood next to her, on the side of the desk where the boss sat. But he couldn't take the seat; Adele was already sitting there.

'What's all this about?' he demanded. 'Is it something to do with your visit to Pete the other day?'

'You'll find out soon enough,' she said, trying to disguise the feeling of trepidation that had her heart doing somersaults. She hoped he hadn't connected the flush in her cheeks with the rush of fear that swept through her.

To Adele's relief Paula soon arrived with another of the barmaids, breaking the awkward atmosphere that hung over the room.

'Come in, take a seat,' Adele said to each of the staff as they arrived, indicating the seats that she had placed at the opposite side of the desk.

'Is everybody here?' she asked, when the office was full.

A few of the staff muttered a 'yes' so she stood up to speak, ignoring her trembling knees. 'As you're probably aware,' she began. 'My brother is currently being held in Strangeways. I'm not about to go into the details right now but I just want you to know that it could be some time before he's back at work.'

She paused, allowing the staff to digest these opening words before she carried on. When the mutterings around the room settled to a lull, she said, 'In his absence he's left me in charge of a number of his businesses.'

Adele couldn't resist a quick peek across at Glynn and

she noticed the stony expression of fury that clouded his handsome features.

'I'll be looking after the nightclub as well as my brother's sunbed salons and the bookmaker's,' she continued. 'So, if you have any problems, you are to take them up with me. Is everybody clear on that?'

When the staff had mumbled their agreement she said, 'Has anybody got any questions?'

'Yes!' said Glynn, his voice booming out. 'When will all this take effect?'

'Immediately,' Adele quickly replied, meeting his eyes and seeing the steely look of hatred that flashed from them. For a few moments he glared at her until she broke his gaze and turned back to address the staff. 'That's all for now,' she said, glad that it was over.

The staff filed out of the office, apart from Glynn, who hung back. As soon as the last of the staff had left he asked, 'When the fuck was all this agreed?'

'When I went to visit Peter,' she replied, trying to hide the slight quiver in her voice.

'Then why the fuck didn't you have the decency to tell me before you told that lot?' he demanded.

'I didn't see any reason why I should,' she said. 'You're a member of staff like everyone else, apart from the fact that you run the *security* business.' She deliberately emphasised the word, 'security', showing her scorn for such a misnomer.

'You're taking the fuckin' piss!' he yelled. 'You've got

no idea how to run a nightclub; you'll buckle at the first fuckin' hurdle.'

'If you've got a problem with me running the business then I suggest you take it up with Peter next time you see him,' she said, trying her best to remain cool. 'But I doubt you'll get very far. Peter was adamant that he wanted to leave me in charge. So, from now on, Glynn, we'll be doing things my way whether you agree with them or not. Now, if you don't mind, I've got a business to run.'

She deliberately turned away from him and logged onto the desk-top computer. But he didn't leave straight away. For a few seconds she could feel him hovering and she willed him to go before her courageous façade slipped.

He still didn't go. Instead he walked over to her and stood with his furious red face only inches from hers. 'You make me fuckin' sick!' he hissed, his eyes bulging and the tendons in his neck taut. She pulled back, alarmed, as a spray of spittle hit her face.

'Just because I'm not screwing you any more, you think you can treat me like a piece of shit. Well, you can have the fuckin' nightclub! It's all yours. The brawls. The violent drunks. The cheating staff. The drug pushers. You can have the fuckin' lot! But you're on your own. You won't get any fuckin' back-up from me. So let's see how you cope with that!'

She felt a stab of fear but tried to hide it. For a few

moments she stared back at him, speechless. Then he stomped through the office and punched the door before storming out, leaving an angry dent in the woodwork.

Adele heaved a sigh of relief as soon as he was gone. Then she loosened the collar of her blouse, which was moist with perspiration. She'd done it. She'd stood up to Glynn and told him who was boss.

After her confrontation with him, Adele was unable to focus on work. She needed something to calm her down. Opening a desk drawer, she pulled out the bottle of brandy that was secreted inside. As she did so, Adele noticed how much her hands were trembling and her heart was pounding. Vowing not to let this become a habit, she poured a generous measure into a mug then drank it.

Although Glynn's venomous words had frightened her, they'd also fired her up. How dare he assume that she wasn't up to the job? She'd soon show him.

As the effects of the brandy took hold, calming her quivering insides, Adele tried mentally to prepare herself for the mammoth task that lay ahead. She had a formidable adversary in Glynn. The man was callous and relentless. And, if Adele was to beat him, she would need something more fiery than alcohol to see her through.

But despite her fear, Adele knew she could do it. After all, she'd had to deal with some tough opponents in the past. And she'd beaten them. So yes, she could do it. She would have to stay strong, though. Because this was going to be one hell of a contest!

Acknowledgements

I would like to thank all the staff at Aria Fiction for their knowledge, expertise and support at every stage. In particular I'd like to thank my publisher, Caroline Ridding, editor, Sarah Ritherdon, Yvonne Holland, Sue Lamprell, Nikky Ward and Sabir Huseynbayli.

I am grateful to Jim Coulson and the staff at insidetime.org for helping me with my research into prison life, and for answering all my questions.

I would like to thank all the readers who have bought my books and recommended them to others. Thanks also go to Kath Middleton and Sophia Carleton for their support.

And last but not least I would like to thank all of my family and friends who have given me words of encouragement and always stood by me throughout my publishing journey.

About Heather Burnside

Heather Burnside previously worked in credit control and accounts until she took a career break to raise her two children. After ten years as a stay at home mum, she decided to move away from credit control and enrolled on a creative writing course.

She started her writing career twenty years ago when she began to work as a freelance writer while studying towards her writing diploma. As part of her studies Heather wrote the first chapters of her debut novel, *Slur*, which became the first book in The Riverhill Trilogy. During that time she also had many articles published in well-known UK magazines.

Heather later ran a writing services business, and through her business, she has ghost-written many non-fiction books on behalf of clients covering a broad range of topics. However, Heather now prefers to concentrate on fiction writing.

If you would like to find out more about the author, you are invited to subscribe to her mailing list. As a subscriber you will be among the first to find out about forthcoming publications.

Hello from Aria

We hope you enjoyed this book! If you did let us know, we'd love to hear from you.

We are Aria, a dynamic digital-first fiction imprint from award-winning independent publishers Head of Zeus. At heart, we're committed to publishing fantastic commercial fiction – from romance and sagas to crime, thrillers and historical fiction. Visit us online and discover a community of like-minded fiction fans!

We're also on the look out for tomorrow's superstar authors. So, if you're a budding writer looking for a publisher, we'd love to hear from you.
You can submit your book online at ariafiction.com/we-want-read-your-book

You can find us at:

Email: aria@headofzeus.com

Website: www.ariafiction.com

Submissions: www.ariafiction.com/we-want-read-your-book

@ariafiction

@Aria_Fiction

@ariafiction